A PARTY TO MURDER

A PARTY TO MURDER

DAVID TORRANCE

A percentage of the profits from this book will be donated to:
Crisis – registered charity in England and Wales (1082947) and Scotland (SC040094)
Macmillan – registered charity in England and Wales (261017), Scotland (SC039907) and the Isle of Man (604)

Special Edition ISBN: 9781786155177
Paperback ISBN (Novel only): 9781786155160
eBook ISBN (Novel only): 9781786155153
eBook ISBN (Recipes only): 9781786155146

Produced by Octavo Publishing Ltd, Cardiff
Printed and bound in the UK by Clays, St Ives Ltd.

CONTENTS

RECIPES FROM THE NOVEL

ACKNOWLEDGEMENTS

My thanks go to my wife Caroline for spending so many evenings on her own whilst I was writing this book and for her help and encouragement throughout. They also go to my son Paul for his objective input, Linda Griffin and Matt Butterworth for their invaluable help on criminal and procedural elements, David Norrington for believing in me and Peter Norrington for his critical evaluation, research support and eye for detail.

For my Dad

*This book is dedicated to my dad who gave me the inspiration
to write it when he was ill.*

Ten percent of all profits from this book will be donated to
Macmillan Cancer Support* in support of the work they do on
behalf of patients with cancer.

A further ten percent of the profits will be given to Crisis* to
help with the life-changing services they provide for homeless
people.

---

* *See imprint page for registration info.*

Hope is in abundance
There for all to see
When the darkness gets here
The lights all shine on in
As the brightness begins to wane
Is there hope for you and me?
Is there hope for me?
Is it a game that I can win?
Perhaps the lights are stars?
Or just a glistening of steel
Am I normal or just insane?
Am I paying for a path of sin?
Is life really such a big deal?
Is it any different to a lovely meal?
Should it be something to fear?

Seven years earlier

The evening sunlight through the bedroom window made the steel blade glisten as it was pressed against the young woman's throat, making her choke. Instead of being subservient to her attacker, she brought her right arm up hard and fast, knocking the knife from his hand and across the room, where it slid over the wooden floor and under the solid oak wardrobe. Her resilience to the threat was commendable but also stupid; as a right hook to the face fractured her eye socket and a knee in her ribs broke them with a loud crack that reverberated around the room. With her resistance shattered the woman lay still and allowed the man to do what he wanted. The ordeal was over within ten minutes and as the bedroom door and then the front door slammed shut behind the attacker, the woman dragged herself up off the floor by holding on to the bed post and tried to make her way onto the landing and down the stairs to get to her telephone in the lounge.

Seven years earlier

CHAPTER ONE

Shona dropped her negligée to the floor and pressed her naked body against the glass of the sliding balcony door of her eighth-floor penthouse. She wasn't sure how many men could see her from the street below. A few that happened to have binoculars maybe, but she didn't care, as her body was the one thing in her life she was proud of. It was the one thing that has ensured she hasn't had to beg on the streets or sleep rough on cold wet nights around the Chapel Walk shopping centre in Worcester during the last few years.

Although Shona earned a decent living at the moment, she was determined to do something other than work as a pole dancer in the Chocolate Elephant, Worcestershire's premier gentlemen's club. Shona wanted to become a powerful high-flier in a world dominated by men and was about to embark on a new career and use her hands in a different way to earn a decent, more respectable living. She knew that it wouldn't be easy but would do absolutely anything to make it happen.

~

Michael, a handsome, dark-haired, thirty-eight-year-old, well-off, freelance journalist, sat at his large square pine table in his sixteen-foot square kitchen, looking at the small ads. He was searching for a good catering company to produce an interesting three-course menu for his sister's forthcoming thirty-fifth birthday party. One advert in particular stood out. Maybe it was the graphics, the colours, the shape of the advert or just the name 'Spice and Slice' that made him pick up the phone and dial their number.

~

Joseph pulled out of the large car park in Langley, Virginia, for the very last time for the next few years.

Joseph, or Jo Jo as his friends and colleagues call him, has been employed by the Central Intelligence Agency for ten years, since he was twenty-six. He had worked diligently within a number of the Directorate of Intelligence's thirteen offices in an attempt to protect US national security interests.

He was now on his way to London to start a secondment with MI5. There is much collaboration between the US and the UK these days, as both countries try to neutralise and eradicate as many threats to public safety as possible, and Joseph had been asked to help Britain in its fight against terrorism.

Jo Jo was going to catch a flight to England in four hours' time for a holiday before starting his new job, but being an efficient person he had time for a nice meal and a beer before he went through security.

~

DCI Graham Laws was working his way through his notes for his Thursday morning briefing. He had been at his desk since 5.30 a.m., looking over the previous weekend's incident reports and preparing a work programme for his team for this Friday, Saturday and Sunday.

The reduction in the number of officers available to him following recent government cuts was making his job virtually impossible, while providing a breeding ground for the scumbags who are out to make life difficult for all the decent people in this beautiful county. Graham was very thorough in everything he did and his analysis work and projections had helped him and his team to predict many crimes before they were committed, catch perpetrators in the act and get many criminals put inside for a long time. Graham was devoted to his job, which is probably why he was still single at the age of forty-two. There was a time a few years ago when he had real ambition to become a chief constable, but that flame had burned out now as he was getting so much enjoyment from being right at the heart of what real police work was all about, making his beloved Worcestershire a much better and much safer place.

~

"It isn't important what type of person you develop into, but that you do all you can throughout your life to be very good at whatever you do," said Justin to the students listening to his speech at the CIA building in Hyde Park, New York.

Justin graduated from the Culinary Institute of America at the age of twenty-five. After spending a little time in England he then spent four years studying Indian cuisine in Bangladesh, before returning to Manhattan to pursue his dreams. Justin always practised what he preached. Over the years, he had spent thousands of hours honing his knife skills to make sure he was the best chef at boning, carving, chopping, filleting and slicing. He had also spent hundreds of hours searching for the ultimate knife manufacturer to ensure that he always had the right tools for every conceivable situation.

"A top chef needs many tools to deliver a perfect plate of food. Whether you go on to become a famous chef with your own chain of restaurants or work in the kitchens of a five-star resort, you must start your journey by equipping yourself with a set of high quality utensils. This will ensure you can create culinary masterpieces, by fusing together all the technical aspects of cooking, with unbelievable taste and deliverable artistic and functional presentation. As far as I am concerned, your first and most important purchase will be a good quality set of kitchen knives, as they can be the fundamental difference between an average cook and a high class cook. I take my kitchen toolbox with my knives in wherever I go, as I never know when I may get the opportunity to use them. As the old adage goes, practice makes perfect and being perfect means being consistent, which in turn means you make few if any mistakes. And as I said at the beginning, you then become very good at whatever you do."

~

Shona rang the quaint robin-shaped bell of the four hundred-year-old picture-book thatched cottage, set back from the country lane and surrounded by woodland, at exactly 9.00 a.m. Although Shona had made and received quite a few phone calls since launching her new business enterprise, this was her first appointment and she was feeling somewhat excited though really nervous. A young twenty-eight-year-old, five-foot-nine-inch-tall, attractive brunette, visiting an unknown householder could be a dangerous experience. Having rung the bell, Shona thought that she really should have put some safety measures in place beforehand.

"Hello," said Michael, upon opening the green, half-glazed, half-oak front door. "You must be…?"

"Shona Green," she said interrupting him quickly. "I am the owner and managing director of 'Spice and Slice', a new high quality catering company that I set up recently."

"I am Michael Black," he stuttered, stunned by the speed of Shona's interruption and her beauty. "You seem a little nervous, but I won't bite, unless you want me to," he added.

"I was trying to remain calm, but I am nervous, as it is scary

4

knocking on the door of a fairly remote house, not knowing the type of person who will answer it," replied Shona.

"Would you like to come in and have a coffee, to help you relax?" asked Michael.

"White without sugar, please," replied Shona, trying to appear more assertive. "I can see that you have a good sense of humour to go with a lovely house in a great location," she added.

"That's very kind of you to say so, and I am sorry if I sounded facetious, but I was trying to help you relax," said Michael.

The cottage was long and narrow and very dark inside due to the low ceilings and small windows. The bright white walls set against the black beams running through them did brighten the appearance a little and somehow seemed to provide a calming but cosy and warm effect.

"We have a lot to go through if I am to give your company the contract to deliver a menu that will make my sister's special day, a very special day," said Michael.

Shona flipped open her project book and wrote Michael Black at the top of the first page and then on the first line, 35th Birthday Party.

"Is the party to be a formal or an informal event?" asked Shona.

"Very informal, with the food being served in the dining room," replied Michael as he gave Shona a tour of the downstairs rooms, including a conservatory that led out onto a large patio that was dominated by four enormous patio heaters.

"I understand it is going to be a cold crisp night on the day of the event and wondered if some nibbles outside on the patio might be fun to start with?" asked Shona.

Michael smiled and stared at Shona while he thought about a suitable reply that didn't involve an obvious innuendo, even though her comment had got his mind racing.

"I think we will just have the party inside, as there can often be a lot of noise and dust in the air these days. There was a time a few years ago when I could sunbathe naked in this two-acre garden, but not anymore. It used to be a very isolated place surrounded by trees on two sides and just the Malvern Hills as a backdrop. The idiots in government, who pretend they are running the country, then launched a ridiculous new housing policy that meant the end of traditional village life as people here knew it. If you had driven another mile down the lane and turned right, you would have come upon a hideous new development of boring houses that I can now see out of my upstairs windows, which are creeping closer to my back garden on a daily basis. All of the original residents are still trying to come to terms with a constant stream of traffic down this once quiet lane and the fact our homes have decreased in value because the government doesn't have a sensible low cost housing or immigration policy."

"Wow! You do say what you think," said Shona.

"I do have this tendency to foist my opinions on people. It's just part of my passionate nature, but it does make me a few enemies occasionally."

"I'm not surprised," replied Shona.

"My character probably stems from my job as a journalist, where I try to make people aware of key issues that affect law-abiding tax-paying citizens. I try to get key decision makers within government departments, councils and large organisations to do the right things, instead of things they believe are politically correct but place enormous pressure on individuals and small businesses."

"I pay my taxes," said Shona, "but in the very short time I have been doing this job, I have been squeezed by some larger companies and local authorities."

"That statement sounds interesting," said Michael.

Shona smiled. "You know very well what I mean."

"I do know what you mean and I think I should stop trying to be funny. Running your own business is an extremely brave and very tough thing to do in the current economic climate. Although I am technically a self-employed journalist, I still have to do all that an owner of a small business does, other than maybe negotiate with a lot of suppliers."

"It was the amount of legislation, the number of forms to complete, the expectations of government departments, solicitors and accountants and the cost of everything that got to me in my first few weeks of trading," said Shona.

Michael grinned. "Now who's voicing their feelings?"

"Your passion is catching and I think it is my turn to say sorry," replied Shona, trying to refocus on the reason she was here and steer the conversation back to the party.

"Now, tell me exactly what you would like me to do for you?"

~

"Good morning, all," said Graham. "Last weekend we had one hundred and twenty reported and observed crimes to deal with within Worcester city centre: forty-seven percent linked to anti-social behaviour, twelve percent to shoplifting, eleven percent were of a violent and sexual nature and eight percent were for criminal damage and arson. On a brighter note, we only had two car thefts, three bicycle thefts and one firearms incident to deal with. We have reason to believe that an organised gang will be doing their utmost to increase the number of crimes related to drugs from our usual eight or nine over a weekend by infiltrating the pubs and clubs in large numbers and selling 'synthetic cannabinoids'. These are herbal smoking mixtures with fancy names such as Amsterdam Gold, Blue Cheese,

Clockwork Orange, Devil's Weed, Mary Joy and Spice. All of those are classified as Class B drugs and can have severe side effects such as accelerated heartbeat, high blood pressure, nausea, hallucinations and more serious symptoms such as epileptic seizures and heart attacks. While carrying out your normal duties, look out for people acting suspiciously and for anyone holding or passing on colourful sachets that are often tea-bag shape."

"Would these be square, circular or pyramid shape bags, sir?" said Constable Paul Curry, a new recruit to the team.

"I don't care if they are dead fucking parrot shape," replied Graham with some annoyance.

"What would that be called?" asked Paul.

"Polygon," said Graham in an aggressive tone.

DCI Graham Laws outlined a few other things his team of officers should watch out for over the weekend as there were going to be thousands of visitors to the city on Saturday with both a county cricket match and horse racing taking place. As he was concluding the briefing, his mobile rang. Graham listened intently and quickly realised that the long arm of the law was about to be seriously stretched.

~

Shona was very embarrassed by her actions and her lack of professionalism. She hadn't intended to sleep with potential clients to get any contracts, but was nervous and desperate to get her business up and running, and old habits die hard.

"That shouldn't have happened. It was very unprofessional and naïve of me," said Shona.

"I am sorry too, but you really shouldn't have asked what you could do for me," replied Michael.

"You took that the wrong way."

"I know, but it was an open-ended question and I thought I

8

would have a bit of fun and try my luck when I realised this was your first time."

"I am glad you didn't think that about the sex," retorted Shona.

She then looked Michael directly in the eyes and added harshly, "you could actually have said no."

"Pigs might fly and I am a man," said Michael.

"Well, why don't you use the larger of your brains and make me another coffee, while I type up the menu we agreed for the party on my iPad," said Shona laughing.

"That's the least I can do other than confirm that you have definitely got your first catering contract and that I will not even try to knock you down."

Michael started to say something else but Shona quickly cut him short with "don't even go there," so he focused on the real reason she was here.

"There will definitely only be six people at the party including myself, and don't forget that everybody is very particular about the use of local produce, such as Herefordshire beef or Worcestershire sauce."

"I hope none of your guests work for the government. It will be a short evening if you upset any of them very early on with any ranting or raving."

"I know politicians are not really idiots, but they do force local councils and businesses to make idiotic decisions without understanding or caring about the long-term consequences," replied Michael.

"Did you really think about the consequences of sleeping with me within an hour or so of meeting me for the first time?"

"I have to admit that I didn't. I took the liberty of looking at your website before I phoned you and also checked you out on Facebook and Twitter. What I observed was a gorgeous young woman with incredible alluring eyes and a wonderful smile. I actually stared at your photograph for some time, almost spellbound by your beauty and knew in my heart that I had to get to know you. As soon as I saw you standing at my front door though, the larger of my brains took over. I have never been a shy, retiring person and have been told that I have a way with women, but honestly, this is the first time I have ever slept with someone before getting to know them," said Michael.

"When I embarked on a change of career, although I told myself I would do anything to make this business successful, this didn't actually include sleeping with customers, as I really wanted to set out on a new path as a different person. I have to admit however, that as soon as I saw you I fancied you and just lost control of the situation," replied Shona.

"I think we both lost control, but we have a lot in common and hope you feel the same as me, in that we chalk this up to experience rather than on a bedpost and get to know each other properly," said Michael.

"I would really like that," replied Shona excitedly.

"Your Facebook page told me you were single but it didn't say if you have ever been married," asked Michael.

"I have never been married but I do have a six-year-old daughter from an unsuccessful relationship. What about you?" asked Shona.

"I haven't been married either and don't have any children, as far as I know," replied Michael, who then wondered, as the schools were closed for half-term at the moment, where Shona's daughter was.

"Does your daughter live with you?" he asked.

"No, it is a long and complicated story for another day, but I wasn't in a position to care for a child when Jade was born for various reasons, so I had her fostered."

"Do you see her at all?"

"Only from a distance and the occasional arranged meeting,

but she doesn't yet know that I am her mother."

"What about her father?"

"I have no idea where he is and he has no idea that he has a daughter. I am very friendly with Jade's foster parents and eventually they would like me to be a proper mum to her."

"Will you then try to find her real dad and try to make a go of it as a proper family?"

"No, certainly not. If I find the right man to settle down with, Jade will have a father, but it will not be her biological one."

~

Justin packed his knives away into his toolbox. He wasn't concerned about the consequences of his actions either. He had a job to do and as a professional he would do it the way he felt best to get the necessary results. He had his team in place; a team of handpicked individuals all with different qualities who specialised in different preparations and techniques, to ensure that timings and delivery were consistent with his expectations. The students had been impressed with his speech and the quality of the dishes presented. He hoped that the next dish he cooked would be presented on a plate to a very special customer and that their reaction would be one of real shock.

~

Shona printed the menu for the dinner party and handed it to Michael to check.

"I will be here at 2.30 p.m. to start the preparation. I will serve the starter at 8.00 p.m. the main course at 8.30 p.m. and the dessert at 9.30 p.m. I do have to leave here by 11.00 p.m."

"That's a full eight-hour day," said Michael. "I guess you will be tired afterwards?"

"Yes, I will be," said Shona. "So the only dessert you will be getting on the day of the party will be a Malvern Pudding or an

11

Eton Mess."

Michael smiled and glanced down at the menu. "Are you sure you can get all the ingredients together within a day?"

"No problem," replied Shona, as she left via the front door to go home and begin her preparations. "It would have been nice to have had more notice though."

"I am sorry. I was going to do the cooking myself, but as soon as my sister Kate decided to invite three other people I knew I was out of my depth."

"Lucky I was available," replied Shona.

Michael thought about making another joke but decided against it.

"See you tomorrow, then," he shouted out of an open window. "Don't forget your outfit."

"Let's hope I bring my chef's outfit and not the one that you would prefer to see me wearing," Shona shouted back.

Michael smiled again and wondered what his guests would make of Shona dressed as a pole dancer with a chef's hat on. He also wondered how the impact Shona had made on him in a few hours would shape his life, affect his behaviour in front of his sister, and if his guests would like the menu chosen.

Asparagus & Mushroom Quiche
Braised Ox Cheeks with Dumplings
Worcester Potato Cakes
Malvern Pudding
or
Eton Mess

CHAPTER TWO

The blast had ripped through the pavilion with the force of a tornado. Remnants of the quaint white building could be seen scattered across New Road and Cripplegate Park.

Graham Laws arrived at the scene to find that his operations team had co-ordinated events quickly and that his officers and the fire brigade had already sealed off the area of the blast and were evacuating the Premier Inn hotel nearby, as well as homes and businesses within a half-mile radius of the incident. He made his way through the cordon to the first response incident room set up in the foyer of the hotel.

"What have we actually got here?" Graham asked Charlie Burnett, the chief fire officer.

"It's a bit early to say yet. There isn't a great deal left of the building and the fire is under control so we should be able to begin the investigation process shortly."

"Our forensics team and the bomb squad are on the way," said Graham.

"I am glad you arranged for the bomb squad to attend, particularly as we now know there wasn't any gas being supplied to the pavilion," replied Charlie.

"So you are of the same mindset as me and think that the blast could have been caused by a bomb?"

"It's a possibility, but I don't see why anyone would blow up the Worcester Cricket Club academy pavilion."

"It could be a warning from a terrorist group?" said Graham.

"That did cross my mind as you were speaking. Maybe it's a warning to a certain cricketer and all other sportsmen and women not to wear articles of clothing supporting or denouncing militant groups."

"That sounds a bit extreme, Charlie, but I'll make a few calls to see what I can find out. Let's hope it wasn't a bomb and there wasn't anybody in that building."

"If there was, this place is going to be crawling with politicians, MI5, the army, TV crews, newspaper reporters and Uncle Tom Cobley."

"We are lucky living where we do and it would seem unlikely that militants would centre any attacks here, but we can't be indifferent to what is happening in the Middle East and imagine it to be a self-contained far away thing that doesn't have the potential to do us harm," said Graham.

"You are right, Graham. Terrorist groups will do whatever they can to publicise their cause, often by fear and intimidation, but it isn't as if a cricket pavilion bears any similarity to the Twin Towers."

"No, but our chief constable has arranged with MI5 for someone from the CIA to come to Worcestershire to talk to us about terrorism, espionage and cyber espionage as part of the West Mercia police force development programme and to shadow me and help me as some compensation for some of the redundancies within the force."

~

Joseph had been on English soil no more than an hour when his phone rang.

"Hello, Joseph. It's Andrew Rankin from MI5 here. How was your flight?"

"Fine, Andrew. Thank you, I wasn't expecting to hear from

14

you for at least ten days though."

"I need to see you before you start your holiday so wondered where you might be at the moment."

"I am just about to pick up my hire car."

"Where are you going to be driving to?" asked Andrew.

"I decided to stay with some friends in the Cotswolds before starting on the assignment in London."

"Perfect," said Andrew. "I will meet you in the foyer of the Moto motorway service station on the M4 at Reading in about two hours. It isn't out of your way as you will be travelling west in any case, and what I have to talk to you about is urgent and sensitive."

Andrew Rankin paged his driver immediately and they left the MI5 offices overlooking Lambeth Bridge within seven minutes of him ending the telephone call to Joseph. Joseph collected his BMW 5 Series hire car, set the satellite navigation system and made his way to the services, where Andrew had pulled a few strings with the site director to obtain a meeting room away from the general public.

"I am glad you are staying in the Cotswolds, as we have something strange occurring in Worcestershire, not too far from there, that I would like you to look into," said Andrew.

"I can see my holiday going out of the window," replied Joseph.

"You could well be right. There was an explosion just outside Worcester city centre this morning at ten minutes past eleven. None of our intelligence sources had warned us of anything happening within the county so I would like you to meet with the chief constable of the West Mercia police force to offer your assistance as and when required, to help them establish the cause of the blast and find out who the perpetrators may be," said Andrew.

"Did you say the bomb went off at 11.10 a.m.?"

"Yes, I did."

"That's extremely odd, as that was the exact time my flight from Washington DC landed at Heathrow airport."

~

Emma Thyme had been the lead forensics officer within the West Mercia area for two years and she had obtained a good reputation for her curious mind and acute attention to detail. Emma and her team play a major role in helping Graham and his officers solve hundreds of difficult crimes every year. Emma specialises in the collection of trace evidence from the scene of a crime and her techniques have enabled the Hereford and Worcester police forces to increase the number of solved crimes by seventy-six percent since she got promoted to the position, at the age of twenty-four. She had got a few lucky breaks when solving some horrific murders early on in her career, which led to her getting a promotion ahead of longer serving colleagues. There were at least three or four instances when she provided the Crown Prosecution Service with hard evidence to secure a conviction at the last possible moment, which led to some rather jealous colleagues giving her the nickname 'Justin'.

"Hello, Graham, hello, Charlie," said Emma as she shook their hands. "What's the score?"

"Pavilion nil, blast one," said Graham. "We need you to weave some magic and help us identify the cause of the explosion."

"I will do my very, Georgie," replied Emma.

"I didn't know you were a United supporter," said Charlie.

"Sorry about that! Which team do you support?"

"For now, let's just say they play in blue."

"So you are either a City fan, a Worcester fan or, heaven forbid, a Chelsea fan?" asked Emma.

"I'll tell you later, as I wouldn't want to upset you, or your concentration, until you have done what you need to do," said Charlie.

Emma walked crime scenes in concentric circles or squares depending on the area concerned to make sure she didn't miss any trace evidence. She had worked this system out over the years and it has held her in good stead on many occasions.

"You are clear to go, Emma," said Charlie. "There wasn't the level of heat intensity that we would have expected from such a large blast."

"What colour was the smoke when you got here?"

"Strangely enough, it was white."

"What has the bomb squad said?"

"I haven't had chance to discuss much with them yet other than to learn that there isn't any likelihood of a second explosion."

"That's comforting to know," said Emma.

"Will you be able to get finished before it gets dark?" asked Graham.

"It's hard to say. I'll walk from the outside to a point that I am happy to call the centre. I'll start from the boundary, then move in a little and walk in progressively smaller circles until I reach the centre. I'll undertake a thorough search of this area and then go from the middle back to the outer point of the crime scene area. This ensures that I collect all material that looks to be out of place."

Emma proceeded to put on her protective suit, gathered her tools and made her way to the pavilion, or what was left of it. Collecting evidence is a slow and time-consuming process. Investigators must use caution to avoid disturbing or destroying it and wear the right clothing, gloves, head coverings and footwear protectors so as not to contaminate the crime scene with their own hair, skin, fingerprints, or footprints. Emma enjoyed the challenge of pitting her skills against those of the perpetrators and as she started the job of finding any particles, fibres or flecks of blood that would act as a silent witness in court she smiled to herself and wondered how proud her father would have been to see her in action doing the work that cost him his life.

~

Michael was busy putting the finishing touches to the table decorations and blowing up some more balloons, just before his guests were due to arrive in a few minutes time at 7.30 p.m. Shona had arrived at 2.00 p.m. and everything was going to plan. She had made the quiche earlier in the day that was now in the fridge ready to be warmed in the oven at 7.45 p.m. for fifteen minutes. The ox cheeks had been in the oven on a low heat since 4.00 p.m. and both desserts were looking magnificent.

"I guess Eton Mess originally got its name from being served at the college?" said Michael.

"Yes it did, although it was originally made with strawberries, bananas and ice cream. The meringue didn't get added until many years later. I have trialled this recipe quite a few times and tell people it gets its name from looking a mess and then being eaten," replied Shona.

"That's very good. Let's hope the dessert is." said Michael.

Michael's sister Kate and her husband Kevin actually arrived at 7.35 p.m., before any of the other guests. They were introduced to Shona in such a way that immediately made Kate suspicious of her brother's relationship with her.

"You're a dark horse," Kate said to Michael quietly out of earshot of Shona and Kevin.

"I don't know what you mean," said Michael.

"I am your sister and I know you and your mannerisms like

18

the back of my hand."

"It's a long story."

"Is it?" said Kate.

"No," said Michael "It's a very short story and I will tell you about it in a few days."

Richard and Amanda Webb who live near to Michael, and Jessica Chalmers who had recently moved to the other end of the village from New Zealand, arrived together at 7.40 p.m.

Shona served all of the courses on time and the evening went really well. It wasn't until halfway through dessert that the topic of work was broached by Jessica.

"I was hoping not to discuss my latest assignments," said Michael.

"I am sorry," said Jessica, who hadn't really said much throughout the evening but now under the influence of many glasses of wine was beginning to open up. "As you know, I only moved into the neighbourhood six months ago and thought it would be useful to know as much as I can about the people I meet."

"Michael is a freelance journalist," said Kevin. "He also has a professional blogging site called *The Black Side*, or *Black Log* or something like that, which aims to be judge and jury within the realms of free speech to try and bring justice to the world and help mankind on a righteous path."

"Do you specialise in any particular area of journalism, Michael?" asked Jessica.

"Much of my focus is on the wrongdoings of the government, local councils and large conglomerates. At the moment I am working on budget cuts within the National Health Service and the benefits or otherwise of NHS England and NICE. I am then going to look into the reduction in local community bus services, issues relating to immigration, the lack of black managers within football and the high cost in more ways than one of HS2, the proposed new high speed rail line."

"Those are all very sensitive issues," said Jessica.

"Yes, they are," said Michael. "They are all issues that touch people's hearts and can have a massive impact on their lives, which is why they aren't always easy topics of conversation for dinner parties and can lead to a nice evening turning bad."

"What you really mean," said Kate, "is that your passion for trying to bring power back to the people can be very intense sometimes and your opinionated nature can upset some people who don't agree with what you believe is right."

"I am not sure if you are my sister or a politician in disguise," replied Michael smiling.

Shona overheard the conversation from the kitchen. As she came into the dining room to collect the dishes she glanced at Michael and smiled to herself, as Kate's thoughts were very much in line with her own.

"Now you can see why I don't talk about my work at social events, Jessica."

"I like hearing about your work though, as it is far more interesting than any of ours," said Amanda.

"I would have thought that a part-time position at St Peters Garden Centre, looking after the plants, pruning trees and serving customers is a great job to have," said Kevin.

"It does have its advantages and gives me a lot of free time to do fun things," replied Amanda in rather a smug way as she glanced at Kate.

The conversation about work started to get boring and moved on to include a fun question and answer session that engaged everybody and involved much debate. As it was Kate's birthday, she got to speak first and asked the group, "Where would you like to live in the world if money was no object?"

This was a difficult question for everybody to answer on the spur of the moment as it is hard to think of all the places in the world that are idyllic and would be the perfect location to live the perfect life, taking consideration of the weather, entertainment, nightlife, personal safety and schools. Jessica, however, knew instantly that she would choose to live on Laucala Island in Fiji. "It has everything I could ever wish for and is probably as close to heaven as you could get to before you get there," she added.

Kate hadn't heard of Laucala Island but chose another island called Bora Bora, one of the most celebrated islands in the South Pacific, just northwest of Tahiti.

None of the men were very specific with their answers and just wanted somewhere where they could watch or play sport and eat and drink in nice restaurants. Michael said loudly, probably so that Shona could hear, that he was happy living where he did. The location wasn't as idyllic as it was a few years ago, but the scenery had improved in the last thirty-six hours.

"Pass me the sick bucket," said Kate.

"Shona's cooking isn't that bad," replied Michael.

"Shona's food is fantastic," said Amanda, who then chose an odd location in Bangladesh as her perfect place to live. This got a strange look from her husband Richard for some reason, who moved quickly on to his question, "What book if any are you reading at the moment?"

It didn't take too long for each of the guests to give Richard their answer as most people were too busy to spend time reading, except for Jessica who seemed to have a lot of time on her hands and had three books on the go at once.

It was then Jessica's turn to ask a question and she wanted to know, "Would you rather have X-ray vision or be invisible?"

This subject was debated for some time and produced much amusement and changing of opinions as different scenarios for having such great powers were suggested. Everybody's final answer centred on them being able to turn their power on or off as and when required.

Amanda then asked, "If you all had to lose one of your five senses, which one would you choose?"

At first all those at the party thought this to be a very hard question, but in the end all six around the table chose smell as their answer.

Kevin was then intrigued to learn which object everyone would save if their house was on fire? Almost without exception everybody chose an item of sentiment, although Kevin also selected a framed football shirt signed by the entire Hereford United first team squad from 1972, for some reason.

"We thought you were a sad bastard, now we know," said Michael.

"Pot, kettle, black," replied Kevin when Michael reverted back into work mode and wanted to know what his guests' ideal career would be?

When his guests started proffering stupid answers, Michael thought it was time to start winding the evening up.

By 11.00 p.m. Shona had washed up, put all of the plates, utensils and cutlery away and tidied up the kitchen.

"Why don't you join us for a drink before you go home? You deserve one or two for serving up such a fabulous meal," said Kate, hoping to get to know Shona a little better.

"Another time maybe, but I do need to go home now, as I have a few things to sort out for tomorrow when I get back."

"I'll show you to your car," said Michael, who was glad of this as he knew what Kate's intentions were.

Outside and out of view of his guests, Michael gave Shona a big hug and kiss. "You looked stunning tonight in that little short apron and I was turned on every time you walked into the dining room."

"You're just saying that."

"Give me your hand," said Michael.

"My word," replied Shona somewhat shocked.

"I want you now," said Michael.

"What about your sister and friends?"

"I don't want them joining in," replied Michael, laughing.

Michael and Shona ran into the orchard where Michael sat on the arbour seat, unzipped his trousers and eased Shona on top of him. Shona groaned with pleasure as she thrust up and down, moving faster and faster as she got nearer to climax. Shona came at the same time as Michael, who then held her tightly and kissed her neck lovingly.

"Oh my God," she said, "I can't believe we just did that or that I initially thought you might be a bit square."

"I can't believe that such a beautiful, intelligent, fun loving woman has walked into my life and stolen my heart within a couple of days," said Michael.

"I think that the smooth-talking man struggling with his zip should go back inside the house and look after his guests so that I can get on my way."

Michael went back inside the house to join his guests, only to find his sister staring at him rather inquisitively.

"That was a long goodbye," said Kate.

"I had to pay Shona for her services this evening."

"Was that just for the catering?"

"Stop it, Kate, we're just good friends."

"So were Paul Nicholas and Jan Francis in the TV series."

"Who would like some coffee?" asked Michael, quickly changing the subject before the hole that was being dug for him got much deeper.

"Let's talk about the NHS budget cuts over coffee," said Amanda.

"You're a bit of a tigress," said Michael.

"You don't want to go there," said Richard, Amanda's

husband, then adding, "How do you think I got these scratches on my neck?"

"That sounds a far more interesting topic than any discussion regarding the National Health Service," said Michael.

"You are too much of a nice guy to want to hear about our sordid sex life," said Amanda.

"Please don't think of me as a nice guy," replied Michael.

"Is that because nice guys always finish last?" asked Kevin.

"No, it's because they usually finish in the shower," said Michael, laughing.

CHAPTER THREE

The point of the blade pressed against her neck. Not enough to cut the skin, but enough for her to feel some pain. Frozen with fear but for a flick of the eyes that could see the masked intruder, she tried to scream, but no sound came from her mouth other than a gurgling noise in the throat.

"You have displeased me, Amanda," said the man. "Scream and you will displease me more, which wouldn't be a good thing to do. In fact, it could be the last thing you ever do."

Although scared for her life, an inner strength enabled Amanda to mumble, "How do you know my name?"

"That doesn't matter, what matters is my mission and unfortunately for you, you are going to play a part in it."

"My husband will be home any minute."

"He won't," said the intruder. "I know he went away to Berlin on business this afternoon."

"If you were going to kill me, you could have done so while I was asleep," stuttered Amanda.

"That would have been too easy. I have been instructed to make sure you die in a specific way."

"If am going to die then you could at least tell me why, and tell me your name?" she asked a bit more calmly.

The intruder hesitated but on thinking Amanda would soon die, he said, "I am not able to tell you why you are to die as I am not privileged to such information, but I will tell you that my name is Baz."

A very apt name for the so-called person standing beside her Amanda thought to herself. An unspecified entity in her mind, who was obviously a low life who should have no place in society. Instead of being brave or even stupid by saying what she really wanted to say, Amanda's survival instincts kicked in and she decided instead to play on the intruder's possible manliness.

"Well, Baz, as you know we are all alone, and nobody is likely to arrive home, call round or phone at this time of night so you might as well take off your mask, and avail yourself of my voluptuous body, naked beneath these sheets."

Baz took a step back from beside the bed and stared at Amanda with a surprised and quizzical look.

"However much I would love to have you, I am not stupid enough to leave any DNA as evidence in this house," said Baz.

"I can see why you were selected for the mission," said Amanda trying to make Baz relax and drop his guard.

"How about I just slide the sheets back and you just watch me play with my breasts instead?"

Baz watched in awe as Amanda pulled the sheets back and began to touch herself. He immediately felt movement between his legs and knew that he should resist the urge to touch or rub himself through his trousers. Unfortunately he couldn't do this, as watching Amanda was very exciting.

Amanda watched Baz out of the corner of her eye, in the dim light from the moon through the blinds, hoping to find the right moment to escape from this difficult situation. She teased him with her finger and hand actions and as she did so, his hand and arm movements got a bit faster with each second that passed. Amanda placed her index finger in her mouth and sucked it before rotating it on her nipples. She then placed two fingers inside herself and thrust them in and out for a few seconds before reaching across to her bedside cabinet and grabbing a large purple vibrator from the top drawer.

Baz stared at her with his eyes wide open as she switched the vibrator on and used it in a way he found unbelievably amazing and exciting. As the minutes passed, Baz started to breathe heavily so Amanda moved her body slightly to the left and brought her feet up towards her body and spread her knees apart to give Baz a better look at the way she was using the vibrator.

The excitement was eventually too much for Baz and he started to move his right hand backwards and forwards with some real speed and just as he reached orgasm and his legs staring shaking, Amanda swung her right leg and kicked him hard in the groin.

As Baz scrunched forwards Amanda grabbed hold of the bedside lamp with her right hand and swung it back across her body hitting him flush on the jaw with it. In that same instant she pushed him with her left hand then scrambled down the bed and ran for the bedroom door some eight feet away.

Baz although stunned, quickly switched the knife to his right hand and lunged at Amanda, stabbing her in the side just as the heavy oak door hit him on the nose, breaking it instantly, causing blood to flow from it and down his throat, making him gasp for breath.

Amanda clutched her side and ran down the stairs. Still naked she opened the front door and sprinted down the drive and out on to the main road.

It was now past 1.00 a.m. in the morning, but luckily the A38 is a busy road and even luckier was the fact that the person driving along as Amanda ran into the road was a business woman on her way home from a charity function in the city on behalf of Birmingham Children's Hospital.

Carly King slammed on her brakes and swerved to the right, narrowly missing Amanda by inches. Amanda placed her hands on the bonnet of the Audi, looked at Carly through the windscreen and somehow managed to find the breath to mouth "Help me."

Carly saw the blood oozing from the naked woman standing in front of her and immediately leapt out of the car and rushed to help her. Carly bundled Amanda into the back of the car, thrust a blanket at her and told her to press it hard against her side. She ran back around the car, leapt back into the driver's seat and pressed the accelerator to the floor.

"We should be able to get to the hospital in about eight minutes," said Carly as she spun the car around almost on two wheels. After a few minutes driving, Carly glanced in her mirror and realised that the woman who was lying bleeding on her back seat was starting to go into hypovolemic shock. Carly knew from the time she was married to a doctor that if the woman's body didn't compensate for this she might die before they got to the hospital.

Carly pulled the car into a lay-by, grabbed some rope from the boot and used it to tie Amanda's ankles to the grab handle above the rear door. This might help to keep more blood in her vital organ areas and her blood pressure up, Carly thought as she raced along the A4440, following the hospital signs.

~

Joseph couldn't sleep as his body clock was still on American time, so he was sitting in his friend Sam's lounge at 2.00 a.m. drinking Ovaltine and reminiscing. They hadn't seen each other for a few years and had much to talk about. Some of this was 'boys stuff' and beyond the comprehension of Sam's wife, who thought that sleep was more interesting. Joseph had been listening to the news during the evening, and as his conscience was getting the better of him, he had decided to drive into Worcester on the morning of the fourth full day of his holiday

28

to see DCI Graham Laws.

"I'm going to see the DCI today," he told his friend Sam, "just to see if I can shed some light on the explosion."

"You're supposed to be on holiday."

"You know me: work gets in the way of pleasure."

"Which is why you have lost your wife and family," said Sam.

"Wife maybe," said Joseph, "but my family is a different issue."

"Where is your brother now?"

"I don't know and don't much care," said Joseph.

"I still find it hard to believe that he could have attacked his own father in your house," said Sam.

"If he hadn't upped sticks and left America immediately, I would have had him arrested, Sam."

"Did you tell him that?"

"I told him that he had twenty-four hours to get out of the country, never to return."

"What did your dad have to say about the incident?"

"My dad said his injuries were caused by an armed robber breaking into the house, trying to get money for drugs."

"Perhaps that was the truth? Perhaps the robber knew you were often away working and that an elderly man was alone in the house at the time?"

"Sorry, Sam, but I don't buy that. Not when it was my brother who had a knife in his hand as I walked in the back door."

"So your dad didn't see his youngest son again before he died?"

"No, he didn't. He died within days of the incident. The doctors said that shock had caused his body to shut down."

"It really is difficult to comprehend."

"My brother was and probably still is a very intelligent

being, but beneath the exterior there was always a black side, and to go with it there was a ferocious temper. We used to have a cute rabbit when we were young, but it disappeared one day. We thought it might have been taken by an urban fox as we found some fur in the back yard. The next day our mother served up a pie that she said was homemade ground beef and veg that Justin had got for her from the local deli store, but it didn't taste like it. On another occasion our neighbours' homesteader shed just went up in flames one afternoon. Guess who was the only person within five hundred yards of it? I could go on and on here, Sam, if you really want me to relay many strange occurrences over a fifteen year period."

"I believe you, Joseph, but without the involvement of the police and a forensics team all of your thoughts are just conjecture."

"I threatened to get them involved many times but it wasn't until the incident with dad that Justin realised I was serious. Anyway Sam, I guess I should try to get some sleep, as I said I would be with Graham by 10.30 a.m. so I will need to be up about 8.00 a.m."

"You can park by the racecourse and walk up the hill to the police station," said Sam.

"Is the car park free?"

"You must be joking. Only air is free in England."

"No, it isn't. It cost me fifty pence at a garage to inflate my tyres yesterday," replied Joseph.

~

Carly King sped into the Worcestershire Royal Hospital grounds, negotiated the roundabouts on what felt like two wheels for the second time in the last ten minutes and screeched to a halt outside the Accident and Emergency department. She then leapt out of her car and rushed through the main doors screaming for help. The triage nurse looked up from her desk and mumbled, "What's the problem?"

"My friend is bleeding," said Carly.

"Let me take some details," said the nurse.

"Details?" said Carly. "There is a woman lying on the back seat of my car who has been stabbed and she needs help urgently."

"What's her name?"

"I have no idea she just ran out in front of me."

"I thought you said she was a friend."

"Stop asking such bloody stupid questions and get a doctor," shouted Carly.

The triage nurse immediately paged someone, looked back towards Carly and said, "Help is on its way."

After a few minutes of waiting Carly shouted at the nurse, "We can't wait any longer. You'll have to help me get her into a treatment room."

Carly ran back to her car, opened the back offside door, untied the rope, and quickly wrapped a thick overcoat around Amanda before starting to drag her out. As she was doing this the triage nurse arrived to help her.

"We are really stretched tonight but a team with a gurney will be here within a couple of minutes," said the nurse.

Amanda was cold to the touch and her skin was now very pale, but she was still conscious although her breathing was very fast. Two young looking medics arrived with the gurney, lifted Amanda onto it and rushed her inside the hospital and into the first available examination room.

"Where did she get her injuries?" said the nurse, who Carly could now see was named Irene.

Carly briefly explained to Irene what had happened.

"I am going to phone the police," said Irene, who then added, "They will need to interview you, so please can you move your car into the A&E car park while I go and get you a nice cup of tea?"

"I think I need something stronger than tea," said Carly.

"Coffee it is then," said Irene.

The police arrived within twenty-five minutes and took Carly to an interview room where they questioned her for another thirty-five minutes. Carly eventually left the hospital just after 4.00 a.m. and drove home in her blood-stained car without knowing what happened to the woman whom she had helped or who she was. She walked in her front door at 4.45 a.m. and went straight to the drinks cabinet where she poured herself a large vodka, but in the light of the evenings events she refrained from adding tomato juice and Worcestershire sauce.

~

Baz recognised the number on his mobile phone and ignored it. He had messed up and didn't like to think of the consequences. He needed to get out of the country fast, as it wasn't going to take the Old Bill long to work out who had attacked Amanda Webb. There was one person whom Baz thought he could trust to help him at such short notice, but he was on the payroll of the man trying to get hold of him now. This was the man who was going to be most upset that the target was probably still alive and that this phase of the mission had failed. This was the man who was only known as 'The DJ'.

~

Emma was desperately waiting for the technicians to get back to her with their analysis. She had been up all Thursday night making sure that her evidence bags were labelled correctly and that everything that she could conclude could provide a link to the cause of the explosion had been listed in her analysis book. She had her suspicions as to the cause of the blast but needed the results from the lab before presenting her findings to DCI Graham Laws. It was now Monday morning, so she was expecting to get something presented to her that she could evaluate before driving into the city this afternoon.

~

Richard Webb was awoken in his Berlin hotel alongside the River Spree by the hotel manager to be informed that the Bundespolizei wished to speak to him downstairs in his office. He got dressed quickly and made his way to the lift on the eighth floor with a suspicion that his meeting later today at the famous KaDeWe store was about to be cancelled. He had chosen the Melia Hotel as it was one of the best places to stay in Berlin. It was twenty minutes from the Brandenburg Gate and half an hour from major attractions such as Checkpoint Charlie and Alexanderplatz, which is where he was supposed to be meeting a client tomorrow.

As the lift descended Richard wondered what could be so urgent for the manager to call him on the phone at 6.00 a.m.

He soon found out as the German officer standing in the manager's office spoke quickly, saying something like: *Herr Webb, es tut mir Leid, Sie zu informieren, dass ein Vorfall in Ihrem Haus. Ihre Frau wurde in ein Krankenhaus gebracht. Ich glaube, dass die Situation ist ernst, und wir sollten Sie zu den Flughafen schnell, so kann man den nächsten Flug nach London.* Richard may have missed the odd word or two as his mind was spinning, but he understood enough German to realise that something terrible had happened to Amanda. The hotel manager translated all that the officer had said to confirm this and then asked his receptionist to telephone all of the airlines and get Richard on the next flight back to England.

~

Michael was chatting with Shona on Skype on his laptop about her next dinner party menu when a text message from Richard came through on his mobile phone. He glanced at it and quickly told Shona that he would have to see her later as he needed to get to the Worcestershire Royal Hospital quickly, as Amanda was critically ill following a serious incident at her home late last night.

CHAPTER FOUR

Graham shook hands with Joseph in the reception area of the Castle Street police station, and then invited him to his office for a chat before introducing him to his superior. "This is Assistant Chief Constable Benjamin Lewis, who is responsible for protective services; that includes amongst other things intelligence, major investigations, operations and the protection of vulnerable people."

"There are a few strange things happening here in Worcestershire at the moment," said Benjamin. "We would appreciate your involvement, as we suspect a terrorist organisation is behind some of the incidents."

"I had a brief discussion with Graham on the phone yesterday and will help where I can. This is a beautiful part of the world and I would much rather be here than with Andrew Rankin in London."

"How is Handy Andy?" asked Benjamin.

"Why do you call him that? Is he a very hands-on sort of person?" asked Joseph.

"You could say that," said Benjamin, "Just work out what rhymes with his surname."

"You don't like him, then?"

"Oh, he's ok," said Graham. "He is very driven and has cleaned up many parts of London, but let's just say that he comes from an upper-class family in Surrey and doesn't bat for them."

"What have you got in mind for me? I am only staying in Bourton-on-the-Water so I could start straight away."

"We would like you to meet up with Emma Thyme, our lead forensics officer, to see if you can establish a link between a blast that occurred on Thursday and any terrorist groups."

"Andrew Rankin mentioned it when I met with him the other day, so I checked with my sources in Washington. Although there is no intelligence to suggest that Worcester is a target, it is possible that a new extremist group could be testing its radicals' capabilities before progressing to more prominent targets."

"I am going to meet up with Emma now, as there was another incident late last night, the aftermath of which requires my attention and her expertise. If you come with me we can have another chat in my car about your role and responsibilities," said Graham.

~

Michael arrived at the hospital to learn that Amanda was having an emergency operation. He was asked to take a seat in the main surgery ward waiting room and told that he might not be given any information for some time, as her procedure was a delicate and long process. He phoned Shona and told her that she would have to go to her next customer appointment on her own, as he should at least stay at the hospital until Richard arrived. Michael wasn't quite sure if he had volunteered to go with Shona to try and help her get another dinner party booking because he was being kind, or because a green-eyed monster was telling him to.

~

The Webbs' mansion was inundated with police vehicles. It was unclear what had happened last night, as Amanda was

36

undergoing surgery and Carly was unable to tell the constables that interviewed her at the hospital any more than from where this mystery woman had ran out in front of her and what she had done to help her. Emma and her team were coordinating a plan of action to try and make sense of the situation when Graham pulled up the drive with Joseph.

"What's going off at the moment?" he asked Emma.

"We are just about to commence a thorough search of the property, sir."

"I am sorry, Emma, I wasn't questioning your actions, I was generalising about us investigating two major crimes within the space of what is now ninety-six hours. I gather from the first response team that the serious incident at this property appears to have occurred in just one room?"

"We should be able to piece together a scenario in a few hours, Graham, but it does appear that there was a forced entry and that the lady of the house, Amanda Webb, was attacked in one of the bedrooms. There is a fair amount of blood spattered over the carpet and furniture. It also looks as if the attacker or attackers have tried to clean up some of the blood, which suggests Mrs Webb may have put up a fight."

"It also suggests the perpetrator or perpetrators may be on a DNA database somewhere," said Graham.

"What have you been able to find out about the owners of the house?" asked Emma.

"Probably the same as you, from what the scenes of crime officers, or should I say crime scene investigators, have learnt from the neighbours, in that Mr and Mrs Webb have lived here for a few years and keep themselves very much to themselves. We understand that they have had quite a few visitors in that time, one of whom we know is Michael Black, the well-known local journalist," said Graham.

"Where is Mr Webb at the moment?" asked Emma.

"We have been informed by our sources that he is on his way back from Germany, having flown there on business yesterday," replied Graham.

"Before you go inside to clarify things for me and gather any trace, let me introduce you to Joseph Johnson. He is over here on secondment from the CIA and has been sent here to Worcester by MI5, to see if he can help us in any way possible following the blast at the cricket pavilion."

"Hello," said Emma, as she shook Joseph's hand.

Graham suggested the three of them meet back at the police station later that day, where they could discuss Joseph's involvement here in the UK and how he could help the West Mercia force before he took up his new role in London.

"Before then, we have a painstaking but essential and vital process to go through here and I think I would like to take a look inside the Webbs' house myself," said Graham.

"What about you, Joseph?" asked Emma.

"I don't think I can offer much in the way of help inside the house, so I will sit in the car and make a few calls to Langley, to see if my Office of Terrorism Analysis friends can help me with anything. I would like to know if there is any collusion between different terrorist groups at the moment, their current locations and any changes to their ideologies that may lead them to this part of England."

"Do you think that the attack on Mrs Webb could be linked to the blast at the cricket pavilion?" asked Graham.

"It's difficult to say at the moment," answered Joseph. "Do you know what line of work Mr Webb is in, as it may well be that the attack has something to do with it?"

"I don't know but I am sure we can find out very quickly," replied Graham.

"One of the SOCOs has already established that he is a salesman," said Emma. "A knife salesman!"

"That's interesting," said Joseph.

Graham looked at Joseph for some elaboration, but with none forthcoming he said he would get his protective suit on and start his search in the kitchen.

"If a knife is missing or out of place it could be that this was a bungled robbery. Maybe Mrs Webb came home and disturbed the intruder and he or she grabbed a knife and attacked her in an attempt to get away? If all of the knives are in the places you would expect them to be, then it could be that the attacker brought their own weapon, with the intention of hurting or murdering her or Mr Webb."

"Strange that Mr Webb just happened to be away from home last night," said Emma.

"I will go and speak with the SOCOs in a little while to see if they have found out from the neighbours if the Webbs' have been having any domestic issues recently. As soon as Mr Webb gets to the hospital I think we should pick him up and take him to the station for questioning."

Graham followed Emma towards the house and nodded to the officers guarding the wooden front door. A large mat had been put down on the floor inside the hallway to minimise any unnecessary contamination of the crime scene by those who were authorised to enter the restricted area.

The house was very large and decorated to a very high standard. The hallway was wide with high ceilings and contained a number of pictures and paintings of places from around the world. The tiles on the floor looked as if they were made from marble, as were those in the adjoining kitchen, which was luxurious and contained both an electric double oven and an Aga. There was also a centre console with over thirty cupboards and drawers, with a slate worktop for writing recipes and lists of ingredients. The expansive lounge, dining room, study and conservatory all had expensive thick shag pile carpet and various unusual ornaments from Africa and Asia. The opulence continued upstairs and when Graham found himself in the main bedroom where the attack took place, he found it difficult to focus on the things he should have been looking at. He decided to leave Emma to it, as he was more of a hindrance than a help once she had decided to put her analytical and scientific head on.

Graham asked Emma to walk the property in her meticulous way, gather up as much evidence as possible and call him with any key observations within the next couple of hours, so that he could add her information to that gathered from the door-to-door enquiries, before he commenced his interview with Mr Webb.

~

Baz had decided not to make contact with 'The Fixer' as he wasn't sure if he would fix him up with a false passport or just fix him. Up until last night, he thought he had performed well and done everything that the DJ and his supporters, for use of a better word, had required of him. One small misjudgement, well actually it was a rather large misjudgement, meant he would have to get away from Worcester and England for good. By the time the Old Bill have completed their investigative work and extracted my DNA from the blood in the bedroom and analysed it, I will be on a flight from Paris to Dhaka thought Baz.

"First, I have to get a taxi to St Pancras to catch the Eurostar," he said to himself.

Baz had just finished packing a light bag when the doorbell rang. The taxi is a bit early he thought; that's good. Baz had only just opened the door a fraction when the taser struck him, relieving him of the control over his muscles. Baz screamed and fell backwards inside his house, hitting his head hard on the slate floor. In an instant, the Fixer was on him and Baz was quickly handcuffed, tied up, dragged outside and bundled into a car waiting in the driveway.

"Your taxi awaits," said the Fixer. "Unfortunately, it isn't taking you to the train station."

~

Shona went to her appointment on her own and was successful in getting a second contract. This time she had no need to ply her charms, as the householders were an elderly couple looking for someone to conjure up a very basic, wholesome, three-course meal, for their son and daughter and their respective partners in celebration of their fiftieth wedding anniversary. Mr and Mrs Campbell had mentioned to Shona on the telephone that they needed a link between Scotland and Canada on the menu, which is exactly what Shona presented, and which she was just typing up on 'Spice and Slice' headed paper, when a call from Michael came through on her mobile.

"I got the job," said Shona, before Michael had time to speak.

"Fantastic," he replied. "I said you didn't need my help when going to see potential customers. Just being yourself should be enough to get you a lot of business contracts, as you come across as a genuine, knowledgeable and friendly person. What menu did you eventually settle upon?"

"As I vaguely told you yesterday, I had to come up with a menu that linked Scotland and Canada and after a bit more research late last night I chose:

Salmon Fishcakes
Teviotdale Pie with Seasonal Vegetables
Maple Sugar Pie
Or Rocky Chocolate Mountain"

"That all sounds lovely," said Michael, before his wicked sense of humour kicked in again and he suggested that he would rather be smearing chocolate on Shona's mountains, instead of sitting in the hospital waiting room reading the same magazines over and over again, waiting for news about Amanda.

"Oh, I am sorry, Michael; I forgot that you were still at the hospital. Have the doctors told you anything yet?"

"Not a great deal except for the fact Amanda has had an operation and is in a recovery room on a monitor."

"Do you know what happened to her?"

"Not exactly, but it seems as if she was attacked at home late last night while Richard was away in Germany."

"That's unbelievable! When will Richard get to the hospital?"

"He sent me a text when he landed at Heathrow, so he should be here within an hour or so. As soon as he gets here I will drive over and meet you at your apartment."

"Great," said Shona. "I'll see if I can conjure up some food for you as you must be hungry."

"Sounds good, and it will be lovely to see you, as every minute we spend together is magical," said Michael.

"Oh, very clever! But your smooth talk doesn't mean that I will allow you to get your rocks off."

"You always have to have the last word, don't you."

"I am a woman, so it's my prerogative. And in any case, you started all of the mucky talk so I finished it."

"I could easily finish your proposed meal, although I don't get the link between the two countries for all of the courses."

"The link for the starter should be obvious," said Shona "as it should be for the chocolate dessert. The pie link is a tenuous one as Teviotdale is the name of a community in Ontario, Canada, and the name of an area of dramatic natural beauty

42

near Hawick, Scotland. The maple sugar pie is a traditional dish from Quebec, which has recently celebrated four hundred years since it was founded. The link between Quebec and Scotland comes from the fact that some of its early settlers were Highland soldiers brought over by General Wolfe to help fight the French in the battle for the city in 1759."

"You certainly do your research," said Michael. "I could use you to help me with my work, as that is often the area I struggle to find the time to do, which means I have many last minute panics before hitting deadline dates."

"There are many things we can do together other than have sex, but at the moment you really do need to do something on your own and get as much information as possible on Amanda's condition before Richard arrives."

It was another fifty-five minutes before Richard got to the hospital, where he was taken straight into an office and told to wait for a few minutes as a Mr Khan needed to speak with him.

"I need to see my wife first," said Richard.

"Mr Khan really does need to speak to you before I take you to see your wife," answered the nurse.

Just at that moment the door opened and a man in a dark blue suit with an NHS identity card around his neck walked in.

"Hello, Mr Webb, I am Mr Khan. I am the surgeon that operated on your wife when she was brought here in the early hours of this morning."

"Where is she now?" asked Richard.

"There is no easy way to say this, Mr Webb, but your wife didn't make it. We did all that we could, but her injuries from the knife wound she sustained when she was attacked were too severe and she died two hours ago."

CHAPTER FIVE

Richard went with Mr Khan and a staff nurse to a side room where Amanda lay. Richard didn't say anything when he looked at her, as he was numb with shock and immersed in his thoughts and grief.

"Would you like us to call anyone to come and help you?" said Mr Khan.

"My friend Michael Black is here in the hospital at the moment," muttered Richard.

"I know where he is," said the nurse. "I'll go and get him."

Alone with his young, beautiful, deceased wife, Richard burst into tears and his heartfelt sobs could be felt by hospital staff in the corridor, such was their intensity.

Michael entered the room. He looked at Richard, then at Amanda, before walking across the floor and hugging his friend tightly. No words were necessary.

The ward charge nurse knocked and opened the door.

"We need to take Amanda down to the morgue, as we have to keep her body cold. Your wife's death will be reported to the coroner and it is likely that a post-mortem will have to be carried out. We don't have any clothes or possessions to give you other than a wedding ring and engagement ring."

"Where are my wife's clothes?"

"I am afraid she wasn't wearing any of her own clothes when she was brought in."

"What?"

"The police will be able to tell you more, but all we know is that Amanda was admitted in the early hours of Monday morning having been driven here by a woman in a white Audi."

Just as the charge nurse finished speaking and as if by magic, two police officers walked into the ward and made a beeline for Richard.

"Mr Webb?" asked one of the officers, looking at both Richard and Michael.

"That's me," said Richard.

"We need you to accompany us to the police station for questioning."

"Questioning? I have just learnt that my wife has died and now I have to tell her mother and father the same sad news."

"I am sure the DCI won't keep you long, sir, but we have a procedure to follow."

"Is Mr Webb under arrest?" asked Michael.

"No," replied the officer.

"Don't you think he should be allowed to go home, freshen up and make a few phone calls before he speaks with your boss?"

"You will not be allowed to return home yet, Mr Webb, as the forensics team are going to need another couple of hours there."

Richard went voluntarily with the officers in a state of bewilderment. As he was leaving the room he gave Michael his car keys and asked him to arrange for it to be collected from the hospital car park and driven to his house once the police had finished their investigations. Once he was outside the hospital building, Michael phoned Shona and told her that Amanda had died and that Richard was on his way to the police station to help them with their enquiries.

Michael waited for Shona to digest what he had just told her and then asked her to meet him at his house in thirty minutes. The line went quiet for what seemed like an eternity before Shona said, "Would you still like me to bring you something to eat?"

"No, not now, as I feel sick to the bottom of my stomach. I can't believe that we were only laughing and joking with Amanda on Friday and now she is dead. It makes you realise how much one should try to enjoy each and every day because you never know what is around the corner."

Shona was shocked to learn of Amanda's death. She didn't really know her and had only met and spoken with her for a short while at Kate's birthday party, but the news still sent a chill down her spine. A chill that she had felt many times before, when she was living rough and having to run, hide and fight off men who thought they could use and abuse her. A chill she also felt sometimes when walking home late at night from the Chocolate Elephant, when it seemed she was being followed.

Shona had learnt kick-boxing at a club in Birmingham for a while, just in case she found herself in a really difficult situation, but she always carried an alarm and some pepper spray that was given to her by an acquaintance a few years ago as back-up.

～

Baz stood blindfolded and rigid on what his senses told him to be the concrete floor of an old disused warehouse.

"Hello, Baz, take a seat," said a man from somewhere behind him. This was a man who Baz knew from his voice to be the DJ. As Baz was registering the words being spoken, he was pushed against a wall and forced to sit on a small wooden chair that was placed next to him.

"What are you doing here?" asked Baz.

"I thought that you could be trusted," said the DJ.

"I can be trusted. I didn't calculate on Mrs Webb proving to be such a beautiful and difficult woman."

"How the hell did you let her get away?" asked the Fixer.

"I didn't mean for that to happen. This is the first time I have ever made any sort of mistake."

"We only have your word for that, as the police have yet to reveal any information regarding the blast or the other job you were supposed to have done for me," said the DJ.

Bugger, I forgot that I was supposed to put some violent and horrific CDs through the letterbox of someone who had angered the DJ thought Baz. His mind was now racing as fast as his heart as he tried to work out how he could get out of this situation without having his throat cut.

"I did what you asked with the CDs and I did stab Amanda," mumbled Baz. "Perhaps the police are deliberately withholding information from the public at the moment to stop any crank calls?"

"We are aware that you stabbed Amanda Webb," said the Fixer, "and we also know that she died a few hours ago."

"Oh! That's ok then," said Baz as he attempted to get up from the chair to go.

"Not quite so fast," said the DJ. "The state of your nose suggests you may have left some tell-tale evidence behind, that could lead back to us. However, you were tasked with killing Amanda and you did manage to do that so I am going to give you another chance."

The DJ swiftly removed the blindfold and thrust a knife between Baz's eyes, the tip just pressing on the bridge of his nose.

"I will let you walk out of here in five minutes and give you one week to prove your loyalty to the mission. You will shortly be contacted by text with another task. Fail to complete this and

I will find you and cut out both your eyes. If the police issue a warrant for your arrest at any point I will also find you and cut out your tongue to stop you talking."

Baz was able to walk out of the empty building unscathed. Once outside, it didn't take him long to realise where he was. He had no intention of posting a CD through the door of one of the DJ's old flames from years ago, or responding to any text sent to him later this week. He knew, should he undertake and fail another task, that it would probably be his last and that his life would be terminated. This crystallised his thoughts somewhat, so he decided to go into hiding while he worked out a plan of action.

The logic Baz was processing in his mind was that he lie low for a couple of weeks and then try to make his way to Dover, to see what opportunities existed for him to smuggle his way out of the country. He smiled to himself as he imagined newspaper sellers shouting "Read all about it – immigrant tries to leave Britain in back of a lorry."

Baz didn't have too many options open to him really. He could change his appearance and keep looking over his shoulder for the rest of his life here in the UK. He could call in a few favours and create a new identity with a new fake passport, but risk being double-crossed, or he could try the lorry route. Hiding away for a while was the easy bit, after he had been back to his rented house and collected some clothes, blankets, money and a few provisions. This would at least give him time to clear his head and work out the best way to stay alive and stay free.

~

Shona was visibly upset by Amanda's death and was struggling to comprehend the fact that the doctors were unable to save her life.

"I don't know the full details until I have spoken with the lady who took her to hospital," said Michael. "From what I can gather by reading between the lines and speaking and listening to the nurses, there was much going on that night and not enough staff to cope."

"Situations like this must make your articles on the NHS cutbacks more personal and more difficult to deliver to your audiences objectively and accurately," said Shona.

"I can't deny that Amanda's death and all other incidents like it make me very angry. It is beyond belief that hospitals are struggling to do everything possible to care for more patients than they have the resources for, following all of the cutbacks, and yet this government can hand out billions in foreign aid to undeserving countries that should be more accountable for their own destiny. I appreciate that there is a need to help other countries on certain occasions but only when we can really afford to. The politicians keep on telling the British public that our economy is in difficulty and that there have to be public-sector cutbacks to help balance the books, and then they go and make decisions that contradict this. Surely to God there should be an onus on those running this country to make sure their own house is in order before they try to tidy up those belonging to others?"

"I think a lot of it stems from the fact many politicians have big egos and want other world leaders to respect them and say how wonderful they are," said Shona.

"In some instances, you are right: why else did the UK keep giving India billions of pounds each year when they didn't need it or actually want it?"

"Why else does the UK provide free health treatment for migrants who haven't lived in the country for at least a year and haven't made any payments towards its cost via Income Tax or National Insurance?" said Shona.

"These are just some of the issues I will be writing about. It is nice to be able to talk to you about them and I hope we can have many more discussions like this in the future."

"My ideas for running the country are a bit off the wall, so you'll have to take them with a pinch of salt," said Shona.

"Give me one," asked Michael.

"It isn't really appropriate considering what has just happened," replied Shona.

"I meant one of your ideas."

"Alright, how about we introduce a law stating that all government department or public-sector expenditure over a certain amount has to be signed off by the British public?"

"It would really be impossible for a country to be run like that, but it would stop the government wasting many billions of pounds of public money over the years on things such as ID cards, the Trident nuclear missile system, almost certainly soon on the HS2 rail link and on many hair-brained schemes, badly thought-out purchases and irresponsible payments. There are hundreds of examples of these over the years, such as new motorcycle test centres, fire control centres, new roads in Bangladesh, unusable rubber bullets, benefits for dead people and even here in the West Midlands, four police officers spent some £2.4 million on a PR campaign."

"£2.4 million pounds?" said Shona. "How many policemen, firemen, ambulance drivers and nurses would that amount of money paid for? It's almost criminal."

"That's very funny," said Michael.

"We've digressed a little from talking about Amanda," said Shona ashamedly.

"Yes, I know, but it's all relative and many of the topics we've discussed will be included in the next report that I am preparing for the tabloids and any other publication that will pay me for it. I will be putting a lot of focus on the reduction in the number of Accident and Emergency departments, their staffing levels and opening hours and the impact the cutbacks have on decent people like you, me and, of course, Richard. Talking of Richard, I asked you over here so that we could go and collect his car from the hospital and then take it to his house."

"That's really kind of you, Michael. I wonder how he is coping at the police station."

"Richard is a tough cookie but he is going to need a lot of support over the next few months."

"You don't think he actually had anything to do with Amanda's murder, do you?"

"Not in a month of Sundays."

"Why would someone want her killed, though?"

"It is all a bit odd and I think we should tell all of our friends and family to be vigilant until the police find who did this."

"Do you know something I don't, Michael?"

"No, not all," said Michael, who thinking quickly added, "the attack was probably the culmination of a robbery that went wrong in the run up to Christmas, but it may mean that any large home within the area could become a target."

"That counts me out as a victim," said Shona.

CHAPTER SIX

Richard was escorted into an interview room by Sergeant Peter Ford, given a plastic cup full of machine coffee and told to wait for a few minutes, while the duty officer went to inform DCI Graham Laws that he was here. Ten minutes passed before Graham entered the room with Constable Jane Small, a trained bereavement officer, and Bea Sharpe, a psychological profiler specialising in kinesics, the study of the way people communicate through stance, posture, movement and gesture. Graham made the introductions before informing Richard that he was sorry for his loss and that he just wanted to have a chat with him at this stage to try and understand if or why Amanda was specifically targeted.

"We will not keep you long, Mr Webb," said Graham.

"I hope not as I have a lot of things to do and a lot of people to speak to this afternoon," replied Richard.

"I understand that your friend Michael Black will be collecting your car from the hospital, so we will take you home afterwards and I am going to suggest that Constable Small goes with you and stays with you for a while, until any of your friends or relatives arrive to keep you company."

"That really won't be necessary."

"It's just something we like to do and almost insist upon, as we know from experience that people can do strange and out-of-character things when in shock. Jane may be able to help you come to terms with things and answer any questions that may occur to you."

"Very well, and thank you," replied Richard.

"You can terminate this interview at any time, Mr Webb, but if it's ok with you I would like to videotape the interview as it may help us to catch your wife's killer."

"I thought you said we were just going to have a chat?"

"You are not under arrest and you are free to go at any time of your choosing, but I am going to interview you under caution as dictated by the Police and Criminal Evidence Act 1984. You do have the right to be represented by your own solicitor or a duty solicitor."

"That will not be necessary. Just carry on, as I would like to get home to inform family members and friends of the terrible tragedy," said Richard.

"That's very understandable but before we commence proceedings I will need you to sign this custody record to confirm that you do not wish to be represented or take legal advice at this point in time. I am legally obliged to and will give you a copy of this record if you require it at any time within the next twelve months."

Richard signed the document and said he didn't feel the need to read the codes of practice at this particular moment in time, so Graham commenced the interview.

"I gather that the German police informed you of the circumstances surrounding your wife being taken to the Worcestershire Royal Hospital," asked Graham.

"Yes, they did, but I still can't comprehend it."

"Am I right in saying, Mr Webb, that you only went to Berlin yesterday, a few hours before your wife was attacked?"

"Yes, that is correct."

"What did you go there for?"

"I'm a salesman and had appointments with customers lined

up for today and tomorrow."

"What do you sell?" asked Graham already knowing the answer.

"Knives. I work for a UK manufacturer that uses German steel, and our range is very popular in Germany itself due to its uniqueness."

"Do you travel the world selling knives?"

"No, I only fly between here and Germany," replied Richard rather quickly and forcibly.

"I guess you earn a pretty good salary?" asked Graham.

"It's ok but I don't see what that has to do with anything,"

"I am just doing my job and trying to get a perspective on things," replied Graham.

Bea listened and watched intently as she would have the opportunity to ask Richard questions at a later date. For now, she was making notes on his voice, eye movements, breathing rate and hand and foot reflexes in response to the questioning. Jane would also have time to speak with Richard later, particularly as she had been asked to drive him home, but for now she was in the room to help and advise him should he break down and be unable to cope with the trauma.

"Do you know of any enemies that you or your wife may have had?" asked Graham, trying to choose his words carefully.

"None that I can think of and as far as I am aware we don't owe any money to any individual or company other than the bank in respect of our mortgage." This pre-empted Graham's next question, so he asked about any marriage problems that Richard and Amanda may have had.

"I would say that we had the perfect marriage, well as near to perfect as any marriage could be," added Richard.

"When did you get married?"

"Fourteen years ago," replied Richard, with a strength that appeared to suggest he was proud of this.

"Past the seven year itch then?"

"That isn't funny and I find the remark very offensive."

"What about a fourteen-year itch?" said Graham still searching for a light in what was likely to be a long tunnel.

Richard looked around the room and shook his head in exasperation while chewing on his lip.

"We spend, rather spent," Richard uttered, "pretty much every day and night together, so if you are asking about an extra-marital affair, the answer is most definitely no."

"I hear that German girls are very pretty?" asked Graham.

"I am sure they are," said Richard loudly and angrily.

"So you have never been tempted while away from home?"

"I would rather not answer that. I do have to go away on business from time to time as this is the nature of my job but I don't like doing so. If I had been at home last weekend my wife would still be alive."

"Do you have any insurance policies?" asked Graham.

"I don't like what you are suggesting," said Richard "so I would like to go home now."

"You are free to go, but I will need to speak with you again. Forensics have been and gone, but your house does have some officers outside as a precaution, should the killer or killers return for any reason and to ensure that onlookers and reporters are kept a good distance away. I will speak with you once we have the lab results if we learn anything of significance, but should you think of anything in the meantime that could help us solve the case, please call me on my direct line."

Graham handed Richard a business card and nodded to Jane to escort him home.

"You were a bit hard on him," said Bea.

"Deliberately," said Graham.

"I needed to check his mindset before he could get home and construct something in his head."

Jane drove Richard home in her new black Mini Cooper with go faster white stripes on the bonnet. Upon entering his house, Richard seemed to freeze and stood, stared and listened almost in hope that he had been dreaming and that Amanda would come running down the stairs to greet him as she often did. He then walked silently throughout each room as if in a trance, until he got to their bedroom, where he broke down and cried. Jane sat Richard down on the bed and went downstairs to make him a cup of tea. After a few minutes Richard wandered downstairs into the kitchen looking like a lost sheep and said, "I don't know what to do."

"Losing a loved one can be confusing, involving many powerful emotions. You will go through many different stages as you try to accept that this has happened, try to adjust to life without Amanda and then eventually move on with your life."

"I don't want to live without her," said Richard.

"Nothing can prepare us for the loss of a loved one, even when they have been seriously ill," said Jane.

"You are going to dream about Amanda and wake up believing that she is lying next to you. You are going to think that you have seen her in town and you will most certainly turn to speak to her on many occasions. You are going to feel sorrow, guilt, anger, longing, loneliness and despair. This may seem like a cliché, but you will get to a point where life takes you on a new route. You will always remember Amanda and will always grieve her loss, but you will find a way to channel your emotions for her into positive things, I promise. I, or one of my colleagues, will be here for you and I am sure you have family and friends who will help and care for you and be there for you, too. I will also give you some telephone numbers of organisations that are available twenty-four hours a day, should you be in desperate need to talk to someone in the middle of the night when things often seem worse and the morning sunrise can seem a long, long way away."

"Oh my Lord," said Richard. "I still haven't got round to informing Amanda's parents of her death. I must phone them immediately, unless you think I should go to their house and tell them in person?"

"If they live close by I will take you to see them, if you would like me to?" said Jane.

"I am really not sure what to do for the best," said Richard.

"You will all need each other in these tough difficult times as you try to come to terms with everything, organise a funeral and unfortunately complete the ridiculous amount of paperwork that the government insist upon way too soon after someone has passed away."

"I don't know where to start in respect of a burial or cremation, as it wasn't something we had ever talked about."

As Richard and Jane were finishing their tea, Michael and Shona arrived having had a bit of difficulty getting through the police cordon. Shona hugged Richard and expressed her condolences.

"If there is anything we can do, just ask," said Michael.

"Will you and Shona drive me to see Amanda's parents and then come back and stay here with me tonight?"

"Yes, of course," replied Michael.

"I will go to see my parents tomorrow, as I can't face telling them today," said Richard.

Jane drove home after telling Richard that she would be back to see him in a couple of days' time to give him some literature to read and details of the organisations she mentioned to him earlier that can help him over the next few weeks, months and maybe even years.

"How did it go at the police station?" asked Michael.

"It felt like I was a suspect."

"I was afraid that might have been the case, but Graham is very good at his job and will follow all lines of enquiry to make sure that his team catch the bastard or bastards who did this."

~

Graham sat down with Bea after Richard left and they discussed what Richard had said and how it had correlated with his body movements, the notes that Graham had written following his visit to the crime scene and the findings of the SOCOs. Bea wanted to review the video before she documented her thoughts but she was certain that Richard had lied, or told a slight untruth in one or two places, particularly when Graham pressed him on any dalliances away from home. She was also fairly certain that Richard had proffered the information about not owing any money to try and deflect the fact that either he or Amanda did have a few money issues.

"Something doesn't add up somewhere, Bea, as a knife salesman can't earn enough money to afford that house and all the trappings that go with it. I would like you to go and see his employers to find out what he earns, how often he does go away on official business and if he was authorised to be in Berlin at the weekend. In the meantime, I'll get a warrant to access his bank statements."

~

Baz locked the back door of his house in Warndon Village and started to walk to the bus stop on Tolladine Road.

He made sure that he wasn't being followed by doubling back on himself a few times around Windermere Drive, Keswick Drive, Ambleside Drive and Grasmere Drive before getting on the bus going to Malvern.

In Malvern, he stamped on his Android phone and then dumped it in a waste bin before going to the supermarket to buy himself a pay-as-you-go mobile. This way Baz knew that he could still make calls but not be tracked by the DJ, the Fixer or the police.

Baz walked up Church Street, then up the steps by the Malvinha Fountain and along Bellevue Terrace before making his way up the ninety-nine steps to St Ann's Well for a coffee in the café there, before continuing his walk up into the hills.

The Malvern Hills encompass three thousand acres of open countryside, but Baz knew the area like the back of his hand and had walked the nine miles across the ridges many times, which is how he had accidentally stumbled upon a small six-foot-wide by eight-foot-high tunnel, some one hundred feet below a broken air shaft located in dense undergrowth that would probably have been used by miners in the mid 1800s. The consensus of opinion is that there are only two tunnels under the Malverns that were originally used by steam trains travelling between Wales and Worcester. The original and smallest of these tunnels was closed around 1920, but Baz was unable to use this as a hiding place as it was home to a large colony of bats. The second tunnel alongside it, which is some one thousand three hundred yards long, is still in use today. The tunnel that Baz had found a year or so before was too small for any form of transport but perfect for people who needed to hide or flee in times of danger many years ago. Baz had no idea when this tunnel was constructed, who had done it, and how it could go under the River Severn, but he did know that it was perfect for what he needed it for now. Baz also knew the next few days or weeks until he had formulated a plan wouldn't be a bed of roses and he wouldn't have any home comforts. A few creatures to comfort maybe, but this was a cross he had to bear to survive upsetting the DJ. The tunnel would enable him to walk directly beneath Great Malvern, probably following a straight line to Spetchley, where he could exit it a short distance from the park and gardens. Halfway along the tunnel there is a T-junction and if Baz turned left and took this route he would end up right beneath Worcester city centre. Baz thought it odd that this tunnel had lain undiscovered for hundreds of years, but to make sure it stayed this way he decided he would, if possible, only ever enter and exit it under the cover of darkness.

CHAPTER SEVEN

Graham was finally able to call an operational meeting with Emma, Joseph, Charlie, Bea, Peter and Paul to discuss the events of the last six days at 4.00 p.m. on Tuesday. Emma had got various results back from the laboratory following the bomb blast and some DNA information from the Webbs' mansion, but some of the analysis was going to take a while longer and no amount of ranting and raving from those upstairs could magic the results any faster. Graham waited silently until everybody was settled in their seats and then flipped a switch to release a shutter on the giant whiteboard affixed to the wall of his office.

"I want us to use the next few hours wisely. I want us to go through all that has happened in chronological order, starting with the bomb blast and have an honest and open discussion on all elements to try to understand what the hell is happening here suddenly. What have we got back from the lab that you can immediately share with us to kick start proceedings, Emma?"

Graham stood with his whiteboard marker poised as Emma got up and stood next to him before she started speaking.

"As Charlie, the chief fire officer, and I suspected at the time, the large amount of white smoke suggested the explosion at the cricket ground was caused by an improvised device. There was very little heat after the explosion and there was a very strong bleach-like smell in the air which probably meant the use of acetone peroxide."

"A white crystalline powder often used by terrorists as it doesn't contain nitrogen and can pass through scanners with less chance of detection," interrupted Joseph.

"Yes, that's correct," said Emma. "The chromatograph and mass spectrometer used by the technicians in the laboratory have definitely identified its use in this case."

Graham wrote acetone peroxide on the whiteboard before putting the top on the marker pen and sucking on the end of it. The team watched quietly and intently for a few seconds, knowing not to interrupt his train of thought. Eventually, Graham turned back to face them before speaking.

"I need to understand more about this substance and the bomb-making process in this instance before I inform the chief constable of these findings. He will want us to proffer some rationale for the blast and be sure we are doing everything possible to try and keep the city safe, until we catch the culprits. We have never experienced anything like this in this city and I can't understand why it has happened. If, as a team having analysed the evidence, we decide this may be an act of terrorism, we must use Joseph's experience and contacts to the full. There is already much focus and scrutiny on us and if we don't deliver satisfactory answers and results quickly, we may find ourselves relegated to more menial tasks in the future or to the dole queue. Let's discuss this further after we've listed all the other evidence on the board."

Emma looked back at her pad and then towards those seated before she continued speaking. "We have spoken with everybody who had been or could have been in or close to the pavilion officially last week. This has enabled me to be clear about the trace evidence collected that can be presented to you today. This includes one size-eight and one size-ten footprint, each with unusual sole treads. We have made plaster casts of these and have a team checking them out to see if they can identify each brand of shoe, if they are new or old styles and just by chance if any shop owner remembers selling any with those treads recently and to whom. We have also gathered fibres from a brown sweater and a black beanie hat, neither of which belongs to the groundsman, as well as what looks to be a grey human hair. We also found a sample of mushroom compost and cannabis and importantly, a partial of a hand print which is currently being digitally analysed to determine if the image can be put through the Automated Fingerprint Identification System to see if we can get a match."

"What about CCTV?" asked Joseph.

"We have a team looking through all video footage from the area between Monday and Thursday. We are also asking people in the locality if they saw anything suspicious last week. The problem we have is that the area is always busy with both people and cars during the day and early evening and it is very easy for criminals to blend in. The positioning of the cricket ground also makes for very easy access from New Road, Bromyard Road, the A449, Cripplegate Park or the path leading from the River Severn," replied Graham.

"We also found a couple of cigarette butts which the lab team are still working on to see if they can get a DNA fingerprint that matches one in our database," said Emma.

"If you don't get a match, I can send the profile to Langley, for them to pass on to the FBI to analyse through CODIS, their computer system that has information from all fifty States." said Joseph.

"Fantastic," said Graham as he continued writing all of the salient points on the board.

Joseph added, "If we don't get a result from CODIS, I can get the profile sent to at least another forty or fifty law enforcement laboratories around the world."

As Joseph finished speaking, Assistant Chief Constable Benjamin Lewis walked into the room to find out how the investigation was progressing.

"Good morning, all," he said, sounding a bit like Dixon of Dock Green. "I hope you have something conclusive to tell me as the chief is trying to fend off reporters from all of the TV channels and most of the newspapers. He has been told that he has to call the Home Office every day to update the minister for police and security on our progress and meet with the police and crime commissioner every other day to discuss strategy, budgets and communication to the public."

Benjamin walked across the room and scanned the whiteboard taking in all of the things Graham had written on it during the last hour.

Bomb Blast

- *Time of Explosion 11.10 a.m. Thursday, 20th November*
- *White Smoke/Acetone Peroxide/unstable*
- *Possible Terrorist Cell/Explosives made locally*
- *Suspects probably Male/Sizes 8 & 10 Footwear*
- *Brown Sweater/Black Beanie Hat Fibres*
- *Charred 2.5cm Donut-Shaped Metal Button*
- *Smoker/Drug User/Gardener*
- *Partial Handprint/Hair Follicles*

"I can see you are making some headway with the top-line stuff on the whiteboard, but I really need something more than this to take upstairs," said Benjamin.

"I understand the chief is under pressure but we have worked hard to get to where we are at the moment, so this is all you are going to get," replied Graham. On reflection, he wondered if his tone was a bit disrespectful so added, "The team in the Pershore control room are reviewing the CCTV tapes from all sixty-six cameras throughout the city and the one hundred or so cameras located throughout the various car parks. Emma's team are working hard with the lab technicians, to see if we can get a DNA match from the trace evidence collected and Joseph has been constantly in contact with Washington to try and find a link between the events here and around the world, that might give an indication as to those responsible."

"What makes you think the perpetrators are male and that the explosives were made locally?" asked Benjamin.

"The depth of the prints in the grass tells us that those responsible are most likely to be male. The explosive used is unstable, particularly at temperatures above ten degrees Celsius, so we think that these men actually made their way to the cricket ground on foot and entered the premises during the night."

"I understand where you are coming from, but why would anyone choose to blow up the academy cricket pavilion?"

"Joseph is trying to establish if this was an act of retribution by a political group still upset by the Moeen Ali 'Save Gaza' wristband saga, or if this is a prelude to something else."

"If that was the case, surely a more prominent target would have been selected and the explosion would have happened some time ago, soon after the ICC got involved?"

"This was our thinking too, sir, but the county cricket ground and the hotel which are guarded night and day have sophisticated security systems and it is likely this has taken a bit of planning and may be the starter before the main meal," said Graham.

"We need to be more vigilant around the city during the next few weeks, Graham. We need to draw up a plan that ensures all of our officers patrol every street day and night looking for anything suspicious."

"With all due respect, sir, we are a little thin on the ground at the moment, having lost some ninety-six officers due to the forced cutbacks, but we will do our best."

"I gather from the tone of your voice, Graham, that 'with all due respect' really means 'bollocks'?"

"All I will say, sir, is that we know as a team what we have to do and we will do everything to the best of our ability."

"Let's hope your team have the ability to interpret all of the information coming your way from the various sources and that we can soon tell the chief what he wants to hear. One other thing, Graham, and it may not seem important in the scheme of things, but when your officers are out and about, I want them to be on the lookout for another illegal synthetic stimulant known as Speckled Cherry. These are white or pink tablets with a cherry or cross logo on them. The Home Office has asked all police forces across the country to try and stop the sale of these in clubs and pubs as well as petrol stations, newsagents and even takeaway restaurants, due to the fact they are extremely dangerous. Our intelligence suggests these drugs will be on sale here in Worcester very soon, if they are not already."

"I thought that the gang who were responsible for pushing drugs in the area from a Kempsey warehouse have just been jailed?" said Bea.

"That's correct," said Benjamin. "Thanks to Graham and his team, plus the odd informant, five men have just received custodial sentences totalling eighty-eight years for their part in smuggling £60 million worth of drugs into the UK. We believe, however, that there is another gang operating on a smaller scale in a different way and we can't afford for all of the good work to be undone."

"It seems to me like your government is putting a huge amount of pressure on police forces across the country?" said

Joseph.

"You should talk to our local journalist, Michael Black," said Benjamin. "He could give you a list of things that make our work difficult. Maybe when you get back home to America you could detail some of the things on that list to your superiors, who with any luck may just mention some of them when speaking with their peers on this side of the pond."

"What you are saying is that the Home Office doesn't listen to its chief constables and this is having a major detrimental effect on the day-to-day demands of police officers?"

"I am not at liberty to discuss things like that in this forum," said Benjamin, who was suddenly feeling a little uncomfortable with the way the conversation with Joseph had turned.

Graham could see Benjamin squirming and understood that his boss didn't want to be seen or heard criticising the police force directly, even though he would like those in high places in London to know his thoughts, so he interjected and brought the focus of the meeting back to the current incidents.

Benjamin relaxed a bit when realising he wasn't going to have to answer any more difficult questions within the meeting room and changed the subject.

"What have we got so far on the Amanda Webb murder? Are you any nearer to solving this crime?" he asked.

"We are just about to write our findings on the board. We have interviewed Mr Webb and we have some results back from the lab, but we are still waiting for the results of the post-mortem."

"When do you think we can expect to get those results?"

"I should think we will get them within the next forty-eight hours," said Emma.

"Ok," said Benjamin walking across the room and throwing another marker to Graham.

"Start writing so that I can see what you have established so far and then we can discuss the next steps to take, as I really want to get this nailed quickly. I don't want this investigation dragging on until Christmas, as I am due some holiday and my wife will kill me if it gets cancelled."

Amanda Webb Murder

- *Time of Attack 1.10 a.m. on Monday, 24th November*
- *Forced Entry/Male Attacker*
- *Bedroom Struggle/Rape?*
- *Blood/Semen Stains*
- *Knife Wound*
- *Skin Flakes/Hair*
- *Black Beanie Hat/Black Balaclava Fibres*
- *Partial Footprint possible Size 8 or 9*

"Interesting! Do you think the same person could be involved or responsible for both crimes?" asked Benjamin.

"Anything is possible," said Emma. "We will know later today or tomorrow morning once we have the DNA results."

"How did Mr Webb come across in his interview, Bea?"

"Mr Webb's body posture was very strong considering the circumstances. He only crossed his arms and legs once near the end of the interview and he didn't once put his finger to his lips, touch his nose or rub his eyes. He kept his palms open most of the time, but did cross his ankle's when questioned about German women."

"What about his eye movements?" asked Benjamin.

"Well," said Bea, "it's interesting you should ask that. When answering the DCI's direct questions he moved his eyes to the left most of the time which suggested he was remembering rather than constructing his answers. Occasionally he did flick

70

his eyes to the right but this could have been when accessing feelings, although he held them in position for a few seconds on two occasions when he was asked about the stability of his relationship with his wife and if he or they owed money to anybody."

"He also tilted the chair back and put his hands behind his head when Graham mentioned insurance policies," said Emma.

"Yes, he did, and I think we should get copies of those to see what they say, as he did look uncomfortable when he was thinking at that point in the interview," replied Bea.

"We have already started the process of getting copies of the Webbs' bank statements to see if we can determine anything from them, sir. Emma and I both felt when looking around the Webbs' house that the furniture and other possessions inside were more expensive than a knife salesman should be able to afford, and his responses at the interview suggest we should dig deeper in this area," said Graham.

"Your thoughts in summary," asked Benjamin.

"In the main, I think he was telling the truth. I don't think that Mr Webb had anything to do with his wife's murder as he does appear traumatised, but a couple of shoulder shrugs and other body movements suggest that he may have a few ideas as to the reason for it."

"I want you all to look into his past and keep him under surveillance. I want to know where he goes and whom he talks to. I also want you to tap up your informants Graham to see if the underworld has anything on Mr Webb. As soon as you have more information, inform me immediately."

Graham looked at his watch and thought that everybody had probably had enough for the day, so he suggested that they all went for a drink or two at a local pub.

"How about we carry on our discussions at the Swan with Two Nicks in New Street as it has some fantastic regional beers

71

on tap every week, and I could sink a few right now."

"That's a strange name for a pub. Does it mean anything?" asked Joseph.

"It dates back to medieval times. The nicks refer to the scratches made on the beaks of swans to identify ownership. This practice is known as swan-upping and is a ceremonial occasion on the River Thames where mute swans are rounded up, caught, marked and then released. Today, only two city companies have the licenses to own and mark swans on the Thames – the Dyers and Vintners. The Dyers' swans are marked with one nick on the beak, while the Vintners' have two. All unmarked swans in open water are owned by the Queen."

"I wish I hadn't asked now, or that I had asked after I had downed six or seven pints," said Joseph yawning.

"I am not sure I could manage that many pints, but three or four sounds good," said Graham.

Looking across the room at Benjamin, Graham said in a deliberate and rather pitiful voice that he could probably manage to fund one round on his current salary.

"After that, I will have to put all the drinks and any food that we eat on my expenses. You wouldn't begrudge us that would you, sir?" said Graham, as the team all filed out of the meeting room, leaving Benjamin standing alone, wishing he was going with them, instead of going upstairs to face a different type of grilling.

CHAPTER EIGHT

Shona and Michael had spent most of Wednesday morning purchasing and preparing the food that Shona needed for the Campbells' dinner party on Thursday. Shona wanted to do as much preparation as possible and get used to a new set of knives the day before the party, as it would make things run more smoothly on the day of the event. She hadn't had that luxury before Michael's party, although she had managed to marinate the ox cheeks and make the Malvern pudding during the evening before.

"Where did you suddenly get the inspiration to learn to cook?" asked Michael.

"A combination of the Masterchef television programme and a former boyfriend," replied Shona. "I had to take the job at the Chocolate Elephant all those years ago and stick with it, as it paid such high wages and I would get almost £50 a night in tips for performing special services, but I knew I couldn't do that type of work forever."

"What were the special services?" asked Michael.

"I'll show you one day for free," replied Shona.

"That sounds interesting, although part of me thinks that I probably shouldn't have asked."

"Does that mean you love me or is it your jealous streak surfacing?"

"You have certainly captured my heart," said Michael. "Why

else would I be trudging around the whole of Worcestershire shopping for food?"

"Because you thought it might get you a shag?"

"Oh! If you insist."

"Tough!" said Shona. "I have a maple sugar pie to make."

Michael decided to go home and leave Shona to do whatever she had to, so that her preparations could be done without any hindrance. Shona was keen to make sure that she put as little stress as possible on the host or hostess and that she delivered each course on time. At the tender stage, which in effect was the time Shona spent with her potential client or clients, she asked lots of questions to get a clear idea of the party's setting, style, size and mood. She needed to know how many people were attending, their likes and dislikes and whether or not the hosts had enough kitchen equipment, utensils, plates, glasses, serving dishes, cutlery, napkins and even chairs. Shona also made sure that she knew if the customer wanted her to provide any accessories, decorative trimmings or finishing touches such as fresh or silk flowers, candles, party poppers, crackers, balloons or even indoor fireworks. Shona also liked to know if the client wanted things to be done in a formal or informal way in respect of place settings, such as couples opposite or next to each other, males and females alternating and how guests would dress so that she could dress accordingly. Shona had learnt a lot from reading many books and attending cookery courses in Bredon, Upton-upon-Severn and Hereford, but there is nothing like actually doing something for yourself in a real-life situation to become perfect at what you do.

The Campbells' fiftieth anniversary dinner party was to be a semi-formal one. None of the guests had any special dietary requirements for gluten-free food, nor had a nut allergy, and they all liked red meat, poultry and fish. Shona had agreed with the Campbells to serve balanced dishes for elderly guests that had strong flavours and were practical for them to eat. Mr Campbell was very insistent that each of the dishes had to be served piping hot, with the exception of the ice cream to go on top of the Rocky Chocolate Mountain. Mrs Campbell was happy to lay the table in their dining room and to pour the wine for her guests. Shona was to serve each course on individual plates, with only condiments in the middle of the table alongside two small vases containing violets. Shona had done her research and suggested violets, as they are associated with fiftieth anniversaries because of their long history: they can be traced back as far as 500 BC when ancient Greeks used them to add flavouring to food and wine and for herbal remedies. Shona had decided to serve the ice cream in an ice bowl containing petals from edible violas as it would make a truly impressive serving dish and would certainly leave a lasting impression on everybody.

Michael was going to pick Shona up at 4.30 p.m. and drive her to the Campbells' house as it was out in the sticks. He was then going to collect her later, as he didn't like the thought of her driving back home along the A422 country road late at night on her own. The whole episode with Amanda had spooked a lot of people throughout the county, who were all trying to come to terms with what had happened and how what used to be known as a relatively safe part of the world, was gradually becoming a dangerous one, infiltrated by bombers and murderers. Michael wasn't so sure the answer was that simple and had other thoughts going through his mind as he sat putting the finishing touches to an article on his blog about the Rooney Rule, and the merit for adopting it outside of the US to ensure that more opportunities presented themselves to potential black managers within the English and Scottish football leagues.

~

Jane knocked on Richard's door just after lunch. She knew from the officers guarding the area, that he hadn't left the house at all on Tuesday or this morning, which was odd since he was supposed to be going to see his parents.

"Hello, Richard, how are you feeling this afternoon?"

"Not too good," he replied. "I was sort of ok until Michael and Shona left the house, but since then I have just been wandering from room to room crying."

"Have you told your mother and father about Amanda yet?"

"No! It was horrific telling Amanda's parents."

"Where do your parents live?"

"In the Cotswolds."

"Would you like me to drive you there now?"

Richard seemed to take an age to answer the question by nodding his head a few times, but eventually they set off towards Moreton-in-Marsh. On the way, Jane got a call on her car phone to tell her that Amanda's body had been released by the coroner, as the post-mortem had been completed and that no further examinations would be necessary. Richard heard this of course and heaved a huge sigh of relief.

"The coroner doesn't see the need for an inquest. This means the cause of death has been identified and the registrar will now be informed. It also means that you and your family must decide if you are going to have a burial or cremation," said Jane. Richard nodded his head again but said nothing for a few minutes until a light bulb went on inside his head.

"I still haven't got round to looking at Amanda's will to see what it says about that, but I do know I have to read it very soon. I am pretty sure that everything in it will be straightforward and that bar the odd sentimental object, everything will have been left to me. I guess therefore that there will not be too much for me to do apart from look at it and give anything listed such as jewellery or things from her childhood that are in the loft to her mother and father. She didn't have any brothers or sisters or any long lost relatives that could come crawling out of the woodwork looking for a payday."

"I am afraid it doesn't work quite like that," said Jane. "Your wife will have named an executor or executors in her will and they will have to administer the estate. As you have property worth, I guess, over one million pounds and, I also guess, savings over five thousand pounds, the executors will have to apply for a grant of probate. There will be many forms to complete at the same time as you will be organising the funeral, which as I said the other day, is very unfair on people who are trying to come to terms with the loss of a loved one."

"Surely, if a will is straightforward, there isn't any need for all of that, is there?"

"Unfortunately there is, as the government has to be sure that the wishes of the deceased are carried out and of course, that they get any inheritance tax that may be due."

"Oh! Yes, I forgot about that," said Richard. "Another tax on top of money that has already been taxed. It really does make you wonder why you bother working hard to earn a decent salary, better yourself and leave a legacy for your children." Richard went quiet and it looked to Jane, as she glanced across at him, as if he had gone very pale and was trembling when he stuttered, "Children that I will now never have."

Jane touched Richard's arm to try and offer him a bit of comfort and to show him she understood how he was feeling, but they continued to drive the rest of the way to his parent's house in silence.

~

The Campbells' dinner party on Thursday evening went according to plan, and Shona was complimented by all the guests on the quality of her food and her ingenuity.

"That Teviotdale pie was magnificent," said Mr Campbell.

"I will leave you the recipe," said Shona. "It would serve you and your wife for three days and is often better and even more tasty for being left in the fridge."

"Can you leave the recipe for both the desserts, too?"

"Of course I can. The Rocky Chocolate Mountain is perfect when you need something light and tasty and don't have much time for preparation as it is cooked in the microwave."

"You're winding me up," said Mr Campbell.

"No, I'm not. There are many great meals that you can produce using a microwave. Many top chefs probably wouldn't admit they use one, but it should be part of any great home kitchen, along with other electrical equipment such as a deep fat fryer, food processer, slow cooker, temperature probe and if you can afford them, a Thermomix and sous vide bath."

"I am a bit old to start using too many gadgets," said Mr Campbell, "but I will try some new recipes from your cookbook."

"I didn't say I had written a book, just that I was thinking about it. I will however be launching an online food blog called *Spice and Slice* in the near future with the help of my boyfriend," said Shona.

On the way home, Shona asked Michael if he would help her to start writing a book on home cooking. "I would like it to be a bit different from a lot of other books in that the recipes consist of basic everyday ingredients that can be purchased at a local farm shop, convenience store or supermarket. I want people to be able to prepare and cook my dishes quickly and easily, following a clear methodology, to ensure they create some interesting, wholesome, exciting food that can be shared with friends on both formal and informal occasions. I also think I should tell the reader what utensils they will need for each recipe as there is nothing worse than starting a job and not being able to finish it."

"I agree with your last sentiment and might consider helping you for a fee," said Michael.

"Are you requiring money or some other form of payment for your services?" asked Shona, smiling.

"What are you offering?"

"What would you like?"

"How about I pull over into the woods and show you how to start and then finish a job."

"You don't have a hope as I am too hungry to think about anything other than food."

Michael tutted. "I read somewhere that there is a strong link between food and sex."

"There is. A well-fed woman is more easily aroused and a hungry one wants nothing to do with you."

"I could rustle up a cocktail?"

"Very funny," said Shona.

"Seriously, I did read somewhere that a chef has produced a cookbook using semen that includes cocktails with names such as Jim and Tonic and Macho Mojito."

"The thought of drinking one of those is disgusting and I can't see that they will ever become big volume sellers in pubs and clubs," replied Shona.

"Stranger things have happened. A smell or taste that is disliked by one person, erotic or otherwise, is sure to be another person's turn on," said Michael.

"That's very true. Another thing that is true, is that food is the way to a man's heart and that I do get great pleasure from cooking a meal for someone I love."

"You've had a long day and it's now late so I couldn't

possibly expect you to start cooking again tonight, but we can stop off and get a takeaway on the way to my house. After an hour or so we can then find out if a well-fed woman does want something to do with me and maybe even provide me with some special services?"

"Bloody hell," said Shona. "You're like an elephant."

"It's nice of you to say so," said Michael.

"I meant because of your memory not your manhood."

"I love you too," replied Michael.

"Prove it," said Shona smiling.

"You said you didn't want sex at the moment."

"Why does a man always have to link love with sex? I meant for you to show your love for me by parking up over there and getting me a lamb biryani and a saag bhaji from that Indian restaurant."

"Oh!" said Michael.

"And just to be clear, I don't want a sheek kebab or anything that resembles one tonight, just in case that thought had crossed your mind," said Shona.

CHAPTER NINE

The long sharp blade was thrust swiftly underneath the sternum with the right amount of force to puncture the man's heart. The victim had been followed silently and stealthily, while he walked his dog through the woods. The man fell to the ground instantly and was quickly dragged from the pathway into the undergrowth. The dog immediately started barking but in the same instant, it was silenced using the same weapon.

The DJ worked quickly to bury the dog beneath some bushes. He then dragged the man further into the trees, where he lowered the body into a pre-dug grave containing a polythene sheet and then covered it with black plastic, leaves and bark. If the Fixer had carried out his part of the operation and kidnapped the man's wife, then the police wouldn't be looking for or finding this man's body until the DJ had had time to leave it as he wanted to. The impending rain should also help keep it hidden for now, as few people would be walking deep in the woods if it was thrashing it down, as predicted by the weather forecaster on the BBC Hereford and Worcester radio station.

~

Joseph enjoyed his time at the Swan with Two Nicks on Tuesday, so thought he would go back there on Friday after work and then try out Drummonds night club at the same time.

He staggered out of the building far later than he had anticipated, having sampled a few too many beers. The taste of the beers was vastly different to those available in Washington, probably due to the way they were produced, and there were far fewer pumps than he was used to in his home city. There, he would have the choice of some thirty taps and three hundred and thirty types of ale, lager, stout and cider at Rustico's restaurant and bar on Slaters Lane, twenty-seven pumps in the The Big Hunt in Connecticut Avenue across three floors, or twelve taps and over one thousand bottled beers from around the world at The Brickskeller on 22nd Street. However, none of those places were as quaint, homely and friendly as the Swan with Two Nicks or any of the many other pubs he had frequented here in England.

Joseph thought back to the other evening when Graham had left the pub with Emma, which made him think that there might be something going on between them. "Lucky devil," he said out loud to himself, as he set off on the walk to his hotel which he had booked earlier in the day, as he didn't believe it would be wise to drink and then drive back to his friends' house in the Cotswolds.

Joseph turned right out the pub instead of left by mistake and found himself on Queen Street and then Angel Street. On his slow walk across the city, Joseph encountered many people sleeping rough. He had heard that Worcester has one of the highest numbers of rough sleepers in the country outside of London, but he didn't expect the situation to be as bad as he was seeing firsthand.

Joseph had spent a lot of time in Washington, working with the homeless in his spare time. People living on the streets are grateful for all the help they can get and were often able to pay him back with vital information passed down the grapevine from those higher up the food chain that they came across on the sidewalks and in bars, clubs and shelters. Some of Jo Jo's informants used to be in full-time employment as computer programmers, security guards and assembly line workers, before they became depressed for various reasons and then succumbed to alcohol and drug abuse.

Some of the people living on the streets near the White House and in particular by St John's Church in Washington, are very talented people and Joseph had helped many of them in various ways over the years. One woman who used to paint still-life pictures on the sidewalk now had her own studio and her own apartment thanks to Joseph. As he walked, Joseph wondered if any of the homeless in St John's Worcester had any talent and if he could help those individuals in some way while he was here. His life at the moment was different and exciting, but also a bit spooky. He had travelled some 3,800 miles from his home in Arlington only to arrive in London at the exact same time a bomb was being detonated in Worcester. He was now ensconced in the middle of a murder investigation and was wandering around a city that he didn't know, but somehow felt he did know, wondering how he could help people here, as he had done at home for the last seven or eight years, since he was twenty-eight or twenty-nine years of age.

Joseph rounded a corner from Angel Place and noticed a flashing sign on the side of a building, advertising dancing girls. He walked a bit nearer to see the Chocolate Elephant fascia above the door and thought it might be fun to top the evening off with a bit of adult entertainment. He put his hand in his coat pocket to get his wallet out to pay the entrance fee, but guilt took over. How could he justify paying twenty-five pounds to enter a lap-dancing club, when there were people begging for money to get food only a few hundred yards away. Joseph turned around and made his way back towards Broad Street, where he came across a young girl sitting in a shop doorway.

As he watched her trying to wrap a blanket around herself to keep warm, she asked him if he could spare some change. Joseph took his lap-dancing money out of his pocket and handed it to her.

"Wow! Thank you very much," said the girl.

"This isn't a safe place for a young girl to be spending the night," said Joseph.

"I don't have much choice," she replied.

"How old are you?" asked Joseph?

"Twenty-two," she said, then added, "Where are you from?"

"The United States of America," replied Joseph.

"Are you on holiday, or should I say vacation?" asked the girl.

"I am here on business before I take up an important post in London."

"I struggle to get twenty or thirty pounds a week from the people who live here and you come all the way from the United States and give me more than I have ever received from anybody before."

"I spend some of my spare time in Washington DC helping people who want to be helped get off the streets, into employment and in turn into accommodation of some sort. I understand how easy it can be for anybody from any walk of life to get into difficulty, not know who to turn to for advice or help and end up living out of a doorway, under a bridge or at best in a park in a small tent."

"There are thirty or forty people living on the streets in Worcester and for many it's the way of life they choose."

"What's your name?" asked Joseph.

"Penelope."

"Well, Penelope, you come across as being quite articulate and sound as if you come from a good background, so how is it that you are sleeping here, and is it your choice to be doing so?"

"It's a long story," replied Penelope.

"I would like to hear it and see if I can help you somehow."

"Really?" asked Penelope with some surprise.

"I'll tell you what," said Joseph, "how about I give you another eighty pounds and you take yourself off to a hotel to get cleaned up and get a good night's sleep?"

"Why would you want to do that?"

"So that in return, you will let me buy you breakfast tomorrow morning in the café by the Elgar statue at 9.00 a.m. to see what help I can offer you, before I drive back to the Cotswolds for the weekend."

"Where are you staying?" asked Penelope.

"At the Travelodge opposite the cathedral," said Joseph.

"Could you get me a room there? So that when I come along later I only have to pick up the key. That way I can pretend that we are together and that I have hiked to the hotel to meet you or something."

"That's a good sign, as it says to me that you don't like the life you have, are embarrassed about it and want to change it," replied Joseph.

Joseph said goodbye to Penelope and that he would meet her in the morning, when they could have a proper chat over a large plate of bacon and eggs and he would see if he was able to help her along a new path.

Joseph admired the fabulous buildings as he walked down the High Street and was really impressed by the architecture of the Guildhall and at how imperious the cathedral looked all lit up. Joseph had read that the cathedral contained a tower with two hundred and thirty-five steps to the top via a winding narrow staircase that proffered fantastic views, should you be fit enough to make the strenuous climb. It didn't take Joseph long, maybe two or three seconds, to dismiss the idea of attempting the climb, but he did think to himself that he would like to take a look around what is supposed to be one of England's loveliest cathedrals, before he went home. A cathedral that was built before America was even discovered by Christopher Columbus and has been a place of prayer and worship for fourteen centuries. The cathedral was badly damaged during the English Civil War between the Parliamentarians (Roundheads) and the Royalists (Cavaliers), and as Joseph got closer to the cathedral he could see some scaffolding over an archway and gathered that restoration was probably an on-going and extremely costly exercise.

~

"Did you find that traitor, Baz?" asked the DJ.

"No, his house is empty," replied the Fixer.

"Start asking around in the pubs and clubs to see if anybody knows where he might be. I gave him a chance and he's let me down. People only ever let the DJ down once."

"He would be pretty stupid to stay around here, but he can't get out of the country without his passport, so it will only be a matter of time before one of our sources locates him. He might then see how unwise his actions have been, or we could make sure he might never be able to see again, full stop," said the Fixer.

"We need to go back to the woods tonight to finish what I started earlier," said the DJ.

"Is it absolutely necessary?" asked the Fixer.

"Yes, it is, as I want to keep the police on their toes and try to understand how good their investigators are."

"This is a bit of a game to you, isn't it?"

"It's a challenge and a fine balance between testing my skills and intelligence and getting revenge."

"Are all of the elements within your game or should I say, mission really necessary?"

"I have a reason for everything I do. If you don't want to be a part of this, you only have to say," said the DJ.

"I don't understand all that goes on in your head but I'm glad we are on the same side," replied the Fixer. "Don't forget I have my own reasons for doing some of these things and you're paying me very well to help you with the others, so I would be stupid to back out now."

The DJ looked at him and smiled in an unnerving way, making the Fixer think he had to see this mission through to its conclusion or else he would be a dead man walking.

"What have you done with the dead man's wife? Is she where we agreed?" asked the DJ.

"Yes."

"Good, but make sure that she isn't harmed yet."

~

Michael and Shona went to see Richard on Friday evening to see how he was and how he had got on when he visited his parents a couple of days previously.

"I haven't been home from there long as I stayed with them for quite a while," said Richard.

"That was good," said Shona, hoping that she was saying the right thing under the circumstances.

"Constable Jane Small took me there and my father brought me home this afternoon. My mother and father seemed to be more upset by Amanda's death than her own parents were, but they are very emotional people, whereas Amanda's parents have always appeared to be very matter of fact about things. Perhaps it was my imagination but I always suspected they tolerated each other because of their relationship rather than enjoying spending time together. They did express a wish for their daughter to be cremated, so that is what will happen. I have a few things to finalise tomorrow because the police want to speak to me again on Monday."

"Surely, Graham doesn't still think that you had something to do with Amanda's murder?" asked Michael.

"Well, they are keeping close tabs on me, so I guess they will continue to think that until they actually catch the killer."

"Do you have any idea why Amanda was targeted on Sunday?" asked Shona.

Richard looked at her and then Michael, before he turned around to look out of the lounge window into the garden and replied, "No, not really."

Michael and Shona looked sharply and quizzically at each other. Michael wasn't exactly sure what Shona was thinking, but he thought in that instant that Richard's response was a little odd and that in line with his own thoughts earlier in the week, it was possible that Richard did have some idea why his wife was killed, even if he hadn't actually committed the crime.

CHAPTER TEN

Joseph awoke to hear a knocking on his hotel bedroom door and sat up straight away while glancing at the clock on his mobile phone. It was 5.30 a.m., so he listened again in case the noise was just part of his dream or in his imagination.

His house in America was situated on the outskirts of Arlington and was fairly isolated on the edge of the Stillaguamish River, so Joseph often heard strange noises that he couldn't account for. His job within the CIA had led to him making quite a few enemies over the years. These were very dangerous individuals who could easily snuff him out if they were ever released from prison, which is why he set the intruder alarm on occasions when he was feeling particularly vulnerable. In the main, Arlington is a very peaceful, friendly city with very little crime and some nice tourist attractions that include a kangaroo farm and golf course named Gleneagles. Although it isn't used for major tournaments like its famous cousin in Scotland, the Arlington course is fairly similar in many ways and very challenging in its own right. As in every part of the world however, Arlington does have individuals living there who have no real concern for others and who would for the right price make sure, that to Joseph CIA meant 'Couldn't Interrogate Again'.

The knocking on his door however was real, so Joseph got up, slipped his dressing gown on and walked across the room.

Keeping the chain on, he quietly opened the door to find Penelope standing there dressed in a coat. Joseph ushered her in and asked her what she was doing at this time of the night.

"I am often awake at this time," she said. "So I thought I would come to see you to say thank you for your kindness."

"We are going to meet at the café across the way in three hours' time," said Joseph.

"Not like this," said Penelope as she unbuttoned her coat and let it fall to the floor.

"Wow!" said Joseph as Penelope stood there totally naked.

"You have been kind to me, so I am now going to give you something in return," she said, moving closer to Joseph and pulling the cord on his dressing gown so that it also dropped to the floor in a crumpled heap.

Penelope started to kiss Joseph passionately, and although somewhat tired and shocked he responded accordingly, their tongues darting furiously into each other's mouths. For a man approaching forty years of age, Joseph had a magnificent physique and his penis was now fully erect in expectation. Penelope knelt down and started to lick it before taking his whole length down her throat. Joseph could feel the warm sensation running throughout his body and desperately wanted to come in her mouth. Instead he pulled back, spun Penelope round and pushed her onto the bed. Joseph couldn't believe his luck, as here lying before him was probably the most beautiful woman he had ever seen, with a fantastic sexy figure and magnificent breasts. Joseph lay down next to Penelope, snuggled up close and pressed himself against her bottom as he kissed her neck and stroked her nipples. He then moved his hand between her legs and gently stroked and rubbed her, making her very wet and bringing her to the point of climax. Penelope started to moan with pleasure and then screamed for Joseph to fuck her. He ignored her request and instead slid down the bed and began licking her, very gently at first and then with some pressure. At the same time, Penelope began stroking herself with her fingers and panting loudly. This gave Joseph time to take his wallet from the bedside cabinet and unwrap a legal tea-bag-shaped packet. Just as he did this Penelope suddenly shouted "now, now," so Joseph rammed his penis powerfully inside her and began to thrust in and out, slowly initially, and then with a bit more force. Penelope wrapped her legs around him tightly and shouted "harder, harder" as the waves of orgasm spread through her body. Joseph came at virtually the same time and they both collapsed in a heap on the bed with their legs quivering and shaking and their chests heaving from excitement and exhaustion.

~

Graham decided to go into work on Saturday morning even though it was his day off. He wanted to look over the post-mortem report in peace and try to make some connections between the events of the last eight or nine days and the evidence that had been gathered. He wished in some ways that his brain was wired differently, and despite being of reasonable intelligence and in many ways a balanced person, he knew he had some form of character disorder. His superiors and his sister, as she was the only family member he had left, had tried to get him to slow down, work fewer hours and take some time out for relaxation and the odd holiday, but he always resisted. His stubbornness could be seen as both a strength and a weakness, but he was determined that he and he alone would determine how he used his time. It was sometimes annoying and painful to see work colleagues going home at a normal hour to wives and families and he had tried to change the way he was, but in reality he was more of a leopard than a flounder. Working hard was the way he had chosen to live his life, so it made no sense for him to be resentful; but there were times when he was playing tennis between his ears. Sometimes Graham sat down and talked to Emma about his behaviour, but their conclusions from these discussions were always the same: working long hours was an inevitable consequence of being dedicated to ridding the world, or in this case Worcestershire, of petty and hardened criminals by whatever means possible.

Graham's sister disagreed with this theory and thought he was the way he was because he liked the power and couldn't bear to abdicate responsibility for fear others would fail or fall below his standards and that this would reflect badly on him and the West Mercia police force. He made himself a strong black coffee at 7.30 a.m. and then sat down in the leather chair at his desk and studied the ten-page report carefully, before adding a couple of things to the whiteboard in respect of the Amanda Webb murder and then making copious notes in preparation for his briefing with Benjamin Lewis and Chief Constable Simon Duncan on Monday morning.

Amanda Webb Murder

- *Time of Attack 1.10 a.m. Monday, 24th November*
- *Forced Entry/Male attacker*
- *Bedroom Struggle*
- *No Rape took place*
- *Blood from Victim Type O*
- *Blood from Attacker Type AB*
- *Semen from Attacker*
- *Knife Wound from 15.0 cm Blade*
- *Bruising suggests 10.4 cm Handle*
- *Skin Flakes/Hair*
- *Black Beanie Hat/Black Balaclava Fibres*
- *Partial Footprint possible Size 8 or 9*

Graham now knew that the murder weapon wasn't a knife from the product range sold by Richard's company, as they didn't manufacture one with a fifteen-centimetre blade. As he checked his emails, including one from the lab, he also now knew the identity of the attacker, who was also most likely to be the murderer. It still didn't rule out the possibility that Richard Webb was the brains, or not as the case may be, behind the murder, but at least he had something positive to tell the chief constable, which should keep the old git happy for a while.

Graham telephoned Emma and asked her to come to the police station to help him prepare his report. He also telephoned Joseph, but his phone just went straight to voicemail for some reason.

~

Joseph met Penny, as she now asked him to call her, in the café by the Elgar statue at 8.30 a.m. As he looked at the statue, Joseph wondered why somebody had put a traffic cone on Elgar's head.

"Good morning, Penny, did you sleep well?" asked Joseph.

"Up until about 5.30 a.m.," she said smiling, "then I had to contend with some banging coming from somewhere."

Joseph bought both himself and Penny a large English breakfast and large latte. They sat at a corner table where they could talk in private. Joseph asked Penny how she had become homeless, how she managed to get through each day, what she did for a change of clothes, if she had any possessions and where she kept them, and what her aspirations were. These were five or six simple questions that would enable him to gain a good understanding of her current situation and how he might be able to help her in the short term and going forwards.

"As I said before, it's a long story but I will summarise it for you as best as I can. I left my parent's home in Camberley, Surrey, to take up a degree course in Animal Biology and Ecology just over two years ago. I didn't apply for a grant as my dad said he would pay the £8,900 per year fee for each of the three years of the course, as he didn't want me owing the state for ever and a day. I did very well in my first year, when I managed to get a good part-time job and move into a nice terraced house with three other students within cycling distance of the city."

"What went wrong?" said Joseph interrupting.

"Around about October last year, a new lad took one of the rooms in the house and from the outset things changed. I often came home from a hard day to find him smoking some substance or another and gradually this habit moved on to harder drugs. Around Christmas, the house got raided by the police and everyone was arrested, even though Eva, Lauren and I hadn't touched any of the drugs. My parents were contacted by the West Mercia Police chief constable and despite my protestations of innocence, my dad informed the chief executive at the university of my arrest and he kicked us all off the course."

"That was a bit harsh," said Joseph.

"The uni has rules that it strictly adheres to."

"I meant it was harsh of your dad to inform the chief executive."

"My parents are real Christian people who have never broken the law in their lives, so they saw it as their duty to do the moral thing."

"It seems a bit odd that they didn't believe what their own daughter was telling them."

"They wanted to, but they saw it as a 'no smoke without fire' scenario and chose to let the management committee decide what to do and then abide by their ruling."

"It's hardly Christian to let their daughter sleep rough, is it?"

"They don't know that I am sleeping rough. I lost my job at the same time as losing my place on the course and my life just spiralled downwards."

"Why didn't you go back to Camberley and live with your parents for a while?"

"They were mortified by the scandal and thought that I had brought shame on the family name, so there was no way they were going to invite me back with open arms."

"What do you do for money?" asked Joseph.

"I get about fifty-eight pounds per week job seeker's allowance, but it doesn't go very far."

"What do you do for clothes?"

"The Maggs day centre for the homeless helps me out from time to time and occasionally, I go and look around the charity shops, but I only ever really have the clothes that I live in and those that I carry in this bag," said Penny, pointing to a small brown holdall by her chair.

"What do you do each day?" asked Joseph.

"I go to the Maggs shelter a few mornings a week, where I have a shower and get something to eat and drink. I talk to the fantastic staff and sometimes when I am a bit down I get involved in some of the activities there. In the afternoon, I often go down by the river and people watch or hang around the shops begging for some change."

"I know how hard and dangerous it is for homeless people living on the streets. I know their life expectancy is around fifty years of age due to the very harsh conditions, lack of nutritious food and in many instances, the drink and drugs. I also know this isn't the way of life for you and I want to help you get back on the right path," said Joseph. "I am going to need a few days to put a few things in place, so I'll meet you back here on Wednesday afternoon at 5.00 p.m."

"I can't see how you can possibly help me in such a short space of time, but I would be extremely grateful for anything that you can do for me," said Penny.

"I have a few ideas and have helped many people in a far worse situation than you."

"Thank you," said Penny.

"Oh, thank you," said Joseph.

~

Michael was spending the morning at home on his own as Shona was planning some new menus in preparation for a few dinner parties that she had booked for later in the month. She was also cooking some of the food that she was going to serve at this evening's event.

Michael was reading through his latest article on black football managers. He knew this was still a very sensitive subject and that he had to be sure to get the tone of the document right if he was going to get it published in a mass media magazine or a tabloid newspaper.

Michael's research had shown that most people within football including the managers themselves, didn't believe there was any racist element in the decision-making process of English and Scottish clubs when appointing a new manager. What it had told him was that football club chairmen are scared of making the wrong choice and often go for the soft option and appoint a manager with experience rather than give an inexperienced person a chance, as this is seen as too much of a gamble. As only a few black managers have ever been appointed to date, the pool from which club chairman can select experienced black candidates from is small. Until more black trainee coaches get the required qualifications and there is evidence to suggest that they would be successful in the manager's role, appointments will be few and far between.

Although research undertaken by the Professional Footballers Association suggested at least twenty percent of trainee coaches are black, the majority are not prepared to spend eight years of their life trying to get their qualifications when there isn't a light at the end of the tunnel. During Michael's telephone interviews with many of the football clubs' directors, they did show an appreciation of the situation but likened this scenario to spending hard-earned cash on a new car that they hadn't purchased before. It is safer and possibly less costly to select a make and model that had a good track record and has stood the test of time. Michael thought this to be an odd way of looking at things but realised that without help from journalists like himself, black candidates will only ever be given managerial positions when more club chairmen behave equitably in accepting and processing applications. At the moment, it would appear that only forward-thinking chairmen are giving black managers a chance, providing they have the right qualifications and come across well at the interview stage.

Michael had decided that the Rooney Rule, named after Dan Rooney of the Pittsburgh Steelers American football team, wasn't the answer. This rule meant that NFL teams had to interview an equal number of black and white candidates when choosing a new manager. Michael felt that this scenario was probably more racist than taking all applications on merit. He also felt that certain ex-footballers were making more of an issue out of this situation than was necessary to raise their own profile again and give themselves a new career.

Michael added some text to conclude his summary page: Football is all about competition for places and if the Football Association tries to change this by introducing the Rooney Rule it could have far-reaching consequences in the long term, as teams will begin to choose the eleven players on the pitch and the substitutes, based on their colour rather than their skill.

Michael added a tongue in cheek paragraph that asked searchingly if this would also lead to a change in the rules with the number of players on the pitch being increased to twelve or as was more likely being decreased to ten so as to have an equal number of black and white team members at any one time.

CHAPTER ELEVEN

Graham was just locking his office door as the clock struck 1.00 p.m. to finally go home and get some rest, when he was approached by an out-of-breath sergeant.

"Practising for a marathon, Peter?" asked Graham.

"I didn't realise you were here until a few minutes ago when I got back and saw your car in the compound. I really needed to catch you before you went home, sir," said Peter.

"I was supposed to be having a day off but came in early before the station officially opened to tidy up a few things in peace. What is it that's so urgent, and where have you been?" asked Graham.

"Grafton Woods. I am afraid to say that we have ourselves another body."

"You are joking, aren't you?" asked Graham, who could now see even a half day's holiday disappearing out the window.

"No, sir. A young man walking his dog around 10.00 a.m. came across an old man sitting upright against an oak tree in Grafton Woods. At first he said good morning to him, thinking that the old man was having a rest. When he didn't reply or look up, the young man went a bit closer and it quickly became obvious to him that the old man was probably dead.

We have a team of officers with the paramedics at the scene and I have sealed off the area within five hundred yards of the body, but it looks as if the old man died from natural causes."

"Why do you think that?"

"There isn't any evidence of foul play and the old man is dressed in clean well-pressed clothes that are not muddy or bloody. It just looks as if he became unwell, sat down for a rest and just passed away."

"That seems a little odd to me. From my experience a person passing away under those circumstances would have been slumped on the floor," said Graham.

"Now you come to mention it, it does seem a little odd, but I didn't get to see the body until after the paramedics had tried to revive him."

"Do we have a time of death?"

"The doctor reckons it was about twenty-four hours ago."

"Twenty-four hours. How come the old man wasn't found earlier, was he off the beaten track?"

"No," said Peter, "but it was raining for most of yesterday, so it is possible that nobody walked along that path again until early this morning."

"Do you know who the dead man is?"

"No, sir, not yet, he doesn't have any ID on him."

"Are you sure that there isn't any suggestion of foul play?"

"There doesn't appear to be any, but we haven't searched the area or examined the old man in any way until we have your authorisation, just in case you wanted Emma and her forensics team to get involved."

"Where is the body at the moment?" asked Graham.

"It is pretty much where we found it but it has been placed in a body bag and covered by a tent."

"Keep the area sealed off, Peter, and get the man's body taken to the morgue. I will speak with the medical examiner to see if we can obtain some identification and cause of death later today and then to Emma to make sure she is ready if and when required," said Graham.

~

Shona was at home in her apartment preparing some of the dishes for her next dinner party later the same evening. Her business was taking off better than she could have hoped for as her diary was filled with appointments for the next few months up until February. The downside of this was the limited time she had for her hobbies, which included astronomy and photography. This Saturday she was serving a six-course meal for a young couple celebrating their end of year exam results. They were going to start a three-month travelling holiday the following week, going from their flat in Pershore to New Delhi in India taking in three continents – Europe, Africa and Asia. Their journey sounded hazardous and dangerous, and Shona was glad that her only involvement was to prepare a menu consisting of some of the food the couple might experience on the way.

Mushroom & Leek Gratin
Spanish Carrot Soup (Crema de Zanahoria)
Algerian Borek
Chicken Tagine
Egyptian Umm Ali
Chocolate Naan Bread

~

Baz found the tunnel surprisingly warm. It reminded him of the tunnels built by Hamas to get across the border into Israel, albeit this was a bit bigger. It was well-constructed using thousands of fairly uniform stones and had straight sides, a curved ceiling and a gravel floor. Baz knew he could survive down in the tunnel having read a book called *The Mole People* about the homeless living in the tunnels beneath New York City. Baz did a lot of reading so it was a good job he had kitted himself out with some powerful torches and lanterns, as without them the days would be as dark as the nights. At first, he found the tunnel rather ghostly, almost as if thousands of eyes were watching him, other than the rats that were going to be his companions for a little while.

Baz pitched a canvas tent to sleep in. He cooked some meals on a small gas stove and lit a fire on the nights he didn't venture out into Great Malvern or Worcester. He made his base near to the air shaft as this was a fairly dry spot compared to parts of the tunnel that he felt were under the River Severn, and it also allowed the smoke from his small fire to escape into the atmosphere.

Baz realised living underground was going to be a difficult thing to come to terms with as humans are not meant to live such an existence. He knew that he would have to try to eat properly and take supplements if he was to stay fit and healthy over the next few weeks as he wouldn't be seeing much sunlight.

Baz ate out in fast food restaurants late at night, mixing with other twenty- to twenty-five-year olds so as not to look con-spicuous. He purchased provisions to eat underground on a daily basis and disposed of all rubbish and scraps in waste bins on his evening forays, so as not to encourage more rats than was necessary.

The one thing Baz really missed at the moment was the drugs. In his own mind he wasn't an addict, but did rely on synthetic cannabinoids, particularly Amsterdam Gold, to help him get through each week. This was probably the most popular drug that he sold around the pubs and clubs, so he always had a supply. He knew the dangers of taking drugs and had seen and heard of many deaths from them over the years, and in recent months there had been a few from those such as Black Mamba, Benzo Fury and Mexxy, which is why he didn't handle these on a regular basis or take them. He also knew the government was clamping down on many of the more dangerous drugs and that handling them could land him with a five-, ten- or even fifteen-year prison sentence. Baz tried to convince himself that by not dealing in the very dangerous substances he did have some morals, but in reality it was the fear of incarceration that really stopped him from doing so. The other thing Baz missed at the moment was having any money coming in. He had one thousand pounds in cash on his person, from under his mattress, but he was eating into this, so to speak, and he knew it wouldn't last long, particularly if he did manage to purchase some drugs.

The Fixer was the linchpin of a complicated drug-pushing network within the West Mercia area, so he would need to be extremely careful if he tried to purchase anything from any source during the next few weeks.

When Baz came to England a few years ago, he had intended to lead an honest life, study hard, work hard, get a girlfriend and save up to buy a flat. Things didn't quite work out as planned after he got mixed up with the wrong crowd. Within a short space of time he got hooked on cocaine and was having to buy and then sell on more and more drugs to pay for the habit. When this income wasn't enough for Baz to live the life he had quickly got used to, he found himself having to do dangerous jobs for 'The Organisation' to supplement this. It was one of these jobs that had landed him with a three-month sentence in HMP Hewell as a Category D prisoner earlier this year. As he looked around him in the tunnel at the pairs of eyes staring at him in the dark, Baz thought he was still in a prison but with fewer privileges.

~

Graham managed to get the old man examined at the morgue late on Saturday afternoon and was astonished by the results. He made a few phone calls and gathered a large team of officers together from across the region to make sure that a much larger area around Grafton Woods was properly sealed off, so that forensics could do their job at first light. He still couldn't get hold of Joseph for some strange reason, so he sent him a text telling him to be at the police station at 6.00 a.m. on Sunday morning, as something urgent had cropped up and he needed to get the team together for an important briefing. Those in high places had told Graham that, no sooner had he finished briefing his team, he had been given the unenviable task of standing before the press, informing them of the recent events and answering all of the journalists' questions. He hated doing this, as there was only so much he was allowed to say and he always seemed to get difficult questions from one or two reporters that thought they could do his job much better than he was doing it.

~

Shona was fascinated by the travel plans of Luke Smith and Kylie Page and just a little envious, as she hadn't been anywhere abroad other than France and Italy. Luke and Kylie were originally going to drive the eight thousand miles from Worcester to New Delhi, but were advised by the British Embassy that, although travelling through Germany, Romania, Hungary and Turkey was safe, to try and pass through Iran, Afghanistan and Pakistan wasn't too advisable at the moment. This was a huge disappointment for the young adventurers, so they decided to change their plans and go south through France down to Monaco and then along the Gulf of Lion coast to Spain. This route would enable them to visit some fantastic cities and take in many famous landmarks and attractions, as well as seeing both the Alps and Pyrenees. Luke and Kylie were then going to stay in Gibraltar for two days before crossing the border into North Africa and driving to Casablanca in Morocco. From there, they would then travel east to Algiers before getting a flight to Egypt. They originally wanted to drive to Cairo through Tunisia and Libya but were also advised not to undertake this journey as Libya isn't safe for British nationals to visit these days either.

Shona could tell that Luke in particular was very annoyed at having to succumb to the threat of terrorists, but deep down he knew he had to accept the things he couldn't change about the world. He felt very sad for the innocent people living in countries badly affected by militant groups and could see no point in all of the violence which was destroying their lives and the future livelihoods of their children. He tried to convince Kylie that by sticking to their original journey plans they would be showing support for those being persecuted and helping their economy in a very small way. Kylie did agree with Luke that violence never solved anything long term and she applauded him for thinking this way but wasn't going to be persuaded to take any unnecessary risks.

"You can be bloody pig-headed at times but you have to know the things that you can change and have the wisdom to know those that you can't," said Kylie.

"Very serene, it's a pity the terrorist groups don't realise there is a difference," said Luke. "Everybody likes to fight for what they believe in, but there is a right way to make things happen and a wrong way."

Once they had come to terms with their new itinerary, both were excited at the prospect of spending three days in Giza, but not so excited at the thought of a nine-hour flight from Cairo to New Delhi in India afterwards, if they couldn't get a direct flight, which was proving to be difficult. Other than this element of uncertainty, the youngsters weren't really concerned about any aspect of their trip apart from the different foods they would have to eat, which would be an unknown entity and might not be to their liking.

Shona's task with her menu was to provide Luke, Kylie and their friends for the evening, with examples of the food the two of them might come across on their journey. She intended to serve them combinations that would tantalise their taste buds and give them the confidence that their food experience in all of the countries would be memorable. Because Shona had prepared a lot of the food at home, it gave her a little time to talk with Luke and Kylie about their trip. She was surprised to learn that they had prepared very thoroughly in respect of their route, petrol stations, hotels, local culture and the dangers they could encounter. She wasn't surprised to learn that the two youngsters had been brought up on burgers, pies, fish and chips and takeaways and hadn't got a clue about food from anywhere else in the world other than America, China and India.

Although Shona hadn't travelled much, she had read books on many countries and had spent many hours researching food culture and cooking techniques to try and achieve perfection and a level of sophistication in her work.

"Have you made a list of sights that you must see?" asked Shona, who wished in one way that she was going with them.

"We are still working on it but it does include the Eiffel Tower, Sagrada Familia, Hassan II Mosque, Kasbah of Algiers, Pyramid of Khufu and Taj Mahal," said Kylie.

"A friend of mine takes a video camera everywhere she goes and commentates on the places of interest and the scenery for future reference," said Shona.

"That's a good idea, as photographs don't always do justice to things," said Luke.

Shona's research enabled her to add a few more places of interest to Luke and Kylie's list and they found her knowledge of the countries of much value. They were also interested in all that Shona had to say about food and how they might improve their cooking skills and diet using fresh ingredients when they got back to England. The issue they had was time, as they were studying all day and working at night, so Shona thought it would be a good idea to give them a free lesson on cooking and planning ahead.

"Start with some easy things," she told them, "such as soup, mince or a casserole. I'll give you some recipes when you are ready and you can try to make meals that spread the workload over a period of time. Homemade soup is very easy to make and it can freeze for up to four months. Bolognese, chilli con carne, shepherd's pie and both meat or poultry casseroles will freeze well for up to six months, as will things such as creamy mashed potato and vegetable purées. Pasta dishes including lasagne or carbonara, steak or chicken pies made with shortcrust pastry and fish cakes can be frozen for two or three months. I will also give you some recipes for great desserts that freeze perfectly, such as apple crumble, baked cheesecake, choux buns, key lime pie and spotted dick."

"That would be much appreciated," said Kylie.

"It will be my pleasure. I'll also provide you with a health benefits sheet. I try to detail in my menus the benefits to health of the majority of the key ingredients that I use, as it may just help some people enjoy a better quality of life."

"At some point in the future, I hope I can cook a meal for you and one or two of your friends?" said Kylie.

"Make sure you look after yourselves and come back safe and sound then," replied Shona.

At the end of the evening, Luke and Kylie both hugged Shona and thanked her for making the evening a success.

"We were a bit sceptical about the naan bread with chocolate as a dessert, as we've only ever dipped one in a tikka masala or korma before," said Luke. "But I have to say it was magnificent, as was the whole meal, which was one of the best I have ever eaten."

"I thought that the Umm Ali was one of the best desserts I've ever eaten," said Kylie.

"I made it with a lot of milk so that it had the consistency of a rice pudding, but you can make it with less so that it eats like a bread pudding."

"If I only had a few days on this earth to live," said Kylie, "I would want that to have been my last ever meal."

CHAPTER TWELVE

Graham gathered the key members of his team together in his office. Emma, Bea, Jane, Peter and Joseph all sat down and looked towards the whiteboard as Graham stood poised with his black marker. He had considered asking the newly appointed PCSO supervisor to attend, but thought it prudent to introduce Frank Archer to the team formally, later in the week, once he had finished his training at Hindlip. Graham wasn't sure which budget Frank's salary was coming from, as he seemed to have been losing officers during the last year rather than gaining any. He had heard that this was a new initiative in conjunction with the Warwickshire force, which probably meant the cost would be shared.

"I am sorry for getting you all here before dawn on a Sunday, as I know for a couple of you that it was to be your day off. It was necessary to do so however as we have ourselves another murder victim and I needed to talk to you before it gets light.

"Yesterday morning, a person out walking his dog found a body in Grafton Woods. The deceased was an old man who we think would have been in his seventies. Someone, most probably the murderer, had gone to a lot of trouble to make it look as if the victim had died of natural causes. The old man was fully dressed in pristine clothes, there was no blood anywhere on him and yet, as I found out late last night, he had actually been stabbed in the heart."

"I gather from that, that you managed to get a post-mortem done yesterday evening?" said Joseph.

"Yes, I did. The medical examiner did me a favour, as I suspected that there was more to the man's demise than initially met the eye."

"Was that down to years of experience?"

"In a way, yes, as the situation was all too surreal. Whoever carried out the murder is an intellectual person and according to the ME, a very skilful person with a knife. At the moment we don't know who the victim is as he wasn't carrying any ID. We don't have any new missing persons on file, so I am going to get his photo released to the press and local news reporters to see if we can get a name. Emma, I need you to get your equipment and however many of your team are available across to Grafton Woods within the next hour to see what trace evidence, if any, can be found."

"No problem," said Emma, "I can call on Bill and Ben."

"Great," said Graham, "but let's hope they can work faster than a tortoise and give me something concrete to add to my report, or else the chief might be placing me on gardening leave to tend my flowerpots."

Emma asked to be excused and left the room as Graham flipped both whiteboards open and wrote the name of a person on each one.

"I can tell you all that we have finally had some results back from the laboratories and the DNA results show us that the same person was at the scene of the bomb blast and the Amanda Webb murder. His name is Basil Reddy. He is of Irish and Indian descent and came to this country a few years ago, from Boston, USA, but for some reason has only appeared on our radar recently. He did spend a bit of time in prison earlier this year for possession of Class B drugs and handling stolen goods but until now we had no indication that he would commit a very serious crime."

"I thought the courts were handing out stiffer sentences, like three to five years for possession of Class B drugs," said Bea.

"Yes, they are, but Mr Reddy had less than a gram in his pocket and it was his first offence," replied Graham. "When he was sent down he stated that he had no fixed abode, so it is possible he could be living rough, crashing with friends or moving from place to place, but somehow we have to find him fast."

"I think I know where he's been living," said Joseph.

"What?" said Graham as everybody turned to face the American, who suddenly seemed embarrassed and under pressure with all the pairs of eyes staring at him in expectation of his revelation.

"How the hell can you know where Basil Reddy could be living when I have only just told you his name?"

"I have my sources," said Joseph, thinking about Penny.

"Baz, as he likes to be called, used to travel to Worcester University every day from a house he shared with a group of students in the village of Warndon."

"Do you know where in Warndon?" asked Graham.

Joseph wrote the address on a piece of paper and handed it to Graham, who in turn handed it to Peter, and said, "Get a team of officers to this address immediately."

Graham walked back to the whiteboard and pointed out all of the new information that had become available to him.

"We know that the Amanda Webb murder weapon wasn't one manufactured by Mr Webb's company. I will have a chat with Richard when he is here tomorrow, to see if he can tell us the possible brand of knife used to stab his wife from the information we have been given by the coroner. I also want to show him a picture of the latest murder victim to see if I get a

111

reaction, and then see if he proffers any information when I tell him that we believe the knife used to kill the old man had a 23 cm blade and a 10.5 cm handle."

"I am not sure he will be in a frame of mind for helping us too much, as it's his wife's cremation next week," said Bea.

"It might work in our favour," said Graham, "as his mind may be a little scrambled and we might just get some information that is of major use."

Graham started a third whiteboard and said to the remaining team members left in the room that he wanted them all to meet back here on Monday morning at 8.30 a.m. sharp.

Grafton Woods Murder

- *Time of Murder 10 a.m. – 11 a.m. Friday, 28th November*
- *Victim/Male aged about 70–80 years old*
- *Stab Wound to the Heart*
- *23 cm Blade /10.5 cm Handle*

As the meeting broke up, Graham pulled Joseph aside and said, "Come on, Joseph, tell me from where that name got plucked?"

Joseph thought again about Penny and said, "I am glad you said plucked!"

"The information has come from an incredible source and this particular person may be of use going forward, but I am going to have to grease her palm."

"So you want some of the West Mercia police force miscellaneous budget, do you?"

"Do you want to wrap these cases up sooner or later?"

"How much do you want?"

"I'll let you know in a couple of days, but it shouldn't be

more than £200 per week."

"Bloody hell, I know things are supposedly bigger and better in America, but you have more chance of getting my blood than that."

"I don't want blood, as enough of that is being spilled around this part of the country at the moment, but I will settle for £150 per week."

"£100 and you have a deal. Now, let's get across to Grafton Woods to see how Emma is getting on."

~

Michael had just got back home after visiting Richard and was happy in an odd sort of way that all of the arrangements for Amanda's cremation had been finalised and that Richard was pleased with the eulogy that he had written.

Michael was also happy that there had been a good reaction to his article about black football managers and that some famous names from places such as Brighton, Carlisle, Huddersfield and London had emailed him to say that his thought process was very refreshing.

As he sat down to start his article about HS2 and the ruination of the English countryside, Michael couldn't help but think his inbox over the next few weeks might get overloaded with emails from 'green' people, excluding those he often received from Shona.

He started to write the opening paragraph of his article with an aggressive statement that would ensure his readers would take notice. The message had to get across how the countryside, which covers about eighty percent of England's green and pleasant land at the moment, is gradually being replaced by more houses than are really necessary, industrial estates, wind turbines, even more roads and now a pointless railway line that will initially thunder from London to Birmingham and destroy the look of the beautiful Chilterns forever.

Michael thought it a good idea to list the pros and cons of HS2 Phase 1 before he structured the article, as this would help his readers more easily understand its true impact. As he started to research this in some depth, he could clearly see that there were very few real benefits to the high speed railway line and many elements of real detriment. The government are telling the public that the project will provide ten to twenty thousand jobs, reduce journey times into London by thirty or forty minutes and ease road congestion. They are not mentioning the ten to fifteen thousand jobs that will not now be available or will be lost along the route, due to proposed new developments being scrapped and hundreds of shops, pubs and factories being bulldozed to the ground. They are also seemingly oblivious to the fact that HS2 will cause hardship to many families, due to the demolition of homes along the route and the devaluation of one hundred and fifty to two hundred thousand properties situated within one mile of the railway line. Michael wondered if those in favour of the project did realise its impact on the health and well-being of people living near the line and its impact on wildlife with the loss of much of their natural habitat.

Michael was unsure if HS2 would increase or decrease the UK's carbon emissions as there were too many variables to take into consideration, including any changes to internal flights and the knock on effect this may have for European flights, so he needed to do more research on this before he would commit pen to paper. He initially included under the pros column a reduction in overcrowding on trains, but even this can't be quantified, even though the politicians will have us believe more people will stop driving their cars to work. For now though, he felt he had gathered enough information, albeit a lot of it contradictory and unstable, to at least put another cat among another lot of pigeons owned by government officials.

~

Graham and Joseph arrived at the crime scene at the same time, even though they travelled in separate cars. After walking a short way into the woods, they found Emma standing over the body of a white highland terrier that now looked like a raspberry split.

"We have a rather interesting situation here, Graham," said Emma. "We have uncovered the body of this dog that we have to assume was the victim's. We have also uncovered what was a temporary grave just over there," she said, pointing to a large tent that was covering the spot where the grave had been dug.

"A temporary grave?" said Graham.

"Yes, it looks as if our killer buried the old man for a while, before returning at a later time to strategically place him against that oak tree over there," she said, while turning around and pointing to the right.

"Why would he, or she for that matter, bother doing that?"

"It would seem as if our killer is playing games with us. It's almost as if they are testing us for some reason."

Graham walked towards the grave and then to the oak tree to get an overall feel for the crime scene and gain an understanding of what this particular investigation would entail. He made a few notes on a pad as he stood and looked around before returning to speak with Emma.

"We need to have a conversation with Bea in the morning to see if she can build a profile of this person. We must then add your findings from today to the whiteboards, to see if we can establish any links to the other crimes."

"I do think that the murderer is likely to be a man, Graham, due to the size and depth of footprints we have found, but I'll let you know more in the morning once I've analysed my evidence bags later this evening. One odd thing that we have found, and it may just be something lost by a child out with their mum and dad, is this small rabbit toy with a skull and crossbones image on its tummy."

"Can I see that?" asked Joseph.

"Do you think that Basil Reddy could be responsible for this murder too, Emma?" asked Graham.

"It is possible but it seems unlikely, unless his carelessness at the Webbs' house has made him think more about his actions, as this was a well-controlled crime that has given us very little to work on. We will know more if we can get any DNA from the trace evidence, but I would say that Basil Reddy will be lying low and that this is the work of a real professional."

"Do you have any thoughts, Joseph?" asked Graham.

"I do have some ideas, even more now that I have seen this toy, but I would like to fire off a couple of emails to some of my colleagues back home before I give you these."

"Ok. Let's leave Emma to finish off here and go to Warndon to see how Peter and his team are getting on. After that, I'm going back to my flat in Diglis to watch the football on the TV."

"Did you say Diglis?"

"Yes, why?"

"Where is Diglis exactly?"

"Not far from the cathedral here in Worcester, in an area called Sidbury."

Joseph's mouth opened and there were a few seconds of silence before he took a deep breath and shouted "bollocks, bollocks and more bollocks," before telling Graham that he had to go somewhere urgently.

"Where would that be?" asked Graham.

"I'll tell you when I see you early tomorrow morning, when I hope to proffer an insight into what's going on around here at the moment."

Joseph hurried off, got in his car and drove away, leaving both Graham and Emma standing looking at each other in disbelief. Then Emma asked, "How much do we actually know about Joseph?"

CHAPTER THIRTEEN

Shona had a free day at last, after a rather hectic and eventful couple of weeks. She had spoken with her daughter's foster mother early this morning and was delighted when she agreed to meet in the park during the afternoon for a chat, while Jade played on the swings. Shona was then going to walk into the city and finally hand in her notice at the Chocolate Elephant. Her boss wasn't going to like it, as Shona was very popular with the customers, but he was going to have to lump it.

As she walked to the park, Shona felt as if she wasn't alone. She had a feeling that someone was once again watching her from very close by. She couldn't see anyone within fifty yards of where she was standing and the people that she could see in the distance all seemed to be going about their daily business. Even though for a bright, sunny day it was a little cold, Shona felt a shiver running down her spine. It was a shiver that made her uneasy, a shiver that couldn't be explained.

Halfway along the path on her route to the park, Shona turned around half-expecting someone to be tailing her. The path was clear other than for a few leaves blowing around and a black and white cat practising the green cross code. Shona smiled and wondered if she would ever have the patience to train an animal. She was going to have to find a lot of patience from somewhere over the next few months though, as she had decided to start the process of bringing Jade back into her life and doing everything in her power to be a proper full-time mum at last.

The park was fairly busy with people walking their dogs, playing tennis or just sitting on wooden benches talking, smoking or eating. Within a few seconds of approaching the play area Shona spotted Jade on the roundabout. She was wearing a nice bright pink coat with fur around the hood and very vivid, red wellington boots. Maisie, her foster mother, was standing watching Jade, looking every bit the proud parent and Shona vowed to make sure that whatever happened in the future, Maisie would play a big part in Jade's life forever.

The person watching Shona didn't know what she was actually thinking, but they had a similar thought process for a different reason.

~

Graham arrived in Warndon to find Peter and two officers sitting in a patrol car outside Basil Reddy's rented house.

"Anything going off here?" asked Graham.

"We found out who owns the property and are now waiting for the landlord to arrive with the keys," said Peter.

"Do you have a team around the back of the house?"

"Yes, so if the suspect is inside we have him trapped."

"Have you looked through any of the windows?"

"Yes, and it seems like the place is empty as there was no sound or movement when we knocked on the door."

"If the landlord doesn't arrive in five minutes we need to go in," said Graham.

"We don't have a warrant, sir," replied Peter.

"It is in the pipeline as we speak."

"How did you manage that on a Sunday?"

"I got a few people out of bed."

~

Baz had deliberately grown both a moustache and beard, but was in desperate need of a bath or shower. He decided to set off early on Sunday morning on the long walk towards the village of Spetchley, where he knew that he could freshen up at the Nightingale public house. He had made friends with the landlord and knew he would be safe there and could feel normal for a little while at least. He realised he wouldn't be able to buy drugs anywhere in the village but thought a few pints of beer would offer some compensation.

It took Baz three hours to walk from his base in the Malvern Hills, but he didn't have too much else to do and was glad of the exercise. Once he had climbed from the tunnel he was also glad to see some daylight for the first time in a few days even if it did take his eyes some time to adjust.

Baz was due to meet up with a Mr Cameron Hunter at the pub, having plucked up the courage to phone the man best known as 'The Chameleon' for his ability to change people's lives or help them blend into society by providing them with a new passport, driving licence or other document – in return for a substantial fee.

Baz was a bit nervous about meeting the Chameleon, but less nervous than he was being surrounded by brown rats, even though he knew deep down that the rats were more scared of him than he was of them. This knowledge hadn't stopped Baz dreaming some nights that he was lying paralysed on the floor of the tunnel while a big rat gnawed away at his jugular vein.

Baz had a shower at the pub and was enjoying his first pint for a couple of days when the Chameleon walked in. Baz knew who it was because of the green taillike swirl of a tattoo that was wrapped around Cameron Hunter's neck.

"Hello, Baz."

"Hello, Cameron, good to meet you," said Baz as he shook the man's hand.

"You seem to have got yourself into a bit of mess again, haven't you?" said Cameron.

"I just had another bit of bad luck."

"Bad luck, bad judgement, bad choice of friends, you see it as you will, but one thing is for certain, you are facing a much longer stretch inside than before, but this time as a Category A prisoner."

"That's why I need your help," replied Baz.

"Get me a beer, Baz, and I'll tell you what I'm prepared to do to help you."

"I suppose you would like a Budweiser?" asked Baz.

"You suppose right, Baz, which is very astute of you."

"Your American drawl gave me a bit of a clue as to where you come from."

Baz ordered two beers from the bar, and as he was walking back to the table he started to laugh, which appeared to unnerve Cameron, causing him to get twitchy and a bit angry.

"What's so funny?" snarled Cameron.

"I've just thought of a joke," replied Baz.

"What?" said Cameron with some bemusement.

"What's the difference between the US President and a chameleon?"

"I don't know," said Cameron.

"One changes its colour to suit its surroundings and the other is a lizard."

"That's very funny, Baz. I am not sure if you are taking the piss out of me, or our great president, but I am sure you wouldn't be in the brown sticky stuff if your reflexes the other night were as sharp as your wit."

"I was caught with my trousers down," replied Baz.

"You could have taken your trousers down at the Chocolate

Elephant for less than five hundred pounds."

"Five hundred pounds for a forged passport?" exclaimed Baz. "That's extortion."

"It's either a monkey... or some bird," said Cameron holding out his hand to take the envelope Baz had in his pocket.

Baz handed Cameron his newly acquired photo from the passport booth located within Boots.

Cameron quickly finished his drink and said to Baz, "Meet me here with the cash in used notes on Tuesday at 1.00 p.m. and I'll give you your documents and possibly your only lifeline out of this mess."

~

Shona waved goodbye to Maisie and Jade with a mixture of thoughts rushing through her head. She was very excited at the prospect of having her daughter come to live with her at last, although she knew that she would probably still have to pass some fit and proper person test before this happened. Shona was very worried too, as good things didn't usually happen to her, and her life at the moment was almost too good to be true. She was also scared that having Jade to live with her might affect her relationship with Michael, and that her new career still involved some evening work, which might not sit well with social services. As she walked past the tennis courts in the park, Shona glanced back at Maisie and felt a pang of guilt and some sadness for Jade's foster mother, as she had looked after Jade very well during the last six years and to have her taken away would leave a big void in her life.

As Shona walked across the bridge and glanced down at the swans bobbing about on the River Severn, eating bread and scraps being thrown to them by the locals and the tourists, she knew that she had made the right decision to change her life around. People will always want to enjoy a great food experience, but as she got a little older and her body became less taut, they certainly wouldn't want her for any sort of sexual experience.

Shona turned left on the other side of the bridge and strolled along the river bank looking at a few homeless people pitching their tents for the evening. She smiled to herself, looked up towards the sky and thanked her lucky stars that she had escaped that desperate, dark and depressing way of life and had a bright future to look forward to.

Darkness was descending rapidly as Shona got near to the Chocolate Elephant. She was going to tell Michael about her decision to quit the club and then be a proper mum to Jade when he came round to see her later that evening. She was also going to ask Michael if they could move in together, as this would significantly help her chances of getting Jade back. Shona puffed out her cheeks and prayed that this was as dark as the day got because her strategy was very risky.

If Michael rejected the idea, Shona would have to consider her options and decide if he was the right man for her. He could, of course, make the decision for her and admit he was only using her for sex like every man she had been out with.

~

Baz left the Nightingale by the kitchen door and backtracked towards the tunnel entrance, making sure that he wasn't being followed. He knew that he now had a huge dilemma. Did he trust Cameron Hunter to just bring him a passport or would he turn up at the pub with the DJ or the Fixer? Could he be sure once he handed over his five hundred pounds that he would get a realistic, usable document? In truth, Baz couldn't visualise what a kosher passport looked like, what colour the cover was or how many pages it should contain. As he walked back along the tunnel he knew he had very few options available, but the thought of having to spend so much money on a passport was causing him pain. He consoled himself with the thought that this pain was far less than that he would have to endure if The Organisation were to catch up with him.

If he was going to have to spend much of the cash he had left on a passport, Baz needed to get some drugs and some more clothes first. The clothes would be easy to obtain, as the tunnel back into the city ran underneath the main high street and there he had found a couple of secret entrances into some of the shops' storerooms. Surprisingly, the storerooms were not alarmed with any form of heat sensor or movement device, so Baz was able to remove some of the blockwork, crawl in, grab various items and crawl back out again. Unless a member of staff was to lie on the floor and look underneath the racking, these entrances would never be discovered. If only Baz had found them before he had pissed off the DJ, he could have made a fortune selling Blue-Xtreme fashion products alongside Blue Extreme cannabinoids.

~

Shona's resignation hadn't been taken too well by Luca, the Chocolate Elephant's general manager, but she didn't care much as she now felt free. Free to make her own choices in life, free to work as and when she wanted and free from the grubby pawing hands of the perverts who watched her perform each night.

The air was cold but the night sky was clear, so the moon could be seen clearly, as could Saturn; even though it was almost eight hundred and ninety million miles away, which meant Shona couldn't see the prominent ring system without her telescope. As she thought this, her mobile phone rang. She half-expected it to be Michael, but instead it was an unknown number. Nobody spoke to her but she thought she could hear breathing on the line, which sent another enormous shiver down her spine. Maybe it was a potential client wanting to book a dinner party? As she had forgotten to answer the call as Spice and Slice, perhaps the person on the other end of the line was unsure what to say, got flustered, thought they had dialled the wrong number and put the phone down? As if to reinforce this belief in her mind and to try and shake off any scary thoughts going around in her head, Shona told herself out loud in no uncertain terms to "stop being paranoid."

She was well aware of the strange things happening in the city at the moment and aware that she was walking close to where a blast had occurred ten days earlier, but deep down she felt her life was really on the up as long as she stayed positive and focused.

Shona had a lot to do later that evening as she was trialling some menus for her fourth dinner party, with Michael being the guinea pig, so she quickened her pace. She told herself, inwardly this time, that walking faster had nothing to do with her having the same feeling as she had had earlier that afternoon. She didn't cut through the park this time though and walked instead around the outside, keeping in full view of the car headlights on the one way system and the people leaving Homebase and McDonalds. She tried to look around, by making out that she was gazing into the night sky and following the stars, but as she turned there wasn't anybody about who appeared to be watching her.

Michael arrived at Shona's apartment at 7.30 p.m., unsure of what he was going to be eating, but sure of what the last course would be. He kissed and hugged Shona who seemed a little edgy for the first time since he had met her.

"Hello, sweetheart, how are you?"

"I'm alright; I have just had a strange day."

"Would you like to tell me about it?"

"I'll tell you about it over dinner."

"What exciting concoction have you got for me tonight other than a wig, some chains and a whip?"

"None of those things are on offer, but I do have a nice meal for you to eat and give me some feedback on."

Creamy Green Peas and Lettuce on French Toast
Haddock and Prawn Cobbler
or
Spinach and Ricotta Pasta
Key Lime Pie
Lime and Coconut Sorbet

"You know I find it difficult when having to choose from a menu, so I think I will just have a bit of both main courses, all in the line of duty."

"I don't like the word duty," replied Shona.

Michael ignored the comment and said, "Everything on the menu is rather green and white."

"It is an engagement party meal for a couple who are semi-vegetarian, if there is such a thing, but have two vegetarian guests arriving. The man comes from Nigeria but now lives in Powick, while his fiancée comes from and still lives in Devon."

"I know that the Nigerian football team play in green but I don't get the Devon link other than maybe the countryside and the surf?"

"You're close, Michael. The Devon flag, which was created in 2003, is made up of three colours: green, black and white. The green represents the colour of the hills, the black represents the moors of Dartmoor and Exmoor and, I believe, the white is meant to reflect the salt of the sea surf from both its coastlines."

"You are a mine of information, my love. However, I bet you didn't know that the flag of Worcestershire has got green and white on it too, as well as two wavy lines of blue to represent the River Severn. We are a bit behind the Devonians though, as our flag didn't get registered until 2013."

"Now who is the mine of information?"

"I have some other news for you as well," said Michael.

"What's that?"

"Richard was pleased with the eulogy I've written about Amanda. I went to see him this morning and it appears that everything is all in place for the cremation on Tuesday. Before that though, he still has to go back to the police station for another interview with DCI Graham Laws."

"Graham was a bit aggressive and heavy handed last time, which seemed a bit odd under the circumstances, so I am hoping Richard is treated a bit better tomorrow. I do suspect that Graham is playing a game with him for some reason."

"I think so too, because as far as we know Richard is still the only suspect and a tough cop, nice cop approach is probably the method Graham often uses to get to the truth, backed up by years of experience of dealing with liars."

Shona walked into the lounge to turn the television on for Michael, so that he would stay out of her way while she was dishing up the starter. As she did so the local news was coming to an end with an appeal for information from the public.

"Oh my God," said Shona.

"What?" said Michael?

"That man on the television screen, the one they've just said has been found dead in Grafton Woods. It's Mr Campbell, who I cooked for last week."

CHAPTER FOURTEEN

Graham had assembled the largest team of officers at his disposal and they were all sitting in the training room waiting for him to arrive. He was currently briefing the chief constable in his office as to the weekend's discoveries.

Graham walked into the room at 9.15 a.m. and everyone could tell he was in a bad mood when he launched into a speech without any pleasantries.

"I have just had my fucking balls chewed by the top brass upstairs," he roared.

'Lucky you don't work for Andrew Rankin at MI5,' thought Joseph, 'as that conjures up a horrible vision.'

"The chief is really pissed off that we haven't been able to arrest anybody for the bombing or the murders," Graham continued in a raised voice. "Even though we now have a mass of information relating to all incidents, the name of a suspect involved in the blast and the Amanda Webb murder and as of very late last night, the name of the second victim killed in Grafton Woods."

There was a murmur among all of the officers before Emma spoke up. "I think that any criticism is really unfair. We have all worked very hard to get to where we are on these cases. It's the chief's fault for being so spineless that we are thin on the ground and having to work twice as hard to get results within their expected timeframes."

"I don't think the chief had much choice as far as the staff cutbacks were concerned," said Bea. "Hobson's choice I suspect, the same as all other police forces in the country."

"Bea is right and if we want to keep our jobs we have to keep on doing our best until things turn full circle, which they will when crime rates get out of hand, terrorist activity increases or we get another prime minister," said Graham.

As quickly as Graham had lost his rag he regained his composure and he now addressed those in the room in a quieter but somehow more forceful way. "Maybe the employment of Frank Archer was a response to my outburst the other day and is a step in the right direction. I am sorry for losing it earlier and I shouldn't have let my anger surface like that, but despite what you all may think, I am human."

This statement brought some light relief to proceedings, which gave Graham a bit more thinking time before he continued speaking using his notes as a guide.

"Last night, I took a call from local journalist Michael Black, who was able to tell me that the old man killed in Grafton Woods was a Mr Harold Campbell. He was also able to tell us where he lived or should I say, used to live with his wife Elspeth. We had officers call round their house around 10.30 p.m. last night to find it empty. We have checked with neighbours and relatives, but nobody seems to know the whereabouts of the man's wife. We are concerned that something sinister may also have happened to Mrs Campbell and have therefore registered her as a missing person. Until we are in possession of more information, we have also issued a warrant for her arrest. The situation is a bit surreal as we know the couple celebrated their fiftieth wedding anniversary last Thursday, but as we don't have a clue why Mr Campbell was murdered, or why the killer left him sitting against a tree out in the open, we must assume with Mrs Campbell missing that she had something to do with it."

"She would have needed an accomplice or would have had to hire a contract killer to have left the body in the position it was found in," said Joseph.

Graham wrote the word accomplice followed by a question mark on the whiteboard and then carried on talking in a very matter-of-fact way that suggested he thought Chief Constable Duncan was listening in the corridor. "We also have an arrest warrant out for Basil Reddy. He hasn't been seen at his rental house in Warndon for more than a week but he still has possessions there, so it's difficult to tell if he knows we are onto him or not yet. We will be keeping a close eye on the premises just in case he returns there. Although we know from his DNA, that Baz, as he likes to be called, was complicit in the bomb blast, we don't know for sure if he's linked to any terrorist group. Before we go over the whiteboards in some detail, does anyone have any information to add to them? What about you, Joseph, after your light bulb moment yesterday?"

Joseph stood up, walked across to the boards and said, "I have been up most of the night talking on the phone to various colleagues around the world and I do think that I may have some answers."

"Basil Reddy isn't part of any terrorist organisation as far as the CIA is aware. He has however recently travelled from Pakistan to Bangladesh. Also in Bangladesh at the same time, supposedly to try and sell German knives to industrial suppliers, was a certain Mr Richard Webb."

There were gasps from all those in the room and they all looked at each other in astonishment. Joseph let them digest the information before continuing. "Another person in Bangladesh at exactly the same time was a Mr Justin Johnson. At this point it is only fair to tell you that Justin is my brother, although these days water is thicker than blood because we fell out many years ago and I haven't seen or heard from him since. He currently works for the CIA. Not the Central Intelligence Agency, but the Culinary Institute of America."

"So he could be good with knives, then?" said Graham.

"I suspect he will be a master. He always had a fascination with knives as a child, so it was no surprise to learn he finally chose a career using them some ten years or so ago."

"What did he do when he first left high school?" asked Emma in a tone of voice that suggested she was really interested for some reason.

"He bummed about for a year or so getting involved with some really bad people and committing a number of petty crimes. When he started a four-year bachelor's degree course at the institute I thought it would be the making of him, but how do you say it over here – he still couldn't seem to get the monkey off his back."

"What are you actually telling us?" asked Graham.

"I am telling you that Justin Johnson used to be a rotten egg which at some point cracked and left a very sticky mess behind for everyone else to clean up."

"Are you going to elaborate?" asked Graham.

"Not at the moment, save to say that his actions caused much trauma, that I can't abide him and wish that we were not related."

"Surely a course at the Culinary Institute would have meant your brother having to shell out a lot more than five hundred notes per year in our money and given him a reason to work hard and stay out of trouble?" said Graham, trying to make a rather pathetic Cockney rhyming slang joke to help everyone relax and focus on what Joseph was saying rather than let their minds wander.

"Money was and maybe still is the root of my brother's evil and as his course would have actually cost around twenty

132

thousand dollars per year, the evil probably stems from those who lent him the cash at a high rate of interest to complete the course," said Joseph.

"From what I can gather, you think that your brother may still be earning illegally as well as legally to fund his lifestyle and pay off any debts?"

"Perhaps he robbed a bank?" said Peter jokingly.

"Nothing would surprise me and it wouldn't surprise me if Justin was involved in all of the crimes that have occurred here in Worcester to get revenge on me or someone else who he feels has wronged him, as that was and could still be his way. Unfortunately, we don't have any knowledge of him being here in England. The last we knew, he was lecturing in New York and is still there. It was, however, the toy rabbit with a skull and crossbones on its tummy found by Emma in Grafton Woods that made me think about Justin, as he would often wear a tee shirt with that logo on when he was younger. I think he bought it from some place in Ohio."

"Why did you and Justin fall out?" asked Emma, again with more than a passing interest in her voice.

"It's a long story and very personal," replied Joseph.

"This is all a bit difficult to take in and I can't see where this line of enquiry is going if your brother is still in America," said Graham.

"You and me both, Graham, so leaving Justin out of the equation for the minute, maybe, just maybe there is a possibility that Richard Webb pissed Basil Reddy off in some way in Bangladesh, so Baz decided to go to his house to get his own back. Amanda just happened to be there alone, things got out of hand and Baz tried to silence her."

"That sounds very plausible, but it doesn't account for the murder of Mr Campbell," said Peter.

"No, it doesn't, but everything we have just talked about

does mean our thought processes need to be channelled in a different way. It may well be that Mrs Campbell knows Basil Reddy or Richard Webb for some reason," replied Graham.

"There is another common denominator here," said Constable Paul Curry, trying to impress and make up for his stupid question about the shape of the herbal smoking mixture sachets, and that is that both murder victims are known to Michael Black."

"You have a point, Paul. I have Richard Webb here for another interview this afternoon, so I'll pay Michael Black a surprise visit afterwards. In the meantime, let's write up everything that we have just established onto the whiteboards to see how things are looking," said Graham.

Bomb Blast

- *Time of Explosion 11.10 a.m. Thursday, 20th November*
- *White Smoke/Acetone Peroxide/Unstable*
- *Possible Terrorist Cell/Explosive made locally*
- *Brown Sweater/Black Beanie Hat Fibres*
- *Charred 2.5cm Donut-Shaped Metal Button*
- *Smoker/Drug user/Gardener*
- *Partial Handprint of Unsub*
- *Suspect 1- Basil Reddy, Size 8 Shoes*
- *Suspect 2 – Unknown with Size 10 Footwear*
- *Motive – Religion?*

Amanda Webb Murder

- *Time of Attack 1.10 a.m. Monday, 24th November*
- *Forced Entry*
- *Bedroom Struggle*
- *No Rape took place*
- *Blood from Victim type O*
- *Blood from Attacker AB*
- *Semen from Attacker*
- *Knife wound from 15.0 cm Blade*
- *Bruising suggests 10.4 cm Handle*
- *Skin Flakes/Hair*
- *Black Beanie Hat/Black Balaclava Fibres*
- *Partial Footprint possible Size 8 or 9*
- *Suspect 1 – Basil Reddy*
- *Suspect 2 – Richard Webb*
- *Suspect 3 – Michael Black*
- *Motive – Revenge?*

Grafton Woods Murder

- *Time of Murder 10 a.m. – 11 a.m. Friday, 28th November*
- *Victim – Harold Campbell, aged between 70–80 years*
- *Stab Wound to the Heart*
- *23 cm Blade/10.5 cm Handle*
- *Highland Terrier killed by same Knife*
- *Bodies Hidden for Hours then Moved*
- *Footprints – Sizes 9 & 10*
- *Unusual Shoe Sole Pattern*

- *Green Polyester Fibres – Scarf?*
- *Toy Skull & Crossbones Rabbit*
- *One Muddy Cufflink with the Number 76 engraved on it.*
- *Suspect 1 – Mrs Campbell*
- *Suspect 2 – Michael Black*
- *Suspect 3 – Justin Johnson*
- *Motive – Unknown*

After he had finished writing, Graham announced that both he and Joseph were going upstairs to speak with Assistant Chief Constable Benjamin Lewis and that the team should all take a look at the boards and evidence bags and come up with some ideas on how to progress with the enquiries.

Graham and Joseph returned to the room after half an hour to find everybody engrossed in conversation.

"Has anyone got any new information or thoughts to tell us?" Graham asked in a hopeful manner that suggested his time upstairs wasn't too enjoyable.

"Not exactly," said Peter, "but I'm a bit of a memorabilia freak and visit a lot of heritage museums around the world. I've recently come back from Albany, where I am pretty sure that I saw something there that was similar to the donut-shaped metal button that's in exhibit bag one."

"Do a bit more digging then, as something small like that could prove to be huge at the end of the day," said Graham. "At the same time, see if you can learn something about any cufflinks that have ever been manufactured with the number 76 on them."

"I'll work on those things immediately," replied Peter.

Graham closed the meeting and announced that he wasn't waiting for Richard Webb to come to the station later in the day as he now had a warrant to search his house immediately.

"I want Bea and Jane to come with me to see Mr Webb, Peter to work on the things we discussed a minute ago and the rest of you, except for Joseph, to see how the research team are getting on trying to gather together more information on the knives, footwear, clothing and cigarettes that were found at each crime scene. I would like you, Joseph, to spend the rest of the day trying to find a common link between our suspects, their victims, terrorist groups, the United States, Bangladesh and Ireland."

"No problem, Graham. I am also going to try and trace my brother's movements during the last couple of years and find out if anyone knows where he is at the moment."

"We must all meet back here at 4.00 p.m. tomorrow afternoon after Joseph and I have been to Amanda Webb's funeral to observe proceedings. As you can all gather, those who must be obeyed want a full update on our progress by close of play tomorrow. I don't really want them to chew my balls for a second time," said Graham, laughing this time.

"I have read somewhere that three minutes of chewing can reduce the levels of hormones associated with stress and the harder you chew the greater will be the relief," said Joseph.

"I'll phone Andrew Rankin this afternoon and tell him of your wisdom and that you would like to offer him your services when he's under some pressure," replied Graham.

"Bollocks," said Joseph.

~

"Hello, Mrs Campbell, how are you today?" asked the DJ.

"Angry, cold, frightened and hungry," replied Elspeth.

"We can probably provide you with another blanket and a bowl of cereal," said the Fixer.

"I want my husband, where is he?" asked Elspeth.

"He is in a different place now," said the DJ.

"Why are you keeping me here in this freezing cold hovel?"

"Hovel, how ungrateful," replied the DJ. "I'll have you know that this is a well-constructed semi-converted barn and that my good friend here and I will make sure that you are much, much warmer very soon and will be able to join your husband."

CHAPTER FIFTEEN

Richard was surprised to find three police officers knocking on his front door.

"Hello, Graham, I was going to come to see you this afternoon, you didn't need to send a squad car to get me."

"We are here with a warrant to search your home as we have some new information that suggests you haven't been entirely truthful with us. Then we are going to take you to the station for a formal interview under caution."

"I do have a funeral to prepare for you know."

"You will be home in time for that if you co-operate, otherwise we may have to hold you in a cell for twenty-four hours," said Graham.

Graham, Bea and Jane went through each room with a fine-tooth comb looking at and for documents in respect of mortgages, endowments and life assurances, as well as bank statements, passports and wills. All current, active paperwork was bagged and taken away for further scrutiny at a later date by the police legal team. Richard was taken away at the same time. He would probably be allowed home later that day, but Graham had an inkling that in the near future he might be taken away for quite some time.

~

"Mr Webb, the last time we sat here in this interview room my team told me that I was a bit harsh on you following the sad loss of your wife. Maybe I was, but today I am going to give you an even harder time, you lying fucking little shit!"

"What are you talking about?" shouted Richard angrily.

"You said to us that you only travelled between here and Germany selling your products. We believe that you have also been to Bangladesh recently."

"Oh!" said Richard.

"Oh!" said Graham sarcastically. "Would you care to tell me about that particular trip?"

"There isn't anything to tell," replied Richard.

"What do you know about a Basil Reddy or a Justin Johnson?"

"I haven't heard of either of them."

"They were in Bangladesh at the same time as you and we have reason to believe that both may have a connection with your wife's murder, which puts you in the frame, too."

"Oh!" said Richard.

"I suggest you stop saying oh! and start telling us what we want to know," said Graham. "We are working extremely hard as a force to try and catch your wife's killer. If you are not the murderer and want to bring to justice whoever is, then I would suggest we get this interview process officially underway with the tape running and you start talking. If you want a solicitor this time you need to say now, otherwise we get started immediately."

Richard declined any legal representation for the second time as he felt he didn't need it. He wasn't sure if this decision was going to be a mistake or not but he didn't think he had anything to worry about, and he didn't care about anything other than giving Amanda a decent send off.

"I appreciate your decision and predicament and hope you

can be back home in a few hours to carry on with your grieving and funeral arrangements. The more you co-operate with us the more likely that will happen. If it does happen, we might be closer to finding a motive and getting the killer put behind bars. It will also give me time to make a surprise visit to another suspect," said Graham in a stentorian tone.

Michael was at home working on a mini-project to try and improve public transport within the Worcester and Hereford area, as council cutbacks were having a massive impact on the elderly. He needed to get a strong message across to the readers of his blog and the local free newspaper, outlining the disgraceful way that the elderly are often treated, considering these same people have spent most of their lives working hard and in many cases fighting for this country to make it what it is today.

As he started to type the opening line of his article, Michael heard his door bell ring. He opened the door to find DCI Graham Laws facing him.

"That's a quaint robin-shaped bell," said Graham.

"Are you here as the caped crusader or is this a social call, Graham?"

"You have helped fight our cause via the media, Michael, and I am here to try to help your cause, as there is growing evidence that you may have some involvement in the two murders that have occurred in Worcester during the last two weeks. I need you to provide me with some answers over a nice cup of tea, or I may have to formally interview you back at the station."

~

Shona was on her way to a farm near Bromyard to discuss a menu with a middle-aged couple who were due to retire shortly, having spent almost thirty years working the land.

Shona turned left off the main road and crossed a cattle grid before driving for what seemed like a mile along a narrow driveway lined by a post and rail fence on either side.

The farmhouse was very large, very imposing and very old. Shona noticed a plaque on the wall above the green wood front door dating it at 1842. The door opened onto a long, narrow slate-tiled hallway with a wooden staircase off to the right. At the far end of the hall was a huge kitchen with an Aga within a brick fireplace on one side and a double electric oven surrounded by an ornate fireplace on the opposite side. Either side of each cooker was an array of cupboards and highly polished granite work surfaces. In the centre of the room was a long, solid oak workbench with a double Belfast sink in the middle.

The dining table with seating for ten people was in a separate alcove and beyond that Shona could see a conservatory leading out into the garden.

If Shona was fairly nervous upon entering this impressive house she was shaking by the time she left a few hours later, as Mr and Mrs Price wanted her to prepare four courses for the guests attending their retirement party on Thursday, with each course having two options.

Mr and Mrs Price were insistent that all of the food that Shona was required to serve had to be grown, laid, reared or shot on the farmland and was as fresh as was physically possible. There had been much negotiation in respect of the dinner party cost because of this, as it meant Shona would need to get to the farm very early in the morning to gather and prepare the ingredients which would make for an extremely long and tiring day. Shona built in the fact she would have done some of the preparation at home anyway and agreed to a further discount when Mr Price offered to pluck and prepare the pheasants. Although the final agreed amount was higher than

Mr Price would have liked, Shona was given the contract instead of two larger but cheaper local companies because Mrs Price liked her attention to detail and the fact she gave her customers the recipes used on the day and a list of the health benefits of most of the ingredients.

It was Amanda's funeral tomorrow afternoon, which meant Shona was going to have to work well into the night to plan her timings for the dinner party and then email them to Mr and Mrs Price in the morning to get their agreement. On Wednesday, Shona would then go back to the farm to make sure that all of the ingredients she needed were going to be or could be made available on the day and in the right quantities.

Shona was really glad that her green and white party this week had been postponed indefinitely. This was very disappointing in one way as she needed all the experience she could get from various situations, but the upside as well as giving her some more time to focus on the Price's party came from the caller informing her that she was still going to be given the balance of her invoice as compensation. Shona thought it was a bit odd that someone had phoned to cancel on behalf of the couple and the call did put her in a bit of a quandary. How did she know that the couple were really ill and wouldn't be waiting for her to turn up tomorrow night? Should she telephone to check? How and when was she going to get paid the balance? Should she cook some of the dishes anyway just in case the couple are not actually ill and that the call was a hoax?

This was a situation that Shona hadn't factored for. Perhaps Michael would know what she should do. What Shona did know was that one door often opens as another one closes and that she must plan her programme of work better and learn when to say no. That last statement applies to my love life too she thought as she walked towards her car parked in the Prices' drive.

Although she needed to earn as much money as possible, this had to be tempered with some rest and relaxation, so she made an instant decision to take on no more than three parties or other catering events per week and if possible to be selective with the ones she would agree to do. A few days ago, she had agreed to cater at an elderly couple's tea party in a month's time, but as cakes were not her strong point she now doubted her decision to say yes, particularly as she would have to spend time practising her baking skills during the evenings. She smiled to herself as another upside came to mind; she could say no to Michael's sexual advances for a few weeks without feeling guilty.

As she drove back along the A44 Shona called Michael on his home phone and his mobile to ask his advice, but to her surprise he didn't answer either. When she got home she found out why, as Michael was waiting for her in his car outside her apartment in a state of shock.

~

Graham left Michael's house and went back to his office to try and comprehend all that had transpired during a long and rather strenuous day. Although he still didn't have any suspects in custody, he did believe that he and his team were getting close to solving all of the cases. As he walked through the main door of the building, Assistant Chief Constable Benjamin Lewis was talking to the desk sergeant in the foyer.

"Just when I thought it was safe to go back in the water," Graham said out loud to himself.

"Graham, my man, we were just talking about you," said Benjamin. "Come up to my office and tell me all about your interviews with Mr Webb and Mr Black."

Graham followed Benjamin up the stairs with some reluctance as he really didn't want to discuss the day's activities until he had gathered his thoughts and written up his notes. Benjamin, who had probably done no more than make phone calls and push a few pens around a desk since he clocked on at 9.00 a.m., was excited at the prospect of obtaining some information before Chief Constable Simon Duncan.

"I am not convinced that Mr Webb or Mr Black were being entirely honest this afternoon Benjamin, but in Richard Webb's case, according to Bea based on her observations during the interview, he was telling me what he had built up in his own mind as being the truth."

"So we may need to wire him up to a lie detector at some point," said Benjamin not expecting an answer.

"He said that he went to Bangladesh to sell his range of knives. Steel by all accounts is a commodity that has to be imported, but most of the imports are milled for use in the construction industry and for export to Africa. The catering industry needs good quality knives and we have confirmation from Mr Webb's employers that he has sold big volumes to many businesses in Dhaka and Chittagong. They have however been concerned for some time that his visits to Bangladesh have been getting too frequent and his reasoning for going has been a bit weak."

"Why didn't he tell us this before?"

"He said it was down to the duress he was under after learning of his wife's death."

"I guess that is understandable in one way," said Benjamin.

"Joseph has had his colleagues at the CIA do a bit of digging and they have been in touch with the Bangladesh authorities to get CCTV tapes from the airport, to see if they can see Mr Webb entering and leaving the country, as this may tell us what he is really up to, if anything," said Graham.

"Do you suspect money laundering, narcotics or human trafficking?"

"If he does have some connection with Basil Reddy then I would plump for the transit of heroin via Pakistan," replied Graham.

"What about Mr Black?"

"Michael Black isn't a criminal, Benjamin, he just happens to know a lot of people mainly through his work as a journalist. I don't think he had anything to do with the murder of Amanda Webb or Harold Campbell as he has an alibi on each occasion. I do think however that he is hiding something from us that could be significant."

~

Michael told Shona about DCI Graham Laws visit to his house. He also told her that he hadn't mentioned her or her catering business during their conversation. What he didn't tell her or Graham was that he suspected the link to the murders could be Shona herself, but he needed more than just a hunch before he mentioned it to anyone, for obvious reasons.

The funeral procession was due to leave Richard's house at 1.00 p.m. and Graham had asked for Joseph to be at the crematorium when it arrived. This meant that Joseph had to leave his friend's home in the Cotswolds at 5.30 a.m. to get to Surrey, to do what he had to do and then get back to Worcester in time for the service.

Joseph had found time to see Worcester University's chief executive during the last couple of days and had persuaded him to change his view of Penelope. Joseph hoped that Mr Warren, Penelope's father, who he had asked to meet, would be just as understanding as to his only daughter's unfortunate predicament and change his stance.

What Joseph hadn't allowed for was a reaction to his visit from Mr Warren that was so different from the conversation he had had with Penny's mother on the telephone.

Mr Warren launched into Joseph with a tirade of abuse in a posh accent that wouldn't have been out of place in Sloane Square. Not that Joseph had ever been to Sloane Square.

It was some five minutes before Joseph was able to speak, but eventually Mr Warren calmed down. Perhaps it was Joseph's speech about the Christian Police Association and their belief that a person is innocent unless there is evidence beyond reasonable doubt that did the trick.

Research is a wonderful thing, Joseph thought as he drove back along the M4, hoping that Penny would be as pleased with what he had done and the outcome that he had orchestrated as Joseph himself was. He made it back to Worcester crematorium just as Graham arrived, which meant they had half an hour to meander around the grounds looking for anything or anyone suspicious before the hearse bringing Amanda's body arrived. Neither man saw anyone acting strangely, but it was difficult to focus on any one individual with so many people milling around as one service followed another. Someone was watching proceedings however, and this person was deciding when to move another piece in their imaginary game of chess.

CHAPTER SIXTEEN

Baz hid in the field opposite the Nightingale watching all customers entering and leaving the pub. He didn't really expect the DJ or the Fixer to turn up but he wouldn't have put it past Cameron Hunter to have grassed him up.

It was 1.15 p.m. when Cameron pulled into the car park, got out of his Audi Quattro and walked into the pub, alone. Baz waited for five minutes and made the decision to enter the pub and hope that the Chameleon hadn't changed from green to the colour of the devil's soul.

~

Almost ninety people attended the one-hour service in memory of Amanda Webb. The eulogy read by Michael Black was very moving and captured the essence of her personality, her outlook on life and the way that all who loved her would remember her.

Once the service had been completed, all of Amanda's friends and relatives filed past her coffin, paying their last respects. They were then led out of a door into a beautiful garden area and wreath terrace where forty-seven bouquets were laid out in eight rows in what was a mass of colour. Graham was probably the only person in the congregation to know this, as he had mild OCD symptoms and would count odd things during his daily routine, such as the number of tiles in the court's public toilets, the number of swans under the bridge at South Quay or the number of windows in The Hive public library. He knew the answer to two of these off by heart but it didn't stop him going through the routine each time he went to those places. It was a good job he didn't need to count sheep to get to sleep at night. The other thing he didn't need to count was the number of times he had had sex during the last month, as it was a very low round number, if nought can be classed as a number.

~

Baz left the pub about 3.00 p.m. with his false passport in his jacket pocket. It had cost him five hundred and seven pounds in total in the end, as Cameron insisted Baz bought him another Budweiser before they went their separate ways. He walked back to the tunnel entrance as he had done last week, continually looking around to make sure that he wasn't being followed. He almost skipped the few miles back to his makeshift underground home, not quite believing that he now had the passport to a new life that was a long way from Worcester, from the DJ and from capture by the police.

Baz had two hundred and thirty pounds left, just enough for a night in a guest house, a good breakfast and his train fare to Dover. He gathered the belongings he was going to take with him, said goodbye to a few rats that were lingering around his tent and climbed the steps of the airshaft ladder. As he stepped from the ladder into the wooded area he heard the crack of a twig behind him.

"Hello, Baz," said the DJ.

Baz spun round to find the DJ towering above him in the gloomy light.

"How the hell did you find me here?"

"We had a passport to success," said the Fixer, coming towards Baz from the opposite direction."

"How stupid of me not to have realised that you had a GPS tracking device put inside this fucking passport," said Baz with much annoyance in his voice.

"Did you really think that you could outwit us, Baz?"

"Maybe not, but I can outrun you."

Baz took off down the hill at the speed of a zillion antelopes, careering through the trees and bushes towards St Ann's Well, where he thought there would be enough people walking around for him to be safe. Once he got to the well he wouldn't be too far from the town of Malvern where he could try to blend in with the shoppers and disappear down one of the side alleys. Baz was going to throw the passport into the trees, but as he was about to do so he realised that it might be prudent to hold on to it for a little while longer.

After half a mile or so, Baz was breathing heavily as his lungs were working extra hard to absorb more oxygen from the air. He was starting to feel the lactic acid building up in his legs and his heart pounding out of his chest, but he knew that he dare not slow down or his pounding heart would cease to do so forever. Baz got to Bellevue Terrace, where he ran across the A449, only just dodging the cars and motorbikes, before sprinting down Grange Road and down Church Street. Halfway down Church Street, Baz deliberately bumped into a middle-aged man and slipped the fake passport into his jacket pocket. He then removed his own jacket and dumped it in a waste bin, before walking up the hill towards Waitrose, where he hoped he could wait in their cafeteria for a while. He would then get a taxi into Worcester where he would have to spend some of the money he had left on a hotel room, unless he was lucky enough to be offered a bed at the YMCA night assessment centre. He didn't dare go to any of the stations in the city now, as he guessed they would be under surveillance and he couldn't really afford the taxi fare to Birmingham. If he could make it through the night, he knew that at first light or maybe an hour or so earlier he would have to make his next move and go with escape plan B or C.

The DJ and the Fixer chased Baz down through the woods until they reached the coffee house at St Ann's Well. At this point they decided that they would draw too much attention to themselves if they continued the chase. The last thing they wanted was to bump into a friendly policeman.

"I can't believe he got away from us," said the DJ.

"He ran like a stuck pig," said the Fixer.

"Somehow we have to find him again and fast, to make sure he doesn't squeal like one if he gets picked up by Graham 'bloody' Laws and his merry men," said the DJ.

Just as the Fixer was about to reply, the DJ said, "That's odd the signal from the transmitter is getting stronger again, Baz must be coming back towards us."

The two men started to walk slowly down the hill in the direction of the GPS device, which just happened to be close to where they had parked their car, when the DJ's mobile phone rang. It was Cameron.

Baz was in a bit of a quandary. As of tomorrow morning, he would only have about one hundred and fifty pounds in cash left out of the one thousand pounds he had a week or so ago. He could not or dare not go back to his house and get any more money from his safe, so his only option was to take a train or hitch a lift somehow to a remote part of the UK and try to start a new life under another name. He really needed to go to his bank in the city and withdraw as much cash as possible and hope that the police hadn't alerted the branch manager of any warrant for his arrest. He eventually decided this was much too dangerous and that it was better to move away from Worcester and try to get cash from whichever town or city he ended up in and then make forays to places a long way from his base to obtain more just in case his account was being monitored.

As Baz took his mobile from his pocket to phone for a taxi to take him into the city, it was snatched from him.

The DJ sat down in a chair alongside Baz and pressed what felt like the sharp point of a blade into Baz's ribs.

"You might be able to run but you can't hide," said the DJ.

"Placing the passport in that man's pocket would have had us fooled if Cameron hadn't seen you from his lookout point in the churchyard. We are now going to get up and walk out of here very slowly, Baz. Any sudden movement or attempt to run away again and it will be the last thing that you do."

"You don't want to kill me," said Baz

"Give me one good reason why I don't?"

"If you kill me then you'll never get to know your daughter."

The DJ sat upright, closed the flick knife and said, "What daughter? I don't have a daughter."

"You do have a daughter and I know where she's living at the moment," said Baz.

"Your survival techniques have been impressive so far, Baz, but lying to me isn't a good one."

"It's the truth, on my mother's life," replied Baz.

The DJ picked up his own mobile and dialled a number.

When the person on the other end of the phone answered, all the DJ said was "Change of plan, I'll explain when I see you later, but for now we do what we agreed we would do tomorrow, but without Baz, although he can stay in the barn tonight."

CHAPTER SEVENTEEN

The postal worker noticed a strange stench coming from the letterbox of the flat. Patricia had been delivering letters and parcels to this block for about eight months, so she knew something was seriously wrong this Wednesday morning.

Just in case her mind was playing tricks, Patricia opened the letterbox again and sniffed the air. The repugnant smell of putrid meat tinged with an aniseed odour made her reel backwards. The most disgusting stink that Patricia had ever encountered before was that of a dead mouse decomposing in a watering can. This smell was one hundred times worse and made her go all light-headed and faint, before she threw up over the balcony onto the pavement below.

Patricia composed herself, wiped her mouth and ran down the steps to her van parked in the car park, where she telephoned her superior at the sorting office.

~

Graham was with Emma going over some more information that had been gathered by the back office team on each of the incidents, when a telephone call came through to his desk phone from a uniformed officer standing outside a block of flats in Pershore.

Graham looking deeply shocked, turned around to face Emma and with some resignation in his voice said, "I don't know what's going on, but we have what looks to be another major incident on our hands."

"You're winding me up, aren't you?" asked Emma.

"I wish I was, but it would appear a postman or woman called in a suspicious incident to her boss while delivering a package to an address in Pershore early this morning. The mailroom team leader phoned our control office who knew of an officer in the area and he has just phoned me to convey his findings. I think it would be a good idea for you to get across there with a team immediately," replied Graham.

Having spoken to the initial response team, Emma was now standing on the first floor balcony outside flat number six preparing herself and her team for what she knew was awaiting them inside. Some of her big burly support team had just finished breaking the door in with a battering ram, and she had just put on her protective suit when the doctor arrived. Dr Roland Bennett, an on-call respiratory specialist from a nearby village, had been contacted half an hour earlier and asked to attend what was then a potential crime scene, as the police doctor for the area was on holiday. Dr Bennett couldn't stay at the scene long as he had urgent patients to deal with at his practice, so Emma broke with protocol and asked him to go inside the flat with her to estimate the time of death of the victims before she walked the walk to gather any trace evidence.

"This is going to be worse than you can imagine. When you got the call to help us earlier I didn't know what you would be letting yourself in for. I now know," said Emma.

The doctor looked rather white with fear as he put on a protective suit and just nodded when asked if he was ready. They pushed open the solid wooden door and entered the hallway. Although the team were wearing masks, the redolence of death hit their olfactory system hard, causing them to choke and turn their heads back towards the fresh air outside.

The first dead body Emma came across was that of Luke Smith, who was lying face up on the kitchen floor. His throat had been cut, and his blood had spilled all over the black and white floor tiles. Hundreds of maggots were crawling over the body and over a part-sealed white envelope that was resting on his chest. The envelope contained a white powdery substance, some sprinklings of which had spilt onto the body.

The doctor was more matter of fact about seeing a person with their throat cut than Emma thought he would be, and he appeared to work in a meticulous way to estimate the time of death without any real reaction to the gruesome sight. The sight of a far more mutilated Kylie Page did get the reaction Emma expected. Blood drained from the doctor's face very quickly, but not to the same degree or the same speed it had drained from Kylie, as her head was half-severed. At the sight of this, the doctor vomited profusely and rushed out of the room leaving Emma with brown, beige and yellow as well as red liquid spillages to contend with in a small confined space.

Emma led the doctor outside onto the balcony and told him to go home, compose himself and confirm by email that both times of death had in his opinion taken place approximately sixty hours ago. She then telephoned Jane and asked her to find out where the doctor lived and call in on him to give him some support if he needed it. Emma then contacted Graham and asked him to come across to Pershore as she thought he might like to look at and study the crime scene himself.

It took Graham two hours to get to the block of flats as he had some paperwork to complete and then got stuck behind a tractor on the A4104. He pulled into the car park to find a large crowd had gathered behind the police cordon and the undertakers sitting in their large, white transfer van having their lunch, waiting to be called into action.

Emma had completed her thorough examination of the crime scene and was standing in the hallway of the flat looking through the notes on her pad when Graham appeared at the door.

"I have my evidence bags in my case and the photographer is working with the sketch artist at the moment. The dusting team are on standby downstairs as are the undertakers."

"I spoke to them outside while they were eating their sausage sandwiches with red sauce," replied Graham.

"Don't tell me you listen to the Danny Baker show on Radio 5 Live on a Saturday morning, too?"

"Of course, even if I'm in the office, it's a given."

"You will be looking at more red sauce if you go in there, Graham. Whoever has done this is a real expert, as we have very little to go on. Considering the murders took place late at night and there would have been a lot of noise, maybe even some screaming and shouting, there wasn't any furniture out of place, every light switch had been turned off and the five-lever mortice on the front door had been locked. The perpetrator has tried to make us believe that the time of death was earlier than it actually was by tipping a lot of maggots over both bodies. They also sprinkled a very small amount of a white powdery substance on to the body of the person we believe to be Mr Luke Smith, leaving the rest in a plain white envelope."

"Do you know what the powder is?"

"No, not yet, but I have to assume it could be toxic."

"When did the murders happen?"

"Based on the body temperatures and their decomposition, the doctor thinks it was late on Sunday night."

"I don't suppose we have any witnesses?"

"If there are any, nobody is proffering any information yet."

Graham decided to take a look around the flat without Emma, but after a few minutes he wished that he hadn't. When he came back out on to the balcony he was shaking his head in disbelief at the scenes he had just witnessed.

"It is all very odd. Just when I feel we are on the right track, something like this puts doubt in my mind. Are we dealing with a sadistic killer, a really clever killer or a psychopath?" he asked Emma.

"It does seem like a mixture of all three people acting out some fantasy act, revenge act or jealous act in there, Graham."

"I am going to see Bea to ask her to give me the profile of the person or persons we are hunting, to see if we can link this with our findings on the whiteboards."

"I'll drive my evidence bags to the lab and wait there all night if I have to, so that I can if possible get any or some results to you by tomorrow morning," said Emma.

"Thanks, Emma. I'll sort out some overtime for you, unless of course you would prefer payment in kind?"

"The chief constable still doesn't take too kindly to signing off overtime as he expects everyone to work eighty hours per week like he does, so I might let you wine me and dine me and then have your wicked way with me if it helps keep the department costs down," replied Emma.

"Sounds wonderful, and it would be nice to get a run on the board to use a cricketing term, but for now we need to go our separate ways. On my way back to the station, I am going to call Joseph and ask him to drive to the morgue this evening. That is if I can beg once more for an out-of-hours post-mortem to be undertaken."

~

The DJ had blindfolded Baz and driven him to a large cottage that he had rented on the outskirts of Ledbury. He had chosen this place as a base as the cottage was situated down a side road off the A449 but concealed from any passing traffic. It was also only seventeen miles from Worcester, eight miles from Great Malvern, twenty-three miles from Pershore, and close to the M50 should he need to get anywhere quickly for any reason.

For the first time since he had known him, the DJ actually needed Baz more than Baz needed him, so he tried to control his annoyance about some of the missions Baz had messed up. The DJ loved the use of the word mission as it made him feel important, powerful and stimulated.

If what Baz had told him was the truth then his next mission was going to be a mission within a mission.

The DJ dragged Baz out of the car and made him walk along the gravel path leading to the front door. Baz thought about removing his blindfold and making a run for it, but realised he might be best served by co-operating at the moment.

"What a lovely morning it is, Baz, a lovely morning to be alive, don't you think?" said the DJ as he pushed Baz into the house and through into the lounge, shutting the front door behind him.

Baz nodded and started to say something, but then thought better of it and allowed the DJ to continue speaking.

"I did say to you a little while ago that I would cut out your eyes and your tongue. One part of me still wants to do that as I believe that what you have done or haven't done in some instances is wrong and if you are not punished I'll be showing weakness, which puts my manhood in question."

Baz remained silent as he didn't have a suitable answer that wouldn't anger the DJ.

"On the other hand, Baz, if I cut you up I won't get to learn where my daughter lives, if I really do have one."

"I am not exactly in any position to lie to you," said Baz, now daring to speak.

"People will say and do anything to stay alive for a little longer. They will even say things that they don't believe, particularly if they have a Samurai sword being waved above their head like this one," said the DJ as he grabbed a Katana off the wall and nicked Baz's neck with its frighteningly sharp blade.

Baz squealed and fell to the floor, fear rushing through his body.

"Sorry about that," said the DJ, "but I am not allowed to draw this sword without drawing blood."

"What the hell are you talking about?" said Baz.

"It's a Samurai tradition that if a sword is drawn it has to spill blood."

"Why did you draw it, then?"

"Just to look at it, as it is so beautiful."

"It's a bloody sword, for Christ sake."

"It is now and it is still beautiful with its long sleek curved shiny blade that took someone three weeks to polish to give it this mirror finish. If you look carefully, Baz, you can see your face in between your blood. It's a shame that you are now useful to me as it would have been fun to see if I really could decapitate you with one long swinging blow."

"Where did you get it from?" asked Baz.

"I gave a friend of mine a brief and they got it made for me in Durham. I then bought it as a present to myself for my birthday, so it would be a shame not to use it, wouldn't it?"

"You just did," said Baz, hoping that it wouldn't be used again anytime soon or even at all.

~

Joseph had spent the day doing some research with Peter and they had established a few interesting facts that they thought were pertinent to the investigation. Before going to see the pathologist in the next two or three hours, he had somewhere else to go.

Penny was waiting outside the café when Joseph arrived just before 5.00 p.m. They went inside and Joseph ordered and paid for two large lattes, which they carried to a small round table near the window.

Penny was astonished when Joseph told her where he had been, who he had spoken to and what he'd done to help her within the previous few days.

Joseph had managed to get Penny a fully furnished flat within the university campus for free, as compensation for her expulsion. Her father was going to fund another three-year course to enable her to get a degree in Animal Biology and Ecology, and she would have a bit of pocket money from the job that Joseph had blagged for her from Graham.

"You want me to be a police informant?" asked Penny.

"You know the workings of this city from the ground level so to speak and all I am asking is that you keep your ears and eyes open for any illegal activity. If you learn of anything, however small you think it may be, phone me for as long as I am here in Worcester and afterwards contact DCI Graham Laws."

"You're not leaving, are you?"

"I'll have to go to London for a while and then back home to America at some point, but I don't know if we're talking about one month or one year yet. I don't want to put you under any pressure, but the more you can help me, the longer I will probably be able to stay here in England. For now, I have to go to the morgue and you need to go to your new flat," said Joseph, handing Penny a set of keys.

"Why do you want me to go to the flat now?"

"Because your father is going to collect you from there in about two hours' time to take you back to Camberley for a few days. You can get yourself together, sort out some clothes, have some quality time with your mother and buy some pens, pencils

162

and notebooks, because you start your course again on Monday."

Penny was almost speechless; but as she kissed Joseph goodbye just before she walked out of the café door, she invited him to dinner at her new flat one day next week.

"I will serve you up something extra special as a token of my appreciation," she said.

Joseph walked back to Castle Street, got in his car and drove to his appointment with the pathologist. This was one part of the job that he didn't like, but he knew he had to take the rough with the smooth. The thought of a bit of rough next week kept him smiling for the rest of the evening.

CHAPTER EIGHTEEN

Graham spent a few hours with Bea reading through her profile of the perpetrators as she saw them and trying to draw conclusions and make predictions. Her document wasn't perfect as all of the incidents were markedly different, but at least they had something to discuss at the next briefing meeting, which he was going to hold tomorrow or Friday subject to both the chief constable and the assistant chief constable being available to attend.

As Bea left for home just before 8.00 p.m., Graham summarised their findings by listing the linked characteristics on a fourth whiteboard in the training room.

Perpetrator:

- *Resents authority – Possibly did from a young age.*
- *Believes violence and aggression are legitimate responses to persecution.*
- *Might display stimulus-seeking characteristics.*
- *Is probably prone to substance abuse.*
- *Likes to be the best at whatever they do, regardless of how this makes them look in the eyes of others.*
- *Will see themselves as a good person.*
- *Has developed grudges that never go away.*

- *Thinks the essence of their beliefs or manhood must be upheld at all times.*
- *Will be seeking revenge.*
- *May be immature and demand attention and affection on a constant basis.*
- *Is likely to be jealous, obsessive and delusional.*
- *Does not like to lose things that are critical to their existence.*
- *Must have what they believe is rightfully theirs.*
- *Will have twisted and psychotic perceptions about what is right and wrong.*

He glanced at the other boards, curled his right hand and put his index finger across his lips in deep thought, but in reality it was too late at night and he decided to lock the door and go and get some food and some sleep.

~

Eric Jones looked out of his bedroom window at 7.55 p.m. He knew exactly what time it was because EastEnders was due to start on the television shortly. In the distance, he could see a flicker of light coming from across the fields. He stood and stared for a few minutes until he realised that the hay barn in Mr and Mrs Thompson's field about half a mile away was on fire.

Mrs Campbell struggled to release her hands from the rope that was holding her tight against a wooden support pillar on one side of the barn. She was very tired, having been forced to stand for so long. She knew that the heat was going to intensify and that the barn roof would collapse on top of her if the fire brigade didn't get here quickly. What she didn't know and couldn't understand, was why her captors had kept her here giving her food and water for five days and were now going to have her killed in a fire.

Charlie and his firefighters received a phone call from Mr Jones at 8.05 p.m. and got to the barn at 8.25 p.m. They could tell instantly that this barn was constructed from heavy timbers and had wooden side walls and a metal sheet roof. They were often built like this to minimise damage and be easy to clean up and re-build should they catch fire. They often did and this was the third time the team had been called to such an incident within the last eighteen months. It was clear when they arrived that this blaze had taken firm hold and had probably reached temperatures somewhere between 700° and 900°C in places. If this was an arson attack using petrol as an accelerant, the heat would get to 1,200° at the point where it had been started. Charlie knew immediately that there was little they could do to save any livestock that might be inside. He hoped that this wasn't the case and that that this barn had only been full of square hay bales stacked tightly from floor to ceiling. This in itself was a recipe for disaster in certain situations and despite his teachings to farmers at certain events throughout the county, his advice wasn't always heeded and they continued to store things in inappropriate ways. The previous two barn fires were primarily caused by the storage of animal bedding and farm machinery together without a physical barrier between them. Any machinery or equipment inside this building wasn't going to see the light of day again.

Charlie and his team would make a token attempt to tackle this fire as in reality, it was beyond their control and he had a philosophy to save what can be saved and not pour tons of water onto a lost cause. If he was to use excessive volumes of water on this barn, the mess would smoulder for many days afterwards and it would be much more difficult to clean up. A burning hay barn will become structurally unsound within a short time and Charlie had seen one of his men killed when tackling one five years ago. He had vowed to the fireman's wife at the man's funeral that he was never going to lose another fireman on his watch again. In any case, there had been too many deaths in Worcestershire recently for his liking. Charlie had joined the fire service twelve years ago and worked his way up from a trainee, to a crew manager and then station manager before obtaining his latest position two years ago. Technically, he was responsible for the day-to-day command of the fire service in the county, but he insisted on attending all major incidents and investigations to take control of difficult situations. Charlie was glad that he could combine his managerial, communication and leadership skills with the practical and physical side of the job as he still believed he inspired confidence in dangerous situations and had the ability to carry out tasks alongside younger and supposedly fitter men and women.

Mr Stephen Thompson, the barn's owner, arrived at 8.45 p.m. having just got back from a five-day break just north of Birmingham, where he had spent time looking at some of the best stables in the world.

"I go away for a week and this is what happens," he said.

"When were you last in the barn?"

"Just before I went on holiday."

"Did you have much in there?" asked Charlie.

"About two hundred bales, which means I've lost around one thousand pounds at today's market prices."

"I am sure your insurance will cover the loss," said Charlie.

"Probably not all of it and certainly not all of the rebuilding cost, although we will fight hard to get as much as we can."

"Do you have any enemies who knew you were away?"

"Not that I know of. Are you suggesting this might have been deliberate?"

"My observations would suggest this could be the case."

"What sick bastard or bastards would do such a thing?" said Mr Thompson.

"It could have been kids, but I think from the way the fire is burning this was started by someone who knew what they were doing," replied Charlie.

"Can you put it out?" asked Stephen.

"There isn't too much we can do here tonight, but I'll leave a team here for a while to make sure it doesn't get out of hand. I'll come back in the morning to see if I can identify the cause."

Just at that moment one of the firemen shouted from the other side of the burning building. "Charlie, there's someone in the barn."

Another fireman then came running towards Charlie shouting, "Someone is in there screaming for help."

In an instant the philosophy changed as there was now a reason for his men to fire up the water jets and put on their helmets and oxygen masks. Four fire engines aimed their hoses at the heart of the inferno as the firefighters tried to work out the best and safest way to rescue the person or persons inside. Charlie hoped that the seven thousand litres of water available to him was going to be enough.

A small section of the roof crashed to the floor missing Mrs Campbell by inches. Somehow within the last hour she had managed to loosen the rope tying her to the thick round pillar. She quickly slid her body down it and stretched her feet out to drag a small part of the hot metal roof towards her body. The pain was excruciating and the smell vile as the metal touched the flesh on her legs, melting her skin, but she knew this was the only way she might be able to escape. With the hot sharp piece of metal now near to the pillar, Mrs Campbell swivelled around and stretched her legs out behind her, leaving her hands and face flat on the floor beside the chunk of metal. She was beginning to feel faint as the thick black smoke swirled around the inside of the barn, but she could just see what she was doing due to the brightness of the flames leaping upwards into the sky and the fact that the smoke and hot air were rising.

Mrs Campbell prepared herself for more pain and then screamed as she placed her hands on to the metal and waited for the rope to burn through.

George and Sam, two of Charlie's most experienced firemen, made a hole low down in the wall of the barn and crawled into it near to where the screams appeared loudest. Fortunately, the fire raged less intently in this corner, probably due to the way the wind was blowing. Everybody within the team tackling the blaze hoped and prayed that this evening's events wouldn't add to this week's unexplained death toll.

~

Michael was going to help Shona tomorrow, so this evening he was completing his article on the impact of the bus service cutbacks in and around Worcester. He was backing a 'Save our Buses' campaign by the Rural Services Network and launching a petition to try to save as many of the eighty services across forty routes as possible. His opening paragraph clarified the fact that councils have a statutory duty to provide free off-peak travel for pensioners and disabled residents through a national concessionary fares scheme. However, as with other things that are important to those living in and around Worcester, which is so far away from London and Parliament that some MPs have never been there, funding has been significantly reduced. Michael then confirmed that the majority of the one million people living in Worcestershire would rather see bus services maintained, pot holes filled, improved cycling facilities and safer road crossings for people and wildlife in the form of green bridges, than more crazy road building schemes that encourage more cars and lorries onto the roads thereby increasing air pollution, traffic congestion and the loss of fields, woodlands and wildlife. The last paragraph in Michael's article outlined the real impact that the bus service cutbacks would also have on local shops. Small retail businesses in particular were already under severe pressure to stay solvent due to very high rents and rates and the loss of sales to internet shoppers. A small calculation suggested that with over one hundred and fifty thousand people aged sixty-five or over in the county, the loss of their expenditure in local shops alone could cost the local economy in the region of £10 million per year. Michael shook his head as he finished typing, wondering just how many ghost towns there would be here in England in a few years' time? He then smiled to himself as he thought about adding that sentence to his article and asking his readers an open question as to the likelihood of them all playing at Cowboys and Indians in their local high street instead of going shopping.

~

George and Sam identified where Mrs Campbell was from the screams and got to her quickly, even though it was difficult for them to see her clearly inside the burning building due to the amount of smoke. As they got to her, another piece of the roof came crashing down behind them, some six feet away. Both firemen knew they had to work fast if they were going to rescue Mrs Campbell. George gave Mrs Campbell some oxygen and asked if she could move her arms and legs. She nodded, but no sooner had she done this she passed out due to the pain and shock from her predicament. It was now going to be extremely tough for the two firemen to get Mrs Campbell to a place of safety. Thinking fast, Sam radioed to his colleagues outside to call for an ambulance. He then picked Mrs Campbell up and guided by George in front of him carried her quickly in a fireman's lift towards the place where they had entered the building. This procedure is being discouraged in some circles, as it has been seen in certain situations to increase spinal injuries or cause asphyxiation, but Sam had no other option open to him and they just got to their exit point when the wooden support pillar that Mrs Campbell had been tied to toppled towards them like a felled Christmas tree. George dived back through the hole fast and then dragged Mrs Campbell out feet first, leaving Sam inside to dodge the pillar by inches.

The ambulance took twelve minutes to arrive, but as all of Charlie's crew were trained in emergency medical services and each engine carried a large first aid kit they were able to give Mrs Campbell the best of care until the paramedics took control. As the ambulance pulled away to take Mrs Campbell to hospital, Mr Thompson prayed harder than anyone else that she would survive.

~

Shona arrived at the farmhouse at 9.00 a.m. as it was going to take her a long time to prepare all of the courses, arrange the dining room as requested and make the cocktails. The menu was certainly going to be challenging, which was why Michael had offered to be her assistant. He wasn't too happy when she told him he had to dress up as a waiter.

"If I have to wear a penguin suit, are you going to dress up as Catwoman?" asked Michael.

"Strange you should say that," replied Shona.

"I got a call from your brother-in-law last night to ask if I would do the catering for a Super Heroes dinner party that he would be hosting at the weekend."

"Kate hasn't mentioned it to me, so I guess I am not invited."

"Kevin said it was to do with his work, so I assume it's for his business associates and their wives or girlfriends."

"It's a possibility, but it's strange that Kate hasn't said

anything to me," replied Michael.

"I'll know more when I speak to Kevin about the menu, but for now we have to get this menu under way, the table laid, the room decorated and the cocktails ready for when the guests arrive."

Michael looked at Shona's notebook under the heading of 'Mr & Mrs Price' and at the number of complex dishes that they had to serve.

Sauted Scallops with Mushrooms & Spinach
Baked Eggs in Roasted Tomatoes
Pheasant in Creamy Mushroom Sauce
Stuffed Loin of Pork
Fresh Fruit Pavlova
Crème Brûlée

"Blimey, how many people are coming tonight – five thousand?"

"No, only four, plus Mr and Mrs Price, but they insisted on having a choice for each course."

"I'll go out to the car and get a doggy bag as there might be some left over," joked Michael.

"First, I would like you to make some cider punch. The recipe is over there on the work surface near my apron. Then I need you to get on and prepare the nibbles."

"Do we have time for that as well?" asked Michael, ducking as Shona went to hit him with a spatula.

CHAPTER NINETEEN

If Graham wasn't in a state of shock from all of the incidents that were taking place in such a short space of time, he was when he received a telephone call from Charlie on Thursday morning informing him of the barn fire and the rescue of Mrs Campbell.

"I'm holding a briefing this afternoon at 3.00 p.m. Charlie, can you come across and tell us all that occurred last night before we get onto other police matters?"

"No problem, Graham. I'm going back to the barn now with a couple of my team to look over the remnants of the fire and try to establish exactly how it started. Unless we are very lucky, I won't have a definite answer for you by this afternoon but I'll have a fair idea about things."

"How is Mrs Campbell?" asked Graham.

"Elspeth Campbell is in a bad way and under sedation. She is struggling to speak and is very short of breath, as her lungs have been damaged by smoke inhalation and a respiratory tract injury means less oxygen is getting to the blood. She is also demonstrating signs of carbon monoxide poisoning by vomiting, fainting and complaining of headaches. A doctor from the hospital told me about half an hour ago that Mrs Campbell is having tests today and that you may be able to interview her tomorrow. He did say that she might not be too coherent or have too much recollection of events as the carbon monoxide poisoning is causing her to have seizures and be very confused."

"What about her burns?" asked Graham.

"I am afraid to say that those on her hands and feet are very severe but at least she is alive, which is more than we can say about her husband."

"Does she know her husband is dead?"

"Not officially, but I suspect she suspects this is the case."

Graham walked across to the coffee machine and poured himself two large espressos. He felt like adding some whisky to them to try and lift his mood, but he knew in reality that alcohol made him sleepy and he needed to focus and concentrate hard as he tried to make some sense of the information that Emma and Joseph had left on his desk half an hour ago.

He decided to detail all the new information that had been handed to him in relation to the Pershore murders on a new whiteboard for the whole team to review, if the chief constable could really be considered one of the team. Simon Duncan was a bit more aloof than Assistant Chief Constable Benjamin Lewis and was far more serious, but at least he didn't try to interfere in any investigation work. Graham didn't much care for spending time in Simon's office however, as it was generally an unpleasant experience in more ways than one, as he always came out itching and scratching. He didn't know why this was, but the chief was always doing it and it made Graham feel very uncomfortable and dirty. Perhaps the chief had a dog or cat at home that had fleas? It was more likely that Simon had a nervous habit due to stress or that fact he didn't like confrontation.

~

Graham flicked through the pieces of paper and was surprised at how little evidence there was from the brutal murder of the two young people. As he wrote the most pertinent facts on the board, one really disturbing but strange thing stood out. Following all of the post-mortems that had been necessary recently, it was clear that the size of the knife used for each attack was increasing. As he reflected on this, Graham considered the possibility should there be another murder, that a knife larger than the one used to kill Luke and Kylie could be a machete.

Pershore Murder

- *Time of Murders 10 p.m. – 11 p.m. Sunday, 30th November*
- *Victim 1 – Luke Smith*
- *Victim 2 – Kylie Page*
- *24 cm Blade/12 cm Handle*
- *Self-Raising Flour on Floor*
- *776 Maggots on the Bodies*
- *No Fingerprints on Envelope*
- *No Footprints in the Blood*
- *Rubber Scuff Mark on External Door*
- *Knife Point Bruising on Victim 1's Throat*
- *Finger Bruising on Victim 1's Chest*
- *Blood from Victim 1 on Stair Post*
- *Finger Bruising on Victim 1's Back*
- *Suspect – Justin Johnson?*
- *Motive – Unknown*

The meeting got underway with Graham summarising all that had happened over the last two weeks.

"Before we get to discuss the latest murders that occurred in Pershore, I need to inform you all that we almost had another one late last night. Before I let Charlie, the chief fire officer, tell you all about a large blaze at a barn between here and Leominster, I can tell you that Mrs Elspeth Campbell is no longer a suspect in her husband's murder."

Charlie's summary of events, told in some detail, as it wasn't often he got to blow his own trumpet, left the team speechless, before a rant from Chief Constable Duncan brought some focus to proceedings. He was usually a man of few words but it was obvious the recent events were taking their toll on him.

Emma then talked through all of her the findings from the flat in Pershore. She had established that the killer knocked on the door of the flat wearing gloves and as Luke opened it, the killer who was probably male, thrust a knife at his throat.

"Luke tried to slam the door shut, but the killer blocked it with his left foot and then pushed Luke backwards into the hallway where he stumbled and hit his head against the stair post. Luke then scrambled down the hall to the kitchen, where we think he tried to open a cutlery drawer in an attempt to grab a knife for defence purposes. The killer was much too fast and too strong and Luke was pushed from behind causing him to fall against the drawer and then on to the floor. I can't be sure of exactly what happened next, but shortly after this Luke was grabbed by the hair and his throat was sliced wide open. He would have died very quickly, possibly from the shock sooner than from his injury."

The team all sat and stared at Emma as if she was the story teller on *Jackanory*.

"It was," she continued, "a different situation as far as Kylie was concerned, because she was sitting in the lounge listening to music on her headphones. The murderer crept up behind her and dragged the knife across her throat twice, killing her instantly and almost severing her head. Maggots were then tipped on to each body to help them decompose much faster. Someone did this to try to make us think that the attack took place a lot earlier than it actually did. This same person or an accomplice then placed an envelope containing self-raising flour onto Luke's body. We don't know why this was done, as of yet."

"I think I do," said Joseph.

"Go on," said Simon.

"During the last few years in America and Canada, politicians and other famous people have been sent envelopes containing flour via the postal service. These were attempts to scare people and make them think that more Anthrax attacks were about to happen following on from those that occurred back in 2001."

"Anthrax was actually sent via the postal service?"

"Yes, it was, Simon, and not long after the September 11th attacks, too," said Joseph.

"Was anybody killed?"

"I'm afraid so."

"Were the perpetrators caught?"

"The honest answer is no, but the FBI would have you believe otherwise."

"What was the point of doing it?"

"I can't remember the rationale given, and I am sure the case files are buried in the archives. From my experiences over the years very few have ever benefited from acts of terrorism. Take a look at all of the fighting around the world in the last twenty years or so. Every country, every government, every citizen and every extremist or terrorist is now worse off than before each conflict started."

"So why do you think the Pershore murderer placed an envelope full of flour and some maggots on to the victim's bodies?" asked Simon.

"I don't know the answer to that question exactly, sir," said Peter piping up from the back of the room, "but I have a theory about the maggots, in addition to what Emma said."

"Go on," said Simon for the second time.

"As you may or may not know, during the last couple of days, I've been looking at the exhibits from the various evidence bags. While doing this I established late last night that the metal donut-shaped button from bag number one found at the cricket ground has both the American and Irish flags on it and is being sold on the same internet site as the cufflinks similar to the one from bag number three that was found in Grafton Woods."

"That is excellent work, Peter, but what is the relevance of your findings to the Pershore murders?" asked Graham.

"The internet seller is based in America. I think that the number of maggots left at the crime scene are linked to the cufflink, and that this is also linked to America."

"How is that so?" asked Graham again.

"The cufflink damaged in the blast, when purchased new, actually has the date 1776 on it, which is technically recognised as the year that America declared independence from Britain. I think the killer is leaving us progressive clues, which suggests a further incident of some sort will occur. I am hoping that not too many people living here in the UK will have purchased either of these items; that even fewer people who have bought them will live in this area and that we may be able to make an arrest before there is another murder."

"Interesting and extremely well thought through," said Benjamin trying to contribute something to proceedings.

"You may need the help of the CIA to persuade the internet seller to give you names and addresses," said Graham glancing at Joseph.

"I now know what Emma and Peter have been doing. What have you and Joseph been working on?" asked Simon.

"Joseph and I have been looking at the knives used and we think that we know which ones they are and who manufactures them," said Graham as Joseph walked to the front of the room and wrote on a blackboard this time:

Knife 1 - Shun Gold utility

- **Paka wood-laminated handle**
- **Made from Damask stainless steel**
- **Asymmetric blade constructed from 32 layers that have been heated, folded and hammered**
- **Each knife has a unique and individual character**
- **This knife doesn't require oiling**

Knife 2 - Seki Magoruku vintage

- **Riveted Japanese Birch handle**
- **Made from carbon steel**
- **Easy to sharpen to get a razor edge**
- **Will stay sharper for longer**
- **Treated with camellia oil to inhibit blade discolouring**

Knife 3 - Shun Premier series

- **Walnut handle**
- **Corrosion-resistant very hard blades**
- **Hand-hammered embellished surface**
- **Convex cut of this blade offers a sharpness that enables the knife to cut tough objects and materials**
- **Can be used by right-handed and left-handed people**

Joseph backed away from the blackboard so that everybody in the room could see what he had written.

"That is all very nice to know, but how does it help us find the killer or killers?" asked Benjamin.

Graham interjected before Joseph could speak.

"Initially, we will outsource a team to contact all kitchen shops and all online knife sellers to see if any of them has sold a set or a few of these knives to any individual during the last year. As we know the make and style used in each attack, we can also show images of these to our informants to see if they have seen anyone or know of anyone who may carry one on them."

"I also know that the cigarette stubs found at the cricket pavilion are from a pack of Marlboro Lights," said Peter, "so this knowledge together with that on the knives may jog someone's memory in our door-to-door enquiries."

"Do you have any information on the shoes?" asked Simon.

"We are fairly certain the shoe imprints found at the cricket ground and Grafton Woods are from the same shoes," replied Peter.

"We are currently narrowing down the possible number of brands," said Graham.

"Surely that's not rocket science," said Simon.

"With only a partial to go on it is difficult to say if the tread is made up of lines and ellipses or includes circles. It is also too early for any of the lab technicians to help with the scuff mark identification even though we have an electrostatic lift from the door," interjected Emma.

"What we do know," added Graham, "was that the partial from the Amanda Webb murder has a blemish that we understand to be some pine resin, which is the same pine resin as Emma found on the cricket pitch."

"So," said Simon, "we are looking for a drug-taking, chain-smoking, ambidextrous gardener who likes cooking or fishing in his spare time and travelling to America and Ireland with a toy rabbit, when he isn't seeking revenge on people who have wronged him."

"You are probably not too far out, sir," said Graham, speaking while jotting some notes on a pad.

"However, we are probably looking for three or even four perpetrators, who may be operating in isolation, as a team, a trio, a group or as part of a gang or terrorist cell."

"Have you got any more information on the whereabouts of your brother, Joseph?"

"If the situation wasn't so serious I would have to laugh as neither CIA knows where he is and the FBI can't locate him either. In his job as a chef he would only work with high quality knives and those identified on the blackboard as being used are some of the best available in the world. If he is here in the UK, I don't know how he would have got here or why he would be committing or organising any crimes."

"Has he ever committed a serious crime before?" asked Simon.

"Graham asked me that the other day and I can't actually say for certain. He has often been in the wrong place at the wrong time but never been convicted of anything serious."

"It seems like he is very lucky or very clever," added Simon.

"That being the case, I have personal reasons for not liking him and would like his luck to run out, or for him to make a mistake if he is responsible in any way. If it is ok with everybody here, I would like to talk to Mr Webb on a one-to-one basis about his time in Bangladesh. He may be a bit more responsive if I talk about my issues with my brother. Before doing so I will have looked through all of the CCTV footage from the airport."

"That's fine by me," said Graham.

"One final thing," said Joseph. "At the funeral of Mrs Webb, I noticed Mr Black with a young woman and although I haven't been to England before she looks familiar. I think I have an idea where I might have seen her before, so if there are no objections, I would also like to talk to Mr Black."

"I think we should bring Mr Black in for questioning immediately," said Simon.

CHAPTER TWENTY

Shona and Michael had to work hard to cater for a very demanding Mr Price, but they managed to produce some good quality food that was well received by his guests. They even found time at the end of the evening to sit and chat with everybody and indulge in a few glasses of wine.

Michael found the conversation riveting and learnt a lot about issues that affect farmers, such as an ageing population, the high capital cost of entry, low farm-gate prices, reduced subsidies, low profit margins and government and council bureaucracy that has necessitated much change within the industry. Mr and Mrs Price had somehow managed to scrape a reasonable living over the years by working eighteen hours per day, but they had only felt comfortable within the last eighteen months following their decision to diversify.

"Was diversification the only option, Albert?" Michael asked Mr Price.

"If we hadn't breathed new life into this place, it would have died and we would probably have died with it."

"How did you decide what to do?"

"Despite having Shona and yourself here tonight, my wife Cheryl is a really good cook and a people person, so it was easy for us to open a bed and breakfast. We then worked on two of the fields and introduced facilities to make them suitable for campers and caravanners before marketing the site to event management companies for festivals."

"What about the llamas in the front field?" asked Michael.

"They started off as a bit of a hobby really. One llama bought to do the job of a guard dog, soon became a pack that allowed us to provide a llama trekking experience for tourists throughout our thirty-five acres of farmland and woodland," replied Albert.

"Llama trekking sounds a lot more fun to me than milking cows. I do find all the issues you've just spoken about fascinating though and I would really like to help the farmers somehow if I can. I have a very important article to complete about the withdrawal of many life-saving cancer drugs by NHS England because they are deemed to be too expensive. Afterwards I'll research the plight of the farmers and see what angle I can adopt that puts pressure on the government to make your life easier and less stressful."

"I'll be happy to work with you on it, Michael, but don't take too long to write the article or there won't be too many farms left. The average age of a farmer is 59 and there isn't a lot of young blood coming through as wages are so low. Couple this with rolling farmland being replaced by housing estates, warehouses, wind turbines, wider roads and railway lines, and it will not be too many years before the English countryside has disappeared."

~

Baz had spent all day Wednesday locked in a bedroom of the DJ's house. He awoke early on Thursday extremely hungry, and thirsty as he didn't like drinking the en-suite tap water. The sun was shining through the bedroom window and Baz took that as a sign there was light at the end of the tunnel. It was also a sign that he could help the DJ and might not be murdered in his sleep.

"Today, you are going to show me where my daughter lives

and where she goes to school. I then have another job for you. Succeed and you can have this passport back," said the DJ, holding up the little burgundy book that contained the tracking device.

"How did you get that?"

"We followed the guy whose jacket pocket you tried to hide it in and took it back."

"What do you want me to do?"

The DJ handed Baz a piece of paper and gave him instructions to go to Dapplegate Farm and kill the land owners.

"I am going to see the Fixer, the Chameleon and the Painter to plan the next stage of the mission."

"Who is 'The Painter'? I haven't heard that name before."

"He is an old friend of mine who is my eyes and ears in and around the city."

"What does he actually do for you, or shouldn't I ask?" asked Baz.

"Fail to kill Mr and Mrs Price on Saturday and you will know what he can do, as he will splash your blood all over the Worcester city walls in true graffiti style."

Baz sat in the passenger seat and directed the DJ to where Jade lived with her foster mother Maisie. They then drove to the school that Jade attended and waited for a bell to signal the end of lessons for the day. Baz pointed Maisie out as she arrived at the school on foot to collect Jade, at which point the DJ turned to him and announced that he had seen her before.

"That is the woman I saw in the park talking to Shona last weekend. It seems as if I was watching my little girl playing on the swings without knowing it. Life often has a habit of surprising you, doesn't it?"

"It certainly does," replied Baz.

"I can't believe that bitch Shona didn't have the courtesy to phone me and tell me that I had a daughter. What did she think

I was going to do to her?" said the DJ.

"Probably what you are thinking of doing as we sit here?" said Baz.

"You don't know what I am thinking," said the DJ.

"I have an idea, but if I am right I don't think it is the answer and I don't understand why you would want to hurt Shona again. You did enough damage the last time from what I heard, and I think you are skating on thin ice coming back here anyway."

"I gave Shona a lot of money that obviously went towards a deposit on her apartment. I now find out that everything I taught her about cooking has held her in good stead for setting up her own business and that she has been keeping a massive secret from me. I returned to England to claim back what was rightfully mine, but if I play this right I can go back home with two or even three trophies."

"I still don't think your approach is the right one."

"Shona keeps on doing things to make me angry and as you know, Baz, I don't take too kindly to people who do that and I have to react in the way I think is appropriate."

"I am not sure she has done too much wrong, really."

"I really tried to be a better person and love her. I gave her much more of myself than I thought possible and then she dumped me, just like that."

"That's because you beat her up and broke her ribs."

"She didn't do what I wanted her to do."

"I can only assume that she was scared for some reason as everybody is when you are around. Sometimes you just have to accept you can't get your own way and if that happens be adult about it. You may well have believed in your own mind that you loved Shona, but how can you tell someone you love them one minute and then punch them the next?"

"I have some switch inside my head that turns on and off on

its own. It normally turns on when my brain gets signals of jealousy or rejection or if it thinks it is being lied to or I am being cheated out of something."

"So it wasn't your fault that you constantly hit Shona and then eventually battered her?"

"No, not really."

"Try telling that to the relatives of the one thousand women that die each year in America at the hands of their husbands, partners or boyfriends."

"You are lying to me now, Baz."

"I am definitely not lying to you. I am no expert but I did some reading on this particular subject at university and it is a fact. You don't come across as a typical wife or girlfriend beater even though you are self-centred, excitable, moody and hasty, because you are also intelligent, articulate and confident, which the typical abuser isn't," said Baz.

"So what are you saying?" asked the DJ.

"I'm in the deep brown sticky stuff because I'm an addict who needs money. I'm not stupid but will do stupid things to get it, like help you, as I don't have too many other options open to me. You, on the other hand, do have options open to you, as you have brains, a good job, a house and lots of money in the bank, so it is bizarre that you are the one who doesn't demonstrate clear thinking at times."

"What you say is probably right, Baz, but in reality we are not too different as we both need psychological help in some way. Maybe I will try and get help at some point, but only after I have my daughter living with me in New York."

"Do you really think you can kidnap your own daughter and then have any sort of meaningful and loving relationship with her afterwards?"

"You are talking like you are some fucking expert, Baz."

"I did study human behaviour at university."

"So you think you really understand my rationale for doing the things that I do?"

"I have a fair idea but I am not about to tell you as I don't want my ribs to be broken or my tongue to be removed."

"Go on, be honest. I won't hurt you. You may even help me become a better person."

"I think your issues stem from your childhood, as mine do. I suspect you didn't trust your parents as they were always letting you down in some way. This manifested itself so that you stopped trusting everyone, which in turn meant you had conflict after conflict with figures of authority. It wouldn't surprise me if you did things in your teenage years to reinforce your feelings, but then as you got older you realised that your parents actually did love you and care for you but were just too busy trying to do their best for you that they lost sight of what was really important."

"You may well be right to a point, but that doesn't explain my inner turmoil at times, does it?" said the DJ.

"I think it does. I think you may have made mistakes in your life and deep down felt guilty about them, so you set out to gain love from your peers in various ways. This love didn't come for whatever reason, but your drive took you down another path, one of competitiveness. This made you good at what you were doing, which brought respect and power which you mistook for love."

"You are right, Baz, you aren't stupid."

"The jury is still out on that one, but it won't be out for long if the police catch up with you," replied Baz.

"I can't abort my mission now."

"That's your choice, but it isn't going to get you what you think you want and as long as you continue to confuse love with power you will never know the difference between wise and foolish."

~

Joseph knocked on Michael Black's door early on Friday morning, but when there was no answer he forced himself to ring what he thought was a rather small and useless bell.

There was still no answer because Michael and Shona had stayed overnight at Dapplegate Farm as they were too drunk to drive home. Michael had then driven to Bristol for a meeting the following morning, while Shona had taken a taxi home as she needed to prepare for Kevin and Kate's superheroes party on Saturday.

Joseph drove away from Michael's house and went to see Richard Webb, who did happen to be at home as he was preparing a work presentation. This surprised Joseph but in a way he understood, as work can be a distraction from heartfelt thoughts and give some structure to each day.

Joseph had looked through the CCTV tapes and had edited all of the relevant sections that he was now going to show Richard on his laptop. His team in Washington had also been in touch with ground agents in Bangladesh and had come up with some very interesting and useful information. Bea joined Joseph at Richard's house as he thought her skill and experience of body motion communication was going to be invaluable.

Joseph was confident that with Bea's help he was going to be able to present Graham with a report that might just give him the breakthrough he had been striving for over the last week or two. Unfortunately, Graham was taking a couple of days' holiday to try and alleviate some stress, so Joseph wouldn't be able to see him until Sunday.

~

The first person to arrive at Kevin and Kate Rogers' superheroes party was the Black Widow. Only Kevin knew the identity of all of the guests, which perturbed Kate somewhat, but she agreed to play along on the assurance that each guest would reveal themselves at the end of the evening. 'What a ghastly thought,' she said to herself, 'unless of course one of the characters is Hugh Jackman or David Beckham.'

Kate thought it was a bit weird having to introduce herself as Catwoman, as it was pretty obvious who she really was, but the dinner party seemed to be important to Kevin so she threw herself into the role and when the Black Widow handed her a bottle of wine she said, "Puuurrrfect."

Kevin was dressed as Captain America and both he and the Black Widow went into some bizarre dialogue that Kate could only assume came from the film.

"This is a fun thing to do on a Saturday night," said the Black Widow.

"Well, all the guys from my barbershop are dead so this seemed like a good idea," said Captain America.

"Shall we play a game?" said the Black Widow.

"What game?"

"Kiss Me."

"What?"

"Does a display of affection make you uncomfortable?"

"Yes."

The Black Widow grabbed Captain America and then kissed him on the cheek before turning to Kate and telling her, "That was our first kiss since 1945."

It was Kate's turn to say "What?"

"It's ok," said Kevin we were just acting out a few scenes from a film.

Kate was a bit shocked by the events of the last few seconds and was glad she had a mask on to hide the fact her eyes were watering. Her feline instincts told her that she might need to sharpen her claws and be prepared for a cat fight.

The next person to arrive was obviously the Hulk. Whoever it was behind the mask had obtained a fantastic suit which was going to be most uncomfortable after a few hours in their warm house. The Hulk walked into the kitchen, handed Captain America a six-pack that looked like Rolling Rock and then looked long and hard at the Black Widow before asking her if she was here to kill him.

"No, of course not, I am here to look for threats," replied the Black Widow.

"Is Captain America on threat watch too?"

"All of the marvellous heroes here tonight are on threat watch to ensure we stay ahead of the enemy."

"Do we know who the enemy is?"

"We now have the CIA and MI5 to contend with," said the Black Widow.

Kate stood in the corner of the kitchen looking totally bemused by the talk and hoped that the evening would be a little more normal once the other guests arrived.

Thor banged very hard on the door with his hammer and shouted, "What realm is this?"

Catwoman opened the front door with a bottle opener in her hand which surprised Thor and made him step back quickly and roar, "You threaten Thor with a puny weapon like that?"

"I also have sharp claws," said Kate.

"You may try to take my soul, death goddess, but I will fight you to the end."

"Wait until after we have had some Asgard soup."

"So be it," said Thor and walked into the house.

Shona was listening to this, trying to work out if the friends were going to keep the acting up all evening. She thought she knew who the final character was going to be from the menu she had been asked to cook. Each guest had been asked to select the name of a starter, main dish or dessert and Shona had to deliver an exciting, tasty dish for them all to share based on its name. She glanced at the menu she had written and made a few notes alongside.

Asgard Soup
Kitka Salad
Quiver of Duck Breast
Captain's Meat Loaf
Bangers & Smash
Chocolate Web Pancakes
Prince of Cheesecakes

When she was given the list of meals to produce, Shona had tried to guess which characters were going to arrive and so far she had been spot on. The pancakes made her think quite hard, as the guest could have been Spiderman, but she wasn't in any doubt when a beautiful young woman in a figure-hugging outfit arrived. If I was considering any lesbian sex, Shona thought to herself, the Black Widow outfit would swing it so to speak. As the doorbell rang to announce the arrival of the fourth guest, Shona thought that she was the one who should have dressed up as Wonder Woman, based on the amount of work she had to do to keep the superheroes entertained this evening.

The final guest, whoever it was, dressed as Hawkeye, should have come as the Joker, as he rang the bell and seemed to disappear. Catwoman had no sooner shut the door thinking that it was the wind that had caused the bell to ring and it rang again. She opened the door once more to find nobody there for a second time. Just as she was about to shut it again an arrow whizzed past her face, gave the bell a glancing blow and thudded into the ground a few feet away. "Shit," said Kate forgetting her character's role for a moment which caused much laughter and helped everybody relax, including Kate herself, as she was still eyeing her husband with suspicion.

~

Baz parked his car down a narrow lane about half a mile from Dapplegate Farm and then walked slowly through a small copse until he could see the farmhouse in the distance. Between him and the house was a large field surrounded by a woven wire fence that had notices attached to it suggesting that it was electrified.

Baz walked along the farm's perimeter to the right of the house looking for an opening or a stile from which he could cross the field and get close to the side of the building.

It was getting dark and there were no lights anywhere other than those coming from the house which Baz was soon to try to enter. He was a bit concerned that the owners would have exterior security sensors and floodlights that triggered CCTV, but it was a chance he had to take.

There didn't appear to be a gap in the fence, and Baz wasn't prepared to walk up the main driveway so he searched for something to help him leap the fence. He found a large log, dragged it next to the fence and leapt over it, in his mind with the skill of Dick Fosbury or Dalton Grant. In the distance between himself and the house he could make out some sheep lying down, so walked towards them slowly. He had got to within 250 yards of one of the farm's outhouses when he saw a large animal that looked like a llama appear from behind a high mound. It suddenly made a high-pitched rhythmic sound like a squeaky bed spring and rushed towards him spitting at the same time. As it did this, more llamas appeared, forcing Baz to turn and run across the field parallel with the main driveway. He stumbled and fell to the ground on a couple of occasions in his desperation to get away but he eventually made it to the bottom of the drive. With his mind scrambled he climbed the fence, forgetting that it was electrified. The high-voltage low-current pulse caused Baz to scream with pain as he fell on to the side of the fence where he started his wild animal adventure some five or ten minutes ago.

Baz lay low in the grass by the side of the fence for ten to fifteen minutes to recover from the shock and to stay hidden, because the commotion had alerted Mr Price who was walking across his yard shining a torch towards the animals in the field. Baz knew he would now need to adopt a different approach and would need to re-think his point of entry so as to avoid the sodding llamas.

~

The DJ was standing in a residential street in a place called Claines, just on the outskirts of Worcester. The street lights were on but a few weren't working, for which he was thankful as it meant he could hide in the shadows. He walked slowly down the road trying not to look conspicuous and trying to work out a plan of action. As he stood outside number twenty-one and looked around, he decided his best option was to carry out his attack and escape from the rear of the property. The house had an extremely long rear garden bordered by wooden fence panels and a variety of trees and shrubs. At the end of the garden was a large shed and behind this was a gate which backed onto a school cricket pitch. How ironic, the DJ thought to himself, that his mission had started on a cricket pitch and here he was three quarters of the way to achieving his goal standing on another one.

The DJ opened the back gate and crept along the edge of the garden right up to the back door and listened for any sounds from inside the house. He knew which room he wanted to get to as he had stood by the shed and watched the toing and froing from upstairs for the last two evenings.

It was very simple for a skilled person like the DJ to pick the back door lock. He had burgled many houses in his younger days and when doing so he was amazed by the number of people who locked their door and then hung the key up on a hook somewhere nearby. It would have been more difficult for him to enter the property if the key had been left in the lock and turned. He didn't have time to dwell on this as he had a job to do here, and fast. He opened the back door slowly and stepped into the kitchen from where he could hear a television blaring out from a room to his left. He took the flick knife from his pocket, in preparation should he need to use it and then moved slowly along a hallway that he thought would lead to some stairs. He prayed that the stairs wouldn't creak, but with the TV being so loud he didn't think the occupants would hear anything as he walked up them and into Jade's bedroom.

CHAPTER TWENTY-ONE

The DJ had given Baz a very large knife for this evening's task for some reason. Baz had measured the length of the blade at 30 cm, which was a big issue when it came to finding a jacket with a pocket long enough to hold it. It became a different issue when the llama was chasing him, as Baz was worried when falling over that he might stab himself instead of Mr and Mrs Price.

Baz crossed the driveway and this time climbed over a post and rail fence that wasn't electrified. He moved swiftly to his left along the edge of a stream within an empty field that was some five hundred yards away from the farmhouse now on his right. He stopped opposite some cow sheds, well out of view of anyone looking out of the farmhouse windows, and well out of view of the llamas.

The house was fairly large and Baz didn't have much idea about the layout or how many people might be inside. The Fixer had told him that Mr and Mrs Price lived alone, that farm hands came and went each day and sometimes there were B&B guests staying in the west wing. Baz knew he probably had to break in and catch the occupants unawares if he was to succeed with this mission, or wait until they were asleep.

He walked slowly into the cowshed, as he was scared of cows, and was pleased to find it empty other than what appeared to be some milking machines. He looked down at the teat cups and wondered what sort of sensation he would get putting one of them on his penis. The thought didn't last long, as walking out the other side of the shed he stepped straight into a cow pat.

"Shit," he said to himself but rather too loudly. The sound alerted a border collie which appeared from the corner of a garage at the back of the cowshed to the side of the house. Baz stood still, pressed himself against the corrugated side of the building and hoped the dog hadn't spotted him.

Unfortunately, the collie had seen Baz and it started barking noisily and aggressively. Another dog that looked like an Alsatian suddenly joined the party, causing Baz to be fearful and forcing him to draw the knife from his jacket pocket.

The Alsatian charged at Baz and leapt at his throat. Despite having a knife, Baz lost the functionality of his right arm but just managed to sway out of the dog's way, causing it to crash into the side of the cowshed. As the Alsatian landed on the floor in a heap Baz kicked it hard, stunning it and forcing it to back off.

The commotion disturbed the household; all of the outside lights came on, the kitchen door opened and a man that fitted the description of Mr Price stepped out of the back door with a shotgun in his hand. Baz quickly disappeared back into the cowshed and hid in one of the stalls.

The dogs stood at the cowshed entrance barking and Baz could see through a gap in the railings that they had been joined by an English Shepherd and an Old English Sheepdog. Baz was now having serious doubts as to his ability to carry out this task, but knew he had to or he would be back to square one, so he stayed silent and prayed.

Mr Price walked to the cowshed entrance and shone a torch around the building for thirty seconds or so and as he didn't see anything he pulled the roller door shut and said something to the dogs that Baz didn't understand. He then started to walk around the outside of the building towards the other entrance. As he got halfway round, Baz suddenly realised what was about to happen.

Baz got up from his hiding place and ran back the same way he had come into the cowshed, getting to the door just as Mr Price and the dogs got there. Baz stood still and watched as Mr Price aimed the shotgun at his head and shouted at him to put his hands in the air where he could see them.

Baz started to do as he was asked, but as he did so he shouted to a pretend accomplice behind Mr Price, who instantly turned round to see who was behind him. In that same instant Baz lunged at Mr Price with the knife. Mr Price saw the movement out of the corner of his left eye and swung the barrel of the shotgun round hitting Baz flush on the temple with bone-crunching power, knocking him senseless to the ground where he landed with a thud.

~

The DJ held a chloroform-soaked cloth in front of his daughter's face for a few minutes to make sure she didn't wake up when he carried her downstairs. He made sure that the cloth didn't totally cover her mouth and nose as this could be fatal for a young person. He also made sure when carrying her down the stairs that her chin was supported and her airways were not obstructed by her tongue. Jade was heavier than the DJ had anticipated, which made the process more difficult and a bit slower than he would have liked, but eventually he got her out of the house and into the rear garden.

It took the DJ less than two minutes to run to his Range Rover, bundle Jade onto the back seat and drive off down the main road. He tried to keep to the speed limits as he didn't want to have to explain to an officious policeman why he had a drugged young girl in the car, particularly as he had gone to the trouble of putting false plates on it.

The DJ drove to his rented house via a few back streets and then carried Jade into a bedroom that he had prepared for her, before telling the newest of his recruits 'The Gatekeeper' that she shouldn't answer the door to anyone bar him. He had chosen this teenage girl to join the gang as she was bright, pretty and desperate, but probably not in that order. She had long brown hair and a lovely orange glow to her complexion from working away from her home in Auckland for a few years as a guide at the Blackwater Coal Centre just north of Brisbane. She had left her home country of New Zealand rather suddenly about seven or eight months ago. She wouldn't say why, but the DJ didn't care as she had an innocence that worked to his advantage in certain situations.

"I am going out for a couple of hours," said the DJ.

"No problem, but what shall I do if Jade wakes up?" said the Gatekeeper.

"She will be a bit drowsy and dizzy and will feel sick and weak for a while. Just tell her that her mum has been taken to hospital and that you are looking after her until she is able to come home. Make her feel comfortable, give her something to eat if she wants anything, but don't let her out of the house."

"No problem, but can I ask where you are going?"

"I am going to punish someone."

~

Michael wondered how his sister was getting on with Kevin's friends and wished that he was there having fun. Instead, he was once again home alone working. Tonight, he was producing a short sharp paper on the issues between NHS England and the National Institute for Health and Care Excellence. Michael had done a lot of work on this in the past after his mum had died from cancer, but new funding guidelines now meant that his public awareness campaign efforts would have to be doubled. His concerns stemmed from the fact that one minute potentially life-saving drugs are being administered to patients and the next there is talk of the treatments available through the Cancer Drugs Fund being axed. Michael was well aware that the UK lags behind other European countries in prescribing certain medicines to cancer patients and he didn't want the situation to get worse. His aim was to try and force the government to change the way NICE and the CDF operate for the benefit of all cancer sufferers.

He knew he was only one of many lone voices all over the country that need to form a very large choir if the situation is to improve, so that deserving tax-paying citizens lives can be saved or they can have a better quality of life in the time they have left.

Michael sat and cogitated for a few minutes before bashing away at the keys of his laptop in an attempt to link together all of his work on the issues relating to the NHS over the last few months. He thought about his correspondence via email, Twitter and Facebook from thousands of people who all agree with Michael in that everything that is wrong about this country is down to the government and their illogical and short-sighted decisions. There doesn't seem to be any consideration for the views of decent honest law-abiding people when it comes to policy making and certainly no consideration for those seriously affected by the decisions.

Michael thought back to his work on HS2 and the feedback he received from the public about this project and it was clear that the majority of people would choose to scrap HS2 and put this expenditure into the health service. Seventy or eighty billion pounds would pay for more doctors, more nurses, more surgeries and more drugs that would ease the pressure on hospitals and would ensure seven days per week total healthcare for all that are entitled. It would also ensure that the Cancer Drugs Fund could continue to help extend patients' lives.

He summarised this in a clear and succinct manner and ended the report by asking readers one question: Is it better that we save lives or save twenty minutes on a train journey?

~

Penny had found the few days with her parents a bit gruelling. Although it was nice to see them, she felt on trial for much of the time and her dad might well have been shining a bright light into her eyes when they were alone.

She decided to come back to Worcester earlier than planned by saying she had some prep work to do before her university course started. In reality, she missed Joseph so had asked him to come round to her apartment on Saturday night when she would cook him a meal.

One of Penny's friends from her original course had given up her day to help Penny purchase basic kitchen and bedroom items as well as a digital radio. Penny wasn't bothered about having a television as she wouldn't have time to watch it because she was going to spend most of her time studying or working as an informant for Joseph.

Joseph was delighted to accept her invitation and said he would be there at 8.00 p.m., as he had an appointment to go to before this.

Joseph was pleased to find Michael at home at last and although he didn't have any real authority to be questioning him, Michael recognised Joseph from Amanda Webb's funeral and let him into his house.

Joseph didn't have time for pleasantries and got straight to the point of his visit.

"I saw you at the funeral the other day with a young woman and would like to know who she is."

"Shona Green," said Michael.

"Jesus Christ," said Joseph.

"No, Shona Green," said Michael.

"I am here on a very serious matter, Mr Black. I don't actually think that all of the murders that have occurred within the last few weeks are a joking matter, do you?"

"What do you mean all of the murders? I know about Amanda and a Mr Campbell," said Michael.

"There were also two people killed in Pershore the other day: a Luke Smith and a Kylie Page."

"I'm sorry," said Michael, paling as the realisation of what he thought may have been happening within Worcestershire recently hit home.

"I had a suspicion that recent events might have been connected to Shona, but it was no more than that. What you have just told me means that all of those that have been killed recently were people who Shona had cooked for in her capacity as a chef."

"Wow, that's some revelation," replied Joseph. "I wasn't aware of that fact, but the recent murders within the last few weeks are starting to make sense to me now. If what you say is true it may help us find the murderer or murderers, one of whom could actually be my brother."

"Your brother?" asked Michael.

"Believe it or not, yes. Shona used to work at a club or pub called the Barley Mow or something like that, and she dated my brother Justin Johnson for some time. He loaned her a substantial amount of money to start a new life but no sooner had she got this money than she dumped him."

"He isn't a chef by any chance, is he?" asked Michael.

"Yes, he is or was. Why, has she mentioned him?"

"Yes, and I think he may be the father of her child."

"Her child?" said Joseph.

"I think she is about six or seven years old," said Michael.

"Does she live with Shona?"

"No, she had her fostered and as far as I am aware if your brother is the father, he doesn't know of his daughter's existence."

"Maybe he does know and if this is the case he'll do everything he can to get back at Shona and anyone else who has harmed him in some way," replied Joseph.

"All I could gather from Shona when she told me about her daughter was that she has no intention of letting the biological father, whoever he is, play any part in his daughter's life at any time," said Michael.

"If Justin is the father and he gets to know this, he will make sure that if he can't have his daughter then no one else will have her either."

"He sounds like a nasty piece of work."

"Do you know where Shona's daughter lives?"

"No, I don't," replied Michael.

"Where is Shona at the moment?"

"She is currently at my sister's house cooking a meal for her husband and a few of their friends."

"I have somewhere to go now," said Joseph, "but I think you need to contact your sister and check that she and her friends are alive and well."

"Reluctantly and worryingly, I think you are right, so I'll phone her immediately," replied Michael.

"You must find a way to warn your sister that she could be in danger, probably not while she has guests, but certainly afterwards, if as I suspect there is a pattern forming here. I'll give you my card in case you need me and will be back to see you tomorrow with DCI Graham Laws. If you can provide me with your sister's address, I'll arrange for an officer to keep an eye on her house for the rest of this evening and early tomorrow morning," said Joseph, as he started to put on his coat.

CHAPTER TWENTY-TWO

Joseph got to Penny's apartment just before 8.00 p.m. to find the table laid for a three-course meal.

"Blimey, this looks impressive. What are you cooking?" he asked Penny.

Penny walked up to Joseph, gave him a kiss and read out the menu.

Avocado & Bacon Potato Skins
Chicken & Brie Pie
Apple & Banana Crunch Pie
or
Chocolate Mousse Cake

"Before we eat I have a surprise for you," said Penny.

As she finished speaking, her friend Tara entered the room wearing nothing but a short figure-hugging dress that left nothing to the imagination. Joseph gulped and turned to Penny with a quizzical look.

"You told me that you had never had a threesome, so now is your chance."

Penny pulled the ties on her chef's apron and let it drop to the floor to reveal a beautiful skimpy halter neck outfit that showed a large amount of cleavage.

"W-wow!" stuttered Joseph as he stood gaping at the sight to behold before him.

"Don't just stand there, do something," said Penny.

Joseph was a bit stunned and not really in the mood, but didn't want to look a gift horse in the mouth. So he slid his hand inside the material and stroked Penny's nipples before bending down and sucking on them hard.

"You remember how I like it, then."

Joseph didn't say anything as he had his mouth full, but even he couldn't have forgotten what she liked in such a short space of time, as it was only a week or so ago that they had made love.

Tara walked over to Joseph, stood behind him, unzipped his trousers and grabbed hold of his already throbbing penis. Penny then dropped to her knees, took Joseph's penis in her mouth, and sucked and licked it for a few minutes as he told her how good it felt. She then got up, stood behind Tara and slid her dress to the floor before pressing her breasts into Tara's back and touching her intimately. Joseph took his trousers and boxers off, pressed himself against Tara's stomach and fondled her large breasts.

"Have you ever been dominated by two women?" said Penny.

"Not like this," said Joseph.

Tara suddenly pushed Joseph away from her, grabbed his hand, led him into the bedroom and told him to lie down on the rug on the floor. She then stood over him letting him see all the way up her long legs to her silky red panties with a small slit in the middle. Tara licked her finger and touched herself with it before offering it to Joseph to suck. Joseph started to sit up, but Tara pressed her foot down on to his chest and said, "It isn't going to be that easy."

"Ow!" said Joseph as his head hit the floor.

"It was lucky I made you lie on the mat or else you really

would have had something to cry out about," said Tara.

"I am not sure I am going to like this domination lark," said Joseph as Tara pressed her foot down a little harder.

"Is that erection uncomfortable?" she said.

"It might be in a while if you don't help me with it."

"Oh, we'll help you, but we're going to have some fun first," said Penny, standing next to Tara, and sliding off her soft pink panties before dropping them onto Joseph's face.

"That's as close as you are getting for now," she said.

Both girls then leaned over and dangled their breasts just above Joseph's face. He thought for a moment that he had died and gone to heaven.

Suddenly, Penny produced a short black whip that could have been a riding crop.

"I will take that as a compliment," said Joseph.

"Don't kid yourself, just roll over onto your stomach and face some punishment," said Tara.

"You really should reverse the letters in your name," replied Joseph.

"That's unkind," said Tara.

"It is also unkind of you to pin me down on the floor and then ask me to turn over. If I do turn over now something may snap and you might have one each," said Joseph fearfully.

"Good point," said Tara laughing.

"Just get up off the floor and bend over the bed then," said Penny.

"I think you should be doing that and then you can decide if I'm a horse or not," replied Joseph.

Tara ignored Joseph and pushed him against the bed, giving Penny the opportunity to spank him with the whip. The light whipping action led to some slight wheal marks on Joseph's skin and a significant decline in the size of his erection. After ten minutes of total domination, the girls had had their fun and decided that it was Joseph's turn to have some pleasure. They ordered him to lie on the bed where Tara kneeled above his face allowing Joseph to do what he wanted to a while ago and taste her. At the same time, Penny lowered herself onto Joseph's once again stiff and throbbing penis, giving him double the fun, which played havoc with his mind as he tried to concentrate on both things and control his excitement.

"That didn't take very long," said Penny. "How are you now going to satisfy Tara?"

"I'll be ready again within an hour and I'm sure that I could perform better after some food and a couple of beers."

Penny served Joseph two bacon and avocado potato skins for his starter as she thought he might have an appetite. He wolfed them down and then devoured the chicken and brie pie with its beautiful puff pastry top with much enthusiasm. When the chocolate mousse cake was placed on the table Joseph looked at Tara and winked.

"Two lots of dessert," he said.

Just as he was about to eat the mousse cake his mobile phone rang. The constable observing the Rogers' house was reporting to him that nothing untoward appeared to be happening. People at the dinner party seemed to be having a good time, albeit they were dressed up in silly costumes. As everything seemed to be normal, he was going to drive around the rest of the village and come back in half an hour.

As Joseph took his phone out of his pocket to answer it, a folded piece of paper containing a picture fluttered to the floor.

"I forgot about this. I brought it to show you as part of your new role. I'd like you to ask around and find out if anyone can put a name to someone living or working around here who may wear or has worn these cufflinks."

"Do I get a bonus if I actually help you catch anyone?"

"It could be arranged."

"Good. Because I know cufflinks like this have been worn by a nasty piece of work who hands out orders to minions around the city's pubs and clubs. I think he provides the drugs and collects the money."

"Do you have a name?"

"He is known as 'The Fixer', but I have occasionally heard someone call him Kevin."

"I don't suppose Kevin wears a donut-shaped button badge, too?" asked Joseph.

"No, but I know who does," replied Penny.

CHAPTER TWENTY-THREE

Everyone was enjoying the superheroes party and Shona was delivering fantastic, fun food on time, or so Kate told Michael, when he phoned to see if the party was going well and that everything was ok. They chatted for a few minutes about various things including family stuff and then both went about their evening with Michael seemingly satisfied that nothing untoward was going on.

Just as Kevin announced to everyone that he had organised some action games in their large back garden, another superhero arrived at the front door.

"The Punisher is here," he announced.

"Better late than never, but at least we have four teams of two now," said Kevin.

"I have to get going now, so maybe Shona can take my place in the game," said the Black Widow.

"She doesn't have an outfit," said Kate.

"She can be Dagger," said the Punisher "as there is a resemblance."

"How do you know that?" asked Kate. "You haven't seen or met Shona yet."

"I saw her through the window doing the washing up."

Kate started to wonder how the man dressed as the Punisher knew the person doing the washing up was Shona and started to ask the question, but changed her mind and went to organise the game with Kevin, who had decided that a game of attack and defence would test all of the guest's logic, agility, skill, cunning and stamina. He split the players into two teams of four; one team were to defend the garden shed and the other team had to get its superheroes into it without being tagged. The attackers consisted of Captain America, Catwoman, Dagger, and Wonder Woman; the defenders were Hawkeye, Thor, Hulk and the Punisher.

The trees and bushes in the garden provided a lot of cover which made the game very interesting. Captain America thought he could use his shield to stop himself being tagged, but Thor's hammer hit it with such force denting it and knocking him over that he got caught a few strides from home.

Catwoman thought she could avoid capture by creeping through the bushes in her dark outfit, but the Hulk with his super astral perception spotted her and charged across the garden at some 700 mph to tag her with ease.

Wonder Woman thought she could get to the shed by running at sub-light speed from the far corner of the garden, but Hawkeye fired an arrow with a trip wire attached into a tree causing her to crash to the ground and hurt her ribs.

The attackers who were tagged and their conquerors went inside the house for some alcoholic liquid refreshment.

This just left Dagger and the Punisher in the garden where they both had the same objective. The Punisher let Dagger get to the shed where he locked the door once she was inside and took off his mask.

"Oh, my God!" said Shona.

"Hello, Shona," said the DJ.

"What the fuck are you doing here?" asked Shona.

"That's not a nice welcome after all of these years, is it?"

"You beat me up good and proper and then raped me, so what did you expect?"

"I am sorry about that."

"You have never been sorry for anything you have done in your whole wretched life."

"I am sorry for what I did and sorry that you stole my twenty thousand pounds."

"You gave that money to me."

"Semantics, my dear. I loaned it to you and then you reported me to the police for grievous bodily harm."

"You broke my ribs and fractured my eye socket. I would have pressed that and a rape charge too if I felt it would have stuck, but as we were in a physical relationship it would have been difficult to get a conviction and I didn't want to have to go through the whole ordeal again in court."

"I thought the police had a warrant out for my arrest?"

"They did. But I stupidly reflected on everything in hospital and decided not to press any charges. I guess I thought you would never have the nerve to return to England with the knowledge that you were a wanted man."

"I guess I should say thank you, but none of that changes the fact that I desperately need that money and want it back."

"I don't have that kind of money just lying around."

"You seem to have done well for yourself in a roundabout way or should I say round a pole in a fun way and now you have a nice new business which is earning you a few bob."

"How do you know about my new business?"

"I have eyes and ears everywhere."

"I still don't have twenty thousand pounds that I can lay my hands on just like that."

"You can always sell your apartment."

"Then what do I do and where would I live?"

"I don't really care."

"That just about says it all really, doesn't it."

"You hurt me emotionally and ruined my dreams of a new

life here in England so I am now back here to ruin yours."

"How the hell can you say I ruined your dreams?"

"I really loved you, Shona, and wanted to make a life with you here in Worcestershire, but that can't happen now as technically I am or could still become a wanted man."

"Tell me: if you thought you were a wanted man, why did you risk coming back to England thinking you might be picked up at any of the airports or the ports?"

"I have a new name and a new passport, as do you, I gather."

"What do you call yourself these days then?" asked Shona, ignoring his question hoping he wouldn't pursue it.

"DJ Macintyre."

"Why?"

"He was someone I met up with in Seattle and then again in Bangladesh. We hit it off and listened to rock music together while we honed our knife skills."

"Why have you come back to search for me now?"

"I had to let the dust settle and time pass so that I wasn't on any radar anymore."

"Why risk it though as you must have established a good life with all of your cookery skills?"

"I had some other business to attend to here and as you know, I can't just let sleeping dogs lie."

"It's a weird coincidence that Macintyre is also the name of a man searching for the missing chef Claudia Lawrence."

"Is it really?" replied the DJ.

"You didn't have anything to do with that, did you?"

"No, of course not, but I may have something to do with the disappearance of a chef standing next to me now."

"I think that six or seven people in that house might just notice if we disappear and my screaming might alert them before that could happen."

"Yes, I know, but it was great to see you looking a bit scared and it would be even better to see you really frightened."

"How did you know I was here? Don't answer that as I assume someone at the party tipped you off."

"You are on the right lines, you could say the party was organised especially for your benefit."

"What are you going to do to me now then, break my arms or my legs or something much worse?"

"None of those things. I'm going to invite you to dinner at my rented house tomorrow lunchtime."

"And what if I decide not to turn up?"

"Oh, you will turn up, if you want to see your daughter again, or should I say our daughter again – alive!"

Shona went white, her eyes widened, her jaw dropped and she was suddenly very frightened.

"How did you find out about Jade?"

"I told you that I have eyes and ears everywhere."

The DJ handed Shona a piece of paper with an address on.

"Be at this address tomorrow at 11.30 a.m. I'll pick you up and drive you blindfolded to my house. If you mention our meeting to anyone, including the police, you know what the consequences will be."

Shona went back into the house feeling somewhat shaken and perplexed. Kate noticed something was up and tried to speak to her, but Shona told her she was tired and needed to go home.

"Where has the Punisher gone?" asked Kate.

"He's disappeared like the Invisible Man," replied Shona.

"Do you know who was beneath the mask?"

"No," said Shona lying. "But just being in his presence gave me the creeps."

"He gave me the creeps too, but I thought I recognised his voice from somewhere," replied Kate.

"Beware of him, Kate. I think his costume name should be

his real name," said Shona, gathering her things together to
leave.

CHAPTER TWENTY-FOUR

"Well, well, well, who have we here then?" said Graham, walking into the interview room to find Basil Reddy sitting in front of him. "You have been a naughty boy, haven't you?"

Baz said nothing, so Graham read him his rights. "Basil Reddy; you are under arrest on suspicion of the murder of Amanda Webb and the arson attack on the Worcester Cricket Club academy pavilion. You are not obliged to say anything unless you wish to do so, but it may harm your defence if you do not mention when questioned something which you later rely on in court. Anything you do say may be given in evidence. Do you understand?"

Baz nodded his head and asked for his solicitor to be called before he would consider answering any questions. Graham had his custody sergeant lock Baz in the cells while they waited for him to be legally represented.

It was a busy Sunday morning at the police station but Graham didn't mind, as at last he had some good news to tell the chief constable at his Monday morning briefing. He also had some bad news to tell him as a report had come in of the disappearance of a young girl. He had despatched a team of officers including Jane to a house in Claines to try and establish what might have happened to her and why.

A child is reported missing every three minutes in the UK which makes it really difficult for the police and social services to know which telephone calls are genuine and need to be investigated and which calls are from parents and carers panicking unnecessarily early. Jane started the questioning in an attempt to find out if Jade had any issues at home or at school that might have encouraged her to run away. Another officer took Jade's laptop away to get it interrogated, to see if she had mentioned running away on her Facebook and Twitter accounts. Consideration had to be given to the fact she might have been groomed by a paedophile, and if this was the case it was imperative to find her fast, as history suggests that the first forty-eight hours are critical to the safe recovery of a missing child.

Graham had asked for a picture of Jade to be sent to him so that he could alert the ports and airports. He also told his officers to canvas all houses within the vicinity and instigate a search of any house where the resident wasn't cooperative or seemed edgy and scared. He also set up some roadblocks so that traffic officers could speak to drivers using the roads near to Jade's house. People are creatures of habit, he told Maisie; someone who uses any of these roads at night may have noticed something out of place and not registered it or seen a car or van driver acting suspiciously.

Jane asked Maisie if she had an ID pack for Jade. Maisie said she had thought about getting one done but hadn't.

"That's a shame, as it would have helped me build a profile of your daughter. As it is, we are going to have to do things the old-fashioned way," said Jane, as she got a notepad from her bag. Jane asked Maisie for Jade's birth date, height, weight, hair colour, eye colour and blood type. She also wanted to know of any medication she was on, any allergies she had, any distinguishing marks or tattoos and any hobbies and interests. Jane also noted down what Jade would have been wearing and the fact that she had fallen asleep wearing some heart-shaped silver stud earrings.

"What time did Jade go to bed last night?" asked Jane.

"She was tired, so it was about 7.00 p.m."

"Who was the last person to see her, you or her father?"

"It was me," said Maisie, but you should know that we are her foster parents not her biological parents."

"Oh!" said Jane. "Do you know or see her real parents?"

"I do see her real mum and recently, we have discussed Jade going to live with her permanently. I don't know and have never seen her dad."

"What's her mum's name?"

"Shona Green. She lives near the city centre. I have her address and phone number in a folder upstairs."

~

Shona wandered around her apartment in a daze as lots of thoughts were going through her head. She wondered who had told Justin she was doing the catering at Kevin and Kate's house last night and how he had found out about their daughter. The only person who knew both of those things was Michael. She then wondered if Michael knew Justin and why Justin would threaten her in the way he had. She thought about phoning Maisie to see if Jade was alright but then started to worry about the consequences of speaking to anyone this morning. She decided to ignore the phone and the doorbell should either of them ring.

~

Joseph arrived at the police station at 10.00 a.m. to find it a hive of activity.

"What time do you call this?" said Graham.

"I am supposed to be having a day's holiday, but I came here instead to give you some very interesting and exciting news that may help us solve these cases."

"I bet it doesn't compare with me telling you that we have Basil Reddy locked up in the cells downstairs," replied Graham.

"How did you manage that, for Crissakes?" asked Joseph.

"I would like to say that it was down to some stupendous police work, but in reality it was just a case of one crime too many. What have you got for me then?" asked Graham.

"If you have time, I would like you to come with me to Michael Black's house. I'll tell you on the way."

Before they left the police station, Joseph wanted to look over the whiteboards to see what trace evidence, if any, Emma had gathered from the barn fire the other day. Emma was upstairs analysing fingerprints from some of the high performance cars that had been recovered out of the one hundred and fifty stolen during the last few months. She took a while to arrive and walked into the room to find Joseph, Graham and Peter chatting and looking at the whiteboard and the bagged exhibits.

Barn Fire

- *Victim 1 – Elspeth Campbell*
- *Ignited by Petrol*
- *Mini-Explosions caused by Butane Gas Canisters*
- *Melted Flick Knife found in the Ashes*
- *Large amounts of Potting Soil collected*
- *Charred Aluminium Foil Fragments*
- *Marijuana Sticks*

Graham looked at Emma, walked towards her and then leant over and kissed her on the forehead.

"You are a magician, Emma. The evidence here on top of what the documentation team established yesterday and Joseph and Peter have just told me, gets us really close to wrapping some of these cases up."

"Are you going to enlighten me?" replied Emma.

"Later today or tomorrow I will, but for now I would like you to figure out how Justin Johnson got into the country, if of course it is him that's behind some or all of the latest crimes. I also want to know where he is now and what he may be planning next."

"I am sure that Basil Reddy will tell Emma with a bit of persuasion," said Joseph.

"I am sure he would, but that isn't going to happen, and I am sure you aren't suggesting we partake in police brutality, are you, Joseph?"

"Not at all, Graham. We Americans don't go in for terrible things like that."

Graham smiled as he and Joseph prepared to leave the building, happy in the knowledge that the jigsaw was coming together and that Peter and Bea might add another piece when they visited Mr Thompson to see what he knew about Butane Hash Oil.

On the way to Michael Black's house, Joseph told Graham more about his interview with Mr Webb. In turn, he learnt of some interesting information passed down by members of Graham's team analysing details of Richard's estate and finances. Graham was stunned when he was told about Shona and even more stunned when he heard about her child. He was in a state of shock when he took Jane's phone call on his mobile at 11.45 a.m., just as they were arriving at Michael's house.

CHAPTER TWENTY-FIVE

Shona found the experience of being blindfolded rather scary. She had done some odd, deviant-like sexual things in her time but always resisted bondage as she didn't like losing control. Sitting in the car with Justin being unable to see anything, she had lost that control but had no choice other than to do what he asked of her. What she did do was try to memorise how many left and right turns Justin took from the place she was picked up from and by counting how many minutes it was in between turns.

Justin tried to talk to her during the journey, but she wasn't in the mood and just answered yes or no until he got the message and stopped trying.

After about thirty minutes, the car pulled to a halt and the ignition was turned off. Justin released the passenger door lock and told Shona that she could remove her blindfold and follow him inside, into what appeared to be a very large house.

Shona got a shock when she walked in to the lounge as Jade was lying on a giant purple microbead cushion on the floor watching television. Sitting in a chair next to Jade reading a book was Jessica.

"What the fu...." Shona stopped herself from saying any more.

"I think you know this little girl and my 'Gatekeeper'," said Justin with a smirk on his face.

"Hello, Shona, have you been to see my mum at the hospital?"

Shona was stunned at all she was being expected to take in and could only mutter a very silent, "No, not yet."

"Jessica says we can all go and see her later today," Jade continued.

"I will be back to see you in a minute sweetie," said Shona, as she pointed her index finger towards Justin who was still standing in the doorway and flicked her head to one side as if to say follow me.

Shona walked through a door to her right into a large dining room and then turned left again into an even larger kitchen.

"I will start again. What the fuck is Jade doing here?"

"I thought you would like to see her."

"Maisie wouldn't have let you take Jade. Oh no! What have you done to her?"

"Nothing, Maisie is fine. I mean she hasn't caused me any harm and has obviously cared for my daughter well for six years since you just gave her away uncaringly."

"It wasn't like that."

"What was it was like then?"

"If you must know, I had Jade fostered as she was born out of the time that you raped me and I couldn't face caring for her every day, as all I could visualise was you looming over me, hurting me and thinking that you owned me."

"I thought you were on the pill as you didn't want children at the time," replied Justin.

"I had actually changed my mind and had stopped taking the pill about six or seven days earlier. I was going to tell you on that fateful night."

"Wow! That's a surprise. If you were considering having children with me then perhaps we could have a go at being a proper family now in America?"

"You really do have a screw loose, don't you. I guess you kidnapped Jade, which means every police force in the country is going to be looking for her."

"I have that covered," said Justin. He walked across the kitchen floor, opened a drawer beneath the marble work surface and handed Shona two passports.

"One for you and one for Jade," said Justin.

Shona opened both the passports to find one in the name of Natalie Macintyre and one in the name of Laura Macintyre.

"How the hell did you get photographs of us in these passports?" shouted Shona.

"You will see that yours is an old photo, but you haven't changed much. I found Jade's passport in her bedside cabinet just by chance, so it made my trusted friend Cameron Hunter's job easy just to change her name."

"I have no intention of going anywhere with you," said Shona.

"Oh you will if you want to see Michael Black again," said Justin with an unnerving grin on his face.

"How the hell do you know about Michael?"

"As I said before, I have eyes and ears everywhere."

"What have you done with him?"

"That's for me to know and you to find out."

"You really are a sick bastard, aren't you?"

"If you and Jade come with me I may let him live."

"What if the passports don't stand up to scrutiny at the control desks?"

"Oh, they will. I have travelled the world on mine as and when I needed to use it. How do think I got into the UK without the authorities being aware that I was here?"

"Where are you planning to take us?"

"We are going to America via Dublin. I have a personal jet organised to take us to Ireland and from there we will travel to

New York as a family."

Shona was visibly stunned by the words she was hearing and was trying to comprehend her best form of action, but the best she could do was to ask Justin when he planned to set out on the trip.

"We will leave soon, when I am ready, but first I am going to cook you a meal. This is a version of a recipe I picked up at a roadside *dhaba* when I was in Pakistan. The food was so good that a friend of mine invested in a Punjab Dhaba mobile truck in Washington, DC. I have tried to get him to park outside my brother's place of work some twenty minutes away from where he lives and serve him up a tasty dish that would be to die for, but as of yet it hasn't happened."

"You wouldn't harm Joseph, would you?" asked Shona.

"You know he forced me out of the family home and threatened to shop me to the police years ago, so I have every right to get some form of revenge."

"You never actually told me why Joseph said and did what he did, but I guess you did something really bad to upset him. I hope you are not going to prepare us food to die for?"

"I promise you, and you can help prepare it if you like, that everything in this menu will be fresh and delicious and won't cause you or Jade any harm."

Chicken Tawa
Chana Masala
Mushroom Pilau Rice
Naan Bread
Chocolate Chilli Tart

"Perhaps Jade would like to help you make the bread if I give you the recipe," said Justin.

"I would like to do lots of things with Jade, but not under

these circumstances. Her mother must be going out of her mind with worry."

"You are her mother."

"You know what I mean."

"You can phone her when we get to Florida."

"Florida. I thought you said New York?"

"I thought Jade might like a trip to Disneyworld."

"Don't you think the FBI will put out an APB for us as soon as I tell Maisie where we are?"

"You will not tell her. All you will say is that Jade is ok."

"I am sorry, Justin, but this is a joke. You really are delusional if you think we can play happy families, and I am not going to stand for it."

Suddenly Justin snapped, grabbed Shona by the throat and forced her down onto a kitchen chair. Shona tried to move sideways and stand up again but Justin squeezed tighter and held her in position. Once Shona sat calmly, Justin let go of her and backed away a couple of paces. He then curled his mouth up at the corner and flicked his eyes up towards the ceiling as if he was thinking what to say next.

"If you want Michael to die, go into the other room, get Jade and walk out of the front door."

"This is all bravado, Justin. Yes, you're a bit of a bully, but I fell for you because of the softer, kinder side of your personality. In the main, I think you are fairly harmless other than the odd temper tantrum and that this talk of killing Michael is an idle threat."

"If I am harmless then Michael is fingerless," replied Justin.

Justin walked across to the fridge, opened the door and took out a metal baking tray, containing what appeared to be four human fingers. Shona recoiled in horror at the gruesome sight and ran across to the sink where she vomited profusely.

"One short, sharp chop with my Santoku knife was all it took

231

to ruin Michael's career as a journalist. A few sharp cuts with my other knives is all it has taken to ruin your business too, Shona."

Shona eventually stopped being sick, got up from the sink and stared straight at Justin with a thoughtful, quizzical look.

"Did you really think I would let you get away with what you did and have a relationship with someone else," said Justin.

"I was moving on with my life, as we only get one," replied Shona.

"Taking my money to buy a property and set up a cookery business using my teachings is one thing. Having my baby and not telling me about it is another thing, but my brain can't comprehend or forgive three acts of treachery."

"This isn't the fucking dark ages, Justin. It's the twenty-first century, where you can't own someone or prevent them from having a relationship that you don't approve of. And you certainly can't make me love you again or get on a plane and go to America with you."

"If you and Jade don't come to America with me you will have nothing here, as your love life is over and your business is over."

"My business is doing well and whatever you have done to Michael won't stop me from being with him or caring for him."

"Your business is over, Shona. Do you think people will hire you to cook for them, if they think they will be murdered the day after their dinner party?"

"What are you talking about?" asked Shona.

"Mrs Webb, Mr and Mrs Campbell, Mr Smith, Miss Page, and Mr and Mrs Price are all dead. One word to the local or national press about this, if they don't know already, and your business is definitely over, finished, kaput."

Reality suddenly hit home as Shona thought back to the day Amanda was attacked and the news bulletin she saw on TV about Mr Campbell. She then had a striking thought about the party at Kevin and Kate's house last night and pleaded with Justin.

"If I agree to come with you, will you agree not to kill Kevin or Kate Rogers or do any further harm to Michael?"

"Oh, I think I can manage that," said Justin.

CHAPTER TWENTY-SIX

Graham and Joseph were surprised to learn that Michael Black wasn't at home, particularly as he had been told of their impending visit. Graham wanted to go and have a chat with Richard Webb again but Joseph thought it more prudent to find out where Shona Green lived. Based on what he had learnt in the last fifteen minutes, he didn't expect to find her at home either, and he was right.

The neighbours told Graham that Shona had left her apartment around 11.00 a.m. and driven off on her own. This probably meant that she didn't kidnap her daughter but might be on the way to meet the person who did. Graham thought for a moment before asking Joseph if he thought the kidnapper could be Michael Black. He then phoned the police station and got the team to put out an alert for a blue Jeep. Even if the neighbour was wrong about the make and model of the car, the PNC data base would confirm the car Shona owns and its registration number. Any ANPR camera that she passed would pick her up, allowing the operators to transmit her location to Graham's team.

Graham and Joseph drove back to Castle Street and parked in the police compound. 'Lucky bastard!' thought Joseph. He hadn't been offered a special car park pass yet, so he still had to park by the racecourse and walk up the hill. Still it was a bit of exercise, which was all he was getting at the moment, other than when he was with Penny.

"Is Basil Reddy's solicitor here yet?" Graham asked Peter as they walked into the reception area.

"No, but I took a call from him to say he would be here about 9.30 p.m., as he has been away for the weekend."

"I won't be here then, Peter, as I've been on duty since 6.00 a.m. and need to be home by 8.00 p.m. as I have a dinner date."

"What does his solicitor look like?" asked Peter.

"He is a big man probably about six feet four inches tall and wide."

"Before I do manage to get away, Joseph and I are going upstairs to write up our notes for the chief's briefing tomorrow. Can you get some cover and join us to add your findings to the document we'll be producing, as we have to be watertight with this."

"No problem, sir. I think you may need this, too," said Peter, handing Graham an A4 envelope containing eight sheets of A4 paper.

Emma's report from the fire, coupled with the other information the team had gathered, was typed up in bullet-point format. Graham put a line through all of the covered whiteboard points at the same time as writing new ones on the board to make sure that all elements and findings were included. It made for very interesting reading.

~

Shona composed herself, left Justin to prepare the meal and went into the lounge to see Jade, who was still watching cartoons on the television.

"How are you, Jade? Have you been on the swings lately?"

"No, not since you met my mum in the park," she replied.

"I am sorry about your mum," said Shona, not really knowing if Maisie was ok or if Justin was telling the truth.

"Where is your dad at the moment?"

"Working away, somewhere abroad as far as I know, although Jessica says he will be home in few days or so when mum gets out of hospital."

"Are you being looked after here?"

"I felt a bit funny when I woke up this morning and was a bit scared, but Jessica assured me everything would be alright. I feel a bit happier now that you are here, Shona."

Jessica turned around to look at the television again and as far as Shona could tell, watch a programme with a character called Gumball. Shona walked across the lounge and sat next to Jessica.

"I didn't see you at Amanda's funeral, Jessica," said Shona very quietly.

"No, I couldn't face it," replied Jessica.

"Why was that? I gathered from over-hearing the conversations at Michael's dinner party that Amanda was your friend."

"No, she wasn't," said Jessica, glancing towards the kitchen.

"That's strange because I heard you talking to her at the party about Kevin Rogers and it seemed to me that some clandestine affair was going on between the two of them. I can't believe that Amanda would have been discussing something as sensitive as that with you if you weren't her friend."

"Did you tell Michael what you heard?"

"No! It was none of my business and I may have misheard what the two of you were saying," replied Shona.

"It's difficult for me to say much," said Jessica.

Shona remained quiet and thoughtful for a few seconds before asking Jessica how long she had lived in England.

"I think it's been about eight months."

"I am starting to get a few things straight in my mind now Jessica. Tell me, how did you meet Justin?"

"I initially tried to get a job at St Peters Garden Centre in Norton where Amanda worked, but they didn't have any vacancies so she got me a part-time job working for Kevin in his offices. Justin's name cropped up four or five months ago in one of my conversations with Kevin. I thought I'd heard Kevin talking to him on the phone quite a few times before that, though. Then out of the blue about two months ago I got a phone call from Justin offering me some extra work."

"As a babysitter?"

"Very funny! My main role is to collect or deliver parcels for him to various addresses throughout the UK, for which I get paid a very reasonable amount of money."

"You do know what was and will be in any future parcels?"

"I have an idea."

"I don't suppose you delivered a parcel to a flat in Evesham recently, did you?" asked Shona.

"Yes. Why?"

"I can't tell you that yet but I can tell you, that even if he didn't physically do it, Justin was somehow involved in the murder of Amanda."

Jessica looked away and then towards the dining room door and the kitchen with some fear in her eyes. Shona continued speaking to her quietly.

"Justin told me that Amanda was killed just to get at me, but he couldn't possibly have known I was cooking for her and Richard that night unless, of course, you told him afterwards?"

"No, I didn't I swear. I didn't even know about you and Justin until two days ago. Perhaps Kevin told him?"

The light bulb that was flickering inside Shona's head suddenly became a lot brighter. She looked at Jade, who was still engrossed watching another cartoon about a blue hedgehog, before turning back to face Jessica.

"My God, you didn't go to Amanda's funeral because you

have an idea or know why she was killed and you couldn't face seeing Richard."

The door from the dining room opened suddenly and Justin stood there with a face like thunder.

"Take Jade upstairs Shona," he said fiercely. "I want to have a word with Jessica, alone."

Shona did as she was told and prised Jade away from the television with a bit of bribery and they went upstairs to find a nicely decorated child's bedroom in neutral colours with various posters on the wall of pop groups and celebrities. There was a computer sitting on a small desk and just for a moment Shona thought she might be able to get a message to the outside world. Unfortunately, the laptop wasn't connected to the internet and Justin had taken Shona's phone off her when he blindfolded her earlier in the day. Shona had been annoyed by this ever since, as she really should have suspected prior to meeting Justin that he might take her mobile and hidden a spare one in one of her socks in case of an emergency.

"You don't happen to have a mobile phone on you Jade, do you? Justin took mine from me earlier to charge it up," said Shona, lying a little bit so as not to scare Jade in any way.

"No," she replied, "but we can play games on Justin's laptop."

Jade grabbed a hand controller and almost instantaneously, a wizard and an angel appeared on the screen. At that very same moment, Justin grabbed Jessica and dragged her outside into the garden.

"I told you not to mention Kevin to anyone," shouted Justin.

"I didn't mean to but Shona suddenly seemed to guess why Amanda was killed and who ordered the killing," replied Jessica.

"I thought I could trust you, Jessica, but I was wrong. I gave that weasel Baz a second chance and I have just heard from Kevin that he has let me down again by failing in his latest mission and has been arrested. He will now have to pay for his failure and pay quickly. I am not prepared to give you a second chance only to be let down at a later date, too."

Justin reached behind his back and with fast arm and hand speed flashed a blade towards Jessica's throat. With incredible reactions, Jessica swayed to the side and away from the knife. She then grabbed a compact from her pocket and threw it to the ground as if the action was part of some ritual and then planted her feet apart and raised her arms in combat mode. Justin stepped back to assess the situation as Jessica roared at him.

"I learnt the art of Maori hand-to-hand fighting, so if you want to kill me, let's see you try. I can tell by your muscle movements exactly where you are going to strike."

Justin planted his left foot and aimed the knife at Jessica's eyes, but she avoided this easily and plunged two fingers into Justin's throat with the speed of a cobra strike, causing him to cough and splutter. It was surprising how much this hurt, and it had the desired effect as far as Jessica was concerned, as Justin stopped the attack to deal with his pain. Jessica then raised her leg and kicked Justin hard on the knee with her heel which made him scream and then fall to the ground. As he fell, Jessica kicked him in the groin which caused the knife to fall from his grip. She then pounced like a tiger and kicked the knife far away towards the bushes, well out of Justin's reach. Jessica then ran down the garden and with the agility of a cat leapt up and over a wooden-panelled fence.

Justin clambered to his feet and thought about giving chase, but as he did so he looked up at the bedroom window to see Shona staring down at him. If he chased Jessica then Shona and Jade could also escape, and that would be a far worse situation, he decided in his somewhat scrambled brain. He went back into the kitchen and made a couple of phone calls to members of his gang, before racing upstairs and telling Shona and Jade in a surprisingly calm voice that they were leaving to go on a little trip within the next ten minutes.

"Aren't we going to eat first?" said Shona.

"No, we don't have time now."

"But I'm hungry," exclaimed Jade.

"We'll grab a Burger King on the way to the airport, petal."

"Are we going on a plane?" asked Jade.

"Yes; we are having a holiday until your mum is better."

"Can I see her before we go?"

"No, she is in quarantine, if you know what that means?"

"Isn't that where animals go sometimes?"

"Yes. Your mum has a virus similar to the Ebola virus and she has to stay in a room on her own until she gets better. You will see her again when we get back, so don't worry."

"Will I miss school?"

"Yes, I am afraid so."

"My mum and dad might get fined if I don't get permission to go on holiday."

"That's a stupid system. Your parents or guardians should be the ones to decide if you can take time away from school. If they aren't capable of doing that, they surely can't be capable or accountable for your general well-being every day or night. I will make sure that your mum and dad don't get a fine, if you quickly go and pack your trolley bag with all of the clothes and toiletries that you want to take with you, said Justin."

"I only have what I am wearing," said Shona.

"I got someone to buy Jade quite a few clothes yesterday. I'll buy you a new wardrobe when we get to America," said Justin.

"Are we going to Disneyworld?" asked Jade.

"Yes, if you get a move on," replied Justin with some exasperation.

"Yippee!" shouted Jade.

"Hurry up then, petal. We don't want to keep Goofy waiting, do we? And I'm not talking about Shona," said Justin, while actually laughing for the first time in a long while, without realising he was still being hurtful.

CHAPTER TWENTY-SEVEN

William Skinner from Skinner and Skinner Solicitors arrived at the Worcester police station at 9.00 p.m. He introduced himself to Adam Osborne, the late shift desk sergeant, and gave him his business card.

"Has my client Mr Reddy been formally charged with any offence yet?" Mr Skinner asked the sergeant.

"He has been arrested on suspicion of the murder of a local woman, Amanda Webb, and an arson attack on a cricket pavilion. The DCI is also considering charging your client with attempted burglary and attempted GBH following an incident on a farm."

"How long has he been held here?"

"Twenty-three hours in total, during which time he has refused to speak or answer any questions without representation and insisted upon his own solicitor, even though we offered to provide a duty solicitor for him."

"You do realise that Mr Reddy will have to be released or charged tomorrow morning?"

"The DCI has applied for an extension, but the plan is to have him charged and up before the magistrate tomorrow afternoon, once he has been interviewed tomorrow morning in your presence."

"Please can you show me where Mr Reddy is being held, as I would like to speak with him before the formal interview."

Adam took William Skinner downstairs to the holding cells, where he opened the door to the cell Baz was being detained in. Baz appeared to be sleeping on a bench facing the wall but stirred upon hearing the door open and started to sit up, so Adam allowed William in and shut the door behind him.

"I'll be back in fifteen minutes," said Adam, as he locked the cell door.

William walked across the floor and stood over Baz, who was surprised to see a huge man in a suit, with a briefcase in front of him.

"Who are you?" said Baz.

"I am your Fairy God Mother," said William.

"Where is Mr Lock, my usual brief," asked Baz.

"He couldn't make it today, so I'm here to stop you from going to prison."

"How are you going to do that?" replied Baz.

William Skinner bent down to get something out of his case and brought out a small syringe, which he stabbed into Baz's arm.

"The DJ wanted me to cut out your tongue with scissors, but I told him that was too messy and that a short sharp injection of potassium cyanide would do the job just the same."

No sooner had Mr Skinner finished speaking, Baz lost control of his muscles and collapsed back on to the bench. William Skinner, also known as the Hulk because of his size, picked Baz up and laid him back down on the bench in the foetal position facing the wall to look like he was still sleeping. He put the syringe back into his briefcase, glancing at the scissors in the side pocket. He would love to cut the end of Basil Reddy's tongue off and give it to the DJ as a trophy, but couldn't take the risk that the blood would be noticed by the desk sergeant.

Adam returned to see Mr Skinner standing in the middle of

the cell punching keys on his tablet.

"Mr Reddy is being childish and refuses to speak to anyone other than Mr Lock," said William.

"Mr Lock was here the last time Mr Reddy was held in these cells," said Adam.

"Can I talk to you in private out of Mr Reddy's earshot for a minute?" William asked Adam.

Adam took a cursory glance at Baz sleeping or sulking and pulled the cell door shut behind them. They walked back up the stairs to the main reception area where William distracted Adam even further by showing him a fake picture of a large house with a beautiful girl standing naked outside the front door.

"This is Mr Reddy's house with his lovely Croatian girlfriend standing outside their front door on a hot summer's day," said William.

"Blimey," said Adam. "They say crime doesn't pay!"

"We know Mr Reddy and we know what he does to earn his money. We also know he is a real scumbag. It hurts to have to defend someone like him when we think he is probably guilty, but he pays well and we are obliged to do our best for him because of this," said William quietly. He then continued in a louder voice to thank Adam for listening before saying his goodbyes and disappearing out of the front door.

Once outside, the Hulk turned left and walked to the top of Castle Street where he turned right onto Foregate Street and then right again down Shaw Street. Just before he entered the nightclub for a pint or three, he phoned the DJ to tell him that the job was done.

"We have another problem," said the DJ, then explaining what had happened with Jessica.

"I'm nearly at Lasham airport near Alton in Hampshire," the DJ informed the Hulk, so you and the Fixer need to deal with

Jessica before she gets to the police."

"What are you doing there?" asked the Hulk.

"I have an acquaintance who works there as an engineer maintaining Boeing and Airbus aircraft. He has his own private Cessna Mustang and is going to take me, Shona and Jade to Dublin. We are going to spend time there before getting a flight to Orlando on Tuesday."

"I'll make a phone call or two, but I do know where Jessica lives so the problem will not exist for too long," said the Hulk.

Shona was sitting in the back of the car with Jade and was glad that her daughter was listening to music with her headphones on rather than listen to Justin as he rambled on and on during their journey from Worcester. It was a journey that seemed to take forever, but it did give Shona time to think and to wonder how such an intelligent man could be such a cruel, sick bastard. She had absolutely no interest in what Justin was saying and often pretended she couldn't hear him speak because of the traffic and road noise. She grunted in the appropriate places where necessary to stop Justin from getting angry, but all the time she was thinking about Michael, where he was being held, if he was really hurt and how she could prevent herself and Jade from getting on the flight to America without Michael being killed. She kept thinking how stupid she had been to believe Michael would have sold her down the river to Justin. She also kept thinking how stupid she was to let Justin take her mobile phone off her, although in reality there was little she could have done to stop him. There was probably little she could do between here and Dublin to get word to her mum and dad or the police, but she hoped that somewhere, at some point in the city, she could get a few minutes away from Justin without him getting suspicious and give him a reason to hurt or kill more people, especially Michael or his sister Kate.

The road signposted to Alton off the M3 was long and

winding with very few street lights, other than in some of the small villages they passed through such as Odiham and South Warnborough. Shona was struggling to come to terms with the way her life had changed in the last couple of days and she wondered what dark, winding road she was really on. She hoped that Jessica could find the right road and report what she knew to the police before her lights were turned off. If Jessica wasn't able to get help and Shona wasn't able to get some time alone within the next twenty-four or forty-eight hours, it might well be that she would never see her friends and relatives or Michael ever again. She was trying to think clearly and logically, but everything was a bit of a blur and her fear of what Justin could do, should everything not go the way he wanted, was unthinkable.

CHAPTER TWENTY-EIGHT

Jessica hoped she could get to the police station, too. After climbing the first fence, she jumped over a few more and ran as fast as she could across some fields before getting to a main road. She didn't dare walk or run along this road in case Justin came looking for her in his car. She didn't dare contemplate thumbing a lift, as knowing her luck it would be Justin who stopped. She didn't dare contemplate going home either, as she knew that the gang knew where she lived and that one of them would most likely be waiting for her. She cut off down a small side road instead and aimed towards some lights in the distance that appeared to come from a village. After about an hour of walking and hiding among bushes, Jessica saw a sign for a guest house with vacancies and decided to knock on the door and rent a room for the night. This would give her time to get her head together and come up with a feasible story that wouldn't land her in trouble and a true story that would get Justin arrested.

~

The shit really hit the fan inside Worcester police station at 7.00 a.m. on Monday morning after Adam went to look in on Baz in his cell and found him dead. DCI Graham Laws went ballistic when he arrived at 7.30 a.m., as did Chief Constable Simon Duncan when he reported for work at 8.00 a.m.

"We will have to report this to the Independent Police Complaints Commission," said Simon. Then looking directly at Adam, he added, "Until such time as there is an enquiry Adam, you are to be suspended from duty."

Adam had been an officer for almost five years, having previously worked within the prison service. He loved his job here at the Castle Street station and the news hit him like a stone, even though he had been expecting it.

"Is that really necessary?" asked Graham.

"You know the rules, Graham. Even if Mr Reddy was a toerag we have to establish how he died, inform his next of kin somehow and inform the coroner and the Crown Prosecution Service."

"I was actually looking forward to this morning's meeting, sir," said Graham.

"It's always the way, isn't it. Experience should tell you not to look forward to anything as it will always be a disappointment," replied Simon.

"I was working well into the night preparing the report that you've been waiting for since the day of the bomb blast. A report that clearly clarifies how and why the events of the last few weeks have come about, and who is responsible. I was actually looking forward to seeing your face when I told you we had one of the perpetrators in a cell downstairs."

"Oh! You saw my face alright, Graham, but it wasn't the one you thought you would see, was it!"

"No, sir."

"How the fuck did this happen, after all the procedures we have put in place over the years? Outside of the Met, there have been sixteen prisoner deaths in police custody this year and we hadn't had one. Until now that is, which is why I am so bloody angry about it."

"The only excuse I can offer is that Adam was very busy and

was under too much pressure last night, due to the lack of resources we have here now following the staff cuts."

"It always comes back to that when we cock up, doesn't it?"

"Adam is a good officer, so it's the only excuse I can offer at the moment. In truth, you could blame me, as I had Peter working on some investigative work to try and get these murders solved and didn't give Adam any cover."

"Let's hope for both our sakes that your report is worth waiting for and is something I can use to alleviate some of the crushing pressure that is going to come my way from all sides this week."

"If you and Benjamin can come to the training room in half an hour, I'll get everybody else together and tell you what we have established."

"Let's make sure we start dead on 9.00 a.m., as I suspect we have about an hour to kill until the pathologist arrives to do the post-mortem on Mr Reddy."

There was a strange atmosphere among those sitting around the table in the meeting room as Graham stood up and opened his notebook.

"Hello, everybody, I am not going to say good morning as the events of the last twelve hours are certainly not good. What I am about to tell you however is good and will help improve morale, which has been rather low of late, as we have struggled to come to terms with the number of crimes that have happened in such a short time frame."

"I am going to start with Mr Basil Reddy, who was here in the cells following his arrest on Saturday night but has since passed away. I am unable to tell you how he died yet, but we have reported the incident and a post-mortem will be carried out this morning. Emma and her team with the help of the lab technicians have confirmed via the blood and semen samples found at Mrs Amanda Webb's house that Mr Reddy was the

251

person who attacked her. We also know with the help of an informant that he was involved in the bomb blast, as the donut-shaped button badge found at the scene had been ordered on the internet as a present for Mr Reddy by a friend of his when he was studying at Worcester University. Within the last twenty minutes I have just taken a very interesting call from a woman named Jessica Chalmers, who intimated that the murder of Amanda Webb was ordered by a Mr Kevin Rogers with whom she was having an affair. By all accounts, he had recently dumped Mrs Webb in favour of another woman, and Amanda was going to tell Mr Rogers wife, who just happens to be the sister of Michael Black, who has recently gone missing. The intriguing thing about this is that Joseph has literally just established that Amanda Webb had already told her husband Richard that she was leaving him. This wasn't as a result of her affair, it was due to the fact they had grown apart and Mr Webb had been spending a lot of money on an Asian girl who was sending him secret posts on Facebook.

"If you are struggling to take all this in and think it's all very confusing so far, it gets much more so.

"Richard Webb travels to Bangladesh on business quite a lot, which is where he met the Asian girl called Amolika. She was a prostitute in the port of Goalundo Ghat where approximately one thousand five hundred women sell sex to over three thousand men each day for very little money. Richard fell in love with Amolika, and in return for many sexual services, he paid her over the odds so that she could pay off her debt to her local madam. This, in effect, bought Amolika her freedom, after which Richard helped her get a job in a knife-making factory in Dhaka. It was at this point that Amolika started badgering and in effect blackmailing Richard via Facebook to help her get to England. Amanda logged on to Richard's laptop one day after he left it at home and happened to see an email sent from the

Dhaka knife factory's web domain by Amolika, which left her in no doubt as to what had been going on. This is why she checked his personal bank account and why she finally made up her mind to leave him."

Chief Constable Simon Duncan interrupted Graham at that point with a very pertinent question.

"You say that Mrs Webb's murder was ordered by Kevin Rogers. It would seem logical to me if Mrs Webb was going to leave her husband that Mr Webb may have commissioned it from a financial point of view."

"We still have to investigate that theory, sir," said Graham, "but there is another element that we can be certain of."

"Thanks to Joseph's chums in the CIA, we know that the knife factory has closed down and that the owner, who was being investigated for an illegal organised kidney trading racket, has disappeared. The Bangladesh government provided the CIA with documentation that confirms the owner took with him some 350,000 Bangladeshi Taka, which is some £3,000 that was paid to him by a Mr Justin Johnson on the recommendation of Richard Webb for the manufacture of a high quality set of kitchen knives. We know that Justin met with Richard in a street café in Goalundo Ghat where he was working as a chef, and under the pretence of meeting food suppliers within the main seating area, was actually arranging the sale of many illegal drugs."

"When you first interviewed Richard Webb he said he didn't know of a Justin Johnson," said Jane.

"That's correct, but he also said his marriage was strong, and that was a lie too," replied Graham.

"We know that there could be a connection between Basil Reddy and Justin Johnson, so maybe it was Justin that sent Baz to Mr Webb's house to send a warning to Richard to pay him back the money the factory owner took," said Emma.

"Baz wasn't known to be a killer, so it could be that the situation got out of control," said Graham.

"If that is the case, why would the phone caller suggest that Kevin Rogers ordered the killing?" replied Emma.

"We don't know the answer to that yet," said Graham.

"What we do know is that the second victim, a Mr Harold Campbell, and his wife Elspeth, were marijuana users and had been since the 1960s. Mrs Campbell is still recovering in hospital but was able to give us a photofit of the man from whom they had been obtaining the drug for the last five years."

Graham held up a police artist's drawing and then handed it to Peter to circulate internally and via the local media to see if he could get a name, but he had a suspicion this was going to be Kevin Rogers.

"Mrs Campbell thinks her husband was murdered because he refused to pay for their last batch, as the quality wasn't up to the usual standard."

"Joseph, however," continued Graham, "thinks that Mr Campbell was murdered by Justin Johnson, as was Luke Smith and Kylie Page, because they selected Shona Green to do some catering for them."

"How do you work that out, Graham?" asked Assistant Chief Constable Lewis.

"A matter of deduction, Benjamin, following a conversation I had with Michael Black the other day. It would appear that all of the people murdered or attacked, and this includes Mrs Webb, had employed Shona Green, who happens to be Mr Black's girlfriend, to provide them with food for their dinner parties."

"Why would that be a reason to kill people?" said Benjamin.

"Shona allegedly fleeced Justin for a substantial amount of money a few years ago in a roundabout way and at this stage I have to assume it was used to set up her business. Justin is certainly one to bear a grudge and Joseph wouldn't put it past him to make Shona pay for her actions."

"Surely, no one could be so callous as to kill innocent people just to get their own back on a person who's wronged them?" said Jane.

"He killed his own father, my wonderful dad," said Joseph, choosing this to be the moment when the team really needed to see what type of person they were after.

A gasp went around the room and everybody sat silently, trying to take in what Joseph had said, before Graham brought proceedings back to the present.

"I am sorry to learn of this Joseph, and everything that is happening here in Worcester at the moment must bring some terrible memories back to you. I did a bit of research the other day when you first mentioned your brother to me, and it would appear he was initially on a wanted list for allegedly committing an assault and a rape on a young woman almost seven years ago. A young woman by the name of Shona Pascoe, as was her name at the time, before she changed it by deed poll a few months after the incident."

Another gasp went around the room, which allowed Emma the time to stand up and speak.

"If I may say something, ladies and gentleman. I have some other important information that's relevant to our investigations. Luke Smith and Kylie Page were also drug users, as we found cocaine in their blood. We couldn't get any trace evidence from the murder scene to help us catch the killer or killers, as those responsible were exceptionally clever and covered every angle. Peter has been doing a bit of digging though and has established that Luke Smith originally came from a place called Sedgefield where his family started importing and then manufacturing martial arts weapons. Peter asked to see records of all recent sales, and what do you know:

intriguingly, a Miss Jessica Chalmers ordered a Roiyaru Katana at a cost of £1,900 about a month ago, and it was collected by a man whose ID suggested his name was DJ Macintyre. There is nothing unusual about that you might think, but he paid for it with a credit card in the name of Justin Macintyre."

"Well, well, well," said the chief constable. "We now have an idea how this Mr Johnson gained entry to the UK and why he doesn't appear on MI5's radar."

"If he's still in the country, we can stop him getting out of it now," said Graham.

"You don't actually have any hard and fast evidence to pick him up though, do you?" said Benjamin.

"We do have some DNA from the skull and crossbones rabbit," replied Graham. "If it does match the DNA from the knife found by detectives in Shona Pascoe-stroke-Green's house all those years ago then we can at least put Justin Johnson at the scene of the Grafton Woods murder. We do believe with some certainty that Kevin Rogers has also been to Grafton Woods recently, because Peter has established that Kevin's wife Kate placed an order on the internet some time ago for a set of cufflinks with, you've guessed, it 1776 stamped on them."

"How are you getting on with the knives, Peter?" asked Chief Constable Duncan, in a matter of fact tone that suggested no praise was forthcoming for the work Peter had put into his research.

"It is a very long process and we haven't had a breakthrough yet, but Peter did a great job getting the information on the Samurai purchase," interjected Graham, trying to keep his team motivated.

"I wondered what a roy-something-or-other was," said Simon.

"It is a high quality Japanese sword and is probably their

flagship model. It features a hand-forged, folded, sharpened and polished high carbon Japanese steel blade with 1,024 layers. The model ordered was a limited edition and it has pure silver fittings with a floral motif that only really appeals to the discriminating collector or serious practitioner."

"Whatever turns you on," said Simon. "But I can think of better things to spend £2,000 on," he added.

"How much was your set of golf clubs, Simon?" asked Benjamin.

"Moving on," replied Simon. "I've heard the name Kevin Rogers bandied about before. What do we have on him?"

"He runs a haulage company, transporting goods all over the UK and Europe," said Graham. "I have suspected him of drug trafficking for some time, but as of yet we haven't been able to get any evidence on him that would stand up in court. We had an inkling that he was pulling the strings of the gang we busted in Kempsey, but nobody would talk. I also suspect he was the supplier of the drugs to Mr and Mrs Campbell."

"How did we find out about that warehouse in Kempsey?" asked Assistant Chief Constable Benjamin Lewis.

"We got a tip-off from Michael Black who happened to have been told about the comings and goings at that particular place by a member of the public who he was interviewing about the NHS in respect of the provision of drugs for cancer patients," replied Graham.

"It's ironic and somewhat hard to understand in this day and age that Mr Black would grass up his brother-in-law and risk upsetting his sister, don't you think?" said Benjamin.

"Mr Black's tip-off never became public knowledge. Either he doesn't like his brother-in-law or didn't know that he had anything to do with that warehouse. What it does say to me is that Michael is more likely to be a victim in all of this rather than being a party to any murder."

"Do we have anything concrete to link Kevin Rogers and Justin Johnson together?" asked Benjamin.

"We're getting there," replied Graham.

"Joseph and I were talking very early this morning in the canteen. All of the links we know about can't just be coincidence but they wouldn't stand up in court yet."

Graham walked across to the whiteboards and added a few more bullet points to them:

Kevin Rogers – Drug Trafficker
Michael Black – Informant
Kate Rogers – Kevin's Wife and Sister
Shona Green – Mr Black's Girlfriend
Justin Johnson – Drug dealer/Shona's former Boyfriend
Jessica Chalmers – May know all of the above people?

"There could be another angle to all of this," said Bea.

"Mr Rogers may have wanted revenge on Mr Black but couldn't hurt him or murder him himself for fear of upsetting or losing his wife. He could however try to punish Michael through Miss Green who somehow just happened to have come into his life at the same time as Joseph's brother was planning his revenge against her."

"That's an interesting notion. I think we should pick Mr Rogers up and see what he has to say. But before that, Bea, I think it is important to tell the meeting what you, Peter and Emma discovered following the barn fire out towards Cradley."

"The barn was being used for the growing of cannabis from which both marijuana and hash were being produced, as was BHO – which stands for Butane Hash or Honey Oil. I'm not an expert and don't pretend to understand all of the processes, but it appears that the use of BHO has grown exponentially over the last few years. It's made by placing marijuana in a container and pushing butane through the container in such a way that it will escape but leave the plant inside devoid of its cannabinoids. Don't ask me to explain any more than to say these are chemical compounds within the plant and that the liquid mixture that escapes the container is allowed to drip into a tray. What people do with the liquid after that is beyond me, but what I can tell you is that the whole process is extremely dangerous and was the cause of the fire at the barn. Mr Thompson, the owner of the barn, is claiming no knowledge of the activities taking place within the barn and at the moment we have no evidence to suggest otherwise. What we do know however is that the barn was being rented by a company called Worcester Global Hauliers whose managing director is Mrs Kate Rogers."

Graham started to wind up the meeting by asking if anybody had any further questions. There were quite a few although most of them related to the death of Basil Reddy and what would happen to Adam.

Just as Graham thanked everybody for attending and was asking Peter and a team of officers to visit Mr and Mrs Rogers at their home, Joseph got a text from Penny. It was short and to the point but it was very apt and very welcome in light of the meeting that was just concluding.

CHAPTER TWENTY-NINE

"We don't need to make a house call, Graham, as my informant has just told me that Mr Kevin Rogers is standing talking to a strange-looking tattooed man on the corner of Pump Street."

Graham rushed along the corridor and barked an order for a team of officers to be despatched to Pump Street via Charles Street, The Shambles and High Street, and for a squad car to be sent down Fish Street. He then rushed down the stairs himself, hoping that this exercise wasn't just a red herring.

The Fixer was talking to the Chameleon when he glanced up to see a number of police officers walking briskly towards the place where they were standing.

"Time to split," said the Fixer, and he set off on a sprint towards the Elgar statue and the cathedral.

As he ran, Kevin wondered if a church or cathedral was still deemed a place of sanctuary. He had an idea, however, that this right was abolished by an Act of Parliament in the seventeenth century. Kevin ran across the road, down College Yard and into the cathedral via the north porch. He knew his way around the building and also knew one or two places where he might be able to hide.

Kevin turned left and ran down past the prayer candle stands and up the quire steps. He then zig-zagged left past St George's Chapel and around behind the high altar until he came to the

Earl of Dudley's tomb. Here, Kevin tried to squeeze between the serpentinite pillars and press himself against the far alabaster end that was partly hidden by some chairs within the Lady Chapel. He didn't feel safe here so he sprinted past Prince Arthur's chantry, which was built in the sixteenth century to house Henry VII eldest son's tomb, and down the stairs of the south aisle into the crypt.

He continued between the Jurassic limestone pillars and into the prayer room where he quickly took a hooded fleece from the holdall he had been carrying and put it on. He sat on a chair in silence with his head bowed for twenty minutes without moving a muscle or attempting to look up or behind. He hoped the police officers would think he had gone back outside the cathedral through one of the exits. Kevin then looked at his watch, stood up and leaving his holdall under the chair slowly made his way out of the prayer room and across the stone floor of the crypt where he turned right and carefully went up the narrow steps and out into the nave. Kevin picked up a leaflet from a nearby display unit and trying to look like a tourist, walked into the cloisters. He thought about having a cup of tea in the café but carried on walking past a little courtyard and out via the south exit towards the college green on the east bank of the River Severn.

'That was close,' Kevin thought to himself as he strolled nonchalantly down the path towards the Severn Way and then along the edge of the river towards the city centre. Just as he got to the St Andrew's Garden of Remembrance, five police officers rushed out from behind some bushes and made a beeline for him. Kevin turned and ran down South Parade where he hoped he could cut up Bridge Street and get lost among the shoppers. He didn't account for some cyclists riding along the path and as he swerved to avoid them Kevin slipped and fell into the ice cold water of the river. He started to swim downstream towards a small pleasure boat that was coming his way, in the hope he could climb aboard and escape by taking control of it. The boat moved faster than he did though and as a result he got nowhere near to it. One of the officers then shouted to him to give himself up as the river is the longest in the United Kingdom at some 220 miles and he would drown before he escaped the long arm of the law, which might not be very long should he start to go under.

~

Yesterday's hour-long flight from Lasham to Dublin actually seemed to take forever, as it started to get dark and then rain heavily. Jade found the whole experience exciting, but Shona was scared of flying, which was the reason she hadn't visited too many places abroad during her lifetime. Shona was glad when it got dark because she struggled to cope with seeing clouds of irregular shapes go past the aeroplane's windows at different angles to the horizon, as this kept making her think they might be going to crash. She knew in her mind that the pilot was well trained and that these thoughts were illogical, but it was the same fear as having a tiny spider placed on your hand and believing that it could hurt you in some way.

The landing was smoother than Shona had anticipated, considering it was rather windy, and she heaved a sigh of relief when the Cessna came to a halt. She hoped in her heart that this whole episode would soon come to a halt, and that somehow she could avoid going to America, even if Jade was looking forward to it. Shona had about twenty-four hours to do something positive and get her and Jade out of the clutches of Justin or whatever his name was now. She hoped that tomorrow would come slowly and that some miracle would happen in the meantime.

~

Jessica hired a taxi to take her to the Castle Street police station. Unfortunately for her, she arrived in the foyer at the same time as Kevin Rogers was being dragged into the building, kicking and screaming and demanding to see his solicitor. Kevin looked across at Jessica and shouted at her, "You evil cow, you're fired."

Kevin was taken to the interview room and made to sit on a wooden chair. Graham walked around the room studying Kevin carefully. He then turned the opposite chair around and sat facing its back while leaning on it with his elbows.

"Your solicitor has been contacted and she will be here in twenty minutes," said Graham.

"You don't have any justification for arresting me," said Kevin aggressively.

"Why did you assume my officers were coming after you and run away then?"

"You lot have always been trying to pin things on me, including that Kempsey drugs haul."

"So you didn't have any drugs on you and you weren't passing some to a Mr C Hunter?"

"No."

"He might look tough with all of his tattoos, but he's a bit of an old woman really and I think he'll squeal if we bargain with him, considering the street value of the drugs he was carrying," said Graham.

"He's a tough man and he won't tell you anything," replied Kevin.

"If we can get the feminine side of him to come out and get him to talk, you might take a look at his name and call him something else," said Graham with a smile on his face.

"I need a cigarette," said Kevin.

"Technically, under the 2006 legislation, this is a place of work so smoking isn't allowed, but I may make an exception as there is only you and me in this room. I will be legally obliged to take it off you when your solicitor gets here. I'll call upstairs to see if anybody has a packet. Do you have a brand preference, Mr Rogers?"

"Marlboro Lights if possible," said Kevin.

Graham smiled to himself as his trick had worked. He had no intention of allowing Kevin to smoke, but it confirmed his suspicions that he was involved with the bombing of the cricket pavilion and he looked forward to the questioning in half an hour or so.

~

A taxi had picked up Justin, Shona and Jade yesterday evening and taken them from the airport, through the city centre, down O'Connell Street, along by the River Liffey and then down past the Guinness Storehouse and along James's Walk before stopping outside some terraced houses.

"I thought we would be staying at a hotel," said Shona when they arrived.

"An associate of mine has an older brother who owns this place, so it makes sense to stay here as it is free and close to all of the tourist attractions for Jade to enjoy. It also has a nice kitchen, which will give you a chance to impress me with your culinary skills."

"We are only here for two nights, so surely it would be better to go out and appreciate some of Dublin's finest eateries such as Chameleon or Quays Irish restaurant?" said Shona.

"I am impressed with your knowledge of the city, Shona, and it would be good to go to Chameleon as a friend of mine owns it, but I need to know if my investment in your business has been a sound one, so I want you to cook Jade and me a lovely

265

three-course meal tomorrow. Tonight, however, I will order an Indian takeaway to compensate for the meal I wasn't able to cook earlier in the day."

Unfortunately for Shona, tomorrow did come sooner than she had hoped. As she got up on Monday morning, she questioned Justin about the day's plan of action and his expectations of her in the kitchen. The more time she had in the city, the greater were her chances of getting help.

"I don't have any ingredients or my set of kitchen knives," said Shona trying to get out of doing any cooking.

"I have my knives in my suitcase and I have arranged for a local company to deliver a number of components and ingredients in the next half an hour or so," replied Justin, handing Shona the menu he wanted her to cook for him later in the day.

Chicken Liver Pâté with Salad
Sea Bream with Crushed Potatoes
Individual Strawberry Cheesecakes
or
Individual Lemon Soufflés

"Jade doesn't like fish," said Shona.

"Well, you'll have to be creative, then. You have a few hours to think about it as we are going to explore Dublin. I thought Jade would like to go to the castle and the zoo," said Justin.

~

Kevin's solicitor, Fiona Connor, arrived slightly earlier than expected, and as Graham knew her, she was allowed five minutes on her own with her client before the formal interview procedure commenced. Kevin was acting a bit cocky at the start of proceedings, but his solicitor advised him to calm down, say as little as possible and only speak when required to do so. Initially, Kevin was certain that the police had little or no evidence to go on and would not be able to keep him at the station for any longer than the time the interview would take. As the minutes ticked by, he became more withdrawn and looked to his solicitor for advice on numerous occasions before answering any questions.

Graham had asked Bea to sit in on the interview as he felt certain she would be able to detect when Kevin was lying, as he knew he would be on a number of occasions. Graham had decided to be straight and to the point this time, giving Kevin some easy questions and some provoking ones which he already knew the answer to. This would help Bea interpret Kevin's own personal body language which in turn would help Graham with his approach throughout the process.

Nobody outside of the police force knew of the death of Basil Reddy yet, which Graham was pleased about as he was going to try and use this to his advantage.

"As well as Cameron Hunter, we have Basil Reddy locked up here," said Graham before asking Kevin the first question.

"Mr Reddy is suggesting that you were helping him out at the cricket pavilion next to the main county ground recently and that it is you who knows how to use acetone peroxide."

"I don't know a Mr Reddy, anything about any bomb blast or what acetone peroxide is," said Kevin.

"I didn't mention a bomb blast," said Graham.

"I heard about it on the news," replied Kevin.

"It seems odd that Mr Reddy says you were there the night before the blast and that the stub of a cigarette we found at the scene is the same brand as the one you have just asked to smoke," said Graham.

"I walk across that cricket pitch a lot," said Kevin.

"I suppose you walk through Grafton Woods a lot too?"

Kevin whispered something to his solicitor who answered the question for his client.

"My client has had the opportunity to walk through that local beauty spot on quite a few occasions."

"Did you happen to lose anything while out walking there recently?" asked Graham.

"I did lose a set of cufflinks a while ago," said Kevin.

"Another oddity then, as we just happened to find one cufflink right next to the tree where the body of an old man called Mr Campbell was found," said Graham.

"That doesn't prove that my client had anything to do with a murder and that is probably just a coincidence," suggested Kevin's solicitor.

"I didn't mention a murder," said Graham having a bit of fun with the two people sitting opposite him.

"I heard about it on the news," said Fiona.

"Is it a coincidence that your client would appear from my earlier observations to take size ten shoes and that imprints of a size ten shoe were found at the cricket ground and in the woods?"

"Lots of people have size ten feet," said Kevin, jumping in with both of his before Fiona could speak.

"We have identified the footwear as being a Nike Air Force 1 training shoe and I believe that you may well be wearing that same said brand at the moment," said Graham rather smugly.

"Lots of people all over the world wear Nike shoes," replied Fiona.

"That is true, Fiona," said Graham. "In the United States, the Air Force 1 is the sneaker most often encountered at crime scenes, turning up in almost twenty percent of cases. Criminals here in the UK are aware of this and other such data and use research to try and beat the legal system. Unfortunately for them, our forensics methods are getting more and more sophisticated. The fact that the imprints left at the scene of both crimes were only partials, would have made identification virtually impossible a few years ago, but today we have the help of a new database called SoleMate, developed by a company in Evesham, that is an enormous help in our battle to get criminals brought to justice."

"That still doesn't prove my client was at the scene of either crime," said Fiona.

"I will be able to tell you one way or the other once we have taken his trainers for analysis," said Graham, who continued to take a hard and tactical line by now switching the questioning to the murder of Amanda Webb. There wasn't any firm evidence to suggest Kevin was physically present on that fateful night, but Graham wanted to test his metal before ordering a DNA test.

"Tell me about your relationship with Mrs Amanda Webb," Graham asked Kevin.

"I knew her fairly well as my wife was her friend," replied Kevin.

"We understand that you were having an affair with her."

"I don't know where you get that idea from."

"So you weren't sleeping with her then?"

"No, I was not!," exclaimed Kevin aggressively.

"In that case," said Graham, taking a stab in the dark through gritted teeth, "we will have to charge you with her murder, because we found some Air Force 1 size ten footprints at the premises and I am sure that some of your hair follicles and skin flakes will be among the trace evidence collected from her bedroom."

"I would like some time to speak with my solicitor alone," said Kevin.

"Interview suspended at 1.25 p.m.," said Graham.

"Come on, Bea, let's go and talk to Mr Hunter in the other room for a while," he added, as the interview room door was closed.

CHAPTER THIRTY

Before Graham could get to speak to Cameron Hunter, Peter suggested he take some time to talk to the young girl who came into the station at exactly the same time as Kevin Rogers. Graham was about to decline the opportunity but changed his mind when told her name was Jessica Chalmers.

"By the way," added Peter, "the pathologist has done his job and Mr Reddy's body has been taken to the morgue. Jane has made contact with members of the deceased's family and they have given us some very interesting information."

Peter handed Graham a piece of paper, which he looked at and then asked Peter to get Joseph onto it straight away.

"Help Joseph pull a few strings and ask him to meet me here in the foyer in two hours' time, with his passport," he added.

"One other thing, Graham, I've had a bit of luck locating a purchaser of three different Kai Shun knives in one single transaction."

"Fantastic, is it anyone we know?" asked Graham.

"The knives were bought from a cookshop in South Molton, Devon, by a Mr Luca Zini, who happens to be the general manager of the Chocolate Elephant round the corner."

"Fucking hell," said Graham, who then took a few seconds thinking time before continuing. "I feel like I've been riding on the Colossus for a lifetime already, Peter, and now there is another twist and turn. Get some officers together and go and pick him up. I don't have time to interview him today, as you are probably aware, so maybe you can do it with the assistant chief constable and Bea, if Benjamin can spare the time?"

"No problem, sir, I'm fully up to speed with everything."

"I doubt Mr Zini has a record of any sort or we would have heard about it. The fact that he has purchased a set of knives maybe coincidental, so you probably won't be able to hold him until I get back," said Graham.

"I will do my best, but if it doesn't happen, I'll make sure that constables Bill Wood and Ben Tyler keep watch on him. I'll also ask Benjamin to get me a warrant so they can poke around in the nightclub."

"You might want to rephrase that sentence," said Graham as he left Peter and headed into a side room to speak with Jessica Chalmers.

~

Justin and Jade enjoyed their day out in Dublin. Shona didn't enjoy her day much, as her whole focus was on other things. She did try to get a bit of time and space away from Justin, but he wouldn't let her out of his sight. He even stood right outside the ladies toilets listening, just in case Shona asked someone to lend her their mobile phone for a minute or two. Shona was uptight and frustrated when they got back to the terraced house and she didn't really have the inclination to cook a three-course meal, but she didn't dare make Justin angry. Her logic told her to play along, keep him sweet, plant one of his knives in his cabin bag so that it got picked up on the scanners at the airport and make her escape among the crowds while he was being questioned.

~

Graham informed Joseph of everything that had gone on in the interview rooms during the previous few hours, while they travelled in the back of a police car making its way north up the M5 and onto the M42. Cameron Hunter was charged with possession of Class B drugs and released on bail, having provided a DNA sample and had his fingerprints taken. Jessica had helped Graham fill in some of the blanks in his thought processes and had made his job of getting Kevin Rogers locked up a little easier. Kevin refuted any notion that he had ordered the murder of Amanda Webb, but he did admit to having an affair with her and to renting the barn near Cradley through his company. He also refused to admit he was involved in the bombing or the murder of Mr Campbell. Graham knew the DNA and forensic reports would prove he was in both places and he was certain the Crown Prosecution Service would take the case to court. Kevin insisted he knew nothing about the manufacture or sale of cannabis, marijuana or any synthetic cannabinoids, but what he didn't know was that Mrs Elspeth Campbell was still alive and could pick him out in an identity parade. Graham had asked Emma to take Bill and Ben with her to check out Worcester Global Hauliers' premises, after they had been to the Chocolate Elephant. He hoped that Michael Black would put in an appearance at some point as he really wanted to question him about his relationship with Kevin Rogers. He was of the same opinion as the chief constable and knew it to be unlikely that Michael had anything to do with the abduction of Jade or any of the murders, but thought it was a little odd that he was missing. Perhaps he has also been killed he muttered to himself, before debating this with Joseph, who may well have been the last person to see Michael alive.

~

Justin was very impressed by the skill that Shona had shown in preparing each of the meals. Although none of the dishes were complex, they all required a level of competence that was beyond many amateur chefs. He smiled to himself as he thought about the number of awful soufflés some of his students had presented to him over the years. Considering Jade didn't eat fish and Shona had very few ingredients to work with, the chicken, bacon and leek pie that she made for her from scratch was delicious, especially the pastry, which was as light as any he had ever tasted.

It was about 8.30 p.m. when Shona and Justin finished the washing up. Shona was just about to get Jade ready for bed and then read her a story, when there was a loud knock on the front door. Justin got up from the chair he was sitting in watching television and went to see who was interrupting his viewing of *The Naked Chef*.

"Hello, bruv," said Joseph.

"Jo Jo! What a surprise, how did you find me here?"

"I don't think you need me to tell you that, do you?"

"Who sold me out?"

"It was a case of elementary deduction and a little help in one way or another from your friends."

"I see you are still the Joker," said Justin.

"And I am Batman," said Graham walking into view from the shadows.

"What can I do for the dynamic duo?" said Justin.

"You can come with us and help us with our enquiries," said Graham.

"Am I under arrest?" said Justin.

"You will be if you don't come voluntarily," said Inspector Sean Wilson of the Garda, stepping into view.

"What am I supposed to have done?"

"Kidnapping a young girl for a start," replied Sean.

"I wasn't aware that taking my daughter on holiday could be classed as a crime."

"As you are not the legal guardian and are not even on the birth certificate, I think we can safely say this is a crime. As is flying into Dublin using a false passport."

"You can't come in here without a warrant," said Justin.

"We don't need one as we have the permission of the owner of the house; a Mr Rohan Reddy, the brother of your now deceased friend," said Sean, who started to force his way in through the door.

Justin tried to stop Sean entering the premises and as a result was immediately arrested. Shona came down the stairs at that point to see what all the commotion was about. Graham walked towards her as he recognised her from the funeral and asked her if Jade was upstairs.

"Yes," replied Shona.

An officer pushed his way past Shona and ran up the stairs to a bedroom from where he shouted, "The girl is here safe and sound."

Graham held up his badge in front of Shona and informed her that she was also under arrest for the abduction of Jade Green.

"I didn't abduct her, it was Justin. I was coerced into being here. He told me if I didn't co-operate then my boyfriend Michael Black would die. Have you seen him recently?"

"Michael Black is still missing but we are not saying presumed dead as of yet. With you helping us with our enquiries back in England tomorrow, we may be able to find him, but for now you will be spending the night in an Irish police cell," said Graham.

Shona and Justin were kept in separate cells, while Jade was looked after by Tusla, the Child and Family Agency, once Masie had been told that her foster daughter was safe.

Graham and Joseph found a local hotel to stay the night in and then went out for a meal to chat about the day's events.

"Would you mind if I spoke with my brother before any formal interview takes place tomorrow?" asked Joseph.

"As long as those in higher places don't know and as long as there is no brutality, I don't have an issue with it," replied Graham.

Graham and Joseph decided to eat at O'Neills, as it was well situated for Temple Bar, was reasonably priced and served up a fantastic Irish beef and Guinness stew. They found a decent table upstairs where they could sit and talk and enjoy a few of the local beverages such as Headless Dog and Molly's Chocolate Stout, while going over all of the crimes from the last couple of weeks or so to make sure nothing of any note had dropped down a hole. Graham, as ever, was well prepared and brought out a small tablet from his jacket pocket which he fired up, and then proceeded to log into his case note files.

"Let's start with the bombing," said Graham. "I think we know that Basil Reddy and Kevin Rogers were responsible for this and I am sure we have enough evidence to get a conviction against Mr Rogers for his part in it. We can't prove that your brother was involved in any way although I suspect as the time of the detonation was the time your flight from Washington DC landed that he was the mastermind."

"I think Justin planned it that way, as he has a sick sense of humour, but we will never be able to prove it unless Mr Rogers talks or we can find evidence of Justin bankrolling the crime. I am sure that Justin used the bombing to make us overthink things and that he has been trying to play with our minds to see if he was more intelligent than us," replied Joseph.

"I have seen many sick bastards over the years but none that have ever murdered their own father. You don't think his intentions are to kill or maim you, then?" asked Graham.

"It wouldn't surprise me and I've been half-expecting him to try something over the years at home. I'm sure he realised this and that he would be a prime suspect, so decided to launch a terror campaign here in England hoping at some point to get me alone."

"If the bomb was planted to get your involvement with the West Mercia police force in Worcester and Justin hasn't tried to kill you, what is he now doing here in Ireland?" said Graham.

"All will become clear, but I can only assume some elements of his plan A didn't go the way he wanted so he decided to move on to option B or C. Justin is very calculating and it could be that he is even on plan I or J."

"If that's the case, he isn't as clever as he thinks he is, as he is now part of my plans I and J – which are to interrogate Justin. Let's move on to the Amanda Webb murder," continued Graham. "We know for sure that Basil Reddy carried out the assault, but we're going to struggle to establish who was paying him to do it. If it was Kevin Rogers then he will never admit it, as it would treble his likely sentence for the other crimes. It could be your brother or it could still be her husband, but I had a call from Chief Constable Duncan about an hour or so ago who said that there is nothing untoward with Richard Webb's insurance or assurance policies or with his or Amanda Webb's wills. If either of them were going to change them then it hasn't happened. I don't really believe Richard would have had his wife murdered, but it has come to light that he has an online account with a building society and someone was transferring two thousand pounds a month into it from abroad for the past three years up until about five weeks ago."

"I will get the guys back at Langley to look into that," said Joseph.

"I don't think we are going to be able to convict your brother for the murder of Mr Campbell either," said Graham.

"The old rabbit toy with the skull and crossbones proves very little. Even if it does have Justin's DNA on it, he could say he lost it, gave it to a child he met in town or had it stolen."

"I will tackle him on it with a level of questioning that he won't expect, to see how he reacts," said Joseph with a bit of toughness in his tone.

"I can't believe Emma didn't find anything in the woods that might hold up in court against him," said Graham.

"I must admit it is a little strange, although Justin really is very clever and will have thought everything through in the finest detail. He will have checked the weather forecast and planned the murder accordingly. He will have been meticulous in planning the murder of both Luke Smith and Kylie Page too, as there was virtually no trace evidence of any substance at that crime scene, if you pardon the pun," replied Joseph.

"Emma thinks the killer wore gloves, plastic overshoe covers and even a hair net and hat to try to minimise the likelihood of detection through contamination. She also put in her report on the barn fire; that the remnants of some ash deposits in one section of the barn could be from fibres similar to the very few that were collected from the Pershore murders. In her opinion it makes it likely that all the clothing worn by the perpetrator in the Pershore attack has been destroyed in the burning building.

"Are you suggesting Kevin Rogers could be responsible for the murder of Luke Smith and Kylie Page?" asked Joseph.

"Unfortunately not, as he has a stone cast alibi for Sunday 30th, but it looks like someone was trying to fit him or someone else up to deflect any attention from themselves."

"Based on the facts we have and what we know about Justin, I get the feeling that he has tried to put quite a few people in the frame for each of the crimes to make sure we can't pin anything concrete on him."

"Have you asked Mrs Campbell about Justin?"

"I showed her a photofit image, but she didn't proffer any positive information. I would go as far as to say, however, that she did look a bit scared for a second before shaking her head when I pressed her about it."

"So at the moment the only thing we may be able to convict Justin of is the abduction of his daughter?" said Joseph.

"Maybe; but from what I've learnt from you, he's sure to have established a way of being exonerated."

"Surely, we can charge him with entry into both the UK and Ireland using a false passport. That must carry a sentence of some sort?" said Joseph.

"The maximum sentence is ten years but it is unlikely the courts would impose that and I would guess if the CPS took the case on and won he might get sent down for eighteen months or two years," replied Graham.

"That's something, I suppose. What about the alleged violent assault and rape of Shona seven years ago?"

"Unfortunately, Shona decided not to press charges at the time, but she could still do so. As there is no Statute of Limitations on sex crimes here in the UK there is a chance we could get a rape case brought to court. There is a slight problem, however, in that Miss Green, previously Pascoe, waited until the day after the event to report the crime, by which time she had put the knife back in her kitchen drawer and taken a bath. Unfortunately, overnight, she also had time to reflect and by the time she got to hospital she was blaming herself for it happening," said Graham.

"Why didn't she report such a severe attack straight away?" asked Joseph.

"I understand she wanted to, but collapsed and passed out on her landing due to the pain. When she came round it was about 4.00 a.m., so she decided to wait until it got light and then clean herself up and get dressed before calling her mum who then persuaded her to tell the police."

"I wish you hadn't told me that," replied Joseph.

"At least Shona dialled 999. There are too many victims who can't for fear of further repercussions from the attacker or fear of having to go through the ordeal again in court months later. If we could just encourage more victims to come forward, we would be able to rid the county of many of the evil bastards who carry out vicious assaults on women time and time again," said Graham.

"Many women are too scared to report an assault but some are just broken with such low self-esteem they think no one will believe what they say."

"What you say is true, Joseph! But if you are going to take the time to phone the police, you would hope the victim would press charges."

"It seemed as if Shona changed her mind during or just after coming out of hospital and there was little your team could have done," replied Joseph.

"I'll take a longer look at the case notes and rationale for things, at some point. There may be something we missed or a technicality we could get Justin on even if Shona still doesn't want to cooperate."

"Perhaps we'll find evidence at the house where Justin's been living that will get him put away for a long period of time?" said Joseph, with some hope.

"Herefordshire and Worcestershire is a big area to cover, Joseph. Jessica Chalmers told me that the place Justin took her to was about a two- or three-hour walk or jog from Worcester, and as it was dark when she escaped from him it will take us some time to locate the property, particularly as we have limited resources these days," said Graham.

"You could try offering your officers more overtime?" said Joseph teasingly.

"Oh, very funny, Joseph!. You know very well that Simon isn't going to let that happen. Not now the papers have publicised the fact that the West Mercia force paid out over £9 million in overtime payments to staff during the last two years."

"Surely, it would have been better to have made fewer redundancies?"

"You tell our wonderful government that," said Graham.

At that moment, his mobile phone rang again. It was Peter. Graham listened intently, rang off and stared up at Joseph with a bemused look on his face.

"Luca Zini, the general manager of the Chocolate Elephant, has admitted buying a set of Kai knives recently, from a place in Devon."

"He admitted buying them?" asked Joseph with some surprise.

"Yes he did, and he then admitted giving the complete set to Shona Green as a leaving present."

"Wow," exclaimed Joseph rather loudly. That revelation really adds another dimension to things."

"What it implies is that Miss Green may well have murdered, or paid someone else to murder her own customers?" said Graham.

"Maybe she has murdered Michael Black, too?" suggested Joseph.

CHAPTER THIRTY-ONE

Justin and Shona were transferred, or rather escorted back to England by Graham and a team of officers from the Garda, on the first available flight out of Dublin. Joseph was going to take a later flight and escort Jade with a person from the Tusla.

Shona was first to be interviewed by Graham, Benjamin and Bea. She decided not to request a solicitor as she couldn't afford one and didn't really think she needed one. The amount of time Shona was in the interview room seemed to her an eternity, but the whole process only took about an hour and a half. Graham asked really tough direct questions, particularly at the start when he asked Shona what it was that made her decide to become a killer. Bea could see that Shona was physically shocked by this accusation and it took her a few minutes to compose herself and gather her thoughts.

"Why are you asking me that? When you have Justin in a cell downstairs," said Shona.

"You and him seem very close."

"Do you really think that I am in collusion with that sick bastard?" replied Shona angrily.

"Where are the knives that Luca Zini gave to you as a present when you left his employment?"

"I left them in the kitchen at Michael Black's house, or so I thought, but he said they were not there when I asked him soon afterwards. How do you know about them and why do you ask?"

"I am the one doing the interviewing here, Miss Green."

"I think I have a right to know," replied Shona.

"Amanda Webb, whom I assume that you knew well as you were at her funeral, a Mr Harold Campbell, a Mr Luke Smith and a Miss Kylie Page, who all employed you to cook for them recently have all been murdered with knives identical to those you now say that you have lost."

"What are you implying?"

"I think you know very well where I am going with this line of questioning. Why did you murder your customers? Was it because they refused to pay you for your services as quickly as the punters did at the Chocolate Elephant?"

"I didn't have anything to do with the murders, but I am pretty sure that Justin did as he as good as told me that."

"At the moment, we only have your word against his, which I suspect will still be the case when we get to speak with him shortly."

"He is a good liar. I'm telling you the truth," said Shona,

"I gather you have only just started your new business, so how did you manage to pick up new clients, bearing in mind the techniques used would have to have been very different to the way you were used to getting business in the past?"

"I was a pole dancer not a prostitute," replied Shona.

"Same difference," said Benjamin butting in.

"In the same way that the assistant police chief constable is an Apache," said Shona.

"What?" said Benjamin.

"Never mind, just think long and hard." added Shona.

"Just answer the original question, please," said Graham.

"I typed up an advertisement and put it in the classifieds section of the local newspaper," said Shona sarcastically.

"Don't you think it a bit odd that you managed to get so

many bookings in such a short space of time?"

"I never thought about it until Justin turned up at a dinner party hosted by a Mr and Mrs Rogers, dressed as 'The Punisher'."

This news made Graham and Benjamin stare at each other in shock. It also made them think that Shona was probably telling the truth. Graham changed tack upon this revelation as he knew that he would be able to use that information later in the day.

"Is it possible that Justin or someone else set all of your dinner parties up in one way or another as part of some revengeful game?"

"That idea started to cross my mind yesterday, but I couldn't imagine that anyone could be forced to have a dinner party," replied Shona.

"In the same way that anyone could force a bright young woman to get on a plane and fly to Ireland?" replied Joseph.

"Point taken," said Shona.

"Do you know a Jessica Chalmers?" asked Graham.

"Yes, why do you ask?"

"She said that she had heard Kevin Rogers talking on the phone to someone who she thought was Justin. We need to make an association between them, and an alleged phone conversation wouldn't stack up within the legal system. Both men being seen physically talking at the same location, together with other information and some of the evidence collected may well help us with our investigations."

"There is one slight flaw with that," replied Shona.

"And what would that be?" asked Graham.

"Justin only took his mask off when alone with me in the Rogers' garden shed, so nobody else saw him to be able to identify him."

"He seems to be too clever for his own good. If only you hadn't waited until the following day to report his attack on you all those years ago and had actually pressed the charges," said Graham.

"I've regretted that ever since as I knew that one day I or someone else would pay the price for it," replied Shona.

"It may still be possible for you to do so retrospectively and I'll look at this with the CPS and get back to you."

Graham continued to blitz Shona with many more questions until it got to a point that her head began to hurt and she couldn't take any more. Benjamin, as one of the observers, could see that Shona was struggling and suggested to Graham that they could all do with a break. Graham had Shona taken back to a holding cell and then walked downstairs to see Peter.

"Miss Green has been very cooperative, Peter, and based on our conversation I have a hunch that may help us. Please can you get hold of the incoming phone records for all of the recent murder victims and those such as Mr and Mrs Price who were fortunate not to be killed. I would also like you to check out the homes of another couple – a Mr Samuel Kalu and a Miss Rose Wickens who booked 'Spice and Slice' a couple of weeks' ago and for some reason cancelled their dinner party at the last minute. We understand from Miss Green that their party was due to be held at Mr Kalu's home in Powick even though Miss Wickens lives in Devon."

~

Jade had said very little to anybody since she was taken from her bed in the house in Dublin. Sean Wilson and his team tried to find out her version of events since she last saw her foster mother and father, as had Vicky O'Connell, from Tusla.

"I think she is frightened to tell us anything," said Vicky to Joseph as they sat on the 9.50 a.m. Air Lingus flight that would land at Birmingham International in one hour's time.

"Justin Johnson will have threatened her in some way,"

replied Joseph. "If Jade doesn't cooperate with us, it will be Justin's word against those of Shona and her foster mother Maisie, as I understand that we haven't been able to pick up anything concrete from any of the roadside cameras to show that she was abducted on Saturday evening."

"That's unusual, isn't it?" said Vicky.

"Justin will have planned it so that he drove down every back street possible to get to wherever his rented house is without passing a single camera."

"Is he that clever?"

"He is certainly that devious and will have tested every route possible before he carried out the abduction."

"What happens when we get to England as far as your job goes?" Joseph asked Vicky.

"Graham's told me that Jane Small will meet us at the airport. I'll then fly back to Dublin on a return flight and a police car will take you both and Jade back to where she lives in Claines."

~

Technology is a wonderful thing thought Peter as he and a few selected officers from those at his disposal began the process of checking through the phone records of all the murder victims and Mr and Mrs Price. It needed a warrant and a lot of cooperation from the service providers, but the new law passed by the House of Lords a few years ago to help the police with their investigations was proving to be a godsend. UK telecoms companies were now required to keep phone call logs for a year, but luckily for Peter and his team, Chief Constable Simon Duncan only requested data from the last four weeks. Thankfully, the number of phone calls to and from each of the numbers was fairly low and it wasn't too difficult, using a new computer program that the West Mercia IT team had devised, to learn that one number was a common denominator. Upon further checks it became obvious to Peter that the person making calls to the victims was Kate Rogers, Michael Black's sister.

~

Jane tried hard to coax Jade to speak in the back of the police car, but even the offer of sweets, clothes or a new computer game, paid for out of her own pocket rather than any police budget, didn't have the desired effect. Jane phoned Maisie as the car exited Junction 6 of the M5 to tell her that they were a few minutes away. As they drove down the A449 with Worcester Rugby club on their right, Jade spoke for the first time since Dublin, but only to say, "My dad goes there some Saturday's. I don't know why though, as he always comes home in a bad mood or drunk."

The avenue was lined with parked vehicles, but Paul, the officer driving the police car, found a space on the opposite side of the road to where Jade lived. Joseph could see Maisie standing expectantly in her front garden, so he opened the passenger door and walked around the back of the car to let Jade out of the nearside door that had the child lock on. Jade got out of the back door and walked towards the front of the car where she then saw Maisie waving. At that point and in an instant, she ran between the parked cars in a straight line towards her foster mum. At that exact moment, a silver Vauxhall Astra travelling at some speed hit Jade full on and threw her up into the air. She came crashing down onto the bonnet and slid up the windscreen before falling onto the road. Time seemed to stand still as everybody tried to comprehend what had just happened. Maisie screamed and ran towards the little girl lying crumpled in a heap. Blood was coming from Jade's nose and ears, which wasn't a good sign, and Jane

288

prayed to God for some divine help as she phoned for an ambulance. Joseph got to Jade at the same time as Maisie to try and help, but it was obvious within a few seconds of reaching her that Jade was dead.

CHAPTER THIRTY-TWO

The news of Jade's death was conveyed to Graham just as he was about to recommence his interview with Shona, but after some consultation with Simon and Benjamin he decided to let Bea take her home instead and have Jane meet her at her apartment.

Graham immediately sent Bill and Ben to Claines to investigate the incident and to help Maisie. He then asked Joseph to make his way back to the police station where they would now interview Justin together.

"I can't come back just yet," said Joseph.

"Why what are you doing at the moment?" asked Graham.

"Constable Paul Curry and I are chasing after the car that ran Jade over," he replied.

"What direction are you going in?"

"I have no idea but Paul can tell you if you contact him on the car radio."

"We are just turning on to the A4133 between Ombersley and Great Witley," said Paul.

Paul was driving at some speed to try and keep the Vauxhall in his sights but he was keeping a reasonable distance back so as not to cause the getaway driver more panic than was necessary through the winding roads. Up ahead, the silver Astra sped along the Holt Fleet road at 80 mph overtaking a red Ford Ka on a slight bend and then leaving the ground as it flew over the narrow bridge by the Wharf Inn. As they neared Great Witley, Paul was a little concerned as the gap between the two cars was increasing and he needed to make sure he could see if the Astra driver turned right onto the A451 to Stourport or kept on the A443 towards Tenbury Wells. Paul just managed to see the Astra go left at the junction with the Stourport road and then swing left again onto the B4203 towards Bromyard. Paul pressed his foot hard on the accelerator and caught up with the Astra just by the entrance to Sapey Golf Club, at which point the getaway driver braked hard and then accelerated again in an attempt to make Paul keep his distance and be less confident about his next move.

As they approached Norton, Paul could see in the distance another squad car coming towards them from the Bromyard direction. The Astra driver saw it too and anticipating capture by being forced off the road, he forked left and raced at breakneck speed down a narrow road towards Warren Wood. This is where his luck ran out as a large green tractor suddenly appeared in front of him. The driver braked harder than before, causing the Astra to snake from left to right, but the distance was too short for him to stop and his only option was to pull hard right on the steering wheel and plough into a field. The Astra crashed through a fence, flipped over onto its roof and skidded along the grass for a hundred yards or so before coming to rest against a tree. Paul, Joseph and the tractor driver ran into the field to find the driver scrambling from the wreckage somewhat shaken. As they approached the Astra, the driver tried to run away across the field, but Paul was faster and stronger and dived towards him, bringing him crashing to the ground with a great rugby tackle.

"I am on my way back to the station now," Joseph said to Graham. "We've arrested the man who killed Jade, although he isn't being too cooperative as you can imagine and is only answering to the name of the Painter."

~

Justin Johnson was taken in handcuffs from his cell up to the interview room. So much was happening in such a short space of time that Graham didn't know if he was coming or going.

Emma brought in some of the evidence bags while Graham waited for Joseph to get back.

"This is Emma Thyme, our forensics expert," said Graham.

"The pleasure is all mine or could be?" replied Justin.

"Her nickname, coincidentally, is Justin, because she always gets her man just in time and in this case, that man is you Mr Johnson."

"I haven't done anything wrong or illegal, so I am not sure why I am even here."

"Before your brother gets here I want to be clear that you are refusing to have a solicitor present at the interview that is to commence in a short while. Is that correct?"

"Why would I need a lawyer?" replied Justin.

Joseph heard what was being said as he marched through the door in an angry and aggressive mood. Emma saw the look on his face and as she wasn't actually required for the interview process, she left the room to get back to some more investigative work along the corridor.

"Because if I had my way you would hang for what you have done, if capital punishment were still an option. And as it isn't here in the UK, I will do my utmost to make sure you rot in prison," said Joseph.

"That isn't a nice way to speak to your brother, is it?"

"You know how I feel about you. You got away with murdering our father indirectly and I am sure as hell not going to let you get away with the things you have done here."

"I think we should start the official interview now as this

dialogue is getting us nowhere and I would like to go home," said Justin.

Graham asked Joseph to start the tape running and commence the questioning while he went upstairs for a couple of minutes to check on a legal matter.

Joseph thought about starting the tape after punching his brother, but decided to hold himself back, do the correct thing and inform those who would listen to the tape at a later date that he was "commencing an interview with Mr Justin Johnson at 3.00 p.m."

"My name isn't Justin Johnson," replied Justin.

Joseph knew that his brother had potentially changed his name, but this statement still surprised him into silence for a few seconds as he thought of a response.

"Who are you then?" was the only thing Joseph could manage to muster.

"My name is DJ Macintyre."

"And I am Sherlock Holmes," said Joseph.

"You're looking good for your age," replied Justin.

Joseph ignored the remark and continued with the questioning.

"So you're saying that you are not my brother?"

"No, I am saying that I officially changed my name a few years ago. I think I may have mentioned this to the nice Irish policeman and Detective Chief Inspector Laws at Dublin airport yesterday. Surely, the CIA would have known that?"

"You travelled to Bangladesh recently as Justin Johnson."

"Did I? Well, that was then and this is now. Ask the nice detective when he comes back what name was printed on my passport earlier today. So, as you can't convict me for entering the UK via a false passport, I would like to leave, now, this minute, pronto."

"You are going nowhere, sunshine, until you've answered all

of our questions," said Graham as he walked back into the room puffing and wheezing having run down the stairs.

"How well do you know a Mr Richard Webb?"

"I know he still owes me a set of custom made chef's knives that I paid him to have made for me."

"You may also know, that we know all about your meetings with Mr Webb in Bangladesh. What we don't know is if you have seen him since you came to England."

"No, not yet, but I have it in my diary to call him."

"Did you know his wife has been killed?"

"No, how did that happen?" said Justin in a somewhat unsurprised voice.

"You had her murdered," said Joseph

"I don't know what you're talking about," replied Justin.

"Do you know a Mr Basil Reddy?"

"Is he Quasimodo's brother?"

"What?" said Graham.

"He rings a bell," said Justin mockingly.

"Just answer the fucking question," said Joseph.

"No, I don't know a Basil Reddy."

"I suppose you don't know anything about the death of a Mr Harold Campbell in Grafton Woods or the attempted murder of his wife Elspeth in a barn fire, either?"

"No."

"Odd that we found this toy rabbit near to the body of Mr Campbell and that we have been able to lift your fingerprints from it."

"Oh! You have found it. I gave Mulder, as I called him, to a little lad that I met in Cripplegate Park about a week ago."

"What is your relationship with Mr Kevin Rogers?"

"I don't know him personally but I do know his wife Kate," said Justin.

"How do you know her?" said Graham.

"Kate was having an affair with Richard Webb."

"What the hell is in the water here in Worcester," said Graham.

"I can't believe that the Rogers and the Webbs were swapping partners without all of them knowing what was going on."

"Perhaps one or two of them did know," said Joseph.

"We should have a word with Mrs Rogers," said Graham.

"Does that mean I am off the hook for the murder of Amanda Webb?"

"No, it bloody well doesn't," shouted Graham angrily.

"You are not off the hook for killing Luke Smith or Kylie Page, either."

"Who the hell are they?"

"Mr Smith's family own a martial arts business in Durham and just by coincidence someone named DJ Macintyre bought a Samurai sword from this company a while ago."

Graham handed Justin some papers to look at for a few minutes before pressing him on the purchase.

"An acquaintance of mine ordered one for me so I just went there to collect it. I have absolutely no idea who owns the business."

"We understand that your acquaintance would be a Miss Jessica Chalmers?" said Graham.

"Yes, I met her in a pub and got friendly with her and she's done some work for me while I've been here."

"Would that have included the delivery of drugs to people in Worcestershire?" asked Joseph.

"I don't know anything about the delivery of any drugs. I recently got a recipe book published and people in England have been ordering it from my website. I am sure my accountant in New York will verify this."

"Why weren't the books delivered directly to the purchasers' homes?" asked Joseph.

"I took an advert out in the local Worcester News a few weeks ago once I knew that I would be visiting this beautiful county again and I had a lot of enquiries. I thought I could make my customers purchase experience a bit special by getting an employee to deliver their book to their home where possible. I hoped that I would get even more sales while I was here to help pay for this part of my trip, so I brought additional books with me. It wouldn't be very professional to have customers wait weeks for their order, would it?"

"Don't you have people back in New York that could post them out for you?" asked Joseph.

"It was more profitable to do it this way."

"What the fuck are we doing talking about a book when we are in the middle of a murder investigation?" said Graham.

"You are right, I have digressed," said Joseph. "Where is your Samurai sword now?"

"It's in my car."

"Where is your car?"

"It was at Lasham airfield. I hope it hasn't been stolen."

"Oh! You are good, aren't you?" said Graham.

"I have always tried to do all that I can throughout my life to be very good at whatever I do," replied Justin.

"You are so sharp you will cut yourself, hopefully," said Joseph.

"Not on my Samurai if some bastard has stolen it together with my car," replied Justin.

"Are you sure it isn't still at the house you have been renting?"

"Oh! Who is good now?" said Justin.

"Just answer the question."

"No, because my rental period expired at the weekend and I understand there is a new tenant in the house now."

"Are you going to tell us where the house is?"

"The address is in my car with my sword."

Graham looked at Joseph and shook his head before announcing to Justin that the interview was suspended at 4.30 p.m.

"I suppose I am free to go as you haven't charged me?" said Justin.

"Not just yet, as there is still the matter of kidnap to discuss and I want to have a word with Mr and Mrs Rogers and someone who will only answer to 'The Painter' before we continue our little chat" said Graham.

"I need to go and get something to eat first as it's been a long day," said Joseph. He phoned Penny to see if she was around and was glad to learn that she was at home.

"I don't suppose you would be able to rustle up some food for me in an hour or so?" he asked.

"Would you like anything else?" said Penny.

"I would but it will have to wait until much later tonight," he replied.

CHAPTER THIRTY-THREE

Joseph got to Penny's place at 6.30 p.m. to find the table laid and a glass of wine next to his place mat.

"You didn't give me much time to prepare anything special so you have three quick and easy to make courses now and the slow hard course later," Penny shouted from the kitchen.

Joseph looked at the little menu card Penny had put next to his glass of wine.

Tangy Avocado Fans
Sea Bass with Risotto alla Milanese
French Fruit Tart
or
Carrot Cake

"The menu looks very exciting. Are you dressing up as a French tart?" asked Joseph, as Penny walked into the lounge carrying two plates.

"You will have to wait and see," replied Penny.

"You are a great cook, considering your age, the fact you are studying animal biology and have spent a lot of time living on the streets. How did you learn to rustle up food like this?"

"My mum taught me when I was fifteen or sixteen years old. She worked as a sous chef at Pennyhill Park in Bagshot, an exclusive five-star spa resort used by the rich and famous."

"If the animal thing doesn't work out you could also do the food thing," said Joseph.

"You have such a way with words," replied Penny.

"I will spell out some three-or four-letter words for you later," said Joseph as he tucked into his avocado without glancing at Penny.

By the time Joseph got back to the police station, Graham had already spent another arduous hour with Kevin Rogers and was just about to interview Kate for the first time.

"I have a few calls to make relating to Richard Webb so can you interview Mrs Rogers with Bea?" Joseph asked Graham.

"No problem, we'll have a catch up in an hour or two."

When Graham walked into the meeting room just before 9.45 p.m., Joseph was writing on one of the whiteboards that was now positioned against the side wall.

"The money that was being paid into Richard Webb's account was coming from an account held at the Agrani Bank by a director of the Gazipur Cutlery Company. This is a subsidiary of the Dhaka factory that was to have made a set of knives for Justin. We think that the money stopped being paid when the cutlery company's building was damaged, when another building collapsed near to it. One of the rooms in Gazipur's factory was being used to check out individuals, sent there as far as we can tell but without any concrete evidence, by a Mr D Webb whom we think to be Richard, to sign up to be paid to have one of their kidneys removed. We can't arrest him and have him charged for that here in the UK as far as I am aware, but I thought it best to add it to the growing list," said Joseph.

Graham walked closer to the board, picked up a marker pen and said, "We can probably put ML for money laundering on there if we can get the evidence against him to stack up. I know the Bangladeshi government will cooperate, as their country has just come out of the Financial Action Task Force grey list of poor performers in anti-money laundering activities."

"Have you had any more thoughts relating to Justin yet?" asked Joseph.

"Kevin Rogers is staying tight-lipped, which is a bit odd as I would have expected him to start blaming Justin for things. I can only assume they made a pact or Justin has made Kevin fear for the life of his family members," replied Graham.

"I can empathise with that," said Joseph.

"Did he threaten you when you threatened to report him for the assault on your father that may have caused his death?"

"In a roundabout way, but I didn't have a wife or children for him to target so it was a bit different."

"We have had more luck getting Kate Rogers to talk and both Bea and I think she has actually told us the truth. It would appear that her brother Michael Black did randomly pick 'Spice and Slice' from an advert in the local paper when selecting a company to do the catering for her birthday. Her husband Kevin seemed to like Shona, so he asked Kate to phone various people that he knew had events coming up, to make sure they contacted Shona and asked for her services. Bill and Ben have found a file at Worcester Global Hauliers containing hundreds of names and amongst them are Mr and Mrs Campbell, Luke Smith and Kylie Page, Mr and Mrs Price and Rose Wickens. Many of the names have been crossed through, so we are assuming this is a debtor's book probably set against the supply of drugs. I still can't establish if Kevin or Justin is the kingpin, but in one way or another they were both achieving their objectives. Kate Rogers told me she has felt scared of her husband for some time now as his personality had changed, and it was this that led to them having marital problems," said Graham.

"If they were having domestic issues, why did she buy him

some cufflinks recently?" asked Joseph.

"I asked her that and she told me Jessica Chalmers suggested they would make a nice birthday gift, as Kevin was often talking about the time he had spent in Philadelphia before he and Kate got together."

"It's a bit odd that a new kid on the block should tell Mrs Rogers what to buy her husband for a present, isn't it?"

"Unless, of course, Miss Chalmers had been primed by your brother to suggest such an item so that one or two of the crimes could be pinned on Mr Rogers?"

"It seems extreme but I wouldn't put it past Justin to mastermind everything so that failure in any way shape or form would mean others taking the rap for his crimes. He does have incredible powers of persuasion and it could be he indirectly got Kate to contact the chosen clients for Shona's parties," said Joseph.

"Perhaps Kate thought she was actually doing her brother and his new girlfriend a favour by getting Shona some bookings and had no idea that she was probably a party to the murder of innocent people."

"Does Kate know where her brother is?" said Joseph.

"No, she said she's been trying to contact him, to no avail."

"Do you think Justin has had Michael murdered out of jealousy and to hurt Shona even more?"

"It's quite possible, Joseph, and I'm glad he is in a place where he can't harm anyone else. There's a chain of events going on and I'm intrigued to know what else Justin had planned before we interrupted his little game."

Joseph had an idea about that. "If we hadn't had Kevin arrested, I think Justin would have somehow convinced Kate Rogers to stab her husband to death, just like Susan Wright did to her husband in Texas on January 13th, 2003."

"I read about that when I was America. She tied her husband

to their bed and stabbed him one hundred and ninety-three times with two different knives," said Peter.

"I can't comprehend anything else today. I am going to give Jane a call to see how the land lies and see where she is. After that, I think it's about time we packed up and went home," said Graham.

"Good idea," said Joseph. "I'll sleep well knowing that we have two criminals under lock and key for the night."

~

Jessica had stayed in Worcester near to the police station as she was required to make a formal statement. Having done this, she asked for a police escort to take her home as she was frightened to go there alone. Due to a shortage of officers this wasn't possible. She needed to get a few things together and then go back to New Zealand for a while, until the dust had settled and any case against Kevin and Justin and any of the other organisation members was brought to court. She had promised to come back to Worcester should she be needed to give evidence. As she opened her front door and walked into the hallway, she switched on the lights and listened intently for any unusual sounds. The house seemed quiet and everything seemed to be in its proper place. Jessica didn't intend to stay the night here as she had booked into a hotel near the airport, but had to get her passport, a few other documents and some clothes. She pushed open her bedroom door and had just started to walk towards her dressing table when something caught her eye in the right-hand corner of the room.

"Hello, Jessica," said the Hulk.

Jessica turned to run back towards the door, but for his size the Hulk was fast and he cut her off. Jessica leapt backwards and jumped on to the bed. The Hulk came towards her again, so she used the bed like a trampoline to scissor kick him on the jaw, causing him to rock to the side and stumble. Most men would have gone crashing to the floor with a strike like that, so I am going to have to outsmart him here she told herself.

"If you want to have mad passionate sex with me you only have to ask," said Jessica.

The Hulk looked at her and Jessica could see his mind ticking over at the options open to him. Jessica then did what all women seem to be able to do to the bemusement of men and took her bra off without removing any other article of clothing. She waved it about in the air and jumped up and down on the bed at the same time, which had the desired effect on the Hulk's levels of concentration. Jessica then threw the bra at the Hulk, whose natural reaction was to catch it. As he did this, Jessica charged passed him and out of the bedroom door.

Jessica's house was rather large with a split staircase and double landing, and as she ran to the top of one staircase the Hulk ran to the top of the other staircase. If she descended he would cut her off halfway to the bottom. She was breathing heavily and was scared but had the presence of mind to press a speed dial button on her mobile in her pocket and hope she could keep this monster at bay until help arrived.

~

Jane was working late into the night as she had driven Shona to see Maisie. The hurt felt by both women was clear for Jane to see and they were doing their best to comfort each other by looking through old photo albums of Jade, as if in denial of the fact she was dead. It was a blessing that they had each other with Maisie's husband still away and Michael Black still missing. Jane was making tea and polite conversation where possible. She would stay the night, here in the house that Jade lived in until a few days ago, or at least until other relatives arrived.

~

Mr Kalu's house in Powick was searched by two officers, who found nothing untoward other than a musky smell of cannabis. The stench that hit Devon and Cornwall police officers as they broke down the door of Miss Rose Wickens four-bedroom detached house was unbearable. The sight that greeted them inside was even worse. Mr Kalu and Miss Wickens had been tied up and gagged and each of them were missing some body parts. Mr Kalu had lost his manhood while Miss Wickens had lost four fingers. It would appear that they had both bled to death or died from shock. Detective Chief Superintendent Tony Hogan telephoned Graham to inform him of what his officers had found and that his forensics team would furbish him with their reports and findings as soon as possible.

~

Jessica and the Hulk stood looking at each other across the stairs for a few minutes before the Hulk made his move and charged down his flight of stairs and up the other flight opposite, shouting that he was going to tear her limb from limb. Jessica ran around the landing to the side the Hulk had come from and stood facing him again. The Hulk charged at her again and this time followed Jessica around the landing. Jessica ran down the stairs towards the lower landing but stumbled on the way down and landed flat on her chest. This mistake gave the Hulk the chance to pounce on her, grab her by the collar of her polo shirt and haul her to her feet.

"It is a long way to fall, Jessica. I've killed one traitor in Baz and now it's your turn to die."

At that moment a police siren distracted the Hulk's attention, which gave Jessica the split second she was hoping for and she rammed her fist into his throat, causing him to stagger backwards. Jessica then pivoted on her left leg, leant her upper body towards the upper staircase and kicked out hard with her right leg with a sudden but smooth motion, sending the Hulk tumbling down the lower staircase where his head hit the floor with a bone-crunching thud. As blood started to seep from the Hulk's nose and ears, Jessica ran down the steps and out of the front door straight into the arms of a police officer.

"Are you ok?" asked Constable Paul Curry.

"I am now that you are here," replied Jessica.

"We heard what was happening and were glad that we happened to be in the area. The boss had a suspicion that you may have made yourself a target."

"The big hairy thug that was trying to kill me is in there lying prone and lifeless at the bottom of my stairs," said Jessica pointing back towards her house.

Paul walked past her and through the open front door to see the Hulk lying on the stone floor exactly as Jessica had described. As he bent down to check for a pulse he took his mobile out of his pocket and phoned Graham.

"The solicitor who got Adam suspended is no longer. It would appear that he tripped over his tongue and fell down some stairs."

"I know that young woman is beautiful, but make sure you write banana skin or roller skate or some such plausible thing in your report," said Graham.

CHAPTER THIRTY-FOUR

Michael was struggling to come to terms with his surroundings and everything that had happened to him, when he felt another sharp needle like pain in his leg. He kicked out hard into the darkness and heard more scurrying and scuttling around him. The rats had been getting braver and closer to him during the last six or seven hours, as he got nearer to what appeared to be a very damp and lower level of what he now knew to be an underground tunnel. Michael could vaguely make out the time and date on his watch at various intervals on his slow walk to somewhere or maybe nowhere, from an occasional chink of light shining through cracks in the earth or rock above.

Somebody had stunned him with a taser and then clubbed him on the head with a baseball bat or truncheon on Saturday night and he had woken to find himself lying in mud in complete darkness. He didn't have any idea what had happened to him during the three missing days of his life but he was glad that he was at least alive. He was very tired and weak through lack of food and water and very cold and wet from the conditions and lack of control over his bodily functions at some point during his experience. Michael knew he needed to get help soon or he would probably die down here in this giant grave.

He was feeling a bit better than earlier in the day, when he had woken feeling extremely confused, dizzy, drowsy and sick.

It was as if he was totally stoned having been given a date rape drug. As he walked, he started to feel panicky as he thought about what else might have occurred down below. Michael had published a document to raise awareness of date rape some time ago and knew of a drug called DMHP that would leave the recipient well out of it for many hours. As his head cleared, he began to fear for Shona and he hoped and prayed he could find some way out of this hell hole, before his body gave out and his only future use in this world would be to excite some archaeologists, who would eventually find his skeleton in years to come.

~

Maisie's husband Victor eventually arrived home early on Wednesday morning to find his wife, Shona and a policewoman talking and looking at photographs of Jade. The grief they both showed was now to be shared by Victor himself. Jade's death had been difficult to comprehend while he was working away, but the reality was now hitting home. Maisie had asked Shona to help with the funeral arrangements once Jade's body had been released by the authorities, but Shona wasn't sure she could cope with the trauma on top of the other thoughts and feelings she was experiencing at the moment.

Shona didn't know whether to fight or take flight, so she asked Jane to take her home so that she could work out in her own mind within the peace and quiet of her own home what she wanted to do.

Once Shona had said goodbye to Jane and shut the front door of her apartment, all she really wanted to do was sit and stare out of the window. She felt her life had lost its meaning and she was feeling very angry and hostile towards everybody and everything, but especially Justin and Michael. Justin because he had taken her daughter and her business from her and Michael because he had deserted her in her time of need.

The thought that Justin may have killed Michael didn't come into the equation. Even if Michael was dead he had deserted her. Jane had tried to help with kind words but there is no such thing as an 'easy death' and that of a child is the most devastating of all. It wasn't long before Shona began to drink brandy and vodka in large volumes. She knew that her goal was to remember Jade rather than forget about her loss, but at the moment forgetting through being drunk seemed the best option.

~

It was early Wednesday evening. Graham and Joseph had been in an all-day meeting with Chief Constable Simon Duncan, Assistant Chief Constable Benjamin Lewis, Caroline Gardener and Hannah Davies from the Crown Prosecution Service, someone from the National Crime Agency and some of the West Mercia police force's legal team, to discuss all of the cases and how best to conclude them.

An enquiry was on-going following the suspension of Adam Osborne for negligence in the line of duty. In light of the death of the Hulk, real name Frederick Pierce, who used to have his own legal practice until he was struck off for using clients' cash to pay for drugs, forging signatures and falsifying documents, it was likely that Adam would only get a warning and be allowed to continue his duties having learnt a valuable lesson.

The consensus of opinion was that a case against Richard Webb could and would be made for money laundering and that he would be brought to trial even though everyone had sympathy for him over the loss of his wife. There was no suggestion that he had anything to do with his wife's murder directly even though he would gain financially from it and it was likely that it happened as a result of his actions.

"We are fairly certain that Justin Johnson or Kevin Rogers

paid Basil Reddy to kill Mrs Webb for reasons we have explained, but as of yet we have no evidence to support either or both of these thought processes, although we are still trying to find some," said Graham.

Basil Reddy, Amanda Webb's murderer, was dead and Graham had been told Baz's family were not going to take action against the police, probably he thought, because any legal action would open a can of worms for the rest of Baz's family, who knew it was really only ever going to be a matter of time before Baz met his maker anyway. Kevin Rogers, despite his protestations and a well-fought battle by his solicitor, was going to be remanded in custody for the bombing of the cricket pavilion, the murder of Mr Campbell and the abduction of Mrs Campbell until his trial came to court. There was no factual evidence to prove who actually started the barn fire, so it was going to be difficult to prove the attempted murder of Mrs Campbell, but there was enough circumstantial evidence for the CPS to try and gain a conviction for this and the manufacture of legal highs.

The committee decided that there was no case to be made against Kate Rogers or Jessica Chalmers, and obviously no case against Basil Reddy or Frederick Pierce now they were deceased. Michael Black was still missing and a warrant had been put out for his arrest. Nobody was really sure of his actual involvement in any of the crimes, or if he was even linked to them, and although Joseph had spoken with him, Graham was going to undertake a formal interview and a DNA test if he was ever found alive and well.

The big debate came when the team were trying to build a case against Justin Johnson, or DJ Macintyre as he was now insisting on being called. Justin had eventually decided to get legal representation having been held in custody for longer than the legally allowed time and his brief was pushing for his release. Graham and Joseph had spent another two hours interviewing him earlier this morning in true good cop, bad cop style and were presenting all of their findings and evidence from the whiteboards to all those present in the room.

"Mr Justin Johnson as we will still call him, as this is what we have known him as throughout our investigations, has been told of the death of his daughter via a hit and run driver. He showed ambivalence to the news so it is hard to determine if this came as a surprise or not," said Graham.

"People react in different ways to sad news so we can't judge him on that or use it against him," said Simon.

"No, sir, but I did get the impression that he knew the driver who we have in custody and who we now know to be a Mr David Painter, a local unemployed artist who was often seen being creative on the pavement in Worcester High Street. The death of Jade Green means that it is just Justin's word against that of Shona Green, the natural mother of the victim, and Maisie Williams her foster mother, as to whether or not Justin kidnapped Jade or had permission to take her away on a so-called holiday."

"I don't see anything on the whiteboards or your report notes to suggest you have any hard and firm evidence to charge Mr Justin Johnson with any crime," said Hannah.

"Why is that Graham?" asked Simon Duncan, in a stern tone that suggested Graham and his team hadn't been thorough enough in their work.

"Justin has been very clever and very lucky, as we have had the best forensic people possible at our disposal dealing with each of the crimes. We have also had the best forensic support from the Devon and Cornwall police in respect of two murders there. Murders that we believe are linked to the murders here, but as of yet don't have a scrap of evidence other than a toy rabbit that could place Justin at the scene of any of the incidents."

"The toy rabbit doesn't constitute enough evidence for you to hold him any longer," said Caroline, "so if you don't have anything further to bring to the table and if everyone in this meeting is in agreement, I would suggest that you release Mr Justin Johnson on bail."

CHAPTER THIRTY-FIVE

"It's been a real shit day," said Joseph to Graham as they sat in the police station canteen drinking black coffee. "That arsehole of a brother of mine gets released and I get a fucking speeding ticket driving into the city."

"Which one upsets you most?" asked Graham.

"At this moment, Justin being released angers me the most, but it will be the ticket when I have to pay the one hundred pound fine in a week or so. I think it is very strange that you complain about having limited resources and yet you can employ an officer to stand by the side of the road pointing a gun at poor unsuspecting motorists who are going about their daily business trying to earn a living. Surely, that officer would be better employed catching real criminals?" said Joseph.

"Maybe, but the speed traps bring in a lot of money," said Graham.

"That's all well and good but you're forgetting the cost of producing and maintaining them and you should also think about the impact your actions have on the general public. With the ridiculous amount of cameras all over the country at the moment, it wouldn't take a fairly good driver too long to rack up enough points on their licence to get a ban, which could in turn cost them their job."

"We believe that speed cameras do help to slow motorists down and in doing so save lives and reduce the severity of any injuries caused by having an accident," replied Graham.

"Maybe you have a point, but I read somewhere that there hasn't been a single example of a collision that would have been prevented by the presence of a speed camera and I actually think they may cause accidents," retorted Joseph.

"Do you have any examples of any accidents that have actually been caused by speed cameras?" asked Graham.

"One all," said Joseph, who then added; "I haven't been here long but what I have observed is that drivers brake suddenly when they see a camera even if they're not speeding. Friends have told me they automatically look at the dashboard to check their speed when they approach a camera thereby taking their eyes off the road. This increases the possibility of an accident should a child or animal run into the road as the driver's reactions would be much slower."

"You really are on your high horse, Joseph. If we can ever find Michael Black and he isn't convicted of any crime, you two could form a double act and write a two hundred or even four hundred word blog about speeding. If you take the right track, you might win a gold medal or two for journalism in the future, too."

"That's a very sharp and very cryptic statement, Graham. I have an idea what you are implying, and I am a little worried that your statement suggests my days working with you here are numbered and that I may be better employed elsewhere?"

"You are a little sensitive tonight, aren't you? I'm really grateful for your help, as we may not have solved these crimes so quickly or even at all without it," said Graham.

"I guess I feel I have failed in one way though, as Justin is soon going to be free to create more havoc wherever he goes."

"He won't be going too far for a while. I have told him to find a place to rent and remain here in the UK and report to this police station every day until I am satisfied that we haven't missed anything and that there really is no evidence against him. I have confiscated his DJ Macintyre passport and issued his photo to Customs here in the UK and throughout Europe, just in case he tries to escape using false documents. I have also asked our operations team to inform all the airlines and ferry companies of his details should he try to book tickets as Justin Johnson or Justin Macintyre."

"That's some comfort, as I'm damn sure with a bit more time we will find some evidence to convict him."

"I agree with you, Joseph, but for now I am going home to get some sleep. Tomorrow I'll go over everything again to try to work out how the hell your brother has managed to get away with bombing, murder, arson and drug dealing."

"I'm going to do the same as I find it hard to believe he has been one step ahead of us all the time. I really thought that his car or his house would provide us with some evidence. I'm still baffled how one has totally disappeared from the face of the earth and the other, found eventually with Jessica's help, was totally empty. It's as if Justin has been mocking us all along, even to the extent of having the same knives that were used in the killings in his toolbox in the Dublin house, but none of them had a single print or mark on them."

~

Shona didn't help with Jade's funeral arrangements but she did attend the service ten days before Christmas and go to the reception afterwards at the local golf club. There were hundreds of mourners in church, including many of Jade's classmates from school, which gave Shona some comfort that her daughter had touched people's hearts and that she would be missed. Jade's body was laid to rest in a special woodland area for children, set away from the main churchyard. Maisie threw a few of Jade's favourite toys into the grave, including a soft squishy penguin wearing a bow tie and a large cuddly hedgehog plush toy that doubled as a pillow and hand warmer. Throughout the service Shona had a strange feeling of being watched. This was the same feeling she had had when walking through the park a few weeks ago. She kept looking around the church and the graveyard but couldn't see anyone acting suspiciously. Justin, however, was there to see the daughter he never really knew buried. The daughter he had had murdered to prevent himself from going to prison. Justin satisfied himself in his mind that he was now in the same position as he was when he arrived here in England. A few weeks ago he didn't have a daughter and today he still didn't have a daughter. There was hope in abundance for him and Shona for a while but those bright lights have now waned and Jade had gone to the stars in the sky.

"Perhaps this is the price of a life of sin," Justin said out loud to himself. It then crossed his mind that this is probably a way of life for many families and that there is a comparison between life and cooking a meal. Some things go right and others don't, but you take the good with the bad and learn from any mistakes that you make. In the main, Justin was happy with his life and believed that he was actually very good at what he did. Hundreds of other people wouldn't agree and would probably say he was insane.

"You can't help the way you are though," he said to himself again rather more loudly as if trying to convince himself that all the things he had done over the years were down to genetics. For a fleeting second, he wondered if he'd had a bit more love and affection from an early age if he would be a different person. Perhaps he wouldn't have had the need to play with knives and hurt people. Perhaps jealousy and revenge had taken away more feelings and emotions than his actions have given him. He was probably too old to change now, although somewhere at the back of his mind he did quite like the idea of using his knife skills in a more appropriate way. The studying and training that he had done all those years ago was more about gaining respect and being the best at something. He just happened to like the glistening of steel and the feel of the various knives in his hands more than the manifestation of his skill with them to produce a meal. If he could somehow convince Shona he had nothing to do with Jade's death and that he would now let her keep the money she owed him if they set up a catering business together in America, she might forgive him. If she was prepared to do most of the hard work cooking and entertaining to earn her keep, he might just forgive her, too.

"If I change a bit and try to be normal, she might actually begin to love me again and maybe I'll win the game and get her back," Justin said quietly to himself, this time as he walked away from the church through the woods and back to a country house about half a mile away that he had checked into a few days ago after his release from custody. He had been lying low since then to try and gather his thoughts and come up with a new plan of action. In normal circumstances, he would have flown home to New York, but until he officially got his passport back this wasn't going to be realistically possible, and he didn't dare ask the Chameleon to forge another one.

~

Michael had somehow staggered for miles, getting weaker and weaker as dehydration and hypothermia set in. His thoughts were becoming confused, but he had needed to make a decision a while ago when he came to a fork in the tunnel. He really didn't know where he was, but chose to go left because the word had fewer letters. His instincts were telling him that he was getting closer to civilisation, as he thought he could feel vibrations and hear faint noises above him. Michael hoped and prayed that he could get help fast.

The floor texture within the tunnel then seemed to change and he felt as if he was going up a slight incline. At the same time, the darkness became less intense for some reason and Michael felt with his hands that the sides of the tunnel were now made of brick rather than stone. As he started touching what appeared to be a section where a door might have been at one time, Michael tripped and crashed to the ground, hitting his head hard and cracking one of his ribs. He yelled in pain and then cried out loudly and gasped for breath as he tried to drag himself back to his feet. The pain and the strain when he tried to stand, was too much for a weakened and dehydrated Michael Black to bear and he could only manage to crawl along on his hands and knees.

After a few hundred yards he came across a metal door and tried to bang on it hard with his fists, but his strength was truly sapped and he could only manage the lightest of taps. Michael tried to stand up again so that he could kick the door instead, but the weakness in his knees meant that he fell back to the floor landing on his bottom and jarring his ribs, which forced him to cry out in agony again before he passed out.

~

Shona was trying to keep busy by making some of her favourite dishes using puff pastry such as beef Wellington and a French fruit tart, before taking them to Maisie and Victor as neither of them could bring themselves to cook. Cooking gave Shona something to do other than visit Jade's gravestone, where she would kneel on the ground and lean on it while plucking the petals from a red rose. Blooming roses are a symbol of happiness, prosperity and long life, and as Shona knew in her heart that she wasn't likely to experience any of these things now, this was her way of communicating with her daughter, and showing her some honour, devotion and love.

As she knelt and looked around, Shona would feel a ghostly presence and she was sure within the swirl of air from the movement of the trees she could see Jade leaning against one of the tree trunks, smiling. Cooking was also a distraction from thinking about Jade and from drinking large volumes of alcohol. Shona had just taken the beef out of the oven and placed it on a cooling rack when she heard a knock at her front door. Upon opening the door she was shocked and unnerved to find Justin standing before her and very pleased that she had managed to get a steel security chain installed two weeks earlier.

"You have a fucking nerve turning up here," said Shona.

"I turned up at Jade's funeral too, although I disguised myself," replied Justin.

"The police told me they had to let you go, but I didn't expect you to still be in Worcester after all that you've done, and especially after you had my daughter murdered."

"I think you'll find that Jade was our daughter and if I had had her killed I would still be in custody awaiting trial. I promise you that I had nothing to do with her being run down and I only came here to say that you can keep the money that you owe me and that when I get my passport back, I will be returning to America."

"What's the catch?" stuttered Shona, still somewhat shocked.

"There isn't one really, only that I would like you to give some thought in the future to coming out to New York to see me and help me with my catering business."

"There isn't a cat's chance that I will have anything to do with you again, and before you arrived here at my door tonight I had already decided to give you your money back. In fact, I'll write a cheque out for you now and you can piss off for good," said Shona aggressively.

As Shona walked into her kitchen to get her cheque book, Justin's mood changed and he kicked the door hard, breaking the chain instantly. He wasn't going to allow Shona to get rid of him that easily. He had an intended outcome for this mission, which was to make Shona dependent on him in one way or another and it wasn't panning out too favourably at the moment. Justin ran towards Shona and when he got close to her he grabbed her by the throat and pushed her against the wall. If being nice and reasonable wasn't going to work he would have to resort to type and 'encourage' her into seeing things his way.

As her head hit the wall, Shona gathered her thoughts and reached across to the work surface with her right hand and with a sideways swipe plunged a carbon steel Japanese slicing knife into Justin's neck. Justin staggered backwards and Shona pushed him hard into the hallway as blood started to spurt over the floor, up the walls and onto the ceiling. Justin stood motionless in a state of shock staring back towards the kitchen. He realised that Shona was going to stab him again, so he turned and ran out of the front door knowing that he needed to get emergency treatment extremely fast or die lying in a gutter or alleyway. Shona slammed her front door shut and put the deadlock on before collapsing onto the floor shaking with fright and horror over the events that had just occurred.

~

Graham had been wondering long and hard how Justin had got away with the crimes he was sure that he had committed. He was sitting discussing this with Joseph at the Swan with Two Nicks on the last night before Joseph went to London to work with Andrew Rankin at MI5 when the possible answer hit him like a stone.

"Emma 'Justin' Thyme," said Graham loudly.

"What?" asked Joseph.

"Your brother has been paying or threatening Emma to conceal evidence against him."

"Or Justin and Emma go way back and she has been in on all of the murders from day one?" said Joseph.

"She did gather a lot of evidence at the bomb site and this helped us make a case against Kevin Rogers though," said Graham, starting to think his thought process was absurd.

"How did her father actually die?" asked Joseph.

"In the line of duty somewhere in a place called Newark, I believe," replied Graham.

"Did the police catch the criminals who did it?"

"Sort of, as they were found dead with their throats cut."

"Are we talking about Newark near Nottingham or Newark near New York?" said Joseph.

"Jesus Christ, I hadn't realised that there were two Newarks, I just assumed he was killed here in England," said Graham.

"I think if you dig a bit deeper into Emma's father's death you may find some answers, not that this will help us get Justin convicted, unless Emma cracks under the pressure of your interrogation," said Joseph.

"I can't interview her," said Graham.

"I guess not as I understand you have been shagging her for a few months," said Joseph.

"How do you know that?" asked Graham.

"It didn't take a genius to work it out," replied Joseph. "And someone in the admin department mentioned it."

"If Emma has been concealing evidence she could go down for a very long time and although I would find it hard to be impartial, I know it's my job to do what I have to do and bring her in for questioning," said Graham.

"Justice has to be served on those that do wrong," replied Joseph. "I think that Kevin Rogers and David Painter will both get life sentences for their crimes and although death isn't a true form of justice in my mind, at least Basil Reddy and Frederick Pierce are no longer a danger to society. I just hope that my scumbag of a brother gets his just desserts, too."

Just as he was about to reply and tell Joseph that he would keep him informed of any key developments relating to Justin, while he was with MI5 in London, Graham's phone rang. It was Charlie sounding agitated and stressed.

Graham listened intently to what Charlie had to say, before putting the receiver down and staring at Joseph with a blank look on his face, before speaking slowly and clearly.

"We have a serious situation happening on the other side of the river. You and I need to get there fast, Joseph, to help Charlie and his firefighters."

CHAPTER THIRTY-SIX

Shona stood fully clothed, wearing her chef's apron, as she pressed her body against the glass of the sliding balcony door of her eighth-floor penthouse. She wasn't sure how many people could see her from the street below. Since stabbing Justin, she had meandered around the various rooms in her apartment, thinking and drinking. She had allowed the beef to cool before plating it, wrapping it in cling film and putting it in a picnic basket ready to take to Maisie. The fruit tart had been placed in an airtight container and was about to be added to the basket, when Shona changed her mind and threw the tart onto the floor in the hall. The juice from the raspberries and strawberries slowly mingled with Justin's drying blood. Her life was in ruins. Everything she had ever loved had gone. Jade was dead. Michael was probably dead. Justin might be dying or had died and her business was unlikely to survive all the bad press, even if she didn't go to prison for her actions an hour or so ago.

All Shona had ever wanted was a normal life, where she could love and be loved within the confines of a secure environment. She had struggled to get to where she was today by meeting and solving problems head on, in the hope that her future life would have meaning. She had never been one to procrastinate in the hope that her problems would go away and she had never taken drugs to help her get through tough times, of which there had been many.

Since Jade's death however, her responses and actions due to the pain inside her body had been different and her mental state had changed, taking her into unknown territory. Territory to some that would seem to be within a neurotic world. Reality for Shona today was a world of anger, anxiety, cynicism, depression, irritability, negativity and sadness, not necessarily in that order. Shona had believed for many years that she was in control of her life, but standing here now she wasn't so sure anymore, as her behaviour was being directed by other forces impacting on her mind, that at the moment were definitely beyond her control. If anyone had asked Shona a few weeks ago if she was a strong person she would have answered in the affirmative. Now, she wasn't so sure what her answer would be. Perhaps all of her big decisions in the past were really based on weakness rather than strength, she thought, as she opened her balcony door and stepped outside into the cold night air.

~

The fire engine raced down Deansway and across the Worcester Bridge leading to New Road. Time was of the essence for Charlie and his men if the reports of a possible attempted suicide being communicated to him were correct. Graham and Joseph were on their way to the same incident, unsure of how they could be of use, but they knew they had to do whatever they could to prevent one more shockwave from hitting the city and the sticky brown stuff from hitting the round whirly thing on their desks.

~

A cleaner at a bar–restaurant in the city centre heard a noise coming from an external door. It was as if someone was banging on it and crying out for help. It was late into the night and Adrijana thought this to be highly unlikely, as the door hadn't been used for years since the redevelopment of the main shopping area, and the fact that barrels of beer were now delivered via a front entrance. Adrijana listened again before running upstairs to get her manager. Pablo came down into the cellar and listened for noises himself, and then satisfied that something was wrong he telephoned the owner of the establishment. George arrived within fifteen minutes and moved some fixtures out of the way before unlocking a heavy steel door that could only be opened from the inside. They all stared in disbelief when the door was opened, as there lying on the floor was a man who was bleeding from what appeared to be a severe head or neck wound.

~

Shona removed her apron and draped it over her small, square folding table, which reminded her of Michael. She hadn't known Michael very long but she loved him more than she thought could ever be possible. It was a different love from that she felt for Jade, as it was probably a love motivated consciously or subconsciously by sex, but deep down she knew it was a love that would have lasted forever.

Shona's love for Jade was deep, very deep in her mind, but not deep enough according to her friends and family, who struggled to understand the rationale for giving her daughter up all those years ago. These were the same people who also didn't understand her next strong, or maybe weak, decision.

Shona had made up her mind that she couldn't carry on living without Jade and Michael and certainly couldn't face a long custodial sentence. She stood on a chair next to her table and stared at the ground some one hundred feet below. With her mind still spinning, she stood on the table and prepared for life in another world. Everything and anyone that had meant anything to her had gone and there was only one way for Shona to put the pieces of the jigsaw back together.

A crowd was starting to gather in the gloom below but Shona didn't notice this as she stepped onto the wall surrounding her balcony and placed her feet beneath the metal hand rail. Some people with binoculars could probably make out what was happening clearly, but she didn't care as there was nothing left in her life for Shona to be proud of, and nobody left in her life who she would miss or who would miss her.

If I can't be a high-flier in the business world, I can at least be a high-flyer Shona thought to herself as she contemplated jumping.

~

As Graham and Joseph crossed the bridge over the river by the cricket ground, Graham took another phone call on his mobile. The person on the other end of the line was clear and succinct in their delivery of nine words: "We have found Michael Black and he is alive." Graham put his foot down hard on the accelerator and within thirty seconds screeched to a halt behind Charlie's fire engine as his crew were unravelling a safety net. A safety net wasn't an official part of their safety kit these days and hadn't been since the mid 1980s, but was something Charlie insisted on keeping for just this type of emergency, where it was evident that a long ladder would be of little use. Graham leapt out of the police car, grabbed a megaphone from one of the fire officers standing on the grass and shouted up towards Shona in as loud a voice as possible: "We have found Michael Black, he is alive."

Shona, somehow among all the noise and commotion, heard what Graham shouted. This caused her to shudder with disbelief and try within her scrambled mind to comprehend if this was a ploy to stop her jumping, or if the information was true. She chose at that point to believe it could be true and stepped back from the wall, but as she did so her foot clipped the hand rail and she lost her balance and toppled forwards. As she fell, her mind seemed to clear for a split second and a reflex action allowed her to spin and grasp the rail with one hand. Shona clung on with an outstretched arm and now shaken out of her daze, her life or death choice had suddenly become difficult.

Charlie and his crew saw what was about to happen so they grabbed the net and sprinted towards the place where Shona would land if her grip on the rail loosened. Graham stood looking upwards aghast at the scene unfolding above him. He hoped and prayed that Shona could hang on until Charlie and his crew or the officers who were at this point breaking her front door down, could get to her and save her from being killed.

A PARTY TO MURDER

-Recipes from the novel-

How to Use the Recipe Book

The aim of this section is to bring the food cooked by Shona, into as many homes as possible – food that is to be enjoyed on your own or as part of a sharing experience with friends and family. Whether you are an experienced cook or have just started on an exciting journey learning how to prepare and serve delicious food, you will find within these pages many recipes and even new, inspiring ingredients to tantalise your taste buds.

The following pages contain recipes for all of the dishes mentioned within the book.

All of the recipes are designed for 6 people. If you have more or fewer people to your dinner party, divide the measure or weight of the ingredients by 6 as best as possible and multiply by the number of guests.

If you make more than you serve up, the majority of the dishes will be just as nice the following day and many of them can be frozen for use at a later date.

It is good practice to taste your food as you go, to make sure the balance and seasoning is to the liking of you or your guests before serving.

All of the timings are an approximate guide and are subject to your experience, organisation, the speed you choose to work at and the efficiency of your oven. They will help you determine which menus are possible to cook before your friends or family arrive, and which are easy to prepare while entertaining. Many of the dishes can be pre-prepared to give you more time on the day.

The key utensils required to prepare each dish are highlighted within the instructions to ensure you don't start something you can't finish and that everything goes smoothly on the day. Some words or phrases within the recipes that may be unfamiliar to some readers are clarified in the glossary at the back of the book.

Shona was able to gain some contracts because of her knowledge of food and its potential health benefits. Her clients were pleased to learn how some of the key ingredients could be beneficial to them in some way and to understand that minor changes to their eating habits could lead to major changes in their health and life expectancy.

Shona often described foods to her clients as being an excellent, high, rich, good or useful source of nutrients. These are scaled terms that help describe the nutritional value of a food to meet the daily requirements of the majority of healthy people within the population, as recommended by the Department for Environment, Food and Rural Affairs' Reference Nutrient Intake paper. Understandably, the RNI for males and females of different ages and for young children and teenagers will vary quite widely to reflect their different and changing needs.

Disclaimer

As is the case with many things, sometimes a little knowledge can be dangerous and the information that Shona proffered and that is provided in this book is included for educational and entertainment purposes only. It is not a substitute for professional medical advice. The information was obtained from a variety of sources and was correct at the time of publication. The information and materials provided are general in nature, and may not apply to all readers in all circumstances as some details may have been omitted. The advice given by Shona is provided "as is" without warranty of any kind, either expressed or implied. In no event shall anyone associated with this book be liable for any damages including, but not limited to, direct, indirect, special, incidental or consequential damages or other losses arising out of the use of or inability to use or understand the information provided.

Please consult your doctor, physician or health care provider before taking any home remedies, supplements or starting a new health regime.

STARTERS

Asparagus and Mushroom Quiche

Preparation Time – 25 minutes
(45 minutes if you make your own pastry)

Cooking Time – 60 minutes

Ingredients

240g Shortcrust Pastry (For recipe, see p.482)
240g Asparagus (24 Spears)
180g White Mushrooms
1 Medium Onion
50g Grated Cheese
3 tbsp Double Cream
3 Large Eggs
1 tsp Worcester Sauce
2 tbsp Plain Flour
2 Garlic Cloves
2 tsp Salt
2 tsp Black Pepper
30g Butter + extra for greasing

Method

1. Roll out the **pastry** thinly. Place this into a pre-greased **20cm flan tin with removable bottom.** Blind bake for 15 minutes. Leave to cool.
2. Wash the **asparagus spears** and cut off the hard ends of the stalks with a sharp knife. Place in a **saucepan** and cover with boiling water. Simmer for 5 minutes until the stems are tender and then drain.

3. Chop the **onion** finely and sauté in a **frying pan** in 20g butter for a few minutes until soft and translucent.
4. Take 12 asparagus spears and cut these 8cm from the top. Set the 8cm stems aside and put the rest of the asparagus into a **processor** with the **mushrooms.**
5. Blend the asparagus and mushrooms for about 15 seconds until semi-pureed and then turn out into a **bowl**. Season with **salt** and **pepper** and then beat in the rest of the **butter, cream, eggs, Worcester sauce, chopped garlic, flour, grated cheese** and the sautéed onion.
6. Pour mixture onto the pastry in the flan tin and spread it out evenly.
7. Decorate with the 12 asparagus spears set aside.
8. Bake in a preheated oven at 180°C for about 35 – 40 minutes.
9. Serve either warm or cold with salad.

Tip – The freshest and tastiest asparagus can be obtained during the British growing season from April to June. It is a good source of fibre, folate and vitamins A, C, E and K as well as being packed with antioxidants.

Salmon Fishcakes

Preparation Time –30 minutes
Cooking Time – 25 minutes

Ingredients

360g Salmon Fillet
600g White Potatoes
1 tbsp Milk
2 Large Onions
3 Garlic Cloves
30g Fresh Coriander
30g Fresh Parsley
1 tbsp Lemon Juice
2 Medium Eggs
2 tsp Black Pepper
3 tbsp Plain Flour
30g Unsalted Butter

Method

1. *Preheat the oven to 180°C.*
2. *Place a knob of **butter** on the **salmon fillet** and wrap it in tin foil.*
3. *Bake the salmon in the oven for about 10 minutes.*
4. *Peel and boil the **potatoes** in a **saucepan** until tender then mash them with a little **milk** and leave to cool.*
5. *Put the cooked salmon in a mixing bowl and flake to make sure all bones are removed.*
6. *Leave the salmon to cool.*
7. *Finely chop the **onions, parsley, coriander** and **garlic***

and add to the mashed potato with the lemon juice.

8. Beat the **eggs** in a bowl and season with **black pepper.**
9. Mix the salmon, eggs and mashed potato mixture together.
10. Form the mixture into 6 even-sized large patties or 12 small patties on a floured pastry board.
11. Heat the rest of the butter in a large frying pan and fry the patties on one side for 2 minutes, then turn them over and fry the other side for the same time.
12. Serve immediately on a plate with a side salad, tartar sauce and some crusty bread and butter.

Tip – Salmon contains omega-3 fatty acids which may help to prevent heart attacks in people with angina, as they prevent the thickening of the arteries and improve blood flow to the heart. Recent studies have found that salmon contains small proteins called bioactive peptides that help to improve bone density and strength. They have also concluded that eating salmon twice a week may significantly decrease the risk of macular degeneration.

Mushroom and Leek Gratin

Preparation Time – 25 minutes
Cooking Time – 30 minutes

Ingredients

420g Cremini Mushrooms
4 Large Leeks
4 tbsp of Virgin Olive Oil
60ml Dry White Wine
300ml Double Cream
1 tbsp of Lemon Juice
80g Breadcrumbs
1 tsp Salt
2 tsp Black Pepper
50g Parmesan Cheese
French Toast

Method

1. *Preheat the oven to 200°C.*
2. *Wash and slice **leeks** into 1cm thick rounds.*
3. *Remove the stalks and slice **mushrooms** approximately 1cm thick.*
4. *Fry leeks in a **frying pan** in half of the olive oil for 3 minutes on medium heat.*
5. *Add half the **wine** and cook for a further 1 minute or until wine has evaporated.*
6. *Stir in half the cream and cook for 2 minutes.*
7. *Place the leeks in an **ovenproof dish** and top with **lemon juice.***

8. *Using the same pan, fry the mushrooms in the rest of the oil for 3 minutes.*
9. *Add the rest of the wine and cream and fry for a further minute.*
10. *Season with the **salt** and **pepper**.*
11. *Place the mushrooms on top of the leeks in the ovenproof dish.*
12. *Sprinkle **parmesan** and **breadcrumbs** to cover the mushrooms and leeks.*
13. *Bake in the oven for 15 minutes.*
14. *Serve on **French toast** on individual plates.*

Tip – Leeks are allium vegetables closely related to onions, garlic and shallots that add a subtle touch to recipes without overpowering other flavours. They are packed with essential vitamins, minerals and antioxidants such as calcium, vitamin C, folic acid and potassium that offer a variety of health benefits. They also contain an impressive amount of flavonoids particularly kaempherol which has been shown to protect blood vessel linings from damage and at the time of writing is under consideration for use in cancer treatment.

Spanish Carrot Soup (Crema de Zanahoria)

Preparation Time – 20 minutes
Cooking Time – 25 minutes

Ingredients

4 Large Carrots
4 Large White Potatoes
1 tsp Salt
1 Large Onion
20g Unsalted Butter
2 Chicken Stock Cubes
500ml Boiling Water
20g Fresh Coriander
330ml Semi-Skimmed Milk
3 tsp Black Pepper

Method

1. Scrape the **carrots** and slice into 1cm thick rounds.
2. Peel **potatoes** and cut into 2cm thick slices.
3. Chop the **onion** and the **coriander** finely.
4. Cook the carrots and potatoes in a **large saucepan** of salted boiling water for about 10 minutes until the carrots are cooked but firm.
5. Drain using a **colander** and leave to cool.
6. Using the same saucepan melt the **butter** on a medium heat, add the chopped onion and sauté for a few minutes until soft and translucent.
7. Crumble the **chicken stock cubes** in a **glass measuring jug** and stir in the boiling water.

8. Place the carrots and potatoes in a **processor** with 100ml of the chicken stock and the coriander.
9. After pureeing for I minute, return the contents to the saucepan now containing the onion and bring to the boil.
10. Stir in the rest of the stock and the **semi-skimmed milk**.
11. Add the **black pepper** and stir until creamy.
12. Simmer for 10 minutes.
13. Serve hot with crusty bread.

Tip – Carrots are an excellent source of beta carotene which the body converts into vitamin A, which is needed for healthy vision. Unlike most other vegetables, carrots are more nutritious when cooked and if eaten daily will actually help to improve your night vision. Recent studies have also shown that a high intake of beta carotene may play a protective role against prostate cancer and damage to the body by free radicals. Grating or peeling carrots will make them taste sweeter as this releases flavours more quickly which also increases antioxidant levels.

Pea and Lettuce Cream

Preparation Time – 15 minutes
Cooking Time – 25 minutes

Ingredients

6 Little Gem Lettuces
1 Medium Onion
20g Unsalted Butter
360g Garden Peas
1 tsp Salt
2 tsp Black Pepper
5g Fresh Coriander
3 tbsp Cold Water
3 tbsp Double Cream
6 Muffins

Method

1. Wash and then slice up the **lettuces** finely.
2. Chop the **onion** and the **coriander** finely.
3. Melt the **butter** in a large **frying pan**.
4. Fry the onion for 1 minute on a medium heat.
5. Add the lettuce, **peas** and **cold water.**
6. Sprinkle on the **salt, pepper** and coriander.
7. Cover the pan with **tin foil** and cook on a low heat for about 15 minutes.
8. Check every few minutes to make sure all of the water hasn't evaporated.

9. At the end of the cooking time, drain off any excess
   water and add the **cream.**
10. Cook for a further 3–4 minutes.
11. Serve hot on buttered **muffins.**

Tip – Peas are free of cholesterol and low in calories, fat and sodium. They feed your brain and benefit your immune system with antioxidant minerals and vitamins that also support blood, bone and muscle health. They also have high fibre content for improved bowel health and contain a carotenoid substance called lutein which has been shown to reduce the risk of age related macular degeneration and cataracts. Lettuce was thought by ancient people to possess medicinal properties. It does have anti-inflammatory properties that can help to protect neuronal brain cells, lower cholesterol levels, reduce anxiety and the risk of diabetes and help prevent the growth of cancerous cells in the body.

Sautéed Scallops with Mushrooms and Spinach

Preparation Time – 20 minutes
Cooking Time – 20 minutes

Ingredients

12 Scallops
240g White Mushrooms
600g Spinach
120g Unsalted Butter
100ml Double Cream
30ml Lemon Juice
3 Garlic Cloves
20g Fresh Tarragon
10g Fresh Parsley
2 tsp Salt
3 tsp Black Pepper
60ml Dry White Wine

Method

1. Melt 50g of the **butter** in a **large saucepan.**
2. Slice the **mushrooms** and cook them in the butter with 30ml of **white wine** for 3 - 4 minutes on a medium heat.
3. Wash the **spinach** and place in a **large dry saucepan** on a medium to high heat for 2 – 3 minutes until the leaves wilt and become soft.
4. Remove the spinach from the pan and place into a

colander. Press down with the back of a wooden spoon to drain off any excess liquid.

5. Place the spinach in the saucepan with the mushrooms, season with **salt** and **pepper** and pour in the **double cream.**

6. Simmer on a low heat for 5 minutes.

7. Chop the **garlic, tarragon** and **parsley** finely.

8. In a **large frying pan**, melt another 50g of the butter over a medium heat with a tablespoon of **olive oil** and the **chopped garlic**.

9. Season the **scallops** with salt and pepper and place them in the pan for 2 minutes without touching them.

10. Turn them over and cook them on the other side for a further 2 minutes basting them continuously until you see a golden brown ring at the edge of each scallop.

11. Place the spinach and mushrooms into individual serving bowls and arrange the scallops on top.

12. Pour the rest of the wine and **lemon juice** into a saucepan, add the rest of the butter, chopped tarragon and parsley and stir for 1 minute on a high heat.

13. Pour over the scallops and serve immediately.

Tip – Scallops are an excellent source of vitamin B_{12}, magnesium and potassium which are important nutrients for cardiovascular health. Studies have also indicated that a high intake of vitamin B_{12} has been shown to protect the cells of the colon from cancer causing chemicals. A deficiency in the body of vitamin B_{12} can cause extreme tiredness, muscle weakness, breathlessness, pins and needles, a sore tongue, headaches and tinnitus.

Baked Eggs in Roasted Tomatoes

Preparation Time – 30 minutes
Cooking Time – 45 minutes

Ingredients

6 Beef Tomatoes
6 Medium Eggs
1 tbsp Olive Oil
2 Garlic Gloves
5g Fresh Chives
½ tsp Rock Salt
1 tsp Black Pepper
15g Parmesan Cheese

Method

1. *Preheat the oven to 160°C.*
2. *Slice the top off the **tomatoes.***
3. *Carefully scoop out the core and the seeds with a **paring knife** and a **teaspoon** without breaking through the flesh and skin of the tomato.*
4. *Invert the tomatoes on some **kitchen towel** for 5 minutes to drain all the excess juice.*
5. *Place the tomatoes in a **baking dish.***
6. *Crush the **garlic cloves** in a **press** and chop the **chives.***
7. *Drizzle some **olive oil** in each tomato and sprinkle on the crushed garlic and chopped chives.*
8. *Roast the **tomatoes** in the oven for 20 minutes.*
9. *Crack one **egg** at a time into a **small jug** and pour each one carefully into each tomato.*

10. Season with **salt** and **pepper.**
11. Bake in the oven for about 15–20 minutes or until the egg white starts to set.
12. Sprinkle some **parmesan cheese** onto each tomato and put back in the oven for about 5 minutes.
13. Serve on a small plate with crusty bread and a garnish of your choice such as fresh parsley, basil or water cress.

Tip – Eggs are one of the most nutritious foods on the planet. Although they are high in cholesterol they don't adversely affect blood cholesterol and frequent consumption can lead to elevated levels of HDL (the "good") cholesterol. Omega-3 enriched and pastured eggs contain significant amounts of omega-3 fatty acids which are known to reduce triglycerides in the blood. High triglyceride levels put you at risk of heart disease and a heart attack. Diabetics are possibly the only group of people who should avoid averaging more than one egg a day.

Bacon and Avocado Potato Skins

Preparation Time – 30 minutes
Cooking Time – 60 minutes

Ingredients

8 Rashers Back Bacon
6 Medium Russet Potatoes
2 Large Avocados
1 tsp Lemon Juice
3 tbsp Unsalted Butter
2 Garlic Cloves
2 Spring Onions
20g Cheddar Cheese
1 tsp Salt and Pepper
150g Sour Cream

Method

1. Wash then bake the **potatoes** in a 200°C oven for 45-50 minutes.
2. Fry the **bacon** in 1 tbsp butter until it starts to go crispy. Remove from **frying pan** and leave to cool.
3. Slice each **avocado** in half by cutting all of the way round the skin with a **paring knife** and remove the pit with a spoon.
4. Using the same knife, cut a criss-cross pattern into the flesh of the avocados then slide the knife beneath the cube shapes, getting as close to the skin as possible.
5. Scoop out the avocado flesh, place it in a **medium bowl** and drizzle with **lemon juice** to stop it going brown.

6. Remove potatoes from oven and slice length ways.
7. Scoop the potato out of the skins and set aside.
8. Place the skins on a **baking tray** and put them in the oven at a temperature of 150°C for 5 minutes to keep crispy.
9. Chop the **spring onions** and **garlic cloves.**
10. Place the potato in a frying pan with the garlic, spring onions and rest of the butter and fry until well coated.
11. Chop the bacon finely and mix in a bowl with the avocado and **sour cream.** Season with **salt** and **pepper.**
12. Remove the potato from the pan and place it into the bowl with the bacon and avocado. Mix together well and then spoon the mixture back into the potato skins.
13. Grate the **cheese** on top of the skins and place them under a medium grill for a few minutes until hot.

Tip – Unlike most fruits, avocados only start to ripen when they have been cut from the tree. They have the highest protein content of any fruit and are a great source of monounsaturated oleic acid that research has shown reduces LDL (the "bad") cholesterol in the blood. They are a good source of potassium that help the body mechanisms control blood pressure and maintain a regular heartbeat and healthy nervous system. Avocados are also a rich source of vitamin E, an antioxidant that helps thin the blood, enhance its circulation to the scalp to promote strong and heathy hair growth and protect the skin from wrinkles and other visible signs of ageing.

Kitka Salad

Preparation Time – 40 minutes
Cooking Time – 15 minutes

Ingredients

9 Mackerel Fillets
3 Large Avocados
6 Large Tomatoes
1 Medium Cucumber
1 Large Onion
50g Unsalted Butter
Sweet Chilli Sauce
12g Fresh Coriander
2 tbsp Lemon Juice
1 Green Chilli
Salt and Pepper
3 tsp Olive Oil

Method

1. Grill the **mackerel fillets** for about 5–6 minutes. Leave to cool.
2. Remove the skin from the fish, flake the flesh using a fork and place this in a **large bowl.**
3. Chop the **onion** and **green chilli** finely.
4. Melt the **butter** and **olive oil** in a **frying pan**, add the **onion** and cook on a medium heat for 3–4 minutes until the onion is soft but not browned.
5. Chop up 3 of the **tomatoes** and the **coriander** finely and add these to the bowl containing the mackerel. Drizzle

*with the **lemon juice** and add the mixture to the pan with the butter and onion.*

6. *Cook on a low heat for about 4 minutes, then remove from the pan and leave it to cool.*
7. *Slice each **avocado** in half by cutting all of the way round the skin with a **paring knife** and remove the pit.*
8. *Peel off the skin, thinly slice the avocados lengthways and set them aside in a **flat dish**. Sprinkle with lemon juice to stop them discolouring.*
9. *Slice the remaining 3 tomatoes and the **cucumber.***
10. *Arrange the avocado, tomato and cucumber slices around the edge of each plate so they form a circle.*
11. *Place the mackerel mixture in the middle of each plate.*
12. *Sprinkle with the chopped chilli and then season with a little **salt** and **pepper.***
13. *Drizzle with **sweet chilli sauce.***
14. *Serve with a crusty roll and butter.*

Tip – There are many benefits of eating oily fish such as mackerel, which contain high levels of omega-3 fatty acids but are low in saturated fats. It can help prevent cardiovascular disease, strengthen the immune system, and improve the function of organs weakened by illness. It can also reduce symptoms of rheumatoid arthritis and improve cognitive function thereby lowering the chance of suffering from Alzheimer's or Parkinson's disease. If you want to use whole mackerel and fillet them yourself make sure you select those from the fish counter with bright eyes and that don't droop when held horizontally by the head.

Asgard Soup

Preparation Time – 20 minutes
Cooking Time – 30 minutes

Ingredients

100g Minced Beef
½ Medium Onion
20g Unsalted Butter
150g Potatoes
550ml Vegetable Stock
60g Celery
60g Mushrooms
75g Medium Carrots
60g Garden Peas
60g Sweetcorn
2 Garlic Cloves
1 tsp Black Pepper

Method

1. *Dry fry the **mince** for 5 minutes in a **frying pan** then drain off any fat, season with **pepper** and set aside in a **bowl.***
2. *Chop up the **onion** finely, fry this in **butter** on a medium heat for 3 minutes until softened and add to the bowl with the mince.*
3. *Peel the **potatoes**, cut them into quarters and boil in a **medium saucepan** in 450ml of the **vegetable stock** for 5 minutes.*

4. Slice the **celery**, **mushrooms** and **carrots** into 1cm pieces.
5. Add these to the saucepan with the potatoes and cook for a further 10 minutes.
6. Transfer only the vegetables above to a **processor** with another 100ml of the stock and blend for 1 minute.
7. Add the **garlic cloves** and then the mince and onions and blend all the ingredients together for about 1 minute.
8. Pour the mixture back into the saucepan; then add the **peas** and the **sweetcorn.**
9. Bring to the boil and then simmer for 5 minutes.
10. Serve with crusty bread and butter.

Tip – Ground beef if eaten in moderation has many nutrients that are good for the body including vitamin B_{12} and vitamin B_6. Both offer many benefits such as maintaining healthy brain and nerve functions, aiding proper digestion, the forming of red blood cells and turning food into energy. Ground beef also contains iron which aids the absorption of oxygen in the blood, phosphorus, which helps to keep bones, teeth and muscles healthy and zinc which can help improve athletic performance and strength, support reproductive health and fertility, boost immune functions and protect against cancer. Make sure when cooking ground beef that it reaches a temperature higher than 160°C as it is susceptible to harmful bacteria such as E coli.

Chicken Liver Pâté

Preparation Time – 30 minutes
Cooking Time – 15 minutes
Chilling Time – 3 hours

Ingredients

350g Chicken Livers
250g Butter
50ml Double Cream
2 Garlic Cloves
2 tbsp Brandy
1 Medium Onion
2 tsp Chopped Thyme
2 tsp Black Pepper
1 tsp Salt
½ tsp Nutmeg

Method

1. *Wash the **chicken livers** under cold water then dry them off with a **paper towel.***
2. *Place the livers on a **chopping board** and trim the connective veins from them.*
3. *Cut the livers into 2.5cm pieces and set them aside.*
4. *Melt half the **butter** in a **pan** over a medium heat.*
5. *Chop the **onion** finely, add to the pan and fry for 2-3 minutes until softened but not browned.*
6. *Crush the **garlic** using a **press.***
7. *Add the livers to the pan with the garlic, **thyme** and **nutmeg** and fry for 5–6 minutes on a high heat until the*

livers are golden brown.

8. *Add the **brandy** and cook for a further 1 minute.*
9. *Pour contents of the pan into a **food processor,** add the **cream, salt** and **pepper** and blend until smooth.*
10. *Add 50g of butter and blend again.*
11. *Transfer the pâté to a **small loaf tin.***
12. *Melt the remaining butter in a clean pan, skim off the froth and then pour the butter over the pâté. This will preserve the pâté until you wish to enjoy it.*
13. *Transfer the loaf tin to the fridge and chill for about 3 hours until set.*
14. *Removing the clarified butter from the bottom of the pâté first, slice into 6 pieces and serve with a side dish of chopped lettuce and tomatoes, and cold toast.*

Tip – Chicken liver is brimming with nutrients including vitamin B12, vitamin A, folate, selenium, iron and niacin, as well as pantothenic acid and riboflavin. Their combined benefits will guard against anaemia, promote good eyesight, support fertility, keep the thyroid and adrenal glands healthy and maintain good skin condition. Although they are very low in fat they do have high dietary cholesterol content so should only be an occasional part of a balanced diet.

Tangy Avocado Fans with Prawns

Preparation Time – 25 minutes

Ingredients

3 Large Avocados
300g Cooked Prawns
90g Watercress
2 tbsp Lime Juice
6 tbsp of Mayonnaise
1 tbsp Double Cream
6 drops of Tabasco Sauce
3 tsp Tomato Purée
1 tsp Worcester Sauce
1 tsp Paprika
1 tsp Black Pepper
½ tsp Salt

Method

1. *Halve each **avocado pear** lengthways by cutting all the way round them with a **paring knife.***
2. *Twist the halves in opposite directions to expose the pit.*
3. *Scoop the pit out with a spoon or by hitting it with the blade of a **sharp kitchen knife**.*
4. *Cut each half in half lengthways so that you have four quarters.*
5. *Peel the skin off each quarter and discard.*
6. *Place the avocado quarters face down and slice lengthways into 2 or 3 even pieces.*
7. *Take 2 quarters per person and fan the 6 or 8 slices out*

opposite each other on a round plate.

8. *Brush with **lime juice** and season with **black pepper**.*
9. *Mix the remaining lime juice with the **mayonnaise, double cream, tabasco sauce, tomato purée, Worcester sauce, paprika** and **salt** and **pepper**.*
10. *Place a spoonful in the middle of the 2 fans.*
11. *Place the **prawns** on top of the mayonnaise.*
12. *Sprinkle the **watercress** over the avocado and prawns.*
13. *Drizzle with a little **olive oil** if required.*
14. *Serve with bread and butter.*

Tip – Prawns are often thought to be a large shrimp but they actually come from different families. There are thousands of different species but only about 10 key economic types including – Banana, Endeavour, King, Tiger, North Atlantic and School. They are a good provider of protein and are low in fat and calories. They contain reasonable amounts of essential fatty acids such as omega-3 but are a very rich source of selenium that is an antioxidant believed to play a role in the fight against cancer. All shellfish are highly perishable and prone to bacterial contamination so must be stored and cooked properly. They are also more likely than any other types of fish or meat to trigger allergic reactions in susceptible people.

MAINS

Ox Cheeks, Dumplings and Worcester Potato Cakes

Preparation Time – 60 minutes (excluding Marinating)
Cooking Time – 4 hours (Oven) 6 hours (Slow Cooker)

Ingredients

Main

700g Ox Cheeks
300ml Red Wine
300ml Beef Stock
440ml Best Bitter
4 Large Carrots
50g Bacon Lardons
2 Large Onions
6 Garlic Cloves
6 Peppercorns
½ tsp Salt
½ tsp Pepper
6 Large Field Mushrooms

Dumplings

120g Plain Flour
100g Shredded Suet
90g Breadcrumbs
1½ tsp Baking Powder
½ tbsp Dried Parsley
½ tbsp Dried Tarragon

Potato Cakes

360g White Potatoes
45g Shredded Suet
45g Plain Flour
1 tsp Baking Powder
1 tsp Black Pepper
½ tsp Salt

Method

1. *Place the **ox cheeks, peppercorns** and 2 whole **garlic cloves** in a **large bowl,** cover with **red wine** and marinate in the fridge for a few hours or overnight.*
2. *Remove ox cheeks from the marinade when ready to use and dry with a **paper towel.***
3. *Slice them into 4cm wide strips and then into 4cm cubes removing as much fat and sinew as possible.*
4. *Brown the ox cheeks in a **frying pan** for 2 minutes and then place them in an **ovenproof dish** or in a **slow cooker bowl** and sprinkle with **salt** and **pepper.***
5. *Chop the **onions** and fry them over a medium heat until soft and translucent. Add 4 chopped garlic cloves and the **bacon lardons** and continue frying for 2 minutes.*
6. *Add the onions, garlic and bacon lardons to the dish or bowl containing the ox cheeks then cover with the wine from the marinade, **beer** and the **beef stock.***
7. *If cooking in an oven, cover the dish with a lid or tightly with **tin foil** and cook at a preheated 150°C for 4 hours. If using a slow cooker, cook on a low heat for 6 hours.*
8. *Peel the **potatoes** and boil them in slightly salted water until floury. Crumble the potatoes up with a fork and*

mix with **suet, flour, baking powder** and **pepper** until you get a smooth firm mixture.

9. Roll the mixture out onto a floured **pastry board** to a thickness of 1cm and cut into 6 squares. Place these on a **tray** or plate in the fridge until required.

10. To make the dumplings, mix the **plain flour, suet, breadcrumbs, parsley, tarragon, baking powder** and a little **water** to form a sticky dough. On a floured board form the dough into 6 large dumplings then place these on a tray in the fridge until required.

11. Slice the **carrots** to 1cm thick and add to the dish or bowl containing the ox cheeks about 50 minutes before you wish to serve up. Add the dumplings at the same time.

12. Slice the **field mushrooms** and add to the ox cheeks 40 minutes before you serve the meal. At this point turn the oven up to 180° or the slow cooker to a high setting.

13. If you require dumplings with a crispy top – remove the lid or foil from the oven proof dish or place the slow cooker bowl in the oven 20 minutes before serving. Check your slow cooker manufacturer's instructions first for oven suitability.

14. Place the potato cakes onto a **baking tray** and put them in the oven for 15–20 minutes until browned and crisp. Serve these on a side plate instead of bread.

15. Serve ox cheeks in a deep bowl with vegetables of your choice.

Tip – Ox cheeks are cuts of meat taken from the cheek muscles of a cow. They contain little or no fat and because of this can be tough if prepared incorrectly. If cooked properly they are extremely flavoursome and are a great food source for protein, iron vitamin B_{12} and zinc.

Teviotdale Pie

Preparation Time – 35 minutes
Cooking Time – 45 minutes

Ingredients

Main

500g Lean Minced Beef
1 tbsp Olive Oil
250g White Mushrooms
2 Medium Onions
3 Garlic Cloves
2 Medium Carrots
300ml Beef Stock
180g Garden Peas
1 tbsp Tomato Purée
1 tbsp Worcester Sauce
1 tsp Salt
2 tsp Black Pepper
20g Unsalted Butter

Suet Crust

250g Self-Raising Flour
25g Cornflour
75g Shredded Suet
300ml Semi-Skimmed Milk
2 tsp Black Pepper
1 tsp Tarragon

Method

1. Preheat the oven to 180°C.
2. Cook the **mince** in a **frying pan** on a medium high heat in olive oil for about 4 minutes until browned. Add the salt and pepper half way through.
3. Chop the **garlic** finely.
4. Turn the heat down a little, add the **Worcester sauce** and chopped garlic and fry the mince for a further 1 minute.
5. Place the mince in a large **casserole dish** and set aside.
6. Slice the **mushrooms** into quarters and chop the **onions** finely.
7. Melt the **butter** in a frying pan. Add the mushrooms and onions and cook on a medium heat for about 2–3 minutes.
8. Slice the **carrots** into 0.5cm thick rounds, add these to the frying pan and cook with the mushrooms and onions for a further 1–2 minutes.
9. Add the mushrooms, onions and carrots to the casserole dish and stir well.
10. Pour the **beef stock** onto the mince and then mix in the **garden peas** and **tomato purée.**
11. Put the **self-raising flour** in a **mixing bowl** with the **cornflour, suet, black pepper** and **tarragon.**
12. Gradually stir in the **milk** to form a thick batter.
13. Pour the batter over the mince mixture and bake in the oven for about 35 minutes until it has risen and browned.
14. Serve with Charlotte potatoes and green vegetables of your choice.

Tip – Although classified as vegetables in the catering world, mushrooms belong to the fungi kingdom. There are more than 10,000 varieties, some of which may be millions of years old. They are one of only a few vegetables to contain selenium and the only vegetable to contain vitamin D. They also contain copper which is the third most prevalent mineral in the body, which can help prevent anaemia, arthritis, infections, osteoporosis, and thyroid disorders. Mushrooms are naturally low in calories, sodium and fat but high in dietary fibre, which promotes good bowel health and acts as a bulking agent in the digestive system, making you feel full for longer, which can help with weight management. Don't wash mushrooms before using them as they absorb water like a sponge. Use a mushroom brush or clean damp cloth instead. Only eat mushrooms that have been cultivated under appropriate conditions as some wild mushrooms can cause severe illness or death.

Algerian Borek

Preparation Time – 45 minutes
Cooking Time – 20 minutes

Ingredients

250g Ground Beef Mince
1 Large Onion
250g Spinach
1 tsp Salt
1 tsp Black Pepper
½ tsp Ground Ginger
2 Small Eggs
12 Filo Pastry Sheets
60g Fresh Parsley
120g Feta Cheese
1 tbsp Olive Oil

Method

1. Heat the **olive oil** in a **large frying pan** over a medium heat.
2. Chop the **onion** finely, place in the pan with the **spinach** and cook on a medium heat for about 3 minutes.
3. Add the **beef, salt, pepper** and **ginger** and cook for a further 8 minutes.
4. Beat the **eggs** in a **small bowl** and then pour them over the beef mixture.
5. Mix everything together and cook for 3 minutes.
6. Turn off the heat, add the chopped **parsley** and stir well.

7. Transfer the mixture to a **large bowl** and leave to cool.
8. Cut the **filo pastry** into 12 oblong sheets 20cm long x 18cm wide.
9. Place equal amounts of the filling along one edge of each of the **filo** sheets and crumble the **feta cheese** onto them.
10. Fold the edge of each sheet nearest to you over the filling and roll a couple of times.
11. Then take the edge of the sheet furthest away from you and bring this over the top of the borek.
12. Continue to roll the borek away from you as tightly as possible.
13. Moisten the edge of the last 2 inches with water and finish rolling.
14. Fry on a medium heat for about 4 minutes and then place on a **baking tray** in a 150°C oven to keep warm until you have made them all.
15. Serve on a bed of lettuce and chopped tomatoes.

Tip – Spinach is an excellent source of vitamin A, C and K. It also contains a rich source of calcium which is essential for bone health. The chlorophyll in spinach helps to detoxify the colon and aid digestion which in turn helps prevent constipation. Spinach also contains alpha-lipoic acid, an antioxidant which has been shown to be of benefit to those with diabetes and eye related disorders. Researchers have recently determined that Popeye was right to eat spinach for muscle strength although it will take about 1kg per day for it to have any real effect.

Chicken Tagine

Preparation Time – 40 minutes
Cooking Time – 55 minutes

Ingredients

6 Large Chicken Thighs
½ tsp Black Pepper
2 tbsp Olive Oil
2 Medium Onions
3 Garlic Cloves
3 Large Tomatoes
30g Unsalted Butter
3 tsp Harissa Paste
1 tbsp Runny Honey
Pinch of Saffron
3 tsp Ground Coriander
2 tsp Ground Cumin
450ml Chicken Stock
240g Chickpeas
3 Medium Carrots
½ tsp Cinnamon
1½ tsp Turmeric
300g White Mushrooms
240g Garden Peas
270g Couscous

Method

1. Skin and trim the **chicken thighs** then season with **black pepper.**
2. Fry the chicken in **olive oil** in a **large crockpot** over a medium heat turning frequently for 6–7 minutes.
3. Remove the thighs from the crockpot and set aside.
4. Slice the **onions, garlic** and **tomatoes** and then fry these in the same pot in **butter** for 2 minutes, scraping the bottom to release sticky bits left from the chicken.
5. Add the **harissa paste, honey** and **saffron** and stir well for a further 1 minute.
6. Add the **coriander, cumin, cinnamon** and **turmeric** and stir for another 1 minute.
7. Add the **chicken stock** and **chickpeas.**
8. Bring to the boil.
9. Add the chicken thighs and simmer for 10 minutes.
10. Slice the **carrots** and **mushrooms** to 1cm thick and add these to the crockpot with the **garden peas.**
11. Simmer on medium heat for a further 30 minutes until chicken is tender.
12. Turn chicken occasionally.
13. Add **cornflour** to thicken sauce if required.
14. Serve with **couscous** or rice.

Tip – Couscous is small pasta made from small granules of semolina flour that has fewer calories than rice or quinoa and is a good source of protein, potassium and selenium.

Haddock and Prawn Cobbler

Preparation Time – 45 minutes
Cooking Time – 45 minutes

Ingredients

Main

600g Haddock Fillets
4 Hard Boiled Eggs
200g White Mushrooms
240g Prawns
60g Unsalted Butter
60g Plain Flour
750ml Semi-Skimmed Milk
4 tsps White Wine Vinegar

For Topping

180g Wholemeal Flour
60g Plain Flour
1 tbsp Baking Powder
40g Unsalted Butter
2 Large Eggs
2 tbsp Milk
1 tsp Tarragon

Method

1. *Preheat the oven to 180°C.*
2. *On the hob bring a **large saucepan** of water to the boil.*
3. *Skin the **haddock** and cut the fish into 5cm chunks.*
4. *Place the fish in the boiling water for 10 minutes.*
5. *Boil the **eggs** in a **medium saucepan** for about 5 minutes.*
6. *Remove the eggs from the pan; leave them to cool for about 10 minutes then remove the shells and slice.*
7. *Refill the pan with 100ml of boiling water. Slice the **mushrooms** about 1cm thick and cook for 3 minutes.*
8. *Drain the water from the pan containing the haddock and place the fish in an **ovenproof dish.***
9. *Make a roux by melting the **butter** in a **small saucepan** on a medium heat until foaming. Remove from the heat then add a little **flour** at a time stirring quickly to form a paste.*
10. *Add the **white wine vinegar** then 150ml of **milk** at a time stirring continuously and bring mixture to the boil.*
11. *Lower the heat and simmer, stirring continuously, until the white sauce is semi-thick, then set aside.*
12. *Sprinkle the **prawns** on top of the haddock and cover with the sliced mushrooms and sliced egg.*
13. *Pour the white sauce over the top.*
14. *For the topping, sift the **flour, baking powder** and **tarragon** in a **large bowl** until they are mixed together well.*
15. *Cut in the **unsalted butter.***
16. *Beat the eggs in a **small bowl** until fluffy.*
17. *Add the **eggs** and the **milk** to the bowl and then bind mixture together with your hands to form dough.*

18. Roll the dough out onto a pastry board until 1cm thick and then cut into 5cm shapes with a **star shape cutter.**
19. Place these on top of the fish mixture and brush them with a little milk.
20. Place the dish in the oven and cook for 20 minutes or until sizzling.
21. Serve with vegetables of your choice.
22. Include crusty bread as a side dish.

Tip – Haddock is a white-fleshed salt water fish that is a member of the cod family. As well as being an excellent source of protein and a good source of vitamin B6 and B12, haddock is diet friendly, as it is very low in fat, carbohydrates and calories. Unlike cod, haddock does not salt well and is preserved by drying or smoking. The town of Arbroath on the east coast of Scotland is famous for its hot smoked haddock that requires no further cooking before eating. Smoked haddock is high in sodium and should be avoided by those with high blood pressure.

Spinach and Ricotta Pasta

Preparation Time – 60 minutes
Cooking Time – 8 minutes

Ingredients

360g '00' Flour
240g Spinach
150g Ricotta
3 Large Eggs
120g Parmesan Cheese
50g Breadcrumbs
2 tsp Salt
2 tsp Black Pepper

Method

1. *Place the **spinach** in a **saucepan** with 2 tablespoons of water and cook on a medium heat for a few minutes until it has wilted.*
2. *Drain the spinach and leave it to cool for about 5 minutes and then squeeze out any excess water.*
3. *Finely chop the spinach and place it in a **large bowl** with the **ricotta, parmesan** and **breadcrumbs.***
4. *Add 1 tsp of **salt** and 2 tsp of **pepper** and mix all of the ingredients together.*
5. *Chill in the fridge until ready to use.*
6. *For the pasta, mix the **flour** and 1 tsp of **salt** together in a large bowl and make a well in the middle.*
7. *Crack the **eggs** into the well and working from the outside fold the flour mix onto the eggs with a **wooden***

spoon and then mix together with your hands until you get a sticky dough. Add a little cold water if required.

8. Cover the bowl with **cling film** and place it to one side for 15 minutes.

9. Turn the dough out onto a **floured board** and knead it for about 10 minutes until it is smooth and elastic. If the dough is too dry add a little water. If it is too wet add more flour.

10. Roll the dough into a large rectangular shape and cut this into 4 strips the width of a **pasta machine.**

11. Starting at the widest setting roll the dough strips one at a time through the pasta machine twice.

12. Reduce the setting on the machine one notch at a time and continue to roll the dough through it until it reaches your desired thickness.

13. Place all 4 pieces onto a **large board** and spoon the filling down the centre of 2 of the pieces.

14. Brush either side of the filling with a little **milk** and then place the other 2 pieces of pasta on top of the filling.

15. Press the sides down gently and then cut the pasta into squares using a **pastry wheel or shaped cutter**.

16. Place the pasta squares into a saucepan of slightly salted boiling water for about 3 minutes.

17. Serve the pasta hot in a bowl and top with a mushroom and herb (p.462) or cheese and tomato (p.464) sauce and grated **parmesan cheese.**

Tip – Ricotta is made from whey – a by-product from cheeses like mozzarella and provolone. You can make ricotta cheese at home by separating the whey from whole milk. Ricotta is extremely delicious but is a mixed bag as far as healthiness is concerned. It is high in calcium and phosphorus and a good source of protein and vitamin B but is also high in cholesterol and fat. The fat content however is, surprisingly, lower than that of cottage cheese, "the dieter's cheese", and half that of cheddar. Cheese can cause an allergic reaction in susceptible people but usually as part of sensitivity intolerance to dairy products.

Pheasant in Creamy Mushroom Sauce

Preparation Time – 35 minutes
Cooking Time – 45 minutes

Ingredients

Main

8 Pheasant Breasts
120g Unsalted Butter
12 Rashers Streaky Bacon
300ml Double Cream
150ml Dry Cider
300ml Beef Stock
250g Chestnut Mushrooms

Sides

360g Baby Carrots
360g Butternut Squash
1 tsp Salt
1 tbsp Olive Oil
1 tsp Black Pepper
24 Asparagus Spears

Method

1. Heat the **butter** in a **frying pan** and cook each **pheasant breast** for 1 minute each side, then remove them from the pan and set aside to rest.
2. Slice the **mushrooms** and put them in a **large saucepan**

with the **beef stock, cream** and **cider** and slowly bring to the boil on a **medium heat**, stirring occasionally.

3. At the same time cut the rind off the **bacon** and fry it in a **frying pan** for 3–4 minutes until cooked.
4. Preheat the oven to 200°C.
5. Peel the **carrots** and **butternut squash**, cut into 1.5cm segments and place these in an ovenproof dish. Drizzle **olive oil** over them, sprinkle with 1 tsp of ground **black pepper** and **salt** then place the dish in the oven for 35 minutes.
6. Slice the pheasant breast into 2cm thick slices.
7. Pour the mushroom mixture into a large ovenproof dish, place the pheasant breast slices into the dish making sure they are all covered.
8. Lay the bacon rashers on top of the pheasant slices and put the dish in the preheated oven for 25 minutes.
9. Trim the ends off the **asparagus spears**; place these in an **ovenproof dish,** brush with olive oil and then bake in the oven for 15 minutes.
10. Serve with Fondant Potatoes (Page 472)..

Tip – Pheasants are protected by the Game Act which gives protection during the close season and only allows shooting from October to February. They are a rich source of iron, protein, selenium and vitamin B but have a relatively high fat content.

Stuffed Pork Loin with Potato Puffs

Preparation Time – 45 minutes
Cooking Time – 45 minutes

Ingredients

Main

2 Pork Tenderloin Fillets
2 Garlic Cloves
40g Unsalted Butter
2 Medium Onions
2 Egg Yolks
360g Spinach
80g Breadcrumbs
2 tsp Black Pepper
20g Chopped Parsley

Potato Puffs

See recipe on p.474.

Sauce

See recipe on p.468 and p.469.

Method

1. *Preheat the oven to 200°C.*
2. *Butterfly both pork fillets (Don't cut them all the way through).*
3. *Open the fillets out, cover with cling film and bash flat with a rolling pin.*

4. Boil the spinach for 2 minutes in a little water until soft. Drain and then squeeze all of the water out.
5. Place the spinach in a bowl and leave to cool.
6. Chop up the onions finely and fry gently in a pan with a knob of melted butter over a medium heat for 3 minutes.
7. Add the onions to the spinach with the breadcrumbs, egg yolks and the parsley and mix together well.
8. Spread the mixture out on top of the pork and season with a little black pepper.
9. Crush the garlic using a press.
10. Roll the pork fillets up, tie with string at equal intervals, hold in between with cocktail sticks then spread the garlic over the top and set aside.
11. Place the fillets on a baking tray with the rest of the butter and place in the oven on the middle shelf for 45 minutes.
12. Make the Potato Puffs, as per the recipe on p.474.
13. Place the potato puffs in the oven on the top shelf for 20 minutes.
14. At this point make a Beef Jus (p.469) or Onion Gravy (p.468), or serve with pre-prepared Espagnole Sauce (460).
15. Let the pork rest for a few minutes before carving it into slices.
16. Serve with vegetables of your choice.

Tip – Pork is the most commonly eaten meat in the world and its use as a food dates back to 500 BC. The religions of Islam and Judaism as well as some Christian denominations forbid pork consumption. Pork tenderloin is however a lean cut of meat that is nutrient dense and lower in calories and cholesterol than chicken breast. It is high in thiamine that is vital for growth, the repair of muscles and nerve tissues and the structure and integrity of brain cells. Deficiency of thiamine is often related to alcohol abuse, over dieting or kidney and liver disorders which can lead to symptoms such as depression, fatigue, loss of appetite, memory loss, nausea, stiffness or tingling in the arms or legs.

Chicken and Brie Pie

Preparation Time – 35 minutes
Cooking Time – 35 minutes

Ingredients

375g Puff Pastry
6 Medium Chicken Breasts
240g White Mushrooms
3 Large Leeks
3 Medium Carrots
120g Red/Yellow Peppers
180g Garden Peas
180g Brie
300g Crème Frais
1 Small Egg (Beaten)
1 tsp Black Pepper
3 tbsp Olive Oil

Method

1. Preheat the oven to 200°C.
2. Line a **baking tray** with baking **parchment paper.**
3. Roll out the puff pastry on a **floured board**.
4. Place a large **oblong ovenproof pie dish** upside down on the pastry and cut round it with a knife.
5. Place the pastry on the baking tray, brush with the beaten **egg** and place in the oven for 10 minutes until puffed up.
6. Trim the stalks off the **mushrooms** if desired and slice each one into quarters.

7. Slice the **leeks** and **carrots** into 1cm rounds.
8. Slice the **peppers** about 0.5cm thick.
9. Heat a little olive oil in a **large frying pan** and fry the mushrooms, leeks, carrots, **peas** and peppers for 4 minutes adding **black pepper** halfway through.
10. Add the **crème fraiche** and simmer for another 4 minutes.
11. Place the mixture in the ovenproof pie dish.
12. Cut the **chicken breasts** into 4cm cubes.
13. Fry the chicken in olive oil for 4 minutes to seal it and then mix this with the other ingredients in your pie dish.
14. Slice the **brie** into thin strips and lay on top of the filling.
15. Place the pastry lid on top and put the dish in the oven for 10 minutes or until the pastry is crisp.
16. Serve with Boulangère Potatoes (p.470), or other potatoes and vegetables of your choice.

Tip – Chickens are believed to be the closest living relative of the Tyrannosaurus Rex. There are hundreds of different breeds that all lay eggs of varying colours. Chicken is a good source of protein and selenium and is rich in niacin that is an essential vitamin for protection against Alzheimer's, dementia and cancer. Chicken meat must be cooked thoroughly as raw chicken contains the Salmonella organism that can make you very ill if ingested.

Quiver of Duck Breast

Preparation Time – 45 minutes
Cooking Time – 60 minutes

Ingredients

Main

6 Duck Breasts with Skin
50g Unsalted Butter

Plum Sauce

1 Large Onion
50ml Olive Oil
600g Ripe Plums
75g Light Brown Sugar
2 Star Anise
3 Garlic Cloves
1 Cinnamon Stick
1 tbsp Soy Sauce
50ml Port or Red Wine
300ml Beef Stock
Salt and Pepper

Sides

500g Pak Choi
1 tbsp Vegetable Oil
125g Spring Onions
250g Asparagus
1.25kg Maris Piper Potatoes (See recipe on p.476)

Method

1. Stone and quarter the **plums.**
2. Chop the **onion** and fry it in olive oil in a **large saucepan** for 3 minutes until soft.
3. Add the plums and the **sugar** and cook for another 5 minutes on a medium heat.
4. Add the **star anise, garlic cloves, cinnamon stick, soy sauce, port** or **red wine** and **beef stock** and then simmer on a medium heat for 20 minutes until thickened.
5. Remove the star anise and cinnamon stick and keep the sauce warm until ready to serve.
6. Preheat the oven to 180°C.
7. Peel the **potatoes** and boil them in a large saucepan for 10 minutes, then follow the recipe for creamy mash on p.476.
8. Trim the ends of the **asparagus spears,** place them in an **ovenproof dish,** brush with olive oil and cook them in the oven for 15 minutes.
9. Dry the **duck skin** with kitchen paper and score with a sharp **chef's knife** every few millimetres making sure you don't cut all the way through.
10. Season the skin with **salt** and **pepper.**
11. Heat a dry **frying pan** on a medium heat, place the duck breasts skin side down and cook for 5–6 minutes.
12. Turn the breasts over, add the butter to the pan and fry for about 2 minutes.
13. Remove from the frying pan, place the breasts with all the juices in an **ovenproof dish** and cook in the oven for another 5 minutes.

14. Transfer the duck to a warm plate and leave to rest for a few minutes.
15. Meanwhile heat the vegetable oil in a wok or large frying pan then add the **pak choi**, the chopped **spring onions** and 1 tbsp of the plum sauce and stir fry for a few minutes until soft.
16. Slice the duck breasts at an angle every 5mm.
17. Place the duck around the edge of the top of the plate then place the asparagus spears down the middle of the plate to form an arrow shape.
18. Place the creamy mash in a **cylindrical ring** on one side of the asparagus and the pak choi on the other side.
19. Serve the rest of the plum sauce in a **jug.**

Tip – Duck is a good source of pantothenic acid which provides a multitude of benefits to the body including the alleviation of stress, depression, anxiety, asthma and hair loss. It may also help the body to lower cholesterol and create red blood cells, sex hormones and chemicals involved in nerve signalling.

Captain's Meat Loaf

Preparation Time – 35 minutes
Cooking Time – 60 minutes

Ingredients

300g Beef Steak Mince
300g Pork Mince
150g Chestnut mushrooms
1 Large Carrot
2 Garlic Cloves
1 Medium Onion
80g Breadcrumbs
1 Sweet Red Pepper
1 Sweet Yellow Pepper
1 tsp Salt
2 tsp Black Pepper
5g Fresh Coriander
1 tsp Paprika
1 Large Egg
2 tbsp Olive Oil

Method

1. Chop up the **carrot, mushrooms, onion** and **garlic** into fine pieces with a sharp **utility knife.**
2. Preheat the oven to 180°C.
3. Heat a little olive oil in a **frying pan** and fry the chopped vegetables for 3 minutes until tender, then set these aside in a **large mixing bowl.**
4. Place 2 slices of bread into a **food processor** to make

the **breadcrumbs.**

5. *Remove the seeds, then slice and dice the **peppers** and place them in the mixing bowl with the other vegetables. Add the breadcrumbs, **mince** and chopped **coriander** and mix together.*

6. *Add the **salt, pepper, paprika** and a beaten **egg** and mix together with your hands until well blended.*

7. *Spoon the mixture into a 500g greased **loaf tin**, compress down and level off until an inch from the top.*

8. *Cover the tin with **baking parchment** and **tin foil** to form a tight seal.*

9. *Place the tin in an **oblong roasting tray** and pour hot water into the tray until it comes halfway up the tin.*

10. *Bake in the oven for 45 minutes.*

11. *Remove the tin foil and parchment, drain off any excess liquid and place back in the oven for 10 minutes.*

12. *Remove from the oven and leave the meatloaf to cool for 10 minutes before turning it out of the tin.*

13. *Serve warm with chips and peas or cold with a salad.*

Tip – Coriander belongs to the carrot family and is an anti-inflammatory that may alleviate symptoms of arthritis. It can also protect against urinary tract infections, lower blood sugar levels, help clear up skin disorders such as eczema and aid digestion and the proper functioning of the bowels.

Bangers and Smash

Preparation Time – 30 minutes
Cooking Time – 45 minutes
Including time for the Mash and Gravy

Ingredients

15 Pork Sausages
2 Medium Red Onions
600ml Beef Stock
1 tsp Dried Mixed Herbs
1 tsp Black Pepper
450g Frozen Peas
Onion Mash (See p.480)

Method

1. *Preheat the oven to 200°C.*
2. *Place the **sausages** in a **roasting tin** in the oven for about 5 minutes. Turn them over and cook for another 5 minutes.*
3. *Slice up the **onions** and add them to the roasting tin.*
4. *Stir the **dried herbs and black pepper** into the stock and pour this over the sausages.*
5. *Cook in the oven for a further 35 - 40 minutes.*
6. *Make the onion mash, following the recipe on p. 480.*
7. *Place the **peas** in a **saucepan** of boiling water for about 3 minutes or **microwave** in a **non-metallic bowl** for the same time.*

8. *To serve place the mash in the middle of the plate and lay the sausages on top. Arrange the peas to the side of the potato and spoon the onion stock over the top of the sausages.*

Tip – Onions possess many active compounds, flavonoids and phytochemicals that are proven to be beneficial for many health conditions. Red onions are the richest source of quercetin, a potent antioxidant flavonoid that has been shown to thin the blood, ward off blood clots, support normal respiratory health and keep colon cancer at bay. All onions contain vitamin C and chromium, a mineral that helps cells respond to insulin thereby helping with blood glucose control. Raw onion eaten in a sandwich or as part of a salad may encourage the production of good cholesterol thus keeping your heart healthy. Onion juice is known to help minimise the pain and burning sensation when applied to a bee sting.

Chicken Tawa

Preparation Time – 45 minutes
Cooking Time – 40 minutes

Ingredients

6 Small Chicken Breasts
50g Unsalted Butter
2 Medium Onions
1 Red Pepper
1 Green Chilli
3 Garlic Cloves
1 tsp Cumin Seeds
1 tsp Ground Ginger
3 tbsp Curry Paste
2 tsp Ground Turmeric
1 tsp Garam Masala
½ tsp Fenugreek
240g White Mushrooms
9 Medium Tomatoes
½ tsp Cayenne Pepper
½ tsp Salt
3g Fresh Coriander
150ml Double Cream

Method

1. Make the **curry paste** as shown on p.404.
2. Cut the **chicken breasts** into 2cm cubes.
3. Heat 30g of **butter** in a **large crockpot** and fry the chicken on a medium heat for about 5 minutes

until it is browned.

4. *Remove the chicken and set this aside.*
5. *Cut the **mushrooms** and the **tomatoes** into quarters.*
6. *Finely chop the **onions, pepper, green chilli** and **garlic.***
7. *Place the crockpot back on the heat, add 20g of butter and fry the **cumin seeds** for 30 seconds until they splutter.*
8. *Add the onions, peppers, chilli and garlic and fry for 2 minutes on a medium heat, stirring occasionally.*
9. *Add the c**urry paste, turmeric, garam masala, ginger, fenugreek** and 150ml of water and cook for 3 minutes.*
10. *Stir in the chopped **coriander, cayenne pepper, salt** and tomatoes and cook for another 3 minutes.*
11. *Add the chicken, mushrooms and **double cream** and simmer for a further 15–20 minutes.*
12. *Serve with pilau rice and chana masala as required.*

Tip – Red peppers are a sweeter, juicier and a more ripe variation of green peppers. They are high in vitamin C and contain over 100% of your required daily intake. They are a rich source of the carotenoid lycopene, which is linked to a reduced risk of bladder, prostate and pan-creatic cancer. They are also a good source of beta-cryptoxanthin, which recent studies suggest holds promise for the prevention of lung cancer due to smoking. Red peppers may even help you lose body weight, as they are very low in calories and are believed to possess substances that increase your body temperature and its need for oxygen.

Chana Masala

Preparation Time – 15 minutes
Cooking Time – 30 minutes

Ingredients

400g Chick Peas (tinned)
90g Tamarind Paste
3 tbsp Olive Oil
1 tsp Cumin Seeds
1 Medium Onion
3 Garlic Cloves
1 Green Chilli
2 tsp Ground Coriander
2 tsp Ground Cumin
½ tsp Salt
1 tsp Garam Masala
300g Vine Tomatoes

Method

1. Top and tail the **green chilli** and chop up finely. Remove the seeds if you don't want the dish hot.
2. Slice and dice the **onion** and crush the **garlic cloves.**
3. Heat the olive oil in a **large frying pan** and fry the **cumin seeds** for about 1 minute until they splutter.
4. Add the chilli, onion and garlic cloves to the pan and fry on a medium heat for about 2 minutes.
5. Add the **ground coriander**, **ground cumin** and **salt** to the frying pan and cook for a further 1– 2 minutes.

6. Chop up the **vine tomatoes.**
7. Add the tomatoes and **tamarind paste** and simmer for 5 minutes.
8. Place the **chick peas** in a **large saucepan** and bring them to the boil.
9. Transfer the contents of the frying pan to the large saucepan, add the **garam masala** and simmer for 15 minutes.

Tip – Chick peas, also known as garbanzo beans, are a rich source of soluble and insoluble dietary fibre that help to lower cholesterol and prevent digestive disorders. They also contain some proteins that your body breaks down into amino acids to maintain tissue health, folate that protects against genetic mutations that contribute to cancer development and manganese that supports bone development and wound healing. If you have insulin resistance or diabetes, chick peas can help you balance blood sugar levels by providing steady slow burning energy. They have a low glycaemic index which means the carbohydrates in them gets broken down and digested slowly which is also good for those looking to lose weight as it controls appetite.

Mushroom Pilau Rice

Preparation Time – 10 minutes
Cooking Time – 25 minutes

Ingredients

300g Basmati Rice
210g White Mushrooms
45g Unsalted Butter
3 Small Onions
3 Garlic Cloves
1 tsp Cumin Seeds
1 tsp Garam Masala
1 tsp Black Pepper
1 Cinnamon Stick
1 tbsp Turmeric
1 tsp Salt
1 tbsp Olive Oil

Method

1. Slice the **mushrooms** and **onions** and then dice them.
2. Crush the **garlic cloves** using a **press.**
3. Heat the **butter** in a **large saucepan** over a medium heat.
4. Add the onions and cook until soft and golden.
5. Add the **cumin seeds** and let them sizzle for 1 minute.
6. Put the **rice** in a **sieve** and rinse under running water.
7. Add the rice, garlic, **garam masala, salt** and **pepper** to the saucepan and stir fry for 1 minute.
8. Pour on boiling water to cover the rice plus 50%. Add

the **cinnamon stick**, stir once and bring to the boil.

9. Put a lid on the saucepan turn the heat down to low and simmer for about 12 minutes until all the water has been absorbed.
10. Fry the mushrooms in a **frying pan** in the olive oil for 2 minutes and then add them to the rice.
11. Add in a teaspoon of turmeric for colour.
12. Remove the rice from the heat, cover the saucepan with a **dry tea towel** and leave for 6–7 minutes.
13. Remove the cinnamon stick from the saucepan.
14. Fluff up the pilau rice with a fork and serve immediately.

Tip – Basmati rice is a long grain rice with a distinct flavour. It is lower in calories than regular long grain rice but is still a high energy food and a good source of carbohydrates. It is also a rich source of vitamins, but low in fat and sodium as well as being gluten and cholesterol free. Basmati has a low to medium glycaemic index which is lower than all other types of rice. It is also high in a type of fibre known as resistant starch that has a prebiotic effect in the bowel, which means it helps it increase its friendly bacteria.

Curry Paste

Preparation Time – 15 minutes
Cooking Time – 6 minutes

Ingredients

15g Cumin Seeds
12g Coriander Seeds
7g Fennel Seeds
7g Fenugreek Seeds
5g Black Peppercorns
5g Dried Crushed Chillies
5 Curry Leaves
4g Hot Chilli Powder
4g Ground Turmeric
30ml White Wine Vinegar
6 tbsp Water
60ml Virgin Oil

Method

1. Put all the **seeds, peppercorns, crushed chillies** and **curry leaves** in a **grinder or mortar and pestle** and grind to a fine powder.
2. Spoon into a **bowl** and add the turmeric and chilli powder.
3. Add the white wine vinegar and mix together with the water to form a smooth paste.
4. Heat the oil in a **frying pan**, stir in the paste and fry on a medium heat for about 5 minutes.
5. When the water has been absorbed and the oil has

risen to the surface remove from the heat and allow to cool.

6. *Spoon into a small sterilised **Kilner jar.***
7. *Heat half a tablespoon of oil in the pan and pour this on top of the paste mix as this will preserve it.*
8. *This will keep in the fridge for a few months and will be enough paste for many curries.*

Tip – Cumin is an excellent source of iron that is instrumental in keeping your immune system healthy and improving cognitive performance. It also contains essential oils that aid good digestion and act as a relaxant to relieve stress and anxiety that can lead to insomnia. It can also give relief for stomach aches when taken with hot water. Chillies originated in the Americas and have been part of the human diet since 7500 BC. There are more than 200 varieties, some of which contain up to 7 times more vitamin C than an orange. They have a range of health benefits including the relief of sinus congestion, migraines and muscle and joint pain. Chillies can be irritating if eaten in excess and extremely hot ones can burn the inside of your mouth or cause pain during a bowel movement.

Pan Fried Sea Bream with Crushed Potatoes and Sauce Vierge

Preparation Time – 35 minutes
Cooking Time – 30 minutes

Ingredients

6 Sea Bream Fillets
Plain Flour for dusting
1 tsp Black Pepper
1 tsp Salt
750g New Potatoes
600g Chantenay Carrots
600ml Boiled Water
100g Unsalted Butter
1 tsp Muscovado Sugar
2 tbsp Caster Sugar
Sauce Vierge (For recipe, see p.466)

Method

1. Cook the new potatoes as shown on p.473.
2. Scrape and trim the carrots and place them in a **large saucepan.**
3. Add the boiling water until the **carrots** are covered.
4. Add 50g of **butter, salt, pepper** and **sugar.**
5. Bring pan back to the boil.
6. Simmer for about 15 minutes.
7. Lightly flour the skin side of the **sea bream** and season with salt and pepper.

8. Heat a **frying pan** on a hob and then add 50g of butter.
9. Once all the butter has started to melt and foam add the sea bream skin side down and cook for 3 minutes.
10. Turn the sea bream over and cook for a further 3 minutes.
11. Place the potatoes in the centre of the plate and place the sea bream on top.
12. Place the carrots around one side of the plate.
13. Serve the **sauce vierge** on the other side of the plate.

Tip – Black pepper comes from the pepper plant that can grow to 33 feet in height in hot and humid climates. After 3–4 years they bear small white flowers that develop into berries known as peppercorns. They are picked when just turning red and then dried whole before being sold. It has long been recognised as a carminative, an agent that prevents or relieves gas within the gastrointestinal tract and may help in the treatment of colic in infants. Cardamom, dill, fennel and fenugreek are also good examples of carminatives that can also increase bile flow and improve digestion of fats.

Pan Fried Sea Bass with
Risotto alla Milanese

Preparation Time – 10 minutes
Cooking Time – 30 minutes

Ingredients

500g Arborio Risotto Rice
6 Sea Bass Fillets
1.2L Chicken Stock
1 tsp Saffron
1 tbsp Olive Oil
60g Unsalted Butter
2 Medium Onions
6 Garlic Cloves
180ml White Wine
100g Parmesan Cheese
10 Sage Leaves
1 tbsp Vegetable Oil

Method

1. Pour the **chicken stock** into a **saucepan.**
2. Chop the **saffron** finely and add to the stock.
3. Bring the stock to the boil then simmer for 6 minutes.
4. Heat the **oil** and half the **butter** in a **large frying pan.**
5. Chop the **onions** and **garlic** and fry in the oil and butter on a medium heat for 3 minutes.
6. Add the **rice** and cook for a further 2 minutes.
7. Add the **wine** and stir until absorbed.

8. Add the rice to the stock and simmer on a low heat for 10 minutes or until all the liquid has been absorbed.
9. Remove from the heat and cover the pan with a **dry clean tea towel** for about 7 minutes.
10. Fry the **sea bass fillet** skin side down in a little vegetable oil and the rest of the butter for 2–3 minutes.
11. Turn the fish over and cook the other side for a further 2 minutes.
12. Stir **parmesan** and chopped **sage** leaves into the rice.
13. Serve the rice in the middle of a bowl or plate and place the fish on top skin side down.
14. Serve with a side dish of garlic bread or salad if desired.

Tip – Saffron is produced from the saffron crocus flower and is the most expensive spice in the world due to the amount of labour involved in its harvesting. As a spice it energises dishes with an earth pungent essence. It can also be used to dye clothing within the textile industry. As a herbal supplement, it offers benefits to women who have irregular periods or suffer from PMS and to men who suffer from premature ejaculation.

Beef Wellington

Preparation Time – 50 minutes
Cooking Time – 50 minutes

Ingredients

For the Main

700g Beef Fillet
500g Puff Pastry
70g Chicken Liver Pâté (*See p.356*)
15g Unsalted Butter
6 slices of Prosciutto
½ tbsp Olive Oil
1 tsp Black Pepper
½ tsp Salt

For the Duxelle

90g Chestnut Mushrooms
80g Shallots
1 Garlic Clove
10g Unsalted Butter
60ml Double Cream
30ml Dry White Wine
1 tsp Black Pepper

For the Glaze

1 Egg Yolk (Beaten)

Method

1. Place the **beef** on a **chopping board** and trim the ends and sides to obtain an even shape.
2. Season the beef with salt and pepper on each side.
3. Heat the **butter** and **olive oil** in a **frying pan** and cook the beef for 1 minute on either side on a medium heat to seal it.
4. Remove the beef from the pan and leave it to cool.
5. When cool wrap the beef in **cling film** and place it in the fridge.
6. Chop the **mushrooms, shallots** and **garlic** very finely.
7. Heat the frying pan back up, add another 10g of butter and cook until the butter is foaming.
8. Add the mushrooms, shallots and garlic and cook on a medium heat stirring occasionally until the liquid evaporates.
9. Add the **cream, wine** and **black pepper** and simmer uncovered stirring occasionally on a low heat for about 15 minutes or until you get a fairly thick purée.
10. Remove the purée mixture (duxelle) from the frying pan and place in a **small bowl** to cool.
11. Roll out the **puff pastry** into a rectangular shape, large enough to wrap your beef fillet in.
12. Spread the **pâté** evenly all over the pastry except for 2.5cm around the edge.
13. Remove the beef fillet from the fridge.
14. Make a cut lengthways three quarters of the way through the beef and fill with the cooled duxelle mixture.
15. Place the slices of **prosciutto** over the cut in the beef and spread a thin layer of the duxelle on top.

16. Place the cut side down onto the pâté in the middle of the pastry.
17. Brush the edges of the pastry with the **beaten egg glaze** and fold over the top of the beef fillet and seal the edge well.
18. Fold the ends up, seal well and then place the fillet parcel seam down onto a **baking tray.**
19. Score the pastry diagonally at 1cm intervals.
20. Bake in the centre of the oven at 220°C for 30 minutes until pastry is golden in colour.
21. Rest for 10 minutes before cutting into thick slices and serving with new potatoes, vegetables of choice and onion gravy (p.468).

Tip – Different countries and cuisines sometimes use the same name for a different cut of beef. There are 12 cuts of beef that are leaner than a skinless chicken thigh. Butchers are likely to stock more cuts and offer more advice on preparing and cooking beef than a supermarket. Buying the best quality beef you can afford is always worthwhile.

DESSERTS

Eton Mess

Preparation/Cooking Time – 30 minutes
2 hours if you make your own meringue.

Ingredients

Meringue

3 Egg Whites
180g Caster Sugar
Pinch of Salt

Filling

240g Fresh Strawberries
240g Fresh Raspberries
510ml Double Cream
1 tbsp of Icing Sugar

Method

1. *Preheat the oven to 110°C.*
2. *Line 2 **baking trays** with **non-stick parchment paper.***
3. *Place the **egg whites** and a pinch of **salt** into a **large mixing bowl** and whip with a light **wire whisk.***
4. *Gradually add the sugar and keep whisking until the mixture forms stiff peaks.*
5. *Use a **spatula** to spread the mixture over the trays.*
6. *Bake in the oven for approximately 1 hour and then check to see if meringue is crisp. If it is remove from the oven. If it isn't, leave it in and check every 15 minutes.*

When it is cooked, turn off the oven, open the door and leave the meringue to cool for 30 minutes.

7. *Place the cream in a mixer with a whisk attachment, add the icing sugar and whip gently until slightly thick.*
8. *Add half the strawberries and raspberries and mix into the cream with a wooden spoon.*
9. *Break the meringue into pieces and add to the mix.*
10. *Layer up the mix in 6 glass tumblers alternating with the other half of the strawberries and raspberries.*

Tip – Strawberries have been popular since Roman times and there are now more than 600 varieties. Their deep red hue is due to their high flavonoid content which is important for the support of our cardiovascular and nervous systems and detoxification of potential tissue damaging molecules. A recent study has shown that regular consumption of anthocyanins, flavonoids found in berries, can reduce the risk of a heart attack in young and middle-aged women by 32%. Strawberries are recommended to those with high blood pressure as they help negate the effects of sodium in the body. They are also a good food for diabetics as they have a lower glycaemic index than most other fruits.

Malvern Pudding

Preparation Time – 30 minutes
Cooking Time – 30 minutes

Ingredients

Base

1kg Bramley Apples
60g Unsalted Butter
60g Light Brown Sugar
Zest of 2 Lemons

Topping

480ml Semi-Skimmed Milk
180ml Double Cream
60g Unsalted Butter
45g Cornflour
30g Granulated Sugar
2 Eggs
Ground Cinnamon (to taste)

Method

1. *Peel, core and slice the **apples**.*
2. *Fry the **butter** and the apples in a **frying pan** on a medium high heat for 5–6 minutes stirring occasionally.*
3. *Add the **brown sugar** and the **zest of 2 lemons** and cook for a further 4–5 more minutes until the apples are nicely softened. Stir occasionally.*

4. Transfer the apples to an **ovenproof dish** and set this to one side.
5. Place **a large saucepan** on the hob on a medium heat and add the **butter.**
6. When the butter melts and starts to foam, remove from the heat, add the **cornflour** and stir quickly until it has thickened to a smooth paste.
7. Put the pan back on the heat and gradually add all of the milk, stirring continuously until boiling, then reduce to a low heat and simmer for 1 minute.
8. Pour in the **double cream**, stir for a further minute and then leave to simmer for 2–3 minutes.
9. Beat the **eggs** in a bowl and mix in the **sugar.**
10. Remove the pan from heat and **whisk** in the egg and sugar mix.
11. Pour the mixture over the apples and evenly sprinkle with 1 level tablespoon of **cinnamon** if desired.
12. Place the dish in a preheated oven at 180°C for about 10 minutes.
13. Serve hot in bowls.

Tip – With over 7,500 varieties, apples are one of the healthiest foods you can eat as they may help prevent anaemia, constipation, diabetes, gallstones, liver disorders, rheumatism and gout. Studies have also shown that apples can help lower cholesterol, prevent breathing problems including asthma, fight colds, boost brain power and reduce the risk of cancer. Much of an apple's antioxidant power is in the peel so eating them the way nature intended will give you a better blend of nutrients and fibre than juicing. In reality an apple a day may well keep the doctor away.

Maple Sugar Pie

Preparation Time – 10 minutes
(30 minutes if you make your own pastry)

Cooking Time – 50 minutes

Ingredients

240g Shortcrust Pastry (See p.482)
125g Soft Brown Sugar
125ml Double Cream
1 Large Egg
100ml Pure Maple Syrup
25g Unsalted Butter
1 tbsp Lemon Juice
3 tbsp Self-Raising Flour
6 tbsp Breadcrumbs

Method

1. *Preheat the oven to 180°C.*
2. *Roll out the **pastry** on a **floured board** and place this into a pre-greased **20cm flan tin with removable bottom** (2.5cm depth).*
3. *Blind bake for 15 minutes.*
4. *Put the **sugar, double cream, maple syrup, lemon juice, butter, self-raising flour, breadcrumbs** and **egg** into a **mixing bowl** and beat well to a smooth paste.*
5. *Pour the mixture into the **cooled flan tin.***
6. *Bake for approximately 35 minutes when it will have*

risen to the top of the flan case.

7. *Remove from the oven and leave to cool.*

8. *Serve with vanilla ice cream.*

Tip – Pure maple syrup is free of any additives or colouring as it is boiled from the tree sap which is harvested from the maple tree. It contains 54 different antioxidants offering many health benefits and a high level of minerals and vitamins, including manganese and zinc, and riboflavin which is important for energy, body growth and red blood cell production. The majority of healthy foods contain riboflavin, which is not stored in your body and must be replenished each day. Deficiency of this vitamin can lead to anaemia, sore throat, swelling of mucus membranes and skin disorders. It is water soluble so any excess intake will be flushed out of your system causing your urine to turn bright yellow.

Rocky Chocolate Mountains

Preparation Time – 20 minutes
Cooking Time – 6 minutes

Ingredients

180g Muscavado Sugar
1 Large Eating Apple
120g Raspberries
180g Soft Margarine
3 Medium Eggs
120g Plain Flour
1 tsp Baking Powder
75g Cocoa Powder
30g Marshmallow pieces

Method

1. Grease **6 x 150ml ceramic microwave-proof ramekins.**
2. Sprinkle the base of each ramekin with a little **muscavado sugar.**
3. Peel and core the **apple**, dice finely and place in a **small mixing bowl.**
4. Add the **raspberries** and mix together well.
5. Divide the fruit equally between the ramekins.
6. Put the **margarine, eggs, flour, baking powder, cocoa powder** and remaining muscavado sugar into a **large mixing bowl** and beat together until you have a smooth paste.
7. Spoon the mixture equally into the individual ramekins on top of the fruit and level the top.

8. Cover each ramekin with loose **cling film** and cook on high power in a **microwave oven** for 5–6 minutes until they have risen.
9. Turn out each one onto a dish and place the **marshmallow pieces** on top.
10. Place a spoonful of vanilla ice cream on top of each pudding and serve immediately.

Tip – Raspberries have been one of the world's most consumed fruits for thousands of years. Red raspberries contain strong antioxidants such as vitamin C, gallic acid and quercetin that help the body fight against cancer, heart disease and age-related decline. They are high in ellagic acid, a phytochemical that prevents the binding of carcinogens to DNA, inhibits mutations within cells and strengthens connective tissues, which may stop cancer cells from spreading. They also contain zeaxanthin that protects the eyes from damaging blue light rays and reduces the risk of macular disease.

Naan Bread with Chocolate Sauce

Preparation Time – 45 minutes
Proving Time – 1 hour
Cooking Time – 10 minutes

Ingredients

340g White Bread Flour
40g Unsalted Butter
15g Caster Sugar
7g Sachet of Dried Yeast
225g Semi-Skimmed Milk
400g Dark Chocolate

Method

1. Place the **strong white bread flour** and **butter** in a **large mixing bowl** and rub together until it looks like breadcrumbs.
2. Stir in the **sugar** and **yeast.**
3. Make a well in the centre of the mixing bowl and add the **milk.**
4. Mix to a dough and roll into a ball.
5. Knead the dough on a **well-floured pastry board** for 10 minutes.
6. Place the dough in a large clean **dry glass bowl** and cover with **cling film** that has been brushed with a little olive oil on the side facing the dough.
7. Leave in a warm place for about an hour until the dough is double in size.
8. Take it from the bowl and knock it back lightly by

repeatedly folding it on itself with the heel of your hand for 1 minute until it is smooth.

9. *Cut the dough into 6 equal pieces. Roll each piece into a ball then flatten them to make a 1.5cm thick circular shape.*

10. *Make fork holes over each piece of bread, place them on a **baking tray** and grill on a high heat for a few minutes each side.*

11. *Place a **small saucepan** of water on the hob, bring to the boil then reduce to a medium heat.*

12. *Break the **chocolate** into chunks into a **heat-proof bowl** and suspend this over the water. Do not allow the bowl to touch the water.*

13. *As the chocolate starts to melt, stir continuously.*

14. *Pour the melted chocolate into individual serving dishes.*

15. *Remove the bread pieces from the grill, cut each piece into triangular shapes and place point down in the chocolate sauce.*

16. *Serve immediately.*

Tip – A plain naan bread is one of the healthier options as an accompaniment to an Indian meal even though it is high in calories, fat and gluten. This is a very indulgent dessert, although there are health benefits from the dark chocolate, and recent research suggests that white bread can boost the number of good bacteria in the gut which helps ward off stomach and bowel diseases.

Umm Ali

Preparation Time – 25 minutes
Cooking Time – 35 minutes

Ingredients

360g Puff Pasty
900ml Semi-Skimmed Milk
150g Granulated Sugar
1 tsp Vanilla Extract
90g Raisins
30g Sultanas
30g Slivered Almonds
25g Pine Nuts
25g Chopped Pistachios
18g Sweet Flaked Coconut

Method

1. *Preheat the oven to 200°C.*
2. *Roll out the **puff pastry**, and place flat on a **baking sheet or tray**.*
3. *Bake for 15 minutes in the preheated oven, or until puffed and golden brown. Leave to cool for a few minutes.*
4. *Break the puff pastry into pieces, and place in a **large bowl**.*
5. *Add the **raisins, sultanas, almonds, pine nuts, pistachios,** and **coconut**, and toss to distribute.*
6. *Pour the mixture into a **large glass ovenproof dish,** and spread evenly.*

7. *Pour the **milk** into a **large saucepan,** and stir in the **sugar** and **vanilla.***
8. *Heat until hot but not quite boiling then pour the liquid over the mixture in the ovenproof dish.*
9. *Bake in a preheated oven for 15 minutes.*
10. *Turn the oven to grill for 2 minutes to brown the top.*
11. *Remove from the oven and let it stand for 5 minutes.*
12. *Serve warm with vanilla ice cream.*

Tip – Raisins and sultanas are dried grapes produced all over the world that offer many health benefits. They contain fibres that help relieve constipation, good levels of potassium and magnesium that reduce acidity and remove toxins from the body and oleanolic acid which provides protection against cavities, tooth decay and other periodontal diseases. Both are a good source of energy as they are high in fructose and glucose which can also help you gain weight and also a good source of an amino acid called arginine that is good for your sex life. They also contain polyphenol antioxidants that provide protection against the development of tumours and in particular, colon cancer.

Key Lime Pie

Preparation Time – 20 minutes
Cooking Time – 30 minutes
Chilling Time – 2 hours

Ingredients

250g Digestive Biscuits
100g Unsalted Butter
6 Limes (120ml of Juice)
Zest and juice of 3 Limes
3 Large Egg Yolks
1 tin Condensed Milk 397g

Method

1. Lightly grease the sides and base of a **20cm diameter x 2.5cm high flan tin.**
2. Break up and crush the **digestive biscuits.**
3. Melt the **butter** in a **frying pan**, add the biscuits and mix together on a low heat for 1 minute.
4. Press this mixture into the base of the flan tin.
5. Bake in the oven at 180°C for 10 minutes then remove and leave to cool.
6. Whisk the **egg yolks** in a **medium bowl** until they are pale and fluffy.
7. Grate the zest of 3 **limes** onto the yolks and mix in well with a fork.
8. Blend in the **condensed milk** for 1 minute, stirring continuously, add the **lime juice** and then whisk everything together for 2 minutes.

9. *Pour the filling onto the biscuit base and return the flan tin to the oven for 15 minutes or until set.*
10. *Leave to cool then turn out onto a serving plate.*
11. *Chill in the fridge for 2 hours until ready to serve.*
12. *Grate some lime zest over the top for decoration and serve with lime and coconut sorbet (See p.431)*

Tip – There are several varieties of lime, which is the sweeter cousin of the lemon and provides a strong flavour that will enhance many recipes. Limes contain a high amount of vitamin C which is needed by the body for the production of collagen to help with growth and the repair of damaged tissues and prevention of arthritis. Vitamin C can also help lower cholesterol in the blood, improve blood flow and regulate blood sugar levels for diabetics. There is no hard evidence to show that vitamin C actually prevents colds from occurring even though it will boost the body's immune system and may lessen the symptoms and shorten the period of illness.

Lime and Coconut Sorbet

Preparation Time – 5 minutes
Cooking Time – 10 minutes
Freezing Time – 3 hours

Ingredients

1 tin (400ml) Coconut Milk
6 Limes (120ml of Juice)
175ml Water
175g Granulated Sugar

Method

1. *Place the **sugar** and water in a **medium saucepan** and bring to the boil.*
2. *Add the **coconut milk**, bring back to the boil and then simmer for 5 minutes stirring regularly.*
3. *Remove from the heat and allow to cool.*
4. *Add the **lime juice** and mix everything together.*
5. *Pour the mixture into an **airtight container** and freeze for a few hours until set.*

Tip – Although a useful source of fibre, coconut milk is high in calories and saturated fats. It is a good milk substitute for those who want to avoid dairy products or are lactose intolerant.

Fresh Fruit Pavlova

Preparation Time – 20 minutes
Cooking Time – 60 minutes
Resting Time – 30 minutes

Ingredients

Meringue

3 Egg Whites
Pinch of Salt
250g Caster Sugar
1 tsp Vanilla Essence
1 tsp White Wine Vinegar

Filling

300ml Double Cream
Fresh Raspberries and Strawberries or fruit of your choice
White Chocolate (grated for topping)

Method

1. *Draw a 23cm diameter circle with a dark pen on **greaseproof paper. Cut this out** and lay the paper dark-circle-side down on a **baking tray.***
2. *Preheat the oven to 180°C.*
3. *Whisk **egg whites** in a **large bowl** with a pinch of **salt** until the mixture is very stiff.*
4. *Gradually whisk in all of the **caster sugar** until it forms*

stiff peaks.

5. Fold in the **white wine vinegar** and **vanilla essence** with a **wooden spoon.**

6. Spread mixture over the circle of greaseproof paper and make a slight hollow in the middle.

7. Bake in oven for 1 hour or until crisp.

8. Turn oven off and leave for 30 minutes with the door open.

9. Take out meringue and leave to cool.

10. Peel off greaseproof paper carefully and place the meringue on a serving plate.

11. Whisk **double cream** until thick, pile on top of meringue and decorate with **fruit.**

12. Sprinkle shavings of **white chocolate** on top.

13. Sweeten any extra fresh fruit with sugar and whisk in a bowl to create some juice to pour on top.

Tip – Double cream is rich in vitamin A which plays a significant role in the normal formation and maintenance of the heart, lungs and kidneys as well as being important for the health of your eyes, bones and skin. Although it is low in cholesterol, salt and sugar it is exceedingly high in calories and saturated fats and should only be eaten in moderation as part of a balanced diet.

Crème Brûlée

Preparation Time – 25 minutes
Cooking Time – 60 minutes
Cooling Time – 60 minutes

Ingredients

750ml Double Cream
60g Caster Sugar
6 Egg Yolks
1 Vanilla Pod
Pinch of Salt
18g Demerara Sugar

Method

1. *Preheat the oven to 150°C.*
2. *Pour the **cream** into a **saucepan.***
3. *Split the **vanilla pod** lengthways and scrape the seeds into the cream.*
4. *Chop the empty pod into small pieces and add these to the cream.*
5. *Bring the cream to the boil, turn hotplate down to a low heat down and simmer for 7-8 minutes stirring continuously.*
6. *Beat the **egg yolks**, **salt** and **caster sugar** in a **large bowl** until fairly pale and fluffy.*
7. *Bring the cream back to the boil and then pour this onto the egg and sugar mixture a little at a time stirring continuously.*
8. *Whisk for a few minutes or until the mixture thickens.*

9. Once slightly thick strain through a **sieve** into a **jug.**
10. Pour the mixture into **6 x 150ml ramekins** to a level just below the top.
11. Place the ramekins into a **large roasting tray** and fill this with enough boiling water from a kettle to come halfway up each one.
12. Bake in the oven for about 45–50 minutes until the custard is firm but a bit wobbly.
13. Turn the oven off and open the door 5 minutes before you remove the ramekins from the oven.
14. Take the ramekins from the oven and set aside to cool in a fridge for about 1 hour.
15. Sprinkle each ramekin with 3g of **demerara sugar.**
16. Caramelise under the grill or with a **chef's blow torch.**
17. Allow the crème brûlée to rest for a few minutes before serving.

Tip – Although sugar lacks any nutritional benefits it does have a positive effect on your life and metabolism. It has a high calorie content that will give your body a short-term energy boost and contains glycolic acid that will help keep your skin fresh and young looking.

Apple and Banana Crunch Pie

Preparation Time – 20 minutes
(40 minutes if you make your own pastry)
Cooking Time – 50 minutes

Ingredients

240g Shortcrust Pastry (See p.482)
3 Braeburn Apples
2 Medium Bananas
30ml Lemon Juice
90gms Plain Flour
90gms Caster Sugar
90gms Unsalted Butter
30g Porridge Oats
60g Granola
1 tsp Cinnamon

Method

1. Preheat the oven to 180°C.
2. *Grease a **20cm round loose bottom flan tin.***
3. *Press **shortcrust pastry** into the flan dish.*
4. *Blind Bake for 15 minutes.*
5. *Peel the **apples** and slice into cubes.*
6. *Peel and slice the **bananas** into 1.5cm thick rounds.*
7. *Place the fruit in a **large bowl;** add the **lemon juice** and leave to stand for 5 minutes.*
8. *Combine the **flour, sugar, butter** and **cinnamon** in a bowl and mix together until crumbly.*
9. *Mix the **porridge oats** and **granola** with the apple and*

banana and place this in the pastry case, pressing it down gently to give you an even top.

10. *Sprinkle the crumb mixture all over and press it down lightly to the level of the top of the flan dish.*
11. *Bake in the oven for 35 minutes.*
12. *Serve with custard or ice cream.*

Tip – Bananas are naturally free of cholesterol, fat and sodium and are low in calories. They contain a high amount of potassium and a good amount of carbohydrates, vitamin B6, vitamin C and manganese. Because the fruit's sugar content is balanced with fibre they can be enjoyed by those with diabetes.

Chocolate Mousse Cake

Preparation Time – 35 minutes
Cooking Time – 25 minutes
Chilling Time – 3 hours

Ingredients

Cake

30g Cocoa Powder
90g Caster Sugar
90g Self-Raising Flour
90g Margarine
1 tsp Baking Powder
4 tbsp Boiling Water
2 Large Eggs

Topping

70g White Chocolate
100g Dark Chocolate
250ml Double Cream
20g Honeycomb Balls

Method

1. *Preheat the oven to 180°C.*
2. *Grease the sides of a **20cm round spring-form tin**.*
3. *Line the base and sides with **greaseproof paper**.*
4. *Put the **margarine** in a **non-metallic bowl** and melt in a*

microwave for about 30 seconds until soft.

5. Measure **cocoa powder** into a **large bowl,** pour on the **boiling water** and mix to a smooth paste.
6. Add the margarine, **sugar, baking powder** and **eggs** to the paste. Beat until smooth then fold in the **flour** until you get a rich even silky consistency.
7. Pour the mixture into the cake tin and level the top.
8. Bake in the oven on a middle shelf for 25 minutes.
9. When the cake is springy to the touch and a skewer inserted in the middle comes out clean, remove from the oven and set aside to cool for 10 minutes.
10. Whip the **cream** for about 5 minutes in a large bowl until it can form soft peaks.
11. Break the **chocolate into squares**, place in a bowl and microwave until soft.
12. Spoon the chocolate from the bowl and fold into the whipped cream until blended together ensuring that mixture isn't streaky.
13. Remove the cake from the tin and smooth chocolate over the top and sides with a palette knife.
14. Top with **chocolate honeycomb balls.**
15. Cover the cake with a bowl or loose **cling film** that isn't touching the mousse topping and place in the fridge to chill for about 3 hours.
16. Serve with raspberries or strawberries.

Tip – White chocolate may offer an alternative for people who are sensitive to dark chocolate as it is free from caffeine. It does contain a good amount of calcium but it is high in calories and saturated fat.

Prince of Cheesecakes

Preparation Time – 45 minutes
Cooking Time – 1 hour 10 minutes
Cooling Time – 40 minutes
Chilling Time – 4 hours

Ingredients

Base

200g Digestive Biscuits
120g Melted Butter
20g Caster Sugar

Filling

700g Cream Cheese
175g Caster Sugar
3 tbsp Cornflour
2 Eggs + 1 Egg White
80ml Sour Cream
1 tsp Lemon Juice
2 tsp Vanilla Extract

Topping

80ml Sour Cream
100ml Double Cream
25g Caster Sugar

Method

1. Grease the sides of a **20cm spring-form tin** and then line the bottom with **greaseproof paper.**
2. Preheat the oven to 180°C.
3. Crush the **biscuits** into fine crumbs and mix these in a **large bowl** with the **sugar** and **butter.**
4. Press the mixture into the bottom of the tin and bake in the oven for 10 minutes.
5. For the filling mix the **cream cheese** and **caster sugar** in a bowl using an **electric whisk** if possible. Note: This makes a thick filling. If you require a thinner filling, use half the ingredients.
6. Blend the **eggs, lemon juice, vanilla extract, cornflour** and **sour cream** into the bowl.
7. Whisk the **egg white** until fluffy and it forms peaks.
8. Fold into the cream cheese mixture.
9. Pour over the biscuit base.
10. Bake in the oven for 40 minutes.
11. Remove the tin and allow the cheesecake to cool for 10 minutes.
12. The butter will run onto the tray so change the tray at this point.
13. For the topping mix the **sour cream, double cream** and **sugar** in a bowl until smooth.
14. Press the cheesecake down lightly to just below the rim of the tin and then spread the topping over the top.
15. Return to the oven for 20 minutes.
16. Turn the oven off, open the door and leave the cheesecake in for a further 10 minutes.
17. Remove from the oven and leave to cool for 30 minutes.

18. Place in the fridge and chill for about 4 hours.
19. Dust with icing sugar on top and serve with a raspberry coulis and ice cream.

Tip – Cream cheese is one of the tastiest and most versatile cheeses and can be used in sweet or savoury dishes. It is made from a mixture of cream and milk and should be eaten in moderation as it doesn't provide too many nutrients and is very high in calories, cholesterol and saturated fat. If you choose to eat this on a regular basis then the low fat or reduced fat variants are healthier. Sour cream is created by adding bacteria to pasteurised cream and heating it to 22°C. Regular sour cream is also high in calories and saturated fat but it is low in carbohydrates and sodium and does provide a limited source of vitamin A, vitamin B2, vitamin B12, calcium and phosphorous.

Chocolate Web Pancakes

Preparation Time – 30 minutes
Cooking Time – 15 minutes

Ingredients

240ml Buttermilk
300g Plain Flour
1 tsp Baking Powder
½ tsp Salt
150ml Cold Water
6 Medium Eggs
72g Lard
150g Dark Chocolate

Method

1. Mix the **flour, baking powder** and **salt** together in a **large bowl** and make a well in the middle.
2. Whisk the **buttermilk** with the **cold water** in **another large bowl.**
3. Pour the buttermilk into the well and gradually fold in the flour.
4. Now add the **eggs** one at a time and mix until you have a smooth batter.
5. Add about 12g of **lard** to a **frying pan** and heat until it is shimmering hot then turn heat down to a medium level.
6. Using 1 **ladle** of batter for each pancake, pour it into the frying pan and swirl it around to fill the pan.

7. Cook for about 1 minute or until the underside is browned and the top is bubbling.
8. Turn pancake over and cook for another 45 seconds.
9. Remove pancake from the pan and place on a warm plate in the oven on a low heat.
10. Place more lard into the pan and continue the process until all the batter is used and all 6 pancakes are made.
11. Place greaseproof paper between each pancake to stop them sticking together while in the oven.
12. Place 150g of **dark chocolate** in a **bowl.**
13. Place this bowl over a **small saucepan** of boiling water to melt the chocolate until you get a runny sauce.
14. Pour the sauce into an **icing bag.**
15. Place 1 pancake in the centre of each serving plate.
16. Pipe the sauce over the top in the shape of a spider's web.
17. If chocolate starts to harden, reheat in a **microwave.**
18. Serve with ice cream and strawberries.

Tip – Traditional buttermilk is the liquid left behind after churning butter out of cream. Prepared in the traditional way it offers health benefits from its probiotic microbes which fight germs and bacteria, help calm the stomach, reduce acidity and aid digestion. It is a rich source of vitamin B12 and gives lactose intolerant people a dose of calcium without causing a reaction.

Chocolate Chilli Tart

Preparation Time – 20 minutes
(40 minutes if you make your own pastry)

Cooking Time – 55 minutes

Ingredients

240g Shortcrust pastry (see p. 482)
270ml Double Cream
100ml Semi-Skimmed Milk
200g Dark Chocolate
100g Milk Chocolate
2 Medium Eggs
2 tbsp Caster Sugar
8 Cardamon Pods
½ tsp Mild Chilli Powder
¼ tsp Salt

Method

1. *Preheat the oven to 180°.*
2. *Grease a **20cm round loose bottom flan tin**.*
3. *Press **shortcrust pastry** into the flan dish.*
4. *Blind bake for 15 minutes.*
5. *Lightly crush the **cardamom pods** and remove husks.*
6. *Crush the seeds and place these in a saucepan with the **chilli powder** and a pinch of **salt**.*
7. *Add the **sugar** and then pour in the **cream** and **milk**.*
8. *Bring slowly to the boil on a medium heat stirring continuously until the sugar has dissolved.*

9. *Remove from the heat, break the **chocolate** into pieces and add to the pan stirring continuously until the chocolate has melted.*
10. *Add the **eggs** and stir until the mixture has a smooth glossy appearance.*
11. *Pour onto the pastry in the flan tin until it reaches the top.*
12. *Bake in the oven for 35 minutes.*
13. *Allow to cool.*
14. *Dust the top with icing sugar.*
15. *Serve with strawberries and ice cream.*

Tip – Dark chocolate is very nutritious and high in antioxidants that can help improve blood flow, reduce blood pressure, lower the risk of cardiovascular disease, enhance the function of the brain and protect the skin from the sun. It is also lower in saturated fats and cholesterol than milk or white variants but should be eaten in moderation as it is high in calories.

Lemon Soufflé

Preparation Time – 35 minutes
Cooking Time – 30 minutes

Ingredients

6 Eggs Separated
210g Caster Sugar
3 Lemons
6 tsp Lemon Curd
24g Unsalted Butter
210ml Semi-Skimmed Milk
2 tbsp Plain Flour
1 tbs Cornflour

Method

1. *Preheat the oven to 160°C.*
2. *Squeeze the juice from the **lemons** using a **juicer**.*
3. *In a **large bowl** beat the 6 **egg whites** until they are stiff.*
4. *A tablespoon at a time, mix in half the **sugar** and then the **cornflour** and set the bowl aside.*
5. *In a **medium bowl** beat the 6 **egg yolks** until thick.*
6. *Add the lemon juice, the **zest from 1 lemon**, **flour** and the rest of the **sugar** and mix to a smooth paste.*
7. *Bring the **milk** to the boil in a **small saucepan**.*
8. *Remove from the heat for 1 minute and then slowly pour the milk onto the egg yolks whisking constantly to prevent yolks from cooking.*
9. *Pour this mixture into the saucepan and stir*

continuously over a low heat until thick.

10. Strain through a **sieve** into a large bowl and whisk in half of the butter.
11. Grease the bottom of **6 x 150ml ramekins** with the rest of the **butter.**
12. Add a teaspoon of **lemon curd** to each ramekin.
13. Fold the stiffened egg whites into the egg yolk mixture and then pour or spoon an equal amount into each of the ramekins almost to the top.
14. Place the ramekins on a **baking tray** and cook for about 25 minutes until the tops are brown.
15. Dust with a little icing sugar and serve immediately.

Tip – The health benefits of lemons have been known for centuries. They are acidic to the taste but alkaline forming in the body so help the body balance its pH levels. They contain citric acid, calcium, flavonoids, limonene, magnesium, pectin and vitamin C that also help the body boost its immune system and fight infection. Lemon juice contains an oil which may help to relieve rheumatism by stimulating the liver to expel toxins from the body. Lemons are often treated with fungicide spray and a wax so must be washed under a warm tap before being grated.

Individual Raspberry Cheesecakes

Preparation Time – 30 minutes
Chilling Time – 1 hour 15 minutes

Ingredients

120g Oat Biscuits
120g Digestive Biscuits
120g Unsalted Butter
480g Cream Cheese
210ml Double Cream
3 tbsp Caster Sugar
420g Fresh Raspberries

Method

1. Crush the **biscuits** in a **large mixing bowl.**
2. Melt the **butter** and add to the crushed biscuits.
3. Mix together thoroughly and then divide the mixture between **6 x 150ml ceramic ramekins.** Press down firmly.
4. Chill for 15 minutes in the fridge.
5. Place the **cream cheese, double cream** and **caster sugar** in a **medium bowl** and mix to a smooth consistency.
6. Spread the mixture evenly over the top of the biscuit bases.
7. Chill for about 1 hour or longer as required.
8. Spread **raspberry jam** over the top of each ramekin.
9. Top each ramekin with 60g of **raspberries** and then serve or turn each cheesecake out onto a plate.

Tip – The origins of butter go back thousands of years. The earliest written reference to it was found on a limestone tablet that was about 4,500 years old. It is generally believed the word butter originates from the Greek word 'bouturon' meaning 'cow cheese'. It is one of the foods that can transform a bland meal into a masterpiece and recent positive studies on its health benefits have seen it gain popularity at the expense of margarine which is a chemically processed product. Butter is a completely natural food that is rich in the easily absorbable form of vitamin A that is essential for thyroid and adrenal health. It also contains lecithin which is a necessary component of every cell in the body and essential for your circulatory and nervous systems. Butter produced from cows that feed on green grass also contains conjugated linoleic acid that helps the body protect itself against cancer and store muscle instead of fat, as well as vitamin K_2, which is rare in the western diet but plays a central role in calcium metabolism that can help prevent heart disease and osteoporosis.

Carrot Cake

Preparation Time – 40 minutes
Cooking Time – 45 minutes
Cooling Time – 30 minutes

Ingredients

For the Cake

240g Self-Raising Flour
90g Sultanas
12g Chopped Walnuts
6g Chopped Almonds
2 tsp Cinnamon
1 tsp Baking Powder
½ tsp Baking Soda
3 Medium Eggs
15g Unsalted Butter
120ml Sunflower Oil
180g Carrots (Grated)
240g Muscovado Sugar

For the Topping

30g Unsalted Butter
180g Cream Cheese
210g Icing Sugar
3 tsp Orange Juice
Orange Zest

Method

1. Heat the oven to 180°C.
2. Place the **flour, sultanas, walnuts, almonds, cinnamon, baking powder** and **baking soda** in a **large bowl** and mix together well.
3. In a separate bowl beat the **eggs** with the **sugar.**
4. Melt the **butter,** then add to the egg and sugar mix and stir in the **sunflower oil.**
5. Make a well in the flour mix, pour in the egg, sugar and sunflower mix and beat together.
6. Stir in the grated carrots.
7. Pour mixture into a **greased 20cm loose bottom tin.**
8. Bake in the oven for about 45 minutes until the top is firm to the touch and a **skewer** comes out clean.
9. For the topping, beat the **butter** in a bowl until soft. Add the **cream cheese, orange juice, and zest** and mix together.
10. **Sieve** and then sift in the **icing sugar.**
11. Place the topping in the fridge.
12. Remove the cake from the oven and leave to cool.
13. After 30 minutes remove cake from the tin, spread the topping over the top and sprinkle with the more zest.

Tip – Walnuts contain the amino acid l-arginine which offers multiple vascular benefits to those with heart disease. They also contain alpha-linolenic acid which may prevent blood clots and minimise the risk of a heart attack, as well as several unique powerful antioxidants that can improve sperm health and reduce the risk of prostate cancer.

French Fruit Tart

Preparation Time – 40 minutes
Cooking Time – 20 minutes

Ingredients

320g Puff Pastry
1 Medium Egg (Beaten)
100ml Fresh Custard (See p.456)
100ml Double Cream
2 Large Bananas
1 Punnet of Strawberries
1 Punnet of Raspberries
1 Bunch Seedless Grapes

Method

1. On a **lightly floured board** roll out the **pastry** to form a rectangular shape.
2. Place this on a **baking tray** and using a small **paring knife** score a 1cm border around the edge making sure that you don't cut through the pastry.
3. Brush some of the **beaten egg** around the pastry border.
4. Prick the pastry with a fork – not the border – and place in the fridge for about 10 minutes.
5. Preheat the oven to 200°C and bake the pastry for 20 minutes until golden brown and the border has risen.
6. While the pastry is in the oven, make the custard.
7. When cooked slide the pastry onto a wire cooling rack and leave to cool for 10 minutes.

8. *While this is cooling, peel and slice the **bananas** and cut about 12 **strawberries** in half.*
9. *Once the pastry has cooled gently press down the centre to leave a raised border.*
10. *Fold the **cream** into the custard and spread this over the centre of the pastry.*
11. *Draw 4 lines down through the custard mixture so you have even sections.*
12. *Arrange one of the fruits in each section as you decide to give contrasting colours.*
13. *If the tart isn't to be served immediately brush some lemon juice onto the banana to stop it going brown.*
14. *Serve with ice cream.*

Tip – There are about 8,000 varieties of grapes; the first were cultivated as early as 5,000 BC. They are high in phytonutrients: plant chemicals with disease-preventing properties. These include resveratrol, which studies have found to play a protective role against cancer, heart disease and Alzheimer's. Grapes are also a rich source of the micro-nutrient minerals: copper, iron and manganese, as well as vitamins B, C and K.

Fresh Custard

Preparation Time – 15 minutes
Cooking Time – 15 minutes

Ingredients

6 Egg Yolks
60g Caster Sugar
250ml Semi-Skimmed Milk
250ml Double Cream
1 Vanilla Pod
1 tsp Cornflour

Method

1. Beat the **egg yolks, cornflour** and **sugar** together in a **bowl** until pale.
2. Place the **milk** and **cream** in a **saucepan**.
3. Split the **vanilla pod** open lengthways, scrape the seeds inside into the milk and cream and bring to simmering point stirring occasionally.
4. Remove from the heat and pour a little of the milk and cream onto the eggs and sugar and mix well with a **whisk.**
5. Pour this back into the pan and, using a whisk, lightly stir continuously on a low heat until it thickens. Do not boil or else the custard will split.
6. When the custard has thickened to the consistency you

*desire remove from heat and pass it through a **sieve** into a bowl or **serving jug.***

7. *The custard can be served immediately or left to cool if using for the French fruit tart recipe.*

Tip - Vanilla pods contain the seeds from the vanilla orchid plant. Vanilla is the second most expensive spice in the world because cultivation is difficult and involves labour intensive processes.

SAUCES AND SIDE DISHES

Espagnole Sauce

Preparation Time – 30 minutes
Cooking Time – 40 minutes

Ingredients

30g Butter
30g Flour
600ml Beef Stock
25g Bacon Fat
60g White Mushrooms
1 Medium Carrot
1 Medium Onion
8 Black Peppercorns
150ml Tomato Pulp
3 tbsp Water
½ tsp Salt
1 tsp Dried Thyme
1 Garlic Clove
1 Bay Leaf

Method

1. Heat the **butter** in a **saucepan** on a medium heat.
2. When the butter has melted, remove the pan from the heat and stir in the **flour.**
3. Put the pan back on the heat and stir continuously until a smooth light brown colour to make a roux.
4. Turn the heat up slightly and add 150ml of **beef stock** at a time stirring continuously.
5. When the stock has all been used, you have a **velouté.**

a) Cut the **bacon fat** into small pieces, fry in a **dry saucepan** for a few minutes and set aside.

b) Place 6 **large tomatoes** in a **bowl** of boiling water for a few minutes then peel off the skin. Cut them in half, remove the seeds and then blend them in a **processor** for about 1 minute.

c) Chop the **onion, carrot** and **mushrooms** into fine pieces and place in the saucepan with the bacon fat.

d) Add the **peppercorns**, tomato pulp, **water** and **salt** then sauté on a medium heat for 2 minutes.

6. Add the mixture above to the velouté with the **thyme, crushed garlic** and the **bay leaf** and stir well.

7. Simmer for 30 minutes or until the volume of liquid has been reduced by half and then strain through a **sieve**.

8. Use immediately, chill or freeze.

Tip – The peppercorn plant is a climber that needs a tree or pole for support. All of the coloured variants come from the same plant but are picked at different stages of maturity. Black peppercorns contain a good amount of minerals such as calcium, iron, magnesium, manganese, potassium and zinc. They also contain piperine which stimulates the nervous system and acts as an anti-depressant.

Mushroom and Herb Sauce

Preparation Time – 15 minutes
Cooking Time – 15 minutes

Ingredients

12 Cremini Mushrooms
40g Unsalted Butter
2 tbsp Plain Flour
30ml Cider
2 tsp Dried Basil
1 tsp Dried Thyme
5g Fresh Parsley
2 tsp Black Pepper
1 tsp Salt
1 tsp Beef Granules
100ml Double Cream
300ml Semi-Skimmed Milk

Method

1. Blend the **mushrooms** in a **processor** for 1 minute.
2. Melt the **butter** in a **saucepan** until it starts to foam.
3. Remove pan from the heat.
4. Add the **flour** and mix to a paste.
5. Add the **cider** and **beef granules** and continue stirring to make a thicker paste.
6. Pour in the **double cream** and **milk** and then add the **basil, thyme, chopped parsley, black pepper** and **salt.**
7. Stir in the mushrooms, then put the pan back on the

hob, bring the sauce to the boil and then leave to simmer for 10 minutes on a low heat.

8. *Add more milk as required for your desired thickness.*

Tip – Parsley has been around for more than 2,000 years and is a giant amongst herbs in terms of its health benefits. Recent studies have shown that myristicin, an organic compound found in its essential oils, has chemopreventative effects on skin cancer and can also neutralise carcinogens in cigarette smoke and inhibit lung tumour formation. Parsley is a good source of calcium, iron, magnesium and potassium and is rich in vitamins A, B_{12}, C, and K. Vitamin K is named after the German word for blood clotting (Koagulation) and is an essential nutrient needed by the body to help it respond to injuries. It also plays a vital role in building strong bones and teeth. Parsley is very low in calories, but its nutrient profile is no less than many high-calorie foods provide and it offers many other benefits including the prevention of bad breath, bladder infection and indigestion.

Creamy Tomato and Cheese Pasta Sauce

Preparation Time – 15 minutes
Cooking Time – 15 minutes

Ingredients

600g Tomatoes
30g Fresh Coriander
150ml Evaporated Milk
150ml Double Cream
40g Unsalted Butter
2 Medium Onions
2 tsp Tamarind Paste
4 tsp Black Pepper
2 tsp Rock Salt
2 tsp Oregano
90g Grated Cheddar

Method

1. Place the **tomatoes** in a **processer** then add the **coriander, evaporated milk** and **double cream** and blend together for 15 seconds.
2. Chop the onions finely. Melt the butter in a **large saucepan** over a medium heat until it starts to foam, then sauté the onions for about 3 minutes until they are soft and translucent.
3. Pour the liquid from the processer over the onions, add the **tamarind paste, black pepper, rock salt** and **oregano** and stir well.

4. *Bring to the boil, and then simmer on a medium heat for 10 minutes.*
5. *Add the grated cheddar and mix together well.*

Tip – Coriander, also known as cilantro or Chinese parsley, is a great source of vitamins A, C, K, calcium, folic acid, iron, magnesium and potassium. The first medicinal uses of the plant were reported by the ancient Egyptians. It is quite effective for curing various skin diseases such as acne, eczema, rashes and inflammation. It also acts as an antiseptic to cure mouth ulcers. It is widely recognised that coriander lowers blood sugar levels by stimulating the secretion of insulation, helps the heart by lowering bad cholesterol and raising good cholesterol and reduces hypertension by lowering blood pressure. The leaves are a good source of roughage that stimulates digestion through peristaltic action thereby helping to prevent flatulence, indigestion and upset stomachs.

Sauce Vierge

Preparation Time – 20 minutes
Cooking Time – 5 minutes

Ingredients

100ml Olive Oil
6 Coriander Seeds
2 Large Tomatoes
1 Garlic Clove
1 tsp Balsamic Vinegar
5g Fresh Tarragon
10g Fresh Chives
10g Fresh Basil
10g Fresh Coriander
10g Shallots
2 tbsp Lemon Juice
1 tsp Black Pepper
1 tsp Brown Sugar

Method

1. Add the **coriander seeds** to a **hot dry pan** and fry them for 1 minute.
2. Place the seeds in a **medium bowl** crush them and then add a **crushed garlic.**
3. Place the **tomatoes** in a **bowl** of boiling water for 2 minutes. Remove from the water; carefully peel off the skins and leave to cool.
4. Chop all of the **herbs** and **shallots** finely.

5. Remove the core and the seeds from the tomatoes and add the flesh to the coriander and garlic bowl.
6. Add the herbs, shallots and **balsamic vinegar** and mash everything together.
7. Warm the **olive oil** in a **small saucepan,** add the mixture and leaving it to simmer for 2 minutes.
8. Add the **lemon juice, black pepper** and **brown sugar,** stir well and simmer for 2 minutes.
9. Spoon the sauce over your fish or scallops.

Tip – Olives are one of the oldest foods known and are thought to have originated from Crete or Syria over 7,000 years ago. Olive oil, which is now a major component of the Mediterranean diet, is rich in monounsaturated fatty acids. These are good fats that offer a host of health benefits compared to the trans fats and polyunsaturated fats found in most processed foods. Diets with good amounts of olive oil can correlate with healthier hearts, fewer strokes, reduced belly fat and weight loss. Recent studies have also shown that women with diets that are high in monounsaturated fats compared to poly-unsaturated and saturated fats suffered fewer incidences of breast cancer. Lately, researchers and nutritionists have concluded that a diet high in monounsaturated fats may be more beneficial for those with diabetes than one containing a low fat and low carbohydrate content.

Onion Gravy

Preparation Time – 10 minutes
Cooking Time – 15 minutes

Ingredients

1 Large Onion (Chopped)
25g Unsalted Butter
25g Plain Flour
350ml Vegetable Stock
2 tsp Black Pepper
1 tsp Salt
1 tbsp Red Wine
½ tbsp Balsamic Vinegar

Method

1. Melt the **butter** in a **saucepan** and add the onions.
2. Cook on a low to medium heat for 4–5 minutes stirring occasionally until the **onions** are soft but not browned.
3. Remove from the heat, stir in the flour and then add the **stock, salt** and **pepper.**
4. Bring to the boil stirring continuously then add the **balsamic vinegar** and **red wine** and simmer on a low heat for about 10 minutes.

Tip – *Balsamic vinegar can improve insulin sensitivity for diabetics, allowing for easier regulation of blood sugar and the reduction of unpleasant side effects from diabetes.*

Beef Jus

Preparation Time – 10 minutes
Cooking Time – 15 minutes

Ingredients

400g Chestnut Mushrooms
50g Unsalted Butter
2 tsp Cornflour
400ml Beef Stock
2 tsp White Wine Vinegar
2 tbsp Port
2 tsp Soft Brown Sugar

Method

1. Blend the **mushrooms** in a **processor** for 1 minute.
2. Melt the **butter** in a **large saucepan** until it starts to foam.
3. Remove the pan from the heat.
4. Add the **cornflour** and mix to a paste.
5. Pour the stock into the pan and stir for 1 minute.
6. Add the **mushrooms** and **sugar** and bring to the boil.
7. Add the **port** and **vinegar** and simmer for 10 minutes.
8. Strain through a **sieve** into a **serving jug**.

Tip – White vinegar can assist the body in the absorption of essential minerals. In particular, it can potentially be very helpful to women who are not absorbing enough calcium to keep their bones healthy.

Boulangère Potatoes

Preparation Time – 30 minutes
Cooking Time – 1 hour 15 minutes

Ingredients

1kg Desiree Potatoes
3 Medium Onions
6 Garlic Cloves
60g Unsalted Butter
600ml Vegetable Stock
3 tsp Sea Salt
3 tsp Black Pepper
5g Fresh Parsley
60g Grated Parmesan

Method

1. *Preheat the oven to 180°C.*
2. *Grease the base and sides of a **large oblong ovenproof dish** (30cm x 20cm x 5cm).*
3. *Peel the **potatoes** and finely slice them.*
4. *Slice the **onions** thinly and chop up the **garlic.***
5. *Line the bottom of the dish with a layer of potatoes.*
6. *Scatter some of the onion and garlic on top.*
7. *Layer up the remaining potatoes, onion and garlic ensuring you season each layer with **salt** and **pepper**.*
8. *Pour the stock all over the potatoes and sprinkle on the chopped **parsley**.*

9. Dot the top with butter all over and then bake in the oven for 1 hour 15 minutes.
10. After 1 hour sprinkle the **parmesan** over the top and cover the dish with foil for the remaining time.

Fondant Potatoes

Preparation Time – 15 minutes
Cooking Time – 35 minutes

Ingredients

6 Large Desiree Potatoes
150g Unsalted Butter
2 Garlic Cloves
400ml Chicken Stock
Salt and Pepper

Method

1. Peel the **potatoes** then cut off the rounded ends to leave a flat top and bottom.
2. Cut out a tall round tube shape with a **pastry cutter**.
3. Melt the butter in a **frying pan** with 2 crushed garlic cloves until it starts to foam.
4. Place the potatoes vertically in the pan and cook on a medium heat for 4 minutes until the bottoms are golden. Turn them over and cook the tops for a further 4 minutes.
5. Place the stock in an **ovenproof dish** and place the potatoes upright in the dish so they are half covered.
6. Season the potatoes with **salt** and **pepper.**
7. Place this dish in the oven at 180°C for 25 minutes.

Crushed Potatoes

Preparation Time – 10 minutes
Cooking Time – 20 minutes

Ingredients

900g New Potatoes
60g Unsalted Butter
5g Fresh Parsley
5g Fresh Coriander
½ tsp Salt

Method

1. *Wash the **potatoes** in cold water.*
2. *Place in a **saucepan** of cold water with a pinch of salt.*
3. *Bring this to the boil then reduce the heat and simmer for 15 minutes.*
4. *Strain and leave to cool for 2 minutes.*
5. *Dry the saucepan and put back on the hob adding the **butter.***
6. *As soon as the butter foams add the potatoes and lightly crush them down with a **masher.***
7. *Add the **chopped parsley** and **coriander.***
8. *Stir while still on the heat and then remove, place in an **ovenproof dish** and leave in the oven on a low heat until ready to serve.*

Potato Puffs

Preparation Time – 20 minutes
Cooking Time – 35 minutes

Ingredients

300g Maris Piper Potatoes
180ml Semi-Skimmed Milk
36g Unsalted Butter
6g Dried Parsley
6g Dried Tarragon
84g Plain Flour
1 Large Egg
30ml Vegetable Oil
Salt and Pepper

Method

1. Peel the **potatoes** then boil them in a **large saucepan** until soft.
2. Mash with 50ml of **milk** and 36g of **butter.**
3. Add in the **parsley** and **tarragon** and a pinch of **salt** and **pepper.**
4. Preheat the oven to 200°C.
5. Whisk the remaining **milk, flour, egg** and another pinch of salt in a bowl to form a batter.
6. Place about 5ml (1 tsp) of veg oil in each of **6 x 150ml ramekins** and place these on a tray in the oven for a few minutes until the oil is hot.
7. Using half of the mixture pour an even amount of the batter into each ramekin.

8. *Add an equal amount of mashed potato to each ramekin and then pour an equal amount of the remaining batter over the top.*
9. *Bake in the oven for 15–20 minutes until the puffs have risen and are a golden brown colour.*
10. *Using a palette knife ease the puffs out of the ramekins and place on the serving plate.*

Creamy Mashed Potatoes

Preparation Time – 20 minutes
Cooking Time – 25 minutes

Ingredients

1.2kg King Edward or Desiree Potatoes
50g Unsalted Butter
180ml Hot Milk
10g Fresh Parsley
1 tsp Black Pepper
Pinch of Salt

Method

1. Peel the **potatoes,** then slice them into equal size pieces before boiling them in a **large saucepan** of salted water for 10 minutes.
2. Remove from the hob and drain the water using a **colander.**
3. Allow the potatoes to cool in the colander for 5 minutes and then run them under a cold tap to remove some of the starch.
4. Bring another **saucepan** of water to the boil and then cook the potatoes on a medium heat for another 15 minutes or until tender but not mushy.
5. Drain very well and mash them with a **masher** until soft. You can use a potato ricer if you have one.
6. Add the **black pepper** and **salt.**

7. Add the **butter** and beat in a little **milk** at a time until you have a smooth thick purée.
8. Mix in the chopped **parsley** and spoon into a serving dish or into a **cylindrical ring** on a plate.

Sautéed Potatoes

Preparation Time – 20 minutes
Cooking Time – 15 minutes

Ingredients

1.2kg Maris Piper Potatoes
90ml Vegetable Oil
30ml Lard
5g Fresh Rosemary
1 tsp Salt
1 tsp Black Pepper

Method

1. Peel the **potatoes** and cut them into slices about 2.5cm thick.
2. Place them in cold water for about 5 minutes.
3. Drain the water off in a **colander** and then rinse the potatoes again under the tap.
4. Drain the water again and then pat the slices with **kitchen paper** until they are completely dry.
5. Heat the oil and lard in a **frying pan** until it gets very hot.
6. Add the potatoes and cook without stirring them for 2 minutes until they start to brown.
7. Turn them over and cook for a further minute to slightly brown the other side.
8. Turn the hob down to a low to medium heat season with **salt** and **pepper** and allow them to cook for

about 10 minutes.

9. *After 5 minutes sprinkle some rosemary onto the potatoes.*

10. *Drain off the oil and serve hot.*

Onion Mashed Potatoes

Preparation Time – 20 minutes
Cooking Time – 20 minutes

Ingredients

1.2kg Maris Piper Potatoes
75g Unsalted Butter
120ml Semi-Skimmed Milk
2 Medium Onions
2 tsp Dried Parsley
1 tsp Black Pepper
5g Fresh Parsley

Method

1. *Peel the **potatoes** and cut them into large chunks.*
2. *Place these in a **large pan** of boiling water for about 15 minutes until tender.*
3. *Chop up the **onions** finely and set them aside.*
4. *Drain the potatoes and leave to cool for 1 minute.*
5. *Return them to the pan, place this back on the heat and stir them for 1 minute using a **wooden spoon.***
6. *Add the **butter, milk** and **dried parsley,** stir for a further minute then mash the potatoes.*
7. *Add the **onions** and **black pepper** and stir into the mash.*
8. *Serve hot with fresh parsley on top.*

Tip – Potatoes belong to the nightshade family and were first cultivated in the Andes region of South America. They are the fourth most consumed crop in the world behind rice, wheat and corn, and are vastly underrated in terms of their nutritional benefit. They are a rich source of vitamin B_6 and a good source of vitamin C, copper, manganese, phosphorus and potassium. They are also a great source of fibre which helps with digestion and prevention of constipation. Vitamin B_6 helps prevent the accumulation in the body of the compound homocysteine which can damage blood vessels and lead to heart problems. It also plays a vital role in energy metabolism by breaking down carbohydrates and proteins into glucose and amino acids. The do however contain carbs that have a high glycaemic load so probably should be eaten in moderation by those with diabetes.

Short Crust Pastry

Preparation Time – 20 minutes
Cooking Time – 15 minutes

Ingredients

150g Plain Flour
60g Unsalted Butter
24g Lard
50ml Cold Water
½ tsp Salt

This makes the base of a 20cm tin.
Use double the quantity for a pie top as well.

Method

1. Sift the **flour** and **salt** together in a **bowl.**
2. Cut in the **butter** and the lard until the mixture resembles breadcrumbs.
3. Gradually add the **water** to make a soft dough.
4. Roll the dough into a ball.
5. Sprinkle a small amount of flour onto a **pastry board.**
6. Flatten the dough with your palm gently to form a round pancake shape.
7. With a **rolling pin** roll out the dough slowly until it is about one and a half times larger than the width of the **20cm flan tin.**
8. Grease the flan tin with butter or margarine.
9. Press the dough into the flan tin making sure that it hangs over the top of the tin.

10. Depending on your filling and its cooking time or if you are going to have a top on your pie, you may need to bake the pastry blind as detailed below.

11. To bake it blind; place some **greaseproof paper** onto your dough in the flan or pie dish to cover the bottom and the sides and fill to the top with **ceramic baking beans.** Bake in the oven for 10 minutes on 180°C, then remove the dish from the oven and leave it to cool slightly before removing the baking beans and the greaseproof paper. At this point prick the base of the pastry only with a fork and put it back in the oven for 5 minutes.

12. If you are not baking blind, the pastry that you have left hanging over the edge will shrink back during the cooking process and you will need to trim this at the end of the cooking time.

13. If you are baking blind you can trim the pastry first as this process stops it from shrinking.

Glossary

Words or phrases within the recipes or the tips sections that may be unfamiliar to some readers and are not clarified are explained below.

Cookery

Butterfly
This means to cut meat or fish almost in two and then spread it out flat.

Roux
Is an equal quantity of melted butter and flour cooked in a pan and used as the thickening base for a number of sauces.

Veloute
One of the five "mother" sauces of classic French cuisine.

Health

Carotenoids
These are colourful pigments found in fruits and vegetables. They are antioxidants that can contribute to good health. Some such as beta-carotene are converted into vitamin A in the body.

Cryptoxanthin
A member of the carotenoid family that provides colour and flavour to fruits and vegetables and helps protect the body from free radicals.

Flavenoids	Molecules found in a variety of fruits and vegetables that are important components of a healthy diet because of their antioxidant activity.
Folate	A general term for a family of compounds derived from folic acid found in many fruits and vegetables that the body needs to make DNA.
Glycaemic Index	A ranking of carbohydrates in foods according to the way they affect blood glucose levels in isolation.
HDL	High density lipoproteins are microscopic particles which transport excess cholesterol in your blood back to your liver, where it is broken down and removed from your body. A high level of HDLs in the body indicates a lower than average risk of heart disease.
LDL	Low density lipoproteins carry cholesterol from your liver to the cells that need it. If there is too much for the cells to use, it can build up in the artery walls leading to disease. A high level of LDLs raises the risk of heart disease.
Niacin	Also called vitamin B3, it helps to convert food into energy and is essential for healthy skin, blood cells, brain and nervous system.
Pantothenic Acid	Also known as vitamin B5, it is found in high concentrations in many foods.

pH	Is the abbreviation for potential of hydrogen. This is the measurement of hydrogen ion concentration in water-based solutions, how acidic or alkaline they are. Human blood stays in a very narrow range, so any deviation means illness or disease.
Phytochemicals	A group of compounds found in all fruits and vegetables. They are non-essential nutrients but can protect humans against various diseases.
Riboflavin	Also known as vitamin B2 and found in most dairy products, fish and fortified cereals, it is essential in small amounts for metabolic reactions within the body.
Thiamine	Many vegetables are high in vitamin B1 that helps with the metabolism of carbohydrates to aid cellular and organ functions and prevent the build-up of toxins.

WE ARE MACMILLAN. CANCER SUPPORT

Crisis

A total of 20% of the profits from this book will be donated to Macmillan Cancer Support and Crisis[*], in support of the work they do.

---

[*] *See imprint page for registration details.*

Coming Soon

REVENGE IS SWEET

The sequel to *A Party To Murder* with a new interwoven plot that will take the reader on an unexpected journey.

Just when you think you know what will happen there is another twist to surprise and shock.

A psychological crime thriller that still manages to combine the author's key ingredients of sex, humour and cookery.

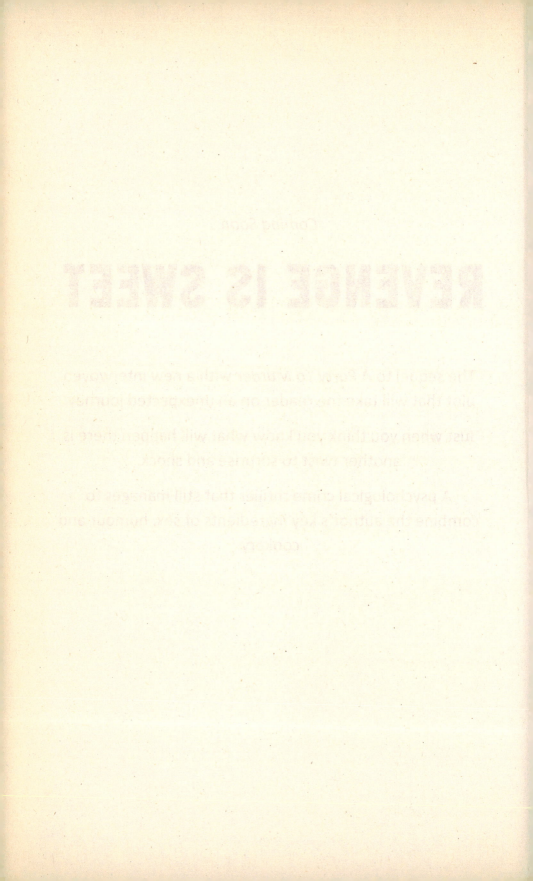

A Party to Murder is also available to purchase in electronic format from all major eBook retailers.